The Last Star

Clifton Wilcox

Fredericksburg, Virginia

Print ISBN: 978-1-969770-34-0

EBook ISBN: 978-1-969770-35-7

Published by Windward Publishing LLC., Fredericksburg, Virginia.

The characters and events in this book are fictitious. Any similarity to real persons, living or dead, is coincidental and not intended by the author.

Wilcox, Clifton

The Last Star

Windward Publishing, LLC

2026

Dedication

I used to think this was about becoming great.
That if I worked harder, moved faster, stayed sharper—I would earn my place.

I was wrong.

This place doesn't give you anything.
It takes what you offer, measures it, and decides whether you're worth keeping another day.

I watched people disappear without explanation.
I learned to correct mistakes before they existed.
I learned that silence isn't calm—it's pressure waiting to be noticed.

If you're reading this, you probably believe there's something on the other side of perfection.
Something worth it.

There isn't.

There is only the standard.
And whether you survive it long enough
to stop remembering who you were before it.

Connor Felwick

Table of Contents

Books by Clifton Wilcox

Fiction

Cool's Last Stand

Where Despair Comes to Play

The Monuments Must Bleed

Keeper of the Fallen Ages

I, Monster

Harvest of Eyes

The Case Against Jasper

Crimson Plume: The Song of Corvus

Framed in Love

Echoes of the Forgotten

Blacktop Harvest

The Plagiarist Game

The Black Forest Protocol

Outcome without Appeal

Deliberation

The Lore Hunter: Brown Mountain

The Pact of Shadows: The Black Orchard

The Black Ledger of Salem

The Four That Bind

Chapter 1

Prologue: The Silent Plate

The maître d' did not look twice at the man who paused just inside the vestibule, as if letting his eyes adjust to the dimness. That was the first mistake, and it was also exactly what the man wanted.

L'Étoile Noire received important people the way it received rain: without surprise, without gratitude, without any visible acknowledgment that the outside world had changed. The glass doors sealed shut behind him with a soft pneumatic sigh. Warmth replaced the street's damp chill. The air carried an expensive quiet, perfumed with beeswax polish and something faintly citrus that never quite resolved into a single note. Nothing here was accidental. Even the scent had been rehearsed.

The man removed his coat with measured movements and handed it over. His jacket underneath was plain, dark, and well cut in a way that refused to announce itself. No bold watch. No jewelry. No visible status markers. He looked like someone who traveled often and preferred not to be remembered.

"Good evening, sir," the maître d' said in a low voice calibrated to the room. "Do you have a reservation?"

The man's smile arrived a moment late, as if it had to be approved internally before it could show itself. "I do," he replied, and gave a name that belonged to no one.

The maître d' did not hesitate. There was a subtle shift in his posture, a microscopic tightening around his eyes that someone trained to see fear could have read as recognition without certainty. He glanced at the book, traced a line with one finger, and nodded.

"Of course."

As he was led through the dining room, the man's footsteps made no sound on the deep carpet. The room was built to swallow noise. Tables were spaced like islands, each one protected by shadows and low lamp light that turned glassware into floating reflections. The walls held art that did not try to be beautiful; it tried to be untouchable. The kind of paintings that suggested the buyer hadn't chosen them for love, but for leverage.

Servers moved with synchronized restraint. Their expressions were pleasant in the same way a locked door could be pleasant: smooth, flawless, uninviting. Conversation from the guests existed only as murmurs. Even laughter was muted, as if the room demanded that joy be tasteful.

The man noted the couples who didn't touch, the businessmen who spoke in short bursts and then watched the room as if it were watching back. He noticed the table near the back where two men sat with their shoulders angled outward, not toward each other, leaving a third chair empty like an unasked question. He noticed the woman at the corner table who never looked at her companion while speaking, addressing her words to the air between them like an arrangement.

He noticed everything, because that was the job.

His table was positioned with careful logic: not the best in the room, but not a punishment either. It offered a partial view of the pass through a slim architectural gap, a deliberate glimpse into the mouth of the kitchen. The restaurant pretended it was transparency. In truth, it was theater. A controlled sliver of labor presented as a privilege.

He sat. A napkin was placed on his lap without him having to move. Water arrived without him asking. A menu was offered like a formal document.

"Would you care to begin with an aperitif?" the server asked.

"Still water," he said. "And I'd like to taste."

There were a dozen ways a diner could say it. The people who truly wanted the tasting menu asked for "the experience." The ones who wanted power asked for "the chef's imagination." This man asked to taste. It was plain, almost bland.

But the server's eyes flickered. The flicker was trained away in most, but not all.

"Of course," the server said, and walked away at a pace that remained steady until he reached the service corridor, where it sharpened by half a degree.

The man's hands rested on the table. Clean nails. No scars. No tremor. The face of a person who had never needed to use his hands for violence and had still learned how to.

He watched the room. The staff, the diners, the choreography of plates delivered and removed. The service here was so smooth it made hunger feel like an interruption. The restaurant did not cater to appetite. It catered to expectation.

From the gap toward the kitchen, he could see motion without sound. Stainless steel flashed. White sleeves moved like the wings of controlled birds. He could not hear the call of orders. He could not hear voices at all. That was unusual. In most kitchens, even refined ones, there was always a hum: a curse under breath, a quick laugh, the rattle of a pan. Here, the silence seemed engineered.

As if noise itself were an imperfection.

He took a sip of water and waited.

In the kitchen, behind the polished facade, the shift had begun hours earlier. The brigade had arrived in layers, each one slipping into position as if the building itself had assigned them a role. The younger cooks had entered with eyes lowered, knives already sharpened, sleeves pulled tight. The senior chefs had moved through them without greeting, checking temperatures, checking labels, checking the clock as if time could be bullied into obedience.

Sofia Alvarez stood at the edge of the prep line, her hair pulled back so tightly it looked like discipline made visible. She had a clipboard she rarely wrote on. She didn't need to. Her memory held mistakes like inventory. She watched hands. She watched wrists. She watched the tiny hesitations that meant weakness.

"Focus," she said, not to anyone in particular, and it didn't matter who heard. Everyone did.

At the pass, Chef Lucien Renaud did not pace. Pacing was for men with energy to waste. He stood as if anchored, his posture straight, his hands still unless they needed to move. His eyes traveled constantly, scanning surfaces, plates, faces, the angle of a quenelle, the sheen of a sauce. He did not need to raise his voice. His attention was the loudest thing in the room.

A commis approached Sofia with a question and stopped two steps short, as if an invisible line on the floor would punish him for crossing.

"Chef," he began.

Sofia's gaze met his and held. The question died in his mouth. She did not speak. She did not have to. He swallowed and went back to his station, trying again to solve whatever problem had made him reach for help.

Renaud's eyes flicked to Sofia, then away. It was not approval. It was confirmation. The machine was running.

Then a figure appeared near the kitchen entrance, a man in a suit that looked like it had never been sat in for too long. Marcus Hale did not belong to the kitchen and yet moved as if it owed him space. He did not wear a jacket. He did not need one. His presence created a draft.

Sofia's jaw tightened almost imperceptibly. She stepped closer to him without rushing.

"He's here," Marcus said quietly.

Renaud did not ask who. He didn't need to. His expression remained unchanged, but something in the air altered, like a pressure system shifting.

Sofia lowered her voice. "Which table?"

Marcus angled his head toward the dining room, toward that controlled gap of visibility. "Center-left. Not the best seat. He'll want to see how we handle being watched without being told."

Sofia's eyes moved, calculating. "No announcement?"

Marcus's mouth twitched. "If you announce him, you turn it into a performance. He's here to see what we are when we think we're alone."

Renaud's gaze lifted slightly, not toward the gap, but toward the idea of it. His voice, when it came, was barely above the hush of refrigeration units.

"Then we are alone," he said.

Marcus leaned closer, just enough to be intimate in a room that forbade intimacy. "You understand what's at stake."

Renaud's eyes did not leave the pass. "It's always at stake."

Marcus studied him for a beat, as if checking for cracks. "No indulgences tonight. No improvisation. No signature flourishes. Clean. Cold. Perfect."

Sofia spoke before Renaud could, the words clipped. "That's already our standard."

Marcus smiled without warmth. "Good. Keep it."

He stepped back, leaving behind the faint scent of expensive cologne and something else: control.

Renaud's fingers tapped the edge of the pass once. Not nervous. A signal. A silent command.

Sofia turned to the line. Her voice did not rise, but it cut through the stillness with surgical clarity.

"Listen," she said.

Every head angled subtly, not fully turning. They did not stop moving, because stopping was also a kind of failure, but attention shifted like a spotlight.

"Dining room has an observer," Sofia continued. "We don't react. We don't change pace. We don't speak unless necessary. We execute. If you make an error, you fix it before it's seen. If you can't fix it, you replace it. If you hesitate, you will be replaced."

No one asked for clarification. No one needed it.

Renaud added one sentence, soft enough that the closest cooks leaned in to catch it.

"Tonight," he said, "the room is listening."

They went back to work with hands that moved faster, cleaner. The knives did not scrape. The towels did not slap against aprons. Even the flames seemed quieter, as if the stoves understood what kind of night this was.

Out in the dining room, the man with the borrowed name received his first course.

It arrived carried by a server whose smile was correct and whose eyes did not meet his. The plate was set down with the gentleness of something sacred. The server described it in language polished to a shine: origin of the ingredient, method of preparation, the reasoning behind the pairing.

The man listened politely, then nodded. "Thank you."

When the server stepped away, the man leaned forward slightly. He did not photograph the dish. He did not immediately taste. He simply looked.

The plate was beautiful in the way a weapon could be beautiful. Minimal, precise, composed with a restraint that felt almost cruel. Everything had a place. Everything had a purpose. It was impossible to tell where the food ended and the message began.

He inhaled, taking in aroma without closing his eyes like a worshipper. His fork cut through the first element with controlled pressure. He tasted.

His face did not change.

From the kitchen's narrow view, Renaud watched the dish disappear from the pass and enter the dining room. He did not watch the diners, not directly. He watched the timing of the runners, the steadiness of hands, the return of empty plates.

But when the first empty plate came back, clean as if it had never held anything at all, his gaze held it for a fraction longer than necessary.

Sofia noticed. She always did.

"He started," she murmured.

Renaud's response was a barely perceptible nod.

In the dining room, the man took another bite, then another. He ate with neither pleasure nor displeasure. He ate with evaluation. Around him, other guests savored, talked, and performed their own rituals of wealth. None of them knew what had just entered the room with them.

And that was the point.

He lifted his glass, watched the candlelight distort through the water, and turned his attention, briefly, toward the narrow gap that offered a view of the kitchen. He could not hear anything from it. He could only see movement.

Silent. Efficient. Controlled.

A kitchen that looked like it had already learned how to hide its panic.

He returned his gaze to the plate in front of him and continued eating, taking his time as if time belonged to him.

In the kitchen, the machine tightened its grip.

Tonight, the restaurant was not serving dinner.

It was being measured.

The second course arrived with the same practiced grace as the first, as if the restaurant were determined to prove that the initial impression had not been a fluke. A different server this time, same expression: smooth, pleasant, emptied of personal thought. The plate was set down precisely at twelve o'clock to the inspector's torso, the rim aligned with an invisible axis in the table grain.

"Langoustine, lightly poached," the server said. "Consommé of roasted shells, young fennel, a reduction of citrus and sea herbs."

The words were delivered like an oath. The server's hands withdrew without tremor.

The inspector nodded once, neither encouraging nor dismissive. When the server disappeared into the dim choreography of the dining room, he did what he had done before. He looked.

The langoustine lay as if it had been placed by instruments rather than fingers, a pale curve caught between shine and translucence. The fennel was shaved into thin crescents, each one identical, staggered like scales. The consommé held a surface tension so perfect it seemed to resist the air.

It was flawless. That was the problem.

He lowered his face slightly, just enough to take in the aroma. Salt, sweetness, a clean mineral note. Beneath it, something citric that should have lifted, should have sharpened. It hovered instead, as if trapped under glass.

He picked up his fork. Cut. The tines met resistance at the wrong moment, subtle but undeniable. Not toughness. Not overcooking. Something else, a textural hesitation that spoke of a second too long in heat, or a cooling window that had opened for a heartbeat and then closed again.

He tasted.

He did not grimace. He did not frown. His expression was trained not to betray the mind behind it. But his eyes, which had been still since he entered, moved once, the smallest flick toward the gap that offered a glimpse into the kitchen.

There, white sleeves flowed. A pan lifted, a sauce poured. Motion without sound.

He ate another bite, slower. Let the broth sit on his tongue. Evaluated the balance. The salt was correct. The acid was correct. The composition was correct. And yet there was a hollowness to it, like a sentence spoken perfectly in a language you did not believe.

He set the fork down.

Around him, the dining room continued its subdued hum. A couple at the next table leaned toward each other, their voices low, expensive. Somewhere behind him a laugh rose and died quickly, caught by carpet and heavy drapery. Glassware clinked faintly, muffled into politeness.

The inspector reached for the folded napkin on his lap and dabbed the corner of his mouth, more out of habit than need. He took a sip of water. Then he sat back.

He could have called the server. He could have offered a comment, asked a question, given the kitchen the smallest rope of explanation. But the point was never to help them. The point was to see what happened when a perfect machine encountered a flaw it could not name.

He waited.

The plate sat untouched for a full minute, the langoustine cooling imperceptibly, the consommé losing its sheen. The inspector did not touch it again. He did not signal. He did not look around as if dissatisfied. He simply let absence do its work.

A server approached, drawn by the timing of things rather than a visible request. The server's eyes flicked to the plate, then up to the inspector's face, searching for a cue.

"Is everything to your liking, sir?" the server asked softly.

It was the kind of question designed to be answered with gratitude. It was also a net.

The inspector looked at the server with a mild, almost absent expression. "No," he said. Just that. No explanation. No anger. No request for replacement.

The server's smile remained in place, but the muscles behind it tightened. "Of course. My apologies."

The server reached for the plate.

The inspector did not stop him. He did not add a word. He watched the plate leave as if it were nothing more than an administrative correction. Then he returned his gaze to the center of the table and waited again, hands folded loosely.

The server moved through the dining room with the careful speed of someone carrying something fragile that could detonate. He kept his posture steady, his steps silent. But there was an urgency in the way he angled toward the service corridor, the way his shoulders held themselves as if bracing for impact.

As he passed the maître d', he did not make eye contact. He did not need to. The maître d' saw the untouched plate and seemed, for the first time that evening, briefly human. His face tightened, then smoothed again as the server disappeared behind the door.

The corridor swallowed sound. The door sealed. The dining room resumed breathing as if nothing had happened.

Inside the kitchen, the change was immediate.

Not a noise. Not a shout. The line did not stop. But the air tightened as if the building itself had sensed the plate crossing the threshold.

The server emerged into stainless steel and heat, the plate held level in both hands. He walked toward the pass with controlled calm, but his throat worked once in a swallow that did not go down easily.

Sofia Alvarez saw him first. She was positioned slightly off to the side, where she could see everything without appearing to watch. Her eyes went to the plate, then to the server's face. In that exchange, information passed: untouched. Returned. No notes.

Sofia did not speak. She stepped closer to the pass, her movements economical.

Chef Lucien Renaud stood at his usual position, anchored behind the heat lamps. He did not turn at the first sight of the server. He waited until the plate was within the perimeter of his control, until it was set down beneath the warming glow like an offering.

Only then did his gaze drop.

A returned plate was not unusual in lesser places. Here, it was a blasphemy. It did not belong in the rhythm of the restaurant. It was an interruption, and interruptions revealed weakness.

Renaud studied it without touching it, his eyes moving over every element: the alignment of fennel, the gloss of consommé, the delicate curve of the langoustine. It looked the way it was supposed to look. That was what made it worse.

He lifted his eyes to the server.

"What did he say?" Renaud asked.

The server's voice was careful. "He said, 'No,' Chef."

Renaud's gaze returned to the plate. The heat lamp's light made the broth shimmer, but as it sat, the surface tension began to break down, a thin line forming where perfection surrendered to time.

Sofia's posture remained composed, but something had changed in her eyes. She understood what this meant. Not just the possibility of a lost star. Something more intimate: control questioned.

Marcus Hale appeared at the edge of the kitchen entrance as if summoned by the disturbance. His presence was subtle but immediate, a man who did not hurry because the world was expected to make room for him. He came close enough to see the plate under the lamp, then stopped, hands loosely at his sides.

"Returned?" Marcus asked quietly.

Sofia answered without turning her head. “Untouched.”

Marcus’s mouth tightened. “Any complaint?”

“No,” Sofia said. “Just… no.”

Marcus looked at Renaud. “He’s testing your response.”

Renaud did not look up. “He’s tasting,” he said, the word almost flat. “He didn’t like something.”

Marcus stepped closer, his voice low enough that it stayed within the triangle of power at the pass. “He doesn’t return dishes unless he wants to see what breaks.”

Sofia’s eyes flicked to the line. The cooks were still moving, still executing, but there were micro-stutters now, tiny hesitations of hands that had noticed the plate’s reappearance. A commis’s knife paused for half a second. A pan was lifted and set down again. No one spoke. They didn’t need to. The returned plate spoke for itself.

Renaud leaned forward slightly, the first visible movement he’d made in minutes. He inhaled, carefully, as if scent might confess what appearance refused.

Then he did something that made Sofia’s jaw tighten.

He reached out and touched the rim of the plate.

His fingertip slid across porcelain, stopping where a drop of consommé had cooled into a barely visible crescent. Not a spill, not a smear. A ghost of a spill, the kind that could happen when a runner turned one degree too sharply, when a hand compensated for a near collision, when a breath changed at the wrong moment.

Renaud's gaze narrowed.

He did not lift the plate. He did not taste. He simply stared as if he could force the dish to reveal which part of the machine had faltered.

Behind him, the heat lamps hummed softly, indifferent.

The server stood frozen, still holding his hands in the shape of the plate he'd carried, as if letting them drop would be a sign of guilt.

Marcus watched Renaud's face, reading for cracks. "We can refire," he murmured. "Send a replacement, complimentary. Keep the pacing smooth."

Renaud did not answer immediately.

Sofia spoke, her voice precise. "Refiring without understanding is guessing."

Marcus's eyes slid to her. "Guessing is sometimes necessary."

Sofia's expression did not change, but the air between them sharpened. "Not here."

Renaud lifted his gaze at last, not to Marcus, not to Sofia, but to the line beyond them. The brigade moved under the weight of his attention like animals under a searchlight, careful not to twitch.

He looked at their hands. Their stations. The placement of tools. The choreography of plating.

His voice, when it came, was quiet enough that it forced the kitchen to lean inward.

"Which station?" he asked.

No one answered. Not because they didn't know. Because knowing was dangerous and speaking it made you complicit.

Sofia's eyes went to the garde manger station, then to saucier. A dish like this passed through multiple hands, touched by multiple points of failure. The whole kitchen was built on shared responsibility until it wasn't.

Marcus let out a slow breath through his nose, controlled. "Lucien," he said, a warning disguised as familiarity. "We don't have time for—"

Renaud cut him off without raising his voice. “We have time,” he said. “We always have time to find the flaw.”

The line tightened further. The cooks moved faster, sharper, as if speed could hide fear.

Renaud’s eyes returned to the plate. He studied the langoustine as if it were evidence at a crime scene. There was nothing visibly wrong. No broken garnish. No misaligned arc of sauce. And yet it had come back untouched, like an accusation.

He straightened slowly.

The kitchen did not breathe.

Renaud’s gaze lifted and pinned itself on a point just beyond Sofia, somewhere in the mass of white jackets and tense hands.

His voice carried, soft but absolute.

“Who plated this?”

No one moved.

The question hung in the air above the heat lamps, above the pass, above the stainless steel and the neat rows of tweezers and squeeze bottles aligned like surgical instruments. It was not shouted. It did not need to be. In this kitchen, volume was for people without authority.

The brigade kept working because stopping would be interpreted as panic. Hands continued to portion, to wipe rims, to drag the edge of a spatula clean with a towel folded to the same width every time. But the rhythm had changed. Every motion now contained the awareness of being watched.

Renaud did not repeat himself. He simply waited; eyes fixed on the line the way a blade fixed itself on a throat.

Sofia stood half a step back from him, her posture composed. She had seen this before. Not the returned plate, not like this, not untouched and without explanation, but she had seen the way Renaud extracted an error from a room full of people who all wanted the error to belong to someone else.

Marcus Hale remained near the entrance, in the borderland between kitchen and corridor. He looked like a man who understood how quickly reputations could be dismantled and how quietly it could be done. His attention flicked once toward the door as if considering how far the tremor of this moment would travel.

"Who plated this?" Renaud asked again, not louder, only more exact. The words were a scalpel, not a demand.

At the garde manger station, a commis's hands shook so slightly that the microgreens he was arranging trembled like something alive. He swallowed hard, eyes locked on his board as if the answer might be written there. Two stations down, a senior chef kept his head down and continued to spoon a purée into a ring mold, face blank with practiced neutrality. No one wanted to be the first to speak. The first voice became a target.

A runner passed behind the line carrying a tray of clean plates, careful not to make noise. His eyes went to the returned dish under the lamp and away again so fast it looked like a flinch.

Renaud's gaze swept across them, not in anger, not in irritation, but with the cold patience of a man who had all night and no mercy. He could wait longer than they could.

It was a young chef who broke first. Not a commis, not brand new, but still new enough that his face had not learned how to hide its fear. He stood at the edge of the poisson station, close enough to the pass that he could feel the heat from the lamps but far enough that he could pretend his work didn't involve that plate.

His name was Julien Morel. Sofia knew it because she kept names the way she kept errors. He had been here nine months. He had stopped talking to other people three months ago. That was usually a sign that someone was trying to survive.

Julien set down the tweezers in his hand. Not with a clatter. Carefully. Deliberately. He lifted his right hand halfway, palm facing inward like a student in a strict classroom.

The entire kitchen seemed to narrow its focus onto him.

"I did," Julien said. His voice was thin, not from weakness, but from the effort it took to push sound through a throat that wanted to close.

Renaud's eyes did not widen. His face did not change. He nodded once, the smallest movement possible.

For a heartbeat, Julien's expression flickered with something like hope. As if admitting it might earn him a chance to explain, to learn, to correct. People came into kitchens believing that truth was valuable. L'Étoile Noire trained that belief out of them.

Renaud did not ask why. He did not ask how. He did not ask what Julien had noticed, what he had felt, what he might have corrected if given a second.

He only said, "Remove him."

Not "fire him." Not "send him home." Not "get him out of here."

Remove.

Two senior chefs moved immediately. Antoine, from the meat station, and a broad-shouldered chef de partie whose name was rarely spoken above a murmur. They approached Julien with the same calm they used to approach a plate that needed correction. Their hands were clean. Their movements were economical.

Antoine didn't grab. He didn't shove. He simply stepped close enough that Julien had to lean back a fraction to keep his space, and that fraction was all the control Antoine needed.

"Apron off," Antoine said, quietly.

Julien hesitated. His eyes went to Sofia first, instinctively searching for an alternative authority, someone who might soften the order into something survivable. Sofia's expression remained neutral. It wasn't cruelty. It was adherence.

"Now," Antoine added, still calm.

Julien's fingers moved to the knot at his waist. His hands shook harder now, the fabric resisting him as if it had its own loyalty. He untied the apron and held it for a moment, not knowing where to put it. The chef de partie reached out and took it from him, folding it once, fast and neat, as if erasing the shape of the body that had worn it.

Julien's mouth opened. A breath came out that might have been the beginning of a protest, an explanation, a plea.

Sofia spoke before he could form words. Her voice was soft, and that made it more final.

"Don't," she said.

Julien looked at her, eyes wet but not crying. Crying was loud. Crying was indulgent. Crying made a mess.

Antoine turned Julien gently by the shoulder and guided him toward the service corridor. The chef de partie walked on the other side, close enough that Julien could not veer off toward the lockers, the staff exit, the back staircase. They kept him centered, contained.

They passed the pass. They passed the returned plate. Julien's gaze flicked toward it as he went by, as if he could see, now, what had been wrong. But the dish revealed nothing. It sat under the heat lamp with its immaculate fennel crescents and its sheen beginning to collapse, indifferent to the human life it had just altered.

Renaud did not follow. He did not watch Julien leave. The removal was not the point. The point was that the machine had rejected a part. The machine would keep moving.

He turned his eyes back to the line.

"Refire," he said.

The word traveled through the kitchen like a release of pressure. Not relief, never relief, but direction. Direction meant survival.

Saucier began again without asking questions. Poisson reset the langoustine. Garde manger shaved fennel to the thickness of a breath. Someone replaced the consommé with a fresh reduction, measured and strained through cloth so fine it might as well have been skin.

Marcus Hale stepped closer to the pass, gaze narrowing as he watched the brigade tighten into compliance. He leaned toward Renaud, voice low.

"That was quick," Marcus said.

Renaud did not look at him. "It was necessary."

Marcus's mouth twitched, a near-smile that held no warmth. "Necessary for whom?"

"For everyone," Renaud replied. "The inspector does not want a story. He wants a standard."

"And now he has one," Marcus said.

Sofia watched the corridor door swing shut behind Antoine and the other chef. The door closed softly, swallowing the last trace of Julien's presence. No shouting echoed back. No argument. No slam. The silence in this place was not just discipline. It was design.

Sofia stepped toward the pass. "Lucien," she said quietly, using his first name only because Marcus was here and because power was being negotiated in half-sentences. "If it wasn't his fault—"

Renaud's gaze cut to her, precise. "Was it his hands on the plate?"

"Yes."

"Then it was his fault," Renaud said. "Fault is not an emotion. It is a position."

Sofia held his gaze. She wanted to say something else, something that would acknowledge the truth she could taste in the air: that the plate could have failed in transit, that a runner could have turned too sharply, that the consommé ghost-mark on the rim suggested a near collision in the corridor. That perfection could be broken by inches and accidents and panic no one confessed to.

But Renaud's kitchen did not deal in accident. Accident was a word that excused.

Marcus tilted his head, watching the exchange like a man watching two blades test each other.

"The inspector will expect a replacement," he murmured. "And he will measure the time between."

Renaud's eyes returned to the new plate being assembled. "He will have it."

They worked with a speed that did not appear frantic, because franticness was another kind of imperfection. The langoustine was poached again, the timing counted in the mind rather than spoken aloud. The consommé was poured with a steadiness that made the liquid look solid. Fennel was placed in identical crescents, not one millimeter off from its intended arc.

Sofia leaned slightly toward the runner who would carry it out. "Twelve o'clock," she said, not because the runner didn't know, but because hearing it reminded the body to obey. "No turns. No pauses."

The runner nodded once, eyes fixed on the plate as if it were already a verdict.

As the plate left the pass, Renaud's hand lifted and hovered for a moment over the empty space where it had been. Not touching, just measuring the absence, as if confirming the machine had corrected itself.

In the corridor, footsteps returned. Antoine came back alone. The other chef did not. Antoine's hands were empty. His face was blank, as if nothing had happened.

Sofia's eyes met Antoine's for a fraction of a second. A question lived there. Antoine did not answer it.

"Where is he?" she asked anyway, quietly, because she couldn't stop herself.

Antoine's voice was barely audible. "He's gone."

Gone where was not asked. Gone could mean the staff entrance. Gone could mean the office. Gone could mean the locked room behind dry storage that most of the younger staff pretended not to know existed. Gone could mean a phone call made in a voice that did not leave evidence.

At L'Étoile Noire, being removed was not always the same as being fired. Fired people returned for their knives, their jackets, their last check. Fired people told stories.

Removed people were edited out. Their names disappeared from schedules. Their locker tags were peeled off. Their employee file stopped existing in the same way a bad memory stopped existing when you convinced yourself it had never happened.

Service did not pause to wonder which kind of gone this was.

In the dining room, the inspector sat with his hands folded, posture unchanged. The returned plate had been cleared without ceremony. The table looked clean, neutral, prepared for the next performance. Around him, other guests continued their murmured conversations, their carefully restrained laughter. The room had not noticed the tiny act of violence occurring behind its walls, and even if it had, it would not have known what it was seeing.

A server approached again, expression perfectly composed.

"Our apologies for the delay," the server said, as if delay was the only possible flaw. "Chef has prepared the course again."

The replacement dish was placed down with the same precision as the first, the rim aligned to an invisible axis, the plate so immaculate it could have been new.

The inspector looked at it. He did not smile. He did not offer reassurance. He did not say, It's fine, don't worry, these things happen.

He simply observed, eyes scanning the surface the way Renaud's had. He inhaled. He tasted.

In the kitchen, Renaud watched the timing. Not directly, not with his eyes on the gap, but by the cadence of returns, by the way the servers moved, by the invisible pulse that connected dining room to pass. He listened for nothing, because nothing would be said. The inspector would not speak until he wrote.

Minutes passed. A plate came back empty. Not scraped, not cleaned aggressively. Simply empty, the way it should be when someone eats without complaint.

No message accompanied it. No server leaned in with a whispered note. No expression betrayed relief.

The machine continued.

Renaud did not exhale. Sofia did not relax. Marcus did not move away from the entrance.

Perfection had been preserved, at least on the surface. A flawed part had been removed. The rhythm had been restored.

And somewhere beyond the kitchen doors, a young chef who had raised his hand was becoming harder to remember, even for the people who had watched him go.

Chapter 2

Entry Through Fire

Connor Felwick arrived three hours before service because he had been told that if you were on time, you were late, and because he could not tolerate the idea of walking into a room like L'Étoile Noire already behind.

The street was still damp from a morning rain that had stopped without clearing the sky. Washington, D.C. wore that particular gray that made stone look older and money look cleaner. The restaurant's facade didn't announce itself the way most famous places did. No gold lettering, no theatrical awning, no indulgent display that begged for cameras. Just dark glass, matte metal, and a name so small it could have been a warning rather than a sign.

L'Étoile Noire.

He stood for a moment on the sidewalk, his knife roll heavy against his palm and watched the building as if it might shift its shape and reveal what it really was. Through the glass, he could see nothing but dimness and the faint suggestion of movement deeper inside, a shadow passing across a corridor, a door closing without sound. The stillness made his stomach tighten.

He told himself that the nerves were good. They meant he cared. They meant he understood where he was.

His phone buzzed with a message from his mother, sent too early from a different time zone: Proud of you. Eat something. He didn't answer. He couldn't afford to invite softness into his hand right now.

He stepped forward and pulled on the door handle.

It opened with a controlled pneumatic sigh, sealing the street behind him like a vault closing. Warmth replaced the wet chill. The air smelled of beeswax and citrus and something clean enough to feel engineered. It was the same scent Connor remembered from the one time he had saved up to eat at a restaurant that wanted to be this one. But here it was more exact, the edges polished until even the perfume of wealth had been disciplined.

A host stand sat to his left like a lectern. No one stood behind it.

He waited anyway.

His shoes made almost no sound on the carpet. That alone unsettled him. He'd grown up in kitchens where floors told the truth, where footsteps slapped and dragged, where speed announced itself in noise. Here, sound was absorbed. Mistakes would be absorbed too, until they weren't.

A door opened from a side corridor and a man in a dark suit stepped out. Not a maître d', Connor realized, because the man's posture wasn't built to welcome. It was built to block.

The man looked Connor over the way a bouncer might, except there was no judgment in his face, only assessment. Thirty seconds of inventory: age, hands, clothes, the knife roll, the expression Connor was trying to keep neutral.

"You're early," the man said.

"Yes," Connor answered. It came out too quick, as if speed could substitute for permission. He cleared his throat. "Connor Felwick. New commis."

The man's eyes did not flicker with recognition. If Connor's name meant anything here, it hadn't reached the front. Or it had, and the man simply didn't care.

He gestured once with two fingers. Not a welcome. A direction.

"Kitchen entrance is through the service corridor. Don't go through the dining room."

Connor nodded. "Understood."

The man stepped aside and let him pass as if granting access through a checkpoint. Connor moved down the corridor, keeping his shoulders from brushing the walls, knife roll tucked in close. There were no framed photos of celebrities, no awards, nothing that said Look what we are. The building didn't celebrate itself. It expected everyone else to.

At the end of the corridor, a plain door waited. No signage. Just a brushed steel handle that had been wiped so often it shone.

Connor paused with his hand on it. Behind it, he could feel heat in the air, a low pressure that suggested stoves already awake. He could not hear anything. That was the strangest part. A kitchen with no sound was like an ocean with no waves.

He opened the door.

Stainless steel and white light hit him first. The room was larger than he expected, not sprawling, but arranged with a kind of ruthless intelligence. Prep stations in exact lines. Shelving that held containers aligned like a laboratory. No clutter. No stray towels. No puddles. Everything clean enough to be suspicious.

And still, no noise.

Not silence in the sense of calm, but silence as a rule. The only sounds were mechanical: refrigeration units breathing, a faint hiss of gas, the soft tick of a timer somewhere too disciplined to ring loudly.

Chefs moved in that silence like parts of a machine. They didn't stroll. They didn't talk. They traveled in straight lines, never colliding, never forcing someone else to shift. Their hands were quick, but not frantic. Knife work had no flourish, only function. Someone was reducing something at a low simmer, stirring without clinking the spoon against the pot. A towel folded into thirds wiped a counter in one pass. A cook adjusted a tray by an inch without looking at it, as if his body knew the measurement.

Connor stepped fully inside, and the air changed around him. It felt like walking into a room where everyone had been talking until you entered, except they hadn't been talking at all. They had been operating. And now the operating table had a new object on it.

He approached what he assumed was the center, the pass, where heat lamps hung like a set of suspended interrogators. The stainless steel there was polished to a mirror. No fingerprints. No smudges. It was too perfect to belong to human hands.

A woman stood slightly off to the side of the main line, watching rather than doing. She was small, tight in posture, hair pulled back hard enough to look painful. She held a clipboard but didn't look down at it. Her eyes moved constantly: hands, boards, the angle of shoulders, the distance between a pan and the edge of a stove.

Connor recognized her from articles and whispers, the way young cooks recognize names the way some people recognize saints.

Sofia Alvarez.

He approached her with the knife roll held in front of him like an offering. "Chef Alvarez?"

Her gaze landed on him and stayed, unblinking. It wasn't rude. It was deliberate. It made him aware of everything: the way his fingers tightened around the roll, the fact that he hadn't shaved as close as he would have liked, the slight sheen of sweat under his collar from walking too fast in the wrong kind of jacket.

"Yes," she said.

"I'm Connor Felwick. I'm supposed to start today." He added, because he couldn't help himself, "Thank you for the opportunity."

Sofia's expression did not soften. She didn't acknowledge the gratitude. She didn't say welcome. Her eyes flicked to his knife roll and back to his face.

"Wash your hands," she said. "Put your things in the lockers. Jacket on. Apron tight. No jewelry. No watch. Hair back. If you don't have a cap, you'll find one. Then you report to garde manger."

"Yes, Chef."

She waited a beat longer, as if checking whether he would fill the silence with unnecessary words. When he didn't, she gave the smallest nod and turned her attention back to the line.

Connor moved away quickly, trying not to look like he was rushing. He found the locker room without being told, guided by the logic of the building. Even here, the lockers were clean, the floor dry. There were no notes taped up, no jokes scrawled in marker. He chose an empty locker with a strip of tape already on it, blank and waiting for a name.

As he changed into his jacket, he noticed something odd: a few lockers had no tape at all, as if their owners had never existed. The absence caught his eye more than any label would have. It felt like a deliberate blank space in a photograph.

He shoved his street clothes inside and closed the door softly. He tied his apron, checked the knot twice, then washed his hands until they felt stripped. When he returned to the kitchen, he moved to the cold station the way he'd been instructed.

Garde manger was always where the new ones went, in Connor's experience. It was treated like the safe station in lesser kitchens, the place where you could be useful without burning anything. Here, it didn't feel safe. It felt precise.

A long-refrigerated counter held trays of herbs, microgreens, thinly shaved vegetables arranged in lines so straight they looked measured with a ruler. Squeeze bottles were labeled in perfect handwriting, the dates written small but legible. A container of salt sat exactly at the corner of a cutting board, aligned with the edge. Even the tweezers were placed as if someone had drawn their outline and demanded they stay inside it.

A tall chef with tired eyes and a face that looked carved from discipline glanced at Connor and then away without greeting. He continued slicing radishes into translucent coins, each one identical enough to make Connor's fingers itch.

Connor swallowed and positioned himself at the open space on the station, waiting for instruction.

Minutes passed.

No one spoke to him.

He resisted the urge to ask what he should do, because Sofia's tone had already warned him: questions were weakness, or at least proof that you couldn't read the room. So he watched. He tracked movements, tried to hear the rhythm everyone else seemed to hear. A chef reached, grabbed a towel, wiped, and returned it to the exact place. Another tasted something without a spoon clink, then adjusted seasoning with two grains of salt between finger and thumb.

Connor chose a task before someone chose one for him. He found a crate of herbs near the back of the station, the kind of prep that always needed doing. He pulled it toward him and began picking through it, separating leaves with careful speed, building neat piles.

For a few minutes, he felt his body settle. Work was work. Work was familiar. He could make himself useful.

Then he noticed the glances.

Not open staring, nothing obvious, but quick checks from the corner of eyes. Assessment. Calculation. The way people looked at a new part before deciding whether it would fit or be rejected.

A tray slid onto the counter near him without warning, stopping with almost no sound. Connor looked up.

Sofia stood there again. Close enough that he could see the faint shadow of flour on her sleeve, like a ghost of labor. Her eyes dropped to his herb piles and held.

He held his breath without meaning too.

After a moment, she reached forward and moved one pile. Not much. An inch, maybe less. But the movement was exact, purposeful. It made Connor's stomach drop because it meant she'd been watching long enough to decide that his spacing was wrong.

"Everything has a place," she said, voice low, as if the words were for him alone even though anyone nearby could hear. "And everything is watched."

"Yes, Chef," Connor managed.

Sofia didn't respond. She turned and walked away, disappearing into the larger choreography of the kitchen.

Connor stared at the adjusted pile for a moment, then corrected all the others to match, aligning them with the same invisible grid. He didn't know what the grid was. He only knew it existed, and that if he didn't find it quickly, someone else would remove him the way you removed a mistake from a plate.

He kept working, fingers moving faster.

At the far end of the kitchen, near the pass, a figure stood still in a way no one else was still. Connor saw him only in fragments at first: a white jacket without wrinkles, hands resting near the edge of the stainless steel, head angled slightly as if listening to pressure rather than sound.

Chef Lucien Renaud.

Even without speaking, he controlled the room. People oriented around him the way metal filings oriented around a magnet. When he shifted his gaze, stations tightened. When he leaned slightly forward, a runner appeared as if summoned. No shouting, no theatrics. Just gravity.

Connor watched him for half a second too long and felt a sudden chill, the sense that looking might be noticed and punished. He forced his eyes back down to his work, but the image stayed with him: Renaud at the center, calm and lethal.

Somewhere deeper in the building, a door opened and closed softly. A corridor swallowed footsteps. Connor remembered the blank lockers and wondered, without knowing why, what kind of kitchen left absences that clean.

He told himself it was normal turnover. High standards. People couldn't handle it, so they left.

But the silence here didn't feel like people leaving. It felt like people being erased.

He adjusted his piles again, matching the invisible order, hands moving with renewed urgency. He could feel the restaurant around him, not like a workplace, but like a system with rules that weren't written down because they didn't need to be.

The air carried heat and disinfectant and the faint metallic scent of knives. The lights were bright enough to reveal flaws and flat enough to make everything look the same. Even time felt controlled, parceled into prep windows and service windows and the thin, dangerous moments between when something could go wrong.

Connor had dreamed of this place. He had chased it through apprenticeships and brutal shifts and instructors who told him he had talent, that he had discipline, that he was ready.

Standing at garde manger with herbs under his nails and Sofia's words still sharp in his ears, he understood his mistake.

He had assumed earning entry meant belonging.

But L'Étoile Noire wasn't a place you joined.

It was a place you survived.

No one officially introduced Connor to anyone else.

That, he realized, was the welcome.

The kitchen accepted his presence the way it accepted a new stainless-steel shelf: by pretending it had always been there and expecting it to meet the same standard of cleanliness. He could feel the others registering him at the edges of their attention, the quick inventory of a new body inside a closed system, but no one offered a name, a station tour, a joke that relieved the pressure. There was no relief in this place. Relief implied slack.

He kept his eyes down, hands moving, learning the pace through observation because asking would mark him as needy. The tall chef beside him continued slicing radishes into coins so thin they curled at the edges like paper. Each slice landed on the board without sound. Connor's own herb prep suddenly felt clumsy, too tactile, too human.

A runner passed behind him. The runner's shoes made no noise on the floor, but Connor still sensed him because the air shifted, a brief draft of motion. The runner set a tray down at the far end of garde manger, then paused with his hands hovering above it as if waiting for permission to withdraw.

Connor glanced at the tray. Tiny porcelain spoons already aligned. A smear of something pale in each bowl, identical in length and thickness.

The tall chef finally spoke, but only to deliver an instruction that had no warmth in it.

"Chervil," he said.

Connor looked up. The chef's gaze did not meet his. It aimed past him, toward the herb piles, as if Connor were a tool and not a person. He added nothing. No please. No explanation.

"Yes," Connor said quietly, and reached for chervil with hands that suddenly felt too large.

He picked leaves, the smallest sprigs, trying to match what he'd seen others do. He placed them into a metal ring on the tray, careful not to touch the smear beneath. The runner remained still. Waiting. Measuring.

When Connor finished the first spoon, he hesitated. Was it right? Was the angle correct? The leaves looked fine to him, but fine was a word that did not belong at L'Étoile Noire.

The tall chef's hand appeared and shifted the chervil by a fraction. Not enough to be a correction you could argue with, just enough to make Connor feel the mistake he hadn't known he'd made.

"Again," the chef said, still not looking at him.

Heat rose under Connor's collar, a flare of embarrassment, but he swallowed it down and restarted. He adjusted the second spoon, then the third, his fingers learning the distance between acceptable and erased. The runner's eyes flicked to Connor's hands once, then away, expression blank.

Connor finished the last spoon. He pulled his hands back as if stepping away from a ledge.

The tall chef inspected the tray without touching it. He gave a single nod toward the runner.

The runner lifted it and disappeared, leaving Connor with a feeling that he had just been tested without being told there was a test.

Minutes later, another tray arrived. Another instruction, barely a word. Fennel. Tarragon. Citrus zest shaved so thin it would dissolve on contact. Connor complied, adjusting his speed to match theirs, learning to move without generating sound.

His knife tapped the board once and the sound landed in the silence like a dropped coin.

Sofia's head turned from across the room, fast as a predator's reflex.

Connor froze for a beat, then forced himself to keep moving, quieter. He could feel the other cooks registering the noise without looking, their bodies tightening slightly, as if sound carried contagion.

A commis at the far side of garde manger slid a towel toward him with the toe of his shoe. The towel stopped neatly at Connor's station line, not crossing into his space. The commis never looked up.

Connor stared at the towel, confused. Then he understood. The towel was folded into thirds, the way everyone else's were. Connor's towel, beside his board, was folded into quarters. It was wrong. He hadn't noticed because it was still a towel. In this kitchen, still a towel meant nothing. There was only correct.

He refolded it into thirds and placed it back where it belonged, aligned with the board's edge. The commis turned away again as if the exchange had not occurred.

The message, Connor realized, wasn't kindness. It was instruction delivered anonymously so it didn't become a relationship.

Relationships created alliances. Alliances created noise.

The service door opened briefly at the back corridor and a puff of cooler air entered, then vanished. A man stepped through with a crate of produce, set it down, and left without a word. The door closed with a soft seal. The kitchen returned to its controlled atmosphere.

Connor caught a glimpse down the corridor as the door shut. A sliver of darkness, the quiet throat of the building. For a second he thought he saw someone standing there, half-hidden by shadow, watching in. But when he looked again, there was nothing.

He remembered the lockers with missing tape. Spaces where names should have been.

He forced the thought away and returned to the tray in front of him.

Time at L'Étoile Noire didn't pass the way it did in other kitchens. It didn't move in a blur of shouted orders and slammed pans. It passed like a metronome ticking inside the skull, each beat another task completed, another small correction absorbed without comment. He checked the clock once and felt guilty for doing it, as if looking at time implied impatience.

Sofia appeared at his station without warning. She did not approach like someone walking. She arrived like a decision.

Connor's hands stopped for half a second before he forced them to continue.

She looked down at the tray he was working on, then at the towel, then at his knife placement. Her eyes were so still that it felt like being photographed.

"You were told not to go through the dining room," she said.

It wasn't a question. Connor's stomach tightened anyway.

"Yes, Chef."

Sofia's gaze lifted to his face. "You were told to report to garde manger. You did."

"Yes, Chef."

She held the silence long enough for him to wonder if he had failed without knowing how.

Then she said, "Do you understand why no one has spoken to you?"

Connor opened his mouth. There were a dozen answers he could offer, none of them safe. Because they're busy. Because standards are high. Because I'm new. Each one sounded like an excuse.

"I don't know, Chef," he said finally. Honesty felt like another kind of risk, but it was the only thing he had that wasn't performance.

Sofia's expression did not change. "Good."

The word landed strangely. Not approval. Not comfort. A marker, like a check on her invisible list.

"This kitchen doesn't welcome," she continued. "It observes. If you need to be welcomed, you're in the wrong place."

Connor nodded, throat tight. "Yes, Chef."

Sofia's eyes dropped again, scanning his station. "Your knife stays here. Not there." She nudged it with a fingertip, aligning it with the board. "Your towel stays here. Always folded the same way. Your hands stay clean enough that no one sees you wash them."

"Yes, Chef."

She paused, then added, softer but sharper for it, "No one will help you here unless they are told to. Help is earned, not offered."

Connor felt the urge to ask what earning looked like, but he caught it before it reached his tongue. He nodded again, a small movement, as if too much motion might draw attention.

Sofia watched him for a long moment. Then, almost as an afterthought, she said, “If you make a mistake, you fix it before it’s seen.”

Connor’s mind flashed, unbidden, to the returned plate story he had heard in school, whispered like a myth. A dish returned at a three-star place. Someone disappeared. No one talked about it afterward. He’d assumed it was exaggeration, a story told to frighten students into discipline.

Standing under Sofia’s gaze, he felt the myth become real.

“Yes, Chef,” he said.

Sofia turned to leave, then stopped and glanced back at him. “Your jacket sleeve,” she said.

Connor looked down. A faint smear of green from herbs, barely visible.

He went cold. It wasn’t even a stain, just a whisper of one, but here whispers mattered.

He grabbed a clean towel, dampened it, wiped the fabric, then wiped it again until the sleeve looked untouched. Sofia watched without helping, without impatience.

When it was clean, she nodded once, almost imperceptibly.

And then she did something that felt more significant than any welcome could have.

She spoke his name.

“Felwick,” she said. “Eyes up. Listen more than you talk. Move like you belong. But don’t assume you do.”

Her attention shifted away as if he’d been filed into the system, categorized, put into a drawer that could be opened or emptied depending on what he did next. She walked back toward the pass, her clipboard still blank.

Connor stood very still for a second, absorbing what had just happened. It wasn’t encouragement. It wasn’t even instruction. It was a warning that he had been acknowledged.

In this kitchen, being ignored meant you were irrelevant. Being acknowledged meant you were visible.

Visible things could be corrected.

Or removed.

He returned to the tray with renewed care, aware now that the unspoken welcome was not silence alone but a set of expectations communicated through absence: no one would cushion him, no one would catch him if he slipped, and any weakness he displayed would not be met with sympathy. It would be met with efficiency.

Around him, the machine continued.

At the far end of the kitchen, Renaud stood at the pass, still as a fixed point. He did not look toward Connor, not directly, but Connor felt the gravitational pull of his presence anyway. He remembered the blank spaces on the lockers. He remembered Sofia's words: if you hesitate, you will be replaced.

Connor adjusted the placement of the garnish with tweezers, matching the invisible grid, and told himself that this was what he'd wanted. This was what greatness looked like.

The kitchen offered no welcome.

Only the chance to prove, moment by moment, that he deserved to remain.

Connor worked until his fingers stopped feeling like fingers and became instruments.

It wasn't the volume of labor that exhausted him at first, not the repetition of plucking herbs and shaving citrus into impossible threads. It was the requirement that every action leave no trace of effort. In other kitchens, speed had come with noise: the percussion of knife against board, the slap of towels, the hiss of someone swearing under their breath. Here, speed existed without sound, as if the air itself punished anything crude.

He began to recognize a pattern in how tasks arrived. Not shouted orders, not explanations, just a tray landing at the edge of the station and a single word spoken by someone who refused to look at him.

"Celeri."

"Apple."

"Endive."

Each word was a door that opened into a precise expectation. Connor learned quickly that the ingredient name was never the full instruction. The rest was assumed knowledge: the cut, the thickness, the placement, the temperature, the timing of when it would be needed at the pass.

At one point, he reached for the mandoline without thinking and set it down with a slightly heavier touch than intended. The plastic feet made a faint tap against stainless steel.

The sound was not loud. In any normal kitchen it would have disappeared under conversation and exhaust fans. Here, it rang like a dropped fork in a church.

Several heads did not turn, but shoulders tightened. The tall chef beside him paused for a fraction of a second, then continued slicing radish as if he'd never heard anything at all. The message was immediate: Connor's mistakes were his alone. The room would register them, record them, but no one would share ownership.

He adjusted his grip, lifted the mandoline again, and lowered it as if placing something fragile and expensive. He forced his breathing to slow. Panic made noise. Panic was visible.

Sofia did not appear, but he felt her awareness from across the kitchen the way you felt a heat source without looking at it. He kept his eyes down and worked with renewed care, aligning thin celeri slices into a neat stack, each sheet so uniform it could have been printed.

When the stack was complete, he moved it to the tray and realized, too late, that he'd set it down a hair off-square to the tray's edge.

He hesitated.

The right action was obvious: fix it before it was seen.

But it was already seen. He felt that too. He could sense the attention on his hands, the quiet measurement of whether he would correct it quickly enough to prove he understood the rule.

He slid the stack one millimeter to the left. Then another fraction. Then stopped, satisfied it was aligned.

A hand appeared beside his, not touching his work, just pointing.

The tall chef finally looked at him. His eyes were the color of tired steel.

“You adjusted twice,” the chef said.

Connor swallowed. “Yes, Chef.”

“One adjustment means you noticed before it existed,” the chef continued. “Two means you noticed after.”

Connor’s stomach tightened with the strange humiliation of being corrected for correcting. “Understood.”

The chef’s gaze dropped to Connor’s towel, still folded into thirds. “Good. Keep it that way.”

Then the chef turned away, already back inside his own tasks.

Connor stood very still, the lesson sinking in like cold water. The goal wasn’t to fix errors. The goal was to move in a way that never created them. Correction was allowed, even required, but it was also evidence. Every small imperfection left a shadow behind it.

The next hour blurred into an exacting rhythm: wipe, slice, align, check, wipe again. Connor learned to keep his station immaculate without looking like he was cleaning it. He learned to rinse a spoon without splashing. He learned to open the refrigerator door with his fingertips, not his palm, so it didn't swing too wide and bump the tray inside. He learned to close it until the seal caught with a soft, controlled pull, not a careless shove.

He also learned that time moved differently depending on who needed what.

A runner appeared beside the cold station, waiting with hands clasped behind his back, posture too rigid to be casual. The runner's eyes held on Connor's tray for a moment, then shifted to the tall chef.

The tall chef lifted his chin once. Permission granted.

The runner leaned in. "Six spoons," he said, barely audible.

"Six," the tall chef replied.

Connor's brain caught on the word. Spoons meant amuse. Spoons meant early course. Spoons meant the pass would want it now, not in ten minutes, not after Connor finished what he was doing.

The tall chef didn't instruct him. He didn't need to. Connor should already understand. Execution, not conversation.

Connor pivoted to the porcelain spoons lined up at the edge of the station. Each spoon already held a pale smear, identical to the earlier tray he'd worked on. A base already set, waiting for finishing.

He reached for the garnish with tweezers and started placing. One sprig, one angle, one breath of distance from the smear's edge. He moved quickly, but not too quickly. His hands wanted to shake. He forced them not to.

Halfway through the fourth spoon, the tweezers slipped and the garnish landed slightly too far forward, just grazing the smear.

It was the kind of mistake no diner would ever identify as a flaw. It was also the kind of mistake that would not survive the pass.

Connor's pulse spiked. He could feel the urge to scrape it off, to smooth it, to make it seem intentional.

But he heard Sofia's voice in his mind: If you make a mistake, you fix it before it's seen.

It had been seen. The runner's eyes flicked to it. The tall chef's gaze tightened almost imperceptibly.

Connor didn't freeze. Freezing would be worse. He lifted the spoon, dumped it into the discard bin without hesitation, and started over with a fresh one.

The motion felt like tearing up money. He forced himself not to think about cost.

He finished the tray. Six spoons, perfect. He set it down at the station's edge with the same alignment as everything else, then stepped back half a pace, hands behind his back, copying the runner's posture without meaning to.

The tall chef inspected without touching, eyes moving like a scanner. He held on Connor's replaced spoon for a beat longer, as if detecting where the mistake had been. Then he gave a slight nod.

The runner took the tray and vanished toward the pass.

Connor exhaled silently. The air left his lungs like he'd been holding it for hours.

He went back to prep, but his body felt different now. Warmer in a way that wasn't relief, sharper in a way that wasn't confidence. He had made a decision fast enough to keep the machine moving. He had chosen waste over visible imperfection. He understood the rule in his bones now: perfection wasn't just the standard, it was the method. You protected it by sacrificing anything that threatened it, including your own ego.

A little later, Sofia appeared at the cold station again. She didn't announce herself. She didn't have to. Connor registered her the way animals registered the shift of a predator's shadow.

She looked at his board, his towel, his tweezers, the tray spacing. Her gaze was quick, economical. Inventory.

"You refired a spoon," she said.

Connor's throat tightened. "Yes, Chef."

"Why?" she asked.

He could have said because it wasn't perfect. That answer would have sounded like begging. He could have said because it touched the smear. That would have sounded like an excuse.

He chose the truth that mattered in this kitchen. "Because it would have been seen."

Sofia held his gaze a fraction longer than usual. "Good," she said, the same word as before, still not comfort.

Then she leaned closer, voice low enough that it stayed inside his space. "Do you know what gets people removed here, Felwick?"

Connor's mind flashed to the blank lockers. Julien Morel raising his hand. The corridor door closing softly behind him. The word remove spoken like a knife.

"Mistakes," Connor said.

Sofia's expression stayed flat. "Everyone makes mistakes."

She let the sentence sit, forcing him to confront it. If mistakes were inevitable, the threat had to be something else.

Connor swallowed. "Being slow to correct them."

Sofia's eyes narrowed, almost approving. Almost. "Being slow," she agreed. "Being loud. Being defensive. Making your problem someone else's. The kitchen can tolerate imperfection for a second. It cannot tolerate hesitation."

Connor nodded once. "Yes, Chef."

Sofia's gaze drifted past him toward the rest of the kitchen, toward the pass where Renaud stood like a fixed star. "Chef doesn't want apologies," she said. "He wants absence. Absence of errors. Absence of noise. Absence of personality when it interferes."

Connor felt the weight of that, the way it made the entire room make a certain kind of sense. It also made something inside him resist, quietly, not enough to show on his face. He had come here to learn, to become better, to earn recognition. The idea of becoming absent felt like a punishment disguised as training.

Sofia's attention snapped back to him. "Show me your cuts," she said.

Connor's heart kicked. "Now?"

"Yes. Now." Sofia reached for a container of peeled apples. She set one on his board. Then a second. Then a third. "Brunoise. Five millimeters. Uniform."

Connor picked up his knife.

In school, they'd taught brunoise like a ritual: square the fruit, slice, stack, cut. Here, the ritual had to happen without theatrics, without pause. He began. His knife moved faster than it had earlier, but he controlled the blade, letting muscle memory do what panic could not.

Halfway through, Sofia's hand came down, not touching his knife, but stopping his forward movement with a flat palm against the board's edge. A silent brake.

Connor froze.

Sofia pointed at his apple sticks. "Those are not squared," she said. "They're close. Close is not squared. Your dice will be inconsistent."

Connor stared, seeing it now: a tiny taper, a slight angle he'd allowed because it felt negligible. Negligible was a word that didn't exist here.

He opened his mouth, then closed it. No defense.

Sofia slid the apple sticks into a neat stack, aligned them, and placed them back in front of him without adding drama. "Again," she said.

Connor started over, stripping away the taper, making the sticks perfect, then cutting them into cubes that looked eerily identical. His hands began to find the tempo. It wasn't his tempo yet, but it was closer.

Sofia watched until he finished the third apple. She didn't praise him. Praise created appetite, and appetite led to indulgence.

Instead, she said, "You can be trained."

Connor's chest tightened with a brief, foolish surge of pride. He kept his face blank.

Sofia's gaze moved to his knife. "But you're still thinking about being good," she added, as if reading him. "Stop that. Be correct."

"Yes, Chef."

Sofia stepped away, already leaving him, already returning to the larger machine. "Service starts in ninety," she said over her shoulder. "Clean your station. Reset everything. When the first tickets come in, you will not be preparing. You will be executing."

Connor watched her go, feeling the strange mixture of dread and hunger she left behind. Ninety minutes. Not long. Long enough to fail in a hundred ways if you didn't understand the invisible grid.

He cleaned, aligned, checked. He rehearsed movements in his head without moving, a mental choreography: reach, pinch, place, wipe. He imagined the spoons leaving his hands, imagined Renaud's eyes on the pass, imagined the returned plate from the prologue story he'd dismissed as myth.

Somewhere in the kitchen, a door opened and closed softly. The corridor swallowed the sound. Connor looked toward it and saw nothing, only shadow and stainless steel.

He thought again of those lockers without tape.

People didn't quit in a kitchen like this, not quietly. They didn't leave gaps that clean. The building had a way of removing evidence.

Connor forced himself back to work. He couldn't afford to stare into the shadows. Not yet. Not when he still didn't know the tempo.

As the minutes bled away toward service, the kitchen's silence didn't soften. If anything, it became more deliberate, as if everyone was conserving sound for the only moments when sound would be permitted.

Connor stood at garde manger, station reset and perfect, hands steady, breathing controlled.

His first lessons in precision had been simple, brutal truths: perfection was not an outcome but a habit; correction was allowed only before anyone noticed; hesitation was the only unforgivable flaw.

He told himself he could do this. He told himself that survival was just discipline taken seriously enough.

Then he glanced once toward the pass and saw Chef Renaud shift his posture by a fraction, the smallest adjustment that somehow changed the entire room.

The machine was about to start moving at full speed.

And Connor was no longer practicing.

Chapter 3

The Brigade

The first tickets did not arrive with a shout.

They slid onto the rail at the pass like a blade drawn halfway from its sheath, quiet and promising violence. Connor saw the movement more than he heard it: a runner's hand, the thin paper, the tiny clamp of metal. Chef Renaud did not announce the beginning of service. He did not need to. The kitchen changed around him the way air changed before a storm.

Connor's station at garde manger was reset and immaculate, every container aligned, every towel folded into the same obedient geometry. His hands were clean enough that they looked newly issued. He kept them close to his body, elbows in, as if space itself was rationed.

A runner appeared at the edge of his vision and stopped precisely at the line of tape that marked where the station ended and the aisle began. The runner's posture was rigid, eyes forward.

"Table seven," the runner murmured.

Not to Connor. To the station. To the air. The words were less instruction than trigger.

The tall chef beside Connor, the one who had corrected him without looking at him, responded immediately. "Heard."

He didn't ask what table seven meant because he already knew. He didn't ask what pace because the pace was fixed. His hands moved. Connor moved with him, not beside him as an equal, but behind him like a shadow.

In culinary school, hierarchy had been explained in clean diagrams. Here, it existed in angles of the body. Who stood closest to the pass. Who spoke without being spoken to. Who touched a plate last.

Connor watched the pass the way you watched a command center. Renaud stood at its core, still enough to look unreal. Heat lamps cast a pale glow onto the stainless steel, turning it into a stage that punished imperfection. Sofia Alvarez moved in and out of the orbit, close enough to speak to him when needed, far enough that it was clear she did not belong to any one station. Her clipboard was absent now. She didn't need it during service. The kitchen itself was her list.

Beyond them were the territories.

Garde manger, Connor's corner of cold precision. Saucier, the heart of heat and reduction, where the air shimmered faintly above pans. Poisson, where fish was handled with a reverence that bordered on superstition. Meat, where Antoine worked, shoulders squared, movements economical, face carved into calm.

Antoine did not look like a man who feared knives or flames. He looked like a man who feared only being seen doing something wrong.

Connor had heard his name earlier, in the prologue story he'd dismissed as myth, attached to the quiet removal of Julien Morel. Seeing Antoine now, present and untroubled, Connor felt the story press itself into reality. The corridor door that swallowed people was not a legend. It was part of the architecture.

Service accelerated without ever becoming loud. Orders moved through the kitchen in clipped phrases, low enough that they felt like private conversations, but the entire brigade responded as if they shared one nervous system.

"Two amuse, walk."

"Heard."

"Fire eight, course one."

"Heard."

The word heard replaced yes, Chef. It meant more than agreement. It meant absorption. An order did not exist until it was heard, and once heard, it became law.

Connor's first task under fire was deceptively small: finishing a set of chilled spoons with a garnish so delicate it looked like it could bruise from breath. His tweezers felt heavier than they had during prep. The spoons were aligned at the station's edge, waiting.

He placed the first garnish. Perfect. The second. Perfect. His hands moved faster now, not because he was calm, but because calm was required. Fear had to be converted into speed.

The tall chef leaned slightly, not looking at Connor, but speaking as if to the air between them. "No pauses."

Connor swallowed and continued, movements tightening. The runner waited, hands behind his back, posture unchanged. The runner did not fidget because fidgeting was noise.

When Connor finished, the tall chef inspected without touching. A brief scan of the tray, then the smallest nod. The runner took the tray and vanished toward the pass as if the floor pulled him.

Connor's chest stayed tight. He realized he had not exhaled properly in minutes.

He risked a glance toward Renaud.

The chef's eyes were on the plates moving across the pass, but his awareness seemed wider than his gaze. He did not speak often. When he did, the words were surgical.

"Wipe."

A runner froze. A plate rim was cleaned. The plate moved again.

"Again."

A sauce was remade, not because it was wrong by taste, but because the sheen had shifted by a degree, because time had touched it.

Renaud did not correct with explanations. He corrected with outcomes. The brigade adjusted without questions, their bodies trained to respond to the smallest cue.

Connor began to see that the kitchen's hierarchy wasn't built on volume of knowledge, but on proximity to consequence. The closer you worked to the pass, the less margin you were allowed. The farther you were, the more you could be replaced without disrupting the machine.

He was very replaceable.

Sofia appeared at garde manger with the suddenness of someone stepping into a spotlight. Her eyes cut across the station in a single glance, inventorying speed, cleanliness, spacing, timing. She did not speak to Connor directly. She spoke to the tall chef.

"Course two, table twelve. Two covers. Allergies?"

"None," the tall chef replied.

Sofia's gaze flicked to Connor for half a second, and Connor felt it like a hand at the back of his neck. Then she was gone again, already moving toward another station.

She did not need to ask Connor if he was keeping up. The answer would show itself.

Minutes bled into each other. Trays arrived. Tasks shifted. Connor's hands learned to move without thinking, because thinking took time, and time here was measured in seconds that could ruin a course.

Then something happened that had nothing to do with food.

A commis from another station stepped too close to the saucier's range, trying to pass behind with a container. He did not bump anyone. He did not spill. He simply stepped into space that wasn't his.

The saucier did not look up. He lifted his elbow slightly, a subtle barrier, and the commis stopped as if he'd hit a wall. He backed away a fraction, rerouted, took the longer path.

No words were exchanged. No one needed to say, This is not your territory. Territory was understood.

Connor felt a chill. In school, stations were assignments. Here, they were borders. Crossing them without permission was a kind of threat.

A few minutes later, Antoine's voice carried from meat, low but sharp. "Behind."

Not a courtesy. A warning. The person behind him moved faster, hugging the edge of the aisle, making themselves small. Antoine continued plating without looking back.

Connor realized the kitchen's language was built to prevent negotiation. Behind, heard, fire, walk. Words that moved bodies without inviting opinion.

Even names were used sparingly.

When Sofia wanted something, she didn't say please. When Renaud wanted something, he didn't say now. The hierarchy was so complete it had eliminated politeness. Politeness implied choice.

At some point, Marcus Hale appeared at the kitchen entrance, half in shadow, half in the sterile light. He didn't wear a jacket. He never did. He watched the pass with the detached attention of someone evaluating an investment.

Connor felt his presence even before he saw him, like a pressure change.

Marcus leaned close enough to Sofia to speak without projecting. Connor couldn't hear the words, but he saw Sofia's jaw tighten, a muscle flickering once near her cheekbone. She gave a small nod and turned slightly toward the pass.

Renaud did not look at Marcus. He didn't have to. The air between them suggested a conversation that had been happening for years without needing sound.

Marcus's gaze traveled, briefly, across the line, and Connor felt exposed, as if he'd been illuminated by a flashlight. Marcus didn't look at him like a chef judging technique. He looked at him like a man judging utility.

Then Marcus was gone again, retreating into the corridor as quietly as he'd arrived.

Connor's hands shook for a moment after, and he tightened his grip on the tweezers until the tremor vanished. Sofia's earlier words returned to him: Everything is watched.

The hierarchy extended beyond the kitchen. It extended into the building's throat, into whatever Marcus represented, into whatever mechanism decided who stayed and who disappeared cleanly enough to leave blank locker tape.

A new ticket hit the rail. The runner called it softly. The tall chef repeated heard. Connor began assembling a plate of chilled elements that required perfect symmetry, a pattern he still didn't fully grasp but could feel in his hands now, like learning the steps of a dance by being shoved into the rhythm.

He placed one component. Then another. The spacing was correct. He knew it because the tall chef did not correct it. That alone felt like a strange kind of praise.

For a few seconds, Connor allowed himself to believe he was matching their tempo.

Then he saw an exchange at the pass that made his stomach drop.

A runner brought a plate forward. Renaud's eyes moved over it once. He didn't touch it. He simply held his gaze on a single point near the rim, expression unchanged.

The runner stiffened as if the chef had spoken.

Sofia stepped in, took the plate, wiped a nearly invisible mark from the porcelain, and set it back down. The plate moved forward again.

No one said anything. No one thanked her. No one acknowledged the correction. But Connor understood the lesson: even a perfect plate could be ruined by a fingerprint, by a smear, by evidence of human presence.

Perfection here meant invisibility. The food had to look as if it had assembled itself.

Connor looked down at his own hands and hated the fact that they existed.

He worked faster. Cleaner. He stopped swallowing so loudly. He stopped shifting his weight. He tried to move like he belonged without assuming he did, the exact contradiction Sofia had given him as instruction.

The hierarchy was revealing itself not as a structure, but as a truth about survival. At the top, Renaud, absolute and silent, the standard personified. Near him, Sofia, the enforcer, the memory, the blade that sharpened everyone else. Around them, station leaders who guarded their territories with quiet brutality. Beneath them, commis and runners moving like blood cells, essential and disposable.

And at the very bottom, new arrivals like Connor, learning that the quickest way up was to stop being a person and become a function.

A plate left garde manger toward the pass, carried by a runner who did not look at it as if afraid his gaze might contaminate it. Connor watched it go and felt a flicker of something that was not pride, not yet. Something closer to hunger.

He had executed correctly. He had not been corrected. He had not been noticed.

In this kitchen, that was the first proof of life.

But as the machine continued, as tickets kept sliding onto the rail and the air stayed tight with controlled heat, Connor understood the darker part of what the hierarchy meant.

If you could be invisible, you could survive.

If you became visible, truly visible, you would either rise or be removed.

And the distance between those outcomes was as thin as a smear on porcelain.

A runner came back to garde manger with an empty tray and did not pause long enough to be thanked. The tray didn't belong to anyone, not really. It was just another piece of the machine returning to be loaded again.

Connor's hands hovered over his station for a fraction of a second, waiting for the next trigger. Waiting was dangerous. Waiting meant you had time to think, and thinking produced hesitation, and hesitation produced noise even when no sound came out of you.

The tall chef beside him spoke again, the same single-word language that had been used all night.

"Terrine."

Connor's eyes flicked to the refrigerated counter where the terrine sat like a sealed document. He didn't ask which one. There was only one terrine that mattered tonight, already portioned, each slice wrapped and held at a temperature that would never be mentioned out loud.

He reached for the tray of portions, lifted one with an offset spatula, and placed it onto a chilled plate. His movements were faster now, not frantic, but trimmed of excess. He could feel the shape of his own speed, the way the kitchen demanded momentum without showing effort.

The tall chef finally looked at him, just once, and Connor felt the scrutiny land.

"Hands," the chef said quietly.

Connor's fingers tightened reflexively, as if grip could substitute for cleanliness. He registered what the chef meant an instant later. Not wash your hands. Not sanitize. Hands as in what your hands leave behind. As in smears on porcelain, warmth on cold garnish, the faint oil of skin on something that should look untouched.

Connor didn't answer. He adjusted his technique instead, using the towel folded into thirds to hold the plate at the edge, letting his fingertips touch only what could be wiped clean without anyone seeing it happen.

The chef's gaze remained on him a beat longer than necessary. Then he turned back to his own work, as if the lesson had been delivered and therefore absorbed.

A runner stopped at the tape line again.

"Table twelve. Two. Walk."

The tall chef responded without looking up. "Heard."

Connor's heart jumped at the word walk. It meant the plate needed to move now, not when it was done, not when it was perfect, but when it was perfect and done at the exact moment required. Timing here wasn't just coordination. It was dominance over time itself.

They assembled in silence. The terrine, the accompaniment, the microscopic garnish placed with tweezers at an angle that felt predetermined by someone else's mind. Connor watched the tall chef's hands to anticipate the next move, because being a half second late made you visible.

On the third plate, Connor reached for the condiment dish and felt the tiniest resistance: the ramekin wasn't where his muscle memory expected it to be. A half inch off. A correction he hadn't made, which meant someone else had, which meant someone else had noticed his layout and adjusted it to their standard without telling him.

The message wasn't hostile. It was worse than hostility. It was ownership.

He slid the ramekins into the new position and didn't let his face change. He plated faster.

When the two plates were complete, the tall chef inspected them the way a person might inspect forged currency. Not because he expected to find something, but because the act of inspection was the only way to prove the kitchen's authority over what left it.

His eyes lingered on Connor's second plate.

Connor felt his throat tighten. He had wiped the rim; he was sure of it. He had held the porcelain at the edge. He had made the garnish angle match. He had done everything right.

The tall chef reached out with one finger and touched the rim near seven o'clock, then looked at his fingertip. Nothing was visible, but something existed. A trace. A possibility.

He did not wipe it. He didn't need to. He simply lifted his gaze to Connor.

"You're sweating," he said.

Connor's body went cold with realization. Not sweat dripping, not dramatic. Just a sheen under the lights that made his skin more human than the kitchen allowed. Sweat meant heat. Heat meant panic. Panic meant loss of control.

Connor forced his breathing down. In through the nose, slow. He shifted his weight in a way that redistributed pressure in his shoes, easing the tightness in his calves without looking like he was shifting. He kept his hands steady, away from his face, away from any impulse to wipe his brow.

"Yes, Chef," he said, and hated the sound of his own voice, the way it seemed too loud even at a whisper.

The tall chef gave the smallest nod, not approval, more like a stamp on a form. He slid the plates forward to the runner.

The runner took them and was gone.

Connor stared at the empty space where the plates had been and understood that garde manger initiation wasn't about learning to plate cold food. It was about learning to eliminate yourself from the plate. Not just your fingerprints, but your temperature, your breath, the fact that you existed at all.

The tall chef spoke again, and this time there was something different in it. Not warmth. But definition.

"Felwick," he said.

Connor's stomach tightened. Sofia had used his name earlier as a warning. Hearing it from someone else felt like a hook.

"Yes, Chef."

The chef reached to the edge of the station and pulled a narrow container toward him. Inside, a pale gel sat in a line, its surface perfectly smooth, like it had never been touched. The chef did not open it fully. He angled it toward Connor like a test.

"Tell me what that is," he said.

Connor's mind raced. He could name ten things it might be based on color alone. The kitchen didn't reward guesses.

"I don't know, Chef," Connor said carefully. "I haven't seen it used."

The tall chef's eyes held on him. The silence that followed was long enough to feel like punishment. Then the chef nodded once.

"Good," he said, echoing Sofia's earlier verdict. "You didn't guess."

He slid the container back into place and then, finally, gave Connor the one thing the kitchen had been withholding.

"Laurent Dumas," he said. It wasn't an introduction. It was a label. "Chef de partie, garde manger."

Connor's mouth went dry. "Yes, Chef Dumas."

Dumas watched him for a beat as if measuring whether the title would make Connor taller or smaller. "You're here," he said. "So, you learn the station."

Connor waited. He didn't ask what that meant. He didn't ask how.

Dumas pointed with his chin toward the refrigerated counter, toward the trays aligned like evidence. "Cold station is not easy," he said. "Everyone thinks it is because nothing burns. That's for amateurs."

Connor nodded, eyes steady.

Dumas continued, voice low enough that it stayed inside the station's borders. "Heat hides. It reduces. It covers. Cold shows everything. Cold keeps everything. If you make something too salty, it stays too salty. If you cut wrong, the cut stays wrong. If your hands shake, the whole plate shows it."

Connor swallowed. "Yes, Chef."

Dumas's gaze dropped to Connor's towel. Still folded into thirds, aligned properly now. "You learn the grid," Dumas said, and Connor felt the word hook into him because it named what he'd been trying to sense since he walked in. "Not your grid. Ours."

"Yes, Chef."

"Rule one," Dumas said. "Nothing leaves your station unless you can defend it with your life."

Connor's pulse spiked. He thought of Julien Morel raising his hand. Of a plate returned untouched. Of the word remove spoken with no emotion.

Dumas watched him as if he could see the thought behind Connor's eyes. "Not metaphor," he added. "Defend it. With facts. Temperature, grams, time. If Sofia asks why something is the way it is, you answer in numbers. Not opinions."

"Yes, Chef."

"Rule two," Dumas said. "You don't touch the pass unless told. You don't cross into another station unless told. You don't correct another chef's plate unless Sofia tells you to. You correct yourself before you're seen."

Connor nodded. "Heard."

Dumas's eyes narrowed slightly at the word heard. Not displeased. Interested. "Good," he said. "You're listening."

A new ticket slid onto the rail. Connor didn't see it, but he felt the shift ripple down the line, the way bodies adjusted without looking away from their work.

Sofia's voice cut through, clipped and exact. "Table nine. Cold course. Four."

"Heard," Dumas replied.

He turned to Connor. "Now you execute," he said.

There was no more explanation. There was only movement.

Connor pulled chilled plates from the stack, his fingers careful not to leave warmth. He placed them on the counter in a line. Four. He reached for the components, each one held at a precise temperature, each one portioned to an exact weight. He didn't know who had portioned them. It didn't matter. Whoever had, had done it correctly, which meant Connor had to keep it correct.

Dumas's hands moved beside his, quick and economical. Not helping, not doing Connor's job, but moving in parallel, a demonstration without instruction. Connor matched the rhythm, letting Dumas's pace drag him forward.

Garnish. Placement. Wipe. Check angles. Wipe again. Connor felt sweat trying to form again under the lights and forced his breathing down. He made his body colder from the inside.

On the third plate, his tweezers picked up a leaf that was a fraction too large. In any other kitchen, it would have been fine. Here, fine didn't exist.

He discarded it instantly and took another without pausing long enough for the action to look like correction. His hands kept moving. The plate did not register the moment of failure. The kitchen would, but the plate would not.

Dumas noticed anyway. Of course he did. He didn't say anything. He only shifted his posture slightly, as if acknowledging that Connor had made the right choice and expecting him to keep making it.

When the four plates were complete, Dumas inspected them, then slid them forward to the runner waiting at the tape line. The runner didn't speak this time. He didn't need to. He took the plates like they were volatile.

As the runner disappeared, Sofia appeared at the edge of garde manger again. Close enough that her presence tightened Connor's spine.

Her eyes moved over the station, then over Connor. A scan. An audit.

Dumas spoke first. "Table nine is walking," he said.

Sofia's gaze flicked to Connor's hands. Clean. Still. Presentable. "He's keeping up?" she asked, as if Connor wasn't there.

Dumas didn't look at Connor when he answered. "So far."

So far. Connor felt the words lodge in his ribs. Nothing here was permanent. Nothing was earned once. Everything was earned every minute.

Sofia's attention stayed on Connor for half a second longer than usual. "Don't chase speed," she said softly, and the softness made it sharper. "Chase absence."

Connor nodded. "Yes, Chef."

Sofia leaned slightly toward Dumas, voice lower, private. Connor caught only fragments. "Hale is here," and then Sofia's eyes went past Connor toward the kitchen entrance, toward the corridor's throat.

Connor didn't turn. He didn't let his face change. But his stomach tightened with the awareness of being watched from beyond the kitchen's hierarchy, from whatever Marcus Hale represented.

Sofia straightened. "Keep him quiet," she said to Dumas, meaning keep Connor quiet, keep his errors quiet, keep his presence from becoming a sound the kitchen had to deal with.

Dumas nodded once. Sofia vanished back into the machine.

Connor returned to his station and began resetting without being told: wiping stainless steel in one pass, aligning containers to the edge, refolding towels even when they hadn't unfolded. He worked as if the act of cleaning was part of plating, part of execution.

In the reflection of the refrigerated counter, he caught a glimpse of himself: young, pale under the lights, eyes too alert. Too human. He remembered the lockers with missing tape. Remembered how absence could be engineered here, how a person could become a blank space without anyone speaking their name again.

Dumas's voice brought him back. "Felwick."

"Yes, Chef."

Dumas looked at him fully now, the first time Connor felt truly seen by someone other than Sofia. "Your initiation is simple," Dumas said. "You will be correct when you are tired. You will be correct when you are afraid. You will be correct when you think no one is looking."

Connor held his gaze. "Yes, Chef."

Dumas's expression didn't soften. It didn't need to. "If you can do that," he said, "you get to stay cold."

Connor didn't know yet whether staying cold was privilege or threat. He only knew it was survival.

Another runner arrived. Another low call. Another plate that would have to look like it had assembled itself, untouched by the sweating hands of the people who made it.

Connor picked up his tweezers.

He executed.

The next ticket came in so quietly Connor almost missed it, but the kitchen reacted before his eyes had fully registered the movement on the rail. That was the first lesson of execution: the body moved on signals the mind was too slow to interpret.

Dumas didn't wait for Sofia to appear. He didn't need to. He angled his head toward the runner at the tape line.

"Cold course is next," Dumas said.

The runner gave a single nod, as if nodding kept the air from hearing.

Connor reached for plates before he was told. Chilled porcelain, dry as bone, stacked in perfect alignment. He separated four with a touch that avoided warmth, set them down, and felt the panic try to climb his throat anyway. Panic made you reach twice for the same thing. Panic made your hands hover, searching. Panic made your breath audible.

He forced his breathing into something smaller.

The components were waiting in their containers like parts in a surgical tray: gel, pickled element, shaved vegetable, a protein so precisely portioned it looked manufactured. Everything had been measured long before Connor arrived, but he understood now that portioning wasn't where control ended. Execution was control preserved under time.

Dumas moved beside him, parallel, not assisting so much as setting a tempo. His hands didn't blur; they simply didn't waste anything. Each movement ended exactly where the next one began.

Connor matched him. Reach. Pinch. Place. Withdraw. Wipe.

On the second plate, Connor's tweezers caught a microgreen sprig at the wrong angle, and his wrist hesitated, a tiny delay. He corrected instantly, but the moment existed, and that meant it could be seen.

Dumas didn't look at him. He said, "No rehearsals."

Connor's stomach dropped. The words were quiet, almost gentle, and that made them brutal. Rehearsal meant uncertainty. Rehearsal meant he was still thinking about his hands rather than letting his hands think for him.

"Yes, Chef," Connor murmured, then regretted speaking. Sound wasn't forbidden, but it was counted.

The plates went out. The runner took them and vanished toward the pass, moving as if the corridor itself could punish a wrong step.

Connor reset immediately, wiping stainless steel in one pass, returning lids, aligning containers to the edge of the counter with the same invisible grid he'd been trying to feel since day one. The station had to look untouched, as if it had been waiting in stillness rather than working under pressure. That was another lesson: execution included erasing evidence of execution.

A runner returned with a note that wasn't a note. Just two words, spoken like a code.

"Table seven."

Dumas answered, "Heard," and Connor felt his shoulders tighten. Table seven had been called earlier in service. Connor didn't know who sat there, but the repetition made it feel important, like a recurring symptom.

Dumas didn't tell Connor what to plate. He pointed at the refrigerated counter with his chin.

Connor opened the drawer, pulled out four identical components, and paused just long enough to confirm the count.

Dumas's voice was low. "How many grams?"

Connor's mouth went dry. He looked at the label, small and clean, dated, initialed. The weight was there, but the question was a test of something deeper. Did he read? Did he check? Did he rely on habit?

"Thirty-eight grams, Chef," Connor said.

Dumas nodded once but didn't let it end there. "Temperature."

Connor touched the side of the container with the back of his fingers, not enough to warm it. He didn't have a probe in his hand. He wasn't allowed time for one unless told. This was about what he could defend, the way Dumas had warned him.

"Four degrees," Connor said, then corrected himself before the correction could look like panic. "Between three and four. It's holding."

Dumas's eyes finally flicked to him. A glance like a blade testing a seam. "If Sofia asks," he said, "you don't say between. You say the number you verified."

Connor nodded, throat tight. "Yes, Chef."

Dumas gestured, and Connor began plating.

The pattern was more complex than the earlier course, a geometry of negative space that made every element look isolated and therefore exposed. There was nowhere to hide. Cold food, Dumas had said, showed everything.

Connor's hands moved steadily. He placed the first component at a precise distance from the rim, then the second, then the third. He wiped without making the wiping visible, towel folded into thirds, always the same. He avoided touching porcelain with bare fingertips unless there was a plan to erase the contact.

The fourth plate was nearly complete when a shadow fell across the station. Not Dumas. Not a runner.

Sofia Alvarez had appeared again, silent as a decision.

Connor didn't look up fast. Looking up fast looked guilty. He kept working, finishing the garnish with tweezers, and then stopped with his hands behind his back, the posture of obedience he'd started copying without noticing.

Sofia's eyes scanned the plates. They didn't linger on the food at first. They lingered on the rims.

Connor felt his pulse in his fingertips.

She reached out and rotated one plate a fraction, aligning it to an axis Connor hadn't known he'd missed. The motion was so small it would have looked like nothing to an outsider. Here, it was a correction as loud as a slap.

Dumas didn't flinch. He waited.

Sofia looked at Connor. "Why is this rotated?" she asked.

It was a simple question. It was also a trap, because there were answers that sounded like excuses even if they were true.

Connor forced his mind to stay cold. "Because I set it down without aligning it to the counter edge," he said.

Sofia's gaze held him. "And why did you do that?"

Because I was rushing. Because I was watching you. Because I'm new. None of it mattered.

"Because I didn't verify before plating," Connor said.

Sofia didn't approve. She didn't soften. But her eyes changed by a fraction, the way a lock might turn a millimeter.

"Correct," she said, and then, without raising her voice, she added, "Execution is not plating. Execution is verification under speed."

Connor nodded. "Yes, Chef."

Sofia's attention moved past him, toward the pass. "Table seven is being watched," she said.

Connor's stomach tightened. Watched by whom? The inspector from the prologue night? Marcus Hale? Someone else entirely?

Sofia didn't explain. She didn't need to. Explanation made the kitchen emotional, and emotion made it loud.

She leaned closer, and her voice dropped so low it felt like it belonged inside Connor's skull. "If you are uncertain, you discard. If you are slow, you are discarded."

"Yes, Chef," Connor said, barely audible.

Sofia stepped back and looked at Dumas. "Walk these," she said.

Dumas slid the plates forward. The runner took them without speaking.

Sofia remained at the station half a beat longer, her eyes on Connor's hands. Clean. Still. Controlled.

"Reset," she said, then vanished into the line as if she'd never been there.

Connor moved immediately, wiping, aligning, returning lids, restoring the illusion of stillness. The kitchen required the station to look like it was always ready, always perfect, even as it bled plates into the dining room.

A few minutes later, the corridor exhaled someone into the kitchen.

Marcus Hale stood at the entrance, half in shadow, half in the sterile white of the line. His suit looked untouched by work. He belonged nowhere near stainless steel, and yet the air made room for him as if he did.

He didn't address the cooks. He didn't look at Connor directly. His gaze traveled toward the pass, toward where Chef Renaud stood unmoving, a fixed point under the heat lamps.

Marcus said something to Sofia that Connor couldn't hear. Sofia's jaw tightened once. She didn't argue. She pivoted, and Connor saw her eyes flick toward garde manger, toward Dumas and him, as if calculating how many weak links existed in the chain at that exact moment.

Then Marcus's gaze did land on Connor, briefly, like a light passing over a wall.

It wasn't a chef's scrutiny. It wasn't technique. It was appraisal.

Connor held his posture and made his face blank. He didn't look away fast, because looking away was fear, and fear was visible. He didn't stare, because staring was challenge. He let his eyes be neutral, his body a function.

Marcus looked away first.

He moved toward the pass, and Connor understood something he hadn't fully named until now: the kitchen's hierarchy wasn't only culinary. It was political. Renaud controlled the plates, Sofia controlled the people, but Marcus controlled the pressure around them, the stakes, the consequences that weren't written on any schedule.

The tickets continued. The machine kept moving.

Dumas leaned slightly toward Connor without looking at him, voice low. "You see him?" he asked.

Connor didn't pretend not to understand. "Yes, Chef."

Dumas's hands never stopped. He was plating something delicate; each element placed with the same cold calm. "Don't try to impress him," Dumas said. "That's not his job."

Connor felt the urge to ask what Marcus's job was, but he swallowed it. Questions were noise.

Dumas finished his plate and slid it aside. "Execution," he said, as if naming the lesson again made it sink deeper. "You do what is required. You do it the same way every time. You don't add yourself to it."

Connor nodded, hands behind his back when idle, moving only when needed.

A runner appeared at the tape line. "Refire. Table seven."

The word refire hit Connor like cold water. Something had failed, somewhere between kitchen and dining room. The prologue story flashed behind his eyes: the returned dish. The untouched plate under the heat lamp. The word remove.

Dumas didn't react outwardly. He simply said, "Heard," and then, to Connor, "What failed?"

Connor's mind raced through possibilities. Garnish wilting. Rim smudge. Temperature. Timing. The worst kind of failure was the one you couldn't name.

"I don't know, Chef," Connor said, and forced the words out cleanly. No guessing. He remembered Sofia's "Good" from earlier, the way not knowing was safer than pretending.

Dumas's eyes flicked to him. "Correct," he said. "So, what do you do?"

Connor swallowed. "You replace everything that could be questioned."

Dumas nodded once. "Now."

They moved. New plates. New components. Everything verified. Connor checked the labels, confirmed grams, checked temperature with a probe only when Dumas handed it to him with a look that meant do it fast and silently.

Connor read the number and committed it to memory.

Dumas watched his hands. "Say it," he said.

"Three point two," Connor replied.

"Again."

"Three point two," Connor repeated, and this time the number felt like armor, something he could hold up if Sofia demanded proof.

They plated in silence, faster now, but without the frantic edge that would show. Execution was speed that looked inevitable.

When the refire was complete, Dumas inspected, then slid the plates forward. The runner took them, and for a moment Connor's gaze drifted toward the pass.

Chef Renaud stood there, as always, still enough to feel unreal. But his eyes were not static. They traveled with the plates like tracking sights. For a brief second, as the runner passed, Renaud's gaze lifted and cut across the line.

It landed on garde manger.

Not directly on Connor. Not a full acknowledgment. Just a passing measurement, like the touch of a ruler against a surface.

Connor felt it anyway, a cold weight in his chest. Being seen by Renaud wasn't a reward. It was exposure.

The plates left. The machine absorbed the disruption. Service continued as if the word refire hadn't been spoken.

Dumas returned to his station and began resetting the ritual of erasing evidence.

Connor mirrored him, wiping stainless steel, aligning containers, folding towel edges into the same obedient thirds. His hands were steady, but inside him something had shifted. He could feel it, the way fear was being converted into function, the way his mind was learning to accept that the work wasn't to cook something good. The work was to produce something unquestionable.

In the gaps between tickets, Connor caught himself listening for sound that never came, for shouting that didn't exist here, for the release of laughter that might have made the pressure survivable.

There was none.

Only the quiet language of a brigade that did not encourage excellence through praise, but through threat.

Dumas spoke again, still without looking at him. "Lesson," he said.

Connor answered automatically now. "Heard."

Dumas's mouth tightened by a fraction, almost approval. Almost. "If you want to survive," he said, "you execute the same when you're calm and when you're hunted."

Connor's throat tightened at the word hunted, because it felt accurate in a way he didn't want to admit.

Another ticket slid onto the rail. Another call came low. Another set of plates needed to leave garde manger looking untouched by human hands.

Connor picked up his tweezers.

He didn't feel like a cook anymore. He felt like part of a mechanism designed to produce perfection and destroy whatever threatened it.

And he understood, with a clarity that made his stomach turn, that the hardest lesson in execution was not learning what to do.

It was learning to do it without being seen doing it at all.

Chapter 4

The First Cut

The night did not end when the rush slowed. It only changed shape.

By the time Connor realized how long he'd been standing, his calves had become a constant ache, not sharp enough to force movement, just present enough to remind him that his body was a liability. Dumas didn't say break. No one said break. The concept existed only as a gap between tasks, a moment stolen while wiping down a counter or switching gloves, a swallow of water taken without lifting the bottle too high.

The tickets kept coming in measured waves, like the dining room breathed in courses and exhaled demands. Connor had started to recognize the pulse: a brief lull after an amuse, a tightening before the first cold course, the sudden compression of time when multiple tables landed on the same sequence.

And with every wave, the kitchen's silence held.

It wasn't calm. It was a rule enforced by the fear of being the first voice that cracked it.

"Four. Cold. Now."

Dumas didn't look at him when he spoke. He didn't have to. Connor's hands moved before his mind finished translating. Plates, chilled. Four. Align. Components out in the same order as always, lids set down in the same place, labels facing outward like evidence ready to be presented.

A runner appeared at the tape line, posture rigid.

"Walk," the runner murmured.

"Heard," Dumas replied.

Connor felt sweat threaten again and strangled it with breath. Slow in. Slow out. The trick wasn't to relax. Relaxation was softness. The trick was to become harder without looking tense.

He plated. Reach, pinch, place. Negative space like a geometric threat. Wipe without making it look like wiping. He didn't glance at the pass. He didn't glance at Sofia. He didn't need to. He could feel the room's attention the way you felt heat through a door.

A tray slid into place beside his board. Not from a runner. From a hand he didn't recognize at first.

Sofia Alvarez stood at the edge of garde manger, a half step inside the station boundary, close enough that her presence shifted the air but not close enough to be accused of interference. Her eyes flicked over Connor's plates, then over the containers, then to Dumas.

"Two more covers just sat," she said. "Table seven. Cold course will stack."

Dumas didn't show reaction, but Connor saw his hands tighten a fraction on the tweezers, a micro-adjustment of grip. Table seven again. The table that had refired. The table that was being watched.

"Timing?" Dumas asked.

Sofia's gaze moved toward the pass; toward the rail Connor couldn't see from this angle. "They're compressing the pacing. Hale wants it tight."

She didn't say Marcus's name like it belonged in the kitchen, but it did. It belonged like a shadow belonged. Connor kept his face blank, but his stomach clenched anyway. Hale meant pressure. Pressure meant mistakes became visible.

Dumas nodded once. "We're ready."

Sofia's eyes slid to Connor. A scan, quick and clinical. She didn't ask if he was ready. She didn't offer reassurance. She only said, "Felwick. When the stack hits, you don't speed up. You remove hesitation."

"Yes, Chef."

"Don't answer me like a student," Sofia said, soft and cutting. "Answer me like someone who will be held accountable."

Connor swallowed. "Heard, Chef."

Sofia's gaze held him for a beat longer, then she was gone, moving away with that same silent decisiveness, already dissolving back into the machine.

Connor finished the four plates and slid them forward. The runner took them and vanished.

For a few seconds, the station was empty except for stainless steel, condensation, and Connor's own pulse trying to make itself known. Dumas reset without needing to be told. Wipe, align, close, wipe again. Connor mirrored him, hands moving in the same ritual, erasing any proof that they'd been under pressure.

"Look at the rail," Dumas said suddenly.

Connor hesitated, a half beat of surprise. He'd been trained not to look toward the pass unless necessary, not to steal attention. But Dumas wasn't asking permission from the kitchen. He was giving Connor a controlled glimpse.

Connor angled his head just enough to see past the aisle, past the bodies moving in strict lines.

The pass was a narrow bright spine of light beneath the heat lamps. Tickets clipped to the rail like a row of small white teeth. Chef Renaud stood at the center, hands still, eyes moving, his presence exerting control without motion. Sofia slipped in and out of that orbit. Runners came forward, offered plates, took them away.

And just behind the pass, at the edge of the kitchen entrance where the corridor swallowed sound, Marcus Hale stood with his arms loose at his sides, watching the flow as if it belonged to him. He didn't speak. He didn't need to. His gaze was pressure in human form.

Connor looked back down.

"Now you know what you're serving," Dumas said.

Connor didn't understand at first. Not fully. Food, he wanted to say. Plates. Guests. But Dumas meant something else.

"The standard," Dumas continued quietly, still working, still resetting. "Not the menu. Not the guests. The standard. That's what gets protected."

Connor nodded once. The motion felt too big in his neck, but he couldn't stop it.

A runner appeared again at the tape line.

“Table seven. Four covers. Cold course. Walk in two.”

Dumas’s voice stayed flat. “Heard.”

Two minutes. It sounded like time until it didn’t.

They began building before the countdown finished. Four plates out. Four sets of components. Connor’s hands moved faster, but he held the speed on a leash, refused to let it show. Every reach was direct. Every placement ended clean.

Dumas spoke without looking up. “You feel it?”

Connor knew better than to ask what he meant. “Yes, Chef.”

“What is it?”

Connor’s throat tightened. This was the kind of question that punished the wrong answer. He searched for what was true and useful. “Compression,” he said. “No margin.”

Dumas nodded once. “Good. That’s service here. It’s not busy. It’s compressed. Busy is noise. Compression is deliberate.”

Connor placed the third element on the first plate, then checked his spacing without appearing to check it. He had learned that looking too closely was a confession of doubt. Verification had to be built into the motion itself.

His tweezers hovered for a fraction of a second over the second plate. The garnish in the container was almost identical sprig to sprig, but not perfectly. One leaf was slightly larger, the stem slightly thicker. In other kitchens, it would have been nothing. Here, it was a choice that could be seen.

Connor discarded it instantly and selected another, not pausing long enough for the action to become a delay.

Dumas didn't comment. But Connor felt, rather than saw, that Dumas had registered it.

The runner returned, as if time had snapped.

"One minute."

"Heard," Dumas replied.

Connor's fingertips tingled. He could feel his body wanting to betray him with breath, with sweat, with the slight tremor that came from holding a posture too long. He locked down his movements. He became smaller inside himself.

They finished the plates. Dumas inspected, eyes moving quickly over rims, angles, negative space. His gaze paused on Connor's fourth plate.

Connor's stomach dropped, the familiar cliff-edge sensation: something is there and you can't see it yet.

Dumas didn't touch the plate. He only said, "Wipe."

Connor didn't reach for the rim like he was scrubbing. He made the wipe invisible, a smooth pass with the towel folded into thirds, as if the towel had never unfolded in its life. He set it back down in the exact position. He didn't breathe differently.

Dumas inspected again. Then he slid the plates forward to the runner.

The runner took them and vanished.

Connor's chest remained tight long after the plates were gone. He tried to exhale quietly, but even the release of breath felt like something the room might record.

"Reset," Dumas said, already doing it.

Connor reset.

This was the baptism, Connor realized. Not his first night in a serious kitchen. Not his first service. But his first time understanding that service here wasn't a series of tasks. It was a continuous test of control under threat, where the threat wasn't fire or knives or time, but visibility. The moment you became visible as human, you were a problem the machine would solve.

A new set of tickets stacked on the rail. The pass looked momentarily crowded with paper, as if the dining room had decided to speak in a single breath. Runners moved faster, but still without noise. Sofia's silhouette tightened near the pass. Marcus Hale didn't move at all.

Then, for the first time, Connor heard Chef Renaud's voice carry beyond the pass, not loud, but clear enough that it changed the line's rhythm.

"Fire."

A single word, and the kitchen pivoted.

Heat stations surged without increasing volume. Cold station tightened. The room narrowed around timing. It wasn't frantic. It was absolute.

Dumas's hands stilled for half a beat, then resumed. "Stack is coming," he murmured, not warning Connor so much as naming the reality.

Connor nodded once. "Heard."

A runner appeared, eyes forward, posture rigid.

"Table seven again," the runner said. Then, after a fraction of hesitation that felt like the runner was risking something by adding extra information: "He's not eating fast."

Dumas's eyes lifted a fraction, the smallest sign that the information mattered. Slow eating meant pacing problems. Pacing problems meant timing errors. Timing errors meant plates dying under lamps, cold elements warming, hot elements tightening, everything slipping into that dangerous space where perfection could be lost without any single person being able to name the moment it happened.

"Who's 'he'?" Connor asked before he could stop himself.

The question landed in the station like a dropped utensil.

Dumas turned his head slightly, not angry, but precise. "Don't ask runners questions," he said quietly. "They carry plates, not stories."

Connor felt heat flood his face. He forced it down. "Yes, Chef."

The runner's eyes didn't flicker. If the runner had heard, he pretended he hadn't.

Dumas leaned in a fraction, voice low enough that it stayed inside Connor's space. "That's your first cut," he said. "You bleed curiosity. It makes you slow."

Connor swallowed. The embarrassment was sharp, but underneath it was something else, colder:

the understanding that the kitchen punished not just mistakes of hand, but mistakes of mind.

"Heard," Connor said.

Dumas nodded once and turned back to the station. "Now," he said, "you execute through the stack."

Connor reached for plates.

In the reflection of the stainless steel, he caught a glimpse of the pass again. Renaud stood unmoving, eyes on the rail. Sofia hovered in his orbit, a blade in human form. Marcus Hale watched it all from the edge like a man watching a lock being picked.

Connor didn't know who was at table seven, or what kind of attention that table drew, only that the table was a recurring pressure point and the kitchen was being forced to bend time around it.

He didn't know yet that bending time always cost someone.

He only knew the stack had begun, and he was about to find out exactly how much speed and silence could be demanded from a human body before it failed.

The stack hit garde manger like a silent wave. Not louder, not messier, just denser. Tickets didn't shout their urgency here; they multiplied it.

Dumas read without looking like he was reading. His eyes moved once, then his hands adjusted the station as if the paper had issued a physical command.

“Six,” he said. “Cold. Two tables.”

A runner hovered at the tape line, waiting for the exact moment he would be needed. Behind him, the aisle remained clear the way a corridor remained clear in a hospital: because bodies knew what happened when they didn’t.

Connor pulled plates from the chilled stack and laid them out, six porcelain circles that looked identical until you learned the kitchen’s private language of orientation. He aligned them to the counter edge, corrected the angle once, then stopped himself from correcting again. One adjustment, not two. Dumas’s voice from earlier lived in his hands now.

Components came out in a sequence that had become muscle memory: container lids placed in the same corner, labels facing outward, the towel folded into thirds, tweezers set down parallel to the board when not in use. It wasn’t cleanliness. It was a ritual that made the body predictable.

A runner’s murmur cut in.

“Table seven. Walk in three.”

Table seven again. Connor felt the number land in him like pressure. The slow eater. The compression Sofia had warned about. The table that triggered refires and tightened jaws.

Dumas didn't react beyond the word that kept the machine moving. "Heard."

Connor's hands accelerated, but he held the speed on a leash. Negative space, placement, wipe, placement, wipe. Cold showed everything. Cold preserved every mistake like a photograph.

On the second plate, Connor reached for the gel container and felt the first real slip of the night: the lid resisted. Not much. Just a fraction, as if the seal had caught at an angle.

His fingers tightened. His mind flashed, stupidly, to force. Force made noise. Noise was visible even when it wasn't sound.

He adjusted his grip, turned more carefully. The lid came loose.

A second had passed.

Maybe two.

He plated faster to compensate, and in doing so almost overreached, his tweezers hovering above the garnish a breath too long.

"No rehearsals," Dumas said, not looking at him.

Connor swallowed and placed the garnish in one motion, decisive. The third plate followed, then the fourth. His breathing stayed quiet, but his pulse was loud inside him, and he hated that it existed.

The runner shifted his weight minutely. A warning disguised as stillness.

"One minute," the runner murmured.

"Heard," Dumas replied, and his voice held no urgency. Urgency was panic in a clean suit. The kitchen didn't allow it.

Connor finished the fifth plate and reached for the sixth. His hand moved to the tray of shaved vegetable, pinched a portion, and stopped.

The portion was wrong.

Not by an amount anyone outside this room would see. A few strands longer. A slightly thicker curl. But it would change the silhouette, the geometry of the plate. It would be visible to the people who mattered, and in this kitchen visible wasn't an aesthetic problem. It was evidence of drift.

He could discard and re-portion. But discarding would take time.

Time they didn't have.

The runner's silence pressed closer.

Connor felt his mind try to bargain. It's close. It's fine. No diner will notice. The most dangerous voice wasn't Dumas or Sofia or Renaud.

It was his own.

He discarded it anyway.

He reached again. Pinched a new portion. This one looked correct. He placed it with tweezers, wiped the rim with a towel folded into obedient thirds, then slid his hands behind his back as Dumas inspected.

Dumas scanned the six plates quickly, eyes on rims first, then angles, then spacing. On the last plate his gaze paused, not because something was wrong, but because time was.

The runner leaned forward a fraction. "Walk," he said, and for the first time there was an edge to it, a thin blade of impatience.

Dumas slid the plates forward. The runner took the first two, then the next two, then the last pair, balancing them with a control that looked effortless only because fear had been drilled into his joints.

As the runner vanished toward the pass, Connor reset on instinct, wiping down the stainless steel in one pass, closing containers, aligning lids, restoring stillness. The station had to look like it had never been busy, never been under threat.

Another runner arrived before Connor had finished wiping.

"Two more. Same course. Table twelve," the runner said.

Dumas answered, "Heard," and Connor pulled two plates, aligned them, began again.

For several minutes the kitchen's rhythm held, compressed but controlled. Plate out. Reset. Plate out. Reset. Connor worked with a growing sense that he was beginning to hear the tempo, that he could move inside it without tripping.

Then the first true disruption arrived, and it didn't announce itself loudly.

It arrived as absence.

The pass, usually a steady drain that swallowed completed plates and returned empty space, stalled. Runners didn't return as quickly. The rail, glimpsed through bodies, held more paper than it should have at this point in the course progression. Heat lamps glowed over plates that sat a beat too long.

Connor noticed because cold station depended on timing more than any other. Cold didn't forgive a delay. Cold warmed. Gel loosened. Crisp elements softened. The plate's perfection didn't shatter; it dissolved.

Dumas noticed too. His shoulders tightened by a fraction.

A runner appeared at garde manger, but not for plates. His eyes were wide in a way the kitchen discouraged.

"Hold," he said.

Hold was not part of their vocabulary. Hold meant the machine had encountered something it couldn't solve cleanly.

Dumas didn't ask why. He simply said, "Heard," and looked toward the pass without turning his head fully.

Connor risked a glance as well, the quickest theft of vision.

Chef Renaud stood at the center as always, but the space around him had changed. It was quieter, and the quiet wasn't engineered. It was threatened. Sofia hovered close, her posture sharpened. Marcus Hale stood near the entrance, still as a courtroom observer.

A plate sat beneath the heat lamps longer than any plate should. Not abandoned, but paused, as if the kitchen had hit a wall and had chosen not to admit it yet.

The runner at garde manger swallowed. "Delayed," he murmured, and the word sounded obscene.

Dumas turned his attention back to Connor immediately. "Two plates ready," he said, voice low. "But you do nothing until called."

Connor nodded. His hands hovered near his station, then folded behind his back. Waiting felt like standing at the edge of a cliff. The body wanted to move because movement was control. Stillness was exposure.

Seconds stretched.

A runner came fast down the aisle, stopped at the tape line. "Walk. Now. Cold course, table seven."

There it was. Table seven again, pulling the kitchen's timing like gravity.

Dumas moved, and Connor moved with him. Two plates already prepared for table seven's next cold course, sitting in the refrigerated drawer like a loaded weapon. Connor pulled them out, checked alignment, wiped rims that were already clean because wiping was not a response, it was a habit.

He slid them to Dumas, who scanned them in a single glance and pushed them forward.

The runner took them and turned away.

And then it happened.

As the runner pivoted, another runner cut across the aisle from the hot side carrying a tray of small plates, moving too fast because the pass had stalled and the backlog was trying to catch up. They did not collide. The kitchen was built to prevent collision. But they came close enough that the runner carrying Connor's plates flinched.

A micro-adjustment of his arms. A correction made on instinct.

The plates stayed level. Nothing spilled. Nothing obvious shifted.

But Connor saw it, because he had been watching hands all night. He saw the flinch travel into the runner's wrists like a tiny shock.

The runner recovered and kept moving, vanishing toward the pass.

Connor's stomach tightened. In another place, it would mean nothing. Here, it was the kind of moment that left ghosts on porcelain.

Dumas said nothing. Sofia was too far to see the exchange, too focused on the pass. The machine continued.

Then a voice cut through the kitchen's silence, not loud, just absolute.

"Stop."

Renaud.

The word didn't come with anger. It came with authority so complete it made motion look like disobedience. The line froze in place without the drama of freezing. Hands didn't drop. Knives didn't clatter. Flames stayed where they were. People simply stopped moving as if the building had issued the command.

Connor felt his own muscles lock. His breath turned to stone in his chest.

Renaud stood at the pass with a plate in front of him. Not a returned plate. Not yet. A plate that had been delayed by seconds and had suffered for it in ways most people would never recognize.

He didn't lift it. He didn't taste. He looked.

Sofia stepped closer, eyes scanning the dish for the flaw Renaud had already seen.

Marcus Hale remained at the edge, watching with that detached intensity, the kind of attention that didn't help but did record.

Renaud's gaze moved along the line like a blade drawn slowly across throats. When he spoke again, his voice was still quiet, but it carried farther because the kitchen had made itself empty to receive it.

“Three seconds,” he said.

No one answered. There was nothing to say. Three seconds was either fatal or irrelevant depending on where you worked. Here, three seconds had weight.

Renaud’s eyes held on the plate, then lifted.

“Again,” he said.

The word landed like a verdict. Not just this plate. Not just this station. The course. The timing. The work that had been done was now waste because time had touched it in the wrong way.

Heat stations began moving immediately, refiring without protest. Saucier reset pans. Poisson reached for new portions. On cold station, Dumas turned to Connor and spoke for the first time with a hint of pressure in his voice.

“Refire components,” he said. “All.”

Connor nodded. “Heard.”

His hands moved fast, but not frantic. He discarded the plates that had been staged, even though they looked perfect, even though a part of him screamed at the waste. The dish wasn’t wrong by appearance. It was wrong by timing. Timing was part of taste here. Timing was part of control.

He pulled new components from the refrigerator, checked labels, checked temperature with the back of his fingers, then with a probe when Dumas handed it to him without a word.

Connor read the display and spoke the number because numbers were armor.

"Three point one," he murmured.

Dumas nodded once. "Go."

Connor plated with hands that felt stripped of personality. Reach, pinch, place. He could hear Renaud's "Again" echoing in the silence, not as volume, but as consequence.

As the new plates formed under his tweezers, Connor understood the subtext of what had just happened. Renaud had stopped the entire line over three seconds not because diners would notice, but because the kitchen had.

Because someone watching from the edge would measure not what the room served, but what it tolerated.

Table seven's slow eater had bent time. The pass had stalled. Runners had compressed movement to compensate. A flinch had traveled into wrists. Three seconds had appeared, and the machine had exposed itself.

Renaud would not allow exposure.

Connor finished the refire and slid the plates forward. A runner took them and vanished.

The kitchen resumed its flow, but it wasn't the same. It had tightened, the way skin tightened over a bruise. No one spoke. No one dared to let the moment become a story.

Connor reset his station again, wiping stainless steel in one pass, aligning containers, refolding towels into obedient thirds even though they had never unfolded. His hands were steady.

Inside, something had been cut open.

He had come into L'Étoile Noire believing perfection was about skill. Tonight he had watched perfection enforced as dominance over time itself, maintained through waste and silence and the threat of being removed for any weakness that made the machine visibly human.

Three seconds.

That was all it took to stop the room.

That was all it took to make Connor understand that the most dangerous errors here were not the ones you made with your hands.

They were the ones you made by letting time slip out of the kitchen's control.

The refire moved through the kitchen like a controlled fever.

No one complained. No one questioned the waste. The remade course emerged with the same cold precision as the first attempt, as if time could be rewound without consequence. Plates left the pass again. Runners flowed out and back. The rail cleared incrementally. Flames resumed their quiet discipline. The machine had corrected itself.

But Connor could feel the bruise under the skin of the room.

For the rest of the push, every runner's path became straighter, every pivot tighter, every hand steadier. The near collision that had made the runner flinch never happened again, not because the corridor widened, but because bodies began moving as if there were no longer any room for error in the laws of physics.

Connor's station was reset to stillness. Containers closed. Labels aligned. Tweezers parallel. His towel folded into thirds with the crispness of a rule. He stood with his hands behind his back, trying to keep his breath invisible, listening for the next call.

Dumas leaned in slightly, not enough to look like conversation. "You saw what did it," he murmured.

Connor's eyes stayed forward. "The delay," he said.

Dumas didn't accept it. "No. The delay is the symptom."

Connor swallowed. He searched for the answer that mattered here, the one that described structure rather than surface. "The flinch," he said. "The runner. He compensated."

Dumas's gaze flicked toward the aisle. "Closer," he said.

Connor felt irritation try to rise, and killed it instantly. Irritation was emotion. Emotion was noise. "Table seven," he said, and the words tasted wrong in his mouth, like naming something superstitious. "He's bending the pacing."

Dumas gave a single, almost imperceptible nod. "Now you're listening."

Connor didn't want to keep speaking, but the question that had cut him earlier came back, not as curiosity, but as the need to map danger. "Who is he?"

Dumas's jaw tightened the way it always did when something brushed against the edge of forbidden. He didn't answer immediately. His hands continued moving, not plating, just checking the station's geometry as if reasserting control over something that had threatened it.

"Doesn't matter," Dumas said at last.

Connor held still. He waited, because he'd learned that silence sometimes forced truth out the way heat forced liquid into steam.

Dumas glanced at him, then back to the room. "It matters because you think your job is food," he added. "You're still thinking like that."

Connor's throat tightened. He wanted to say he understood. He didn't. Not fully.

A runner approached the tape line. "Garde manger. Two. Walk."

Dumas responded, "Heard," and nodded toward the refrigerator drawer.

Connor moved. Two plates out. Quick check. Cold porcelain. No warmth from fingers. Components arranged with negative space that felt like threat. His hands moved without stutter, but his mind kept chewing on Dumas's words.

They built the plates, wiped rims, slid them forward. The runner took them and vanished. The station reset itself again under Connor's hands, the ritual of erasing labor. Only when his movements had returned everything to perfect stillness did Dumas speak again.

"You want to know what dominance is?" Dumas asked quietly.

Connor didn't answer. Any answer would sound eager. He held his posture and listened.

Dumas's voice stayed low. "Dominance is controlling what everyone else thinks is real. In a kitchen, people think reality is food. Taste. Pleasure."

Connor stared at the refrigerator seam as if it might open and offer a clue. He said, "But it is."

Dumas's eyes went to him. A quick, sharp glance. "That's why it works," he replied. "Because you believe it."

From the pass, Renaud's presence remained a steady gravitational force. Connor could see him only in fragments through bodies moving in strict lines: the white jacket unwrinkled by labor, the posture anchored, the hands near the stainless edge as if the pass belonged to him by deed.

Dumas continued. "Renaud doesn't dominate with anger. He dominates with stillness. He makes everyone else move faster so he never has to."

Connor felt the truth of it in his bones. The entire room accelerated around that fixed point. Even Sofia, who moved like a blade, still orbited him.

"And Hale?" Connor asked before he could stop it, then regretted it instantly. Marcus Hale was not kitchen vocabulary. He was something else, something that made Sofia's jaw tighten and made runners swallow their words.

Dumas didn't rebuke him this time. He just looked past Connor toward the entrance where the corridor swallowed sound, toward where Marcus often stood half in shadow, watching.

"Hale dominates with consequence," Dumas said. "He doesn't care if it tastes good. He cares if it stays untouchable. He's not here for dinner. He's here for the story the dinner creates."

Connor felt a coldness behind his ribs. "The stars," he said, remembering Sofia's phrase, the man who keeps the stars.

Dumas gave a small nod. "Stars, investors, reputations. The kind of things people kill for without using knives."

The word kill landed too close to the prologue story Connor had dismissed as myth, the corridor door that swallowed Julien Morel. Gone. Not fired. Edited out.

A subtle shift rippled near the pass. Connor looked up just enough to see Sofia step close to Renaud, speak a sentence too low for anyone else to hear, then move away again. Her face remained composed, but there was a tightness at the corners of her mouth that hadn't been there earlier.

Dumas watched the exchange without appearing too. "They're tightening the pacing again," he said.

Connor felt it too. The rhythm began compressing, not with tickets stacking, but with the way the room held itself, the way runners moved faster in anticipation, as if time had become a hostile element.

Another call came from a runner. "Table seven. Cold course. Walk in four."

Connor's stomach tightened. Table seven again. It wasn't just a table now. It was a lever being pulled over and over, testing the machine's response.

Dumas turned to Connor. "Build it," he said.

"Yes, Chef," Connor replied, and kept his voice low enough to be nearly nonexistent.

They plated four. Connor's hands moved cleanly, but he felt the pressure of those earlier three seconds like a phantom hand at his wrist. He made no wasted motions. He didn't correct twice. He didn't hover. He didn't rehearse.

Dumas inspected, then slid the plates forward.

The runner took them, and as he turned, Connor saw his eyes flick, just for a fraction, toward the corridor. A reflexive look, like a person checking the position of a gun.

Connor's chest tightened with the urge to look too.

He resisted at first. Then, as he wiped the counter, he let his gaze rise a millimeter, just enough to catch the edge of the entrance.

Marcus Hale stood there.

He wasn't in the kitchen fully, not crossing the threshold. He didn't need to. He was positioned exactly where he could be seen by the pass and by anyone who dared look, while still remaining technically outside the brigade's territory. A man who owned the border.

His expression was mild, polite. His eyes weren't. His eyes were doing inventory the way Sofia did, but with a different ledger.

He watched a runner pass. He watched a plate leave. He watched Renaud's stillness. And when his gaze moved, it landed briefly on Connor.

Not a stare. Not a challenge. A measurement. The kind of look that asked a single question: Would the system miss you?

Connor kept his face blank. He lowered his eyes back to his station, hands moving in the ritual of stillness, as if he hadn't been caught looking.

Dumas murmured, "Don't feed him."

Connor's throat tightened. "Yes, Chef."

"What happened with three seconds?" Dumas asked.

Connor replayed it, not as drama, but as mechanics. "Renaud stopped the line," he said. "He made everyone refire."

Dumas's gaze held on Connor for a beat. "And why did he do it?" he pressed. "Not the obvious answer."

Connor felt his mind reaching for the safe response: because perfection, because standards, because timing matters. None of those were wrong. None of those were enough.

He looked toward the pass, where the heat lamps glowed like interrogators. He thought of the inspector in the dining room from the earlier story, unimpressed, returning a plate untouched just to see what broke. He thought of Hale's presence, consequence made human.

"He did it," Connor said slowly, "to show the kitchen that time belongs to him."

Dumas's mouth tightened, almost approval. Almost. "Again," he said.

Connor swallowed. "He did it so Hale could see the kitchen doesn't negotiate," Connor continued. "That it would rather burn money than accept drift."

Dumas nodded once. "That's dominance," he said. "You make the cost so high that no one else sets the terms."

A runner returned, empty-handed, but the shape of his body was wrong. Shoulders slightly tighter. Breath held too close to the chest.

He stopped at the tape line, eyes on Dumas. "Chef," he murmured.

That single word, Chef, directed to Dumas, was unusual. Runners didn't bring feelings to stations. They brought commands.

Dumas's eyes sharpened. "Speak," he said, low.

The runner swallowed. "Table seven asked for the course to be slowed," he said. "He said he doesn't like to be rushed."

Connor felt his stomach drop. The dining room making demands on pacing. That wasn't a preference. It was an attempt to seize control of the machine's time.

Dumas didn't react outwardly. He simply said, "Heard," and the word sounded like a blade being sheathed.

The runner hovered, then added, even lower, "Hale said to comply."

Connor's skin went cold. Hale said. Not requested. Not suggested.

Dumas's gaze flicked toward Sofia, who was near the pass now, listening to something Renaud said without moving her face. There was a tight, invisible conversation happening at the center of the kitchen, and Connor could feel the pressure waves from it even from cold station.

Dumas leaned toward Connor, voice so low it nearly disappeared into refrigeration hum. "Now watch," he said.

Connor didn't ask what. He simply stood still, hands behind his back, eyes up just enough to observe without appearing to.

Sofia moved from the pass with controlled speed, not hurried, but exact. She approached the corridor entrance, stopping just short of Marcus Hale. She didn't smile. She didn't soften.

Connor couldn't hear her words, but he saw her posture, the angle of her shoulders, the way she held her head. Deference without submission. A negotiation in body language.

Marcus answered with a small tilt of his head, a gesture that looked almost courteous. Sofia's jaw tightened, and she returned to the pass.

Renaud did not turn. He did not step toward Hale. He remained at his position as if leaving the pass would be conceding territory.

The machine continued plating.

And yet, as the next tickets came, Connor noticed a change. Not in volume. Not in pace. In intent.

The kitchen began moving as if it were doing two things at once: serving the dining room and resisting it. Holding the line without appearing to. Complying with the instruction to slow table seven's course while preserving the illusion that the kitchen still controlled time.

Connor felt a strange admiration rise in him and then fear behind it.

Dominance, he realized, wasn't only forcing others to obey. It was making obedience look like your choice.

Dumas's voice cut in quietly. "You see it?"

Connor nodded once. "Yes, Chef."

"What does it cost?" Dumas asked.

Connor looked at the immaculate station, the waste bin holding discarded near-perfect elements, the constant refires, the way bodies moved without resting, the way fear had been trained into silence.

He thought of blank locker tape and Julien Morel's raised hand.

"It costs people," Connor said.

Dumas didn't deny it. He didn't soften. "Good," he replied. "Now you understand what you're in."

Another runner arrived. "Garde manger. Table seven. Hold plating until call. He wants the plate at the moment he finishes the previous bite."

Connor felt the absurdity of it and swallowed it immediately. Absurdity was an opinion. Opinions were useless here.

Dumas said, "Heard," and turned to Connor.

"Now," Dumas said, "you'll learn the second part."

Connor's hands tightened behind his back. "Which is?"

Dumas's eyes held him, tired steel. "How to dominate without being seen doing it," he said. "Because that's what they're all watching for. Not whether you can plate. Whether you can control."

Connor stood very still, the cold station lights bleaching everything into clarity. He felt the kitchen's invisible grid tighten around him, felt time become something alive and hostile, something that could be owned by the person strong enough to claim it.

He had thought the first cut was the moment Renaud stopped the line.

Now he understood it was deeper than that.

The cut had been made inside him, slicing away the belief that this place rewarded skill alone.

Skill was entry.

Control was survival.

Dominance was the only language that mattered, and it was spoken fluently here, in silence, with plates that looked like they had assembled themselves and people who disappeared cleanly enough to leave no story behind.

Connor kept his hands behind his back and waited for the call, watching the pass, watching Sofia, watching Renaud's stillness, watching Hale's shadow at the corridor mouth.

And for the first time, he didn't only fear being removed.

He feared what it would mean if he learned how not to be.

Chapter 5

Invisible Rules

Connor stood at garde manger with his hands clasped behind his back, posture borrowed from runners and made rigid by fear. The plates for table seven were not plated, not yet. Components sat in their containers like sealed evidence. A chilled stack of porcelain waited at the station's edge, perfectly aligned, as if alignment could substitute for readiness.

"Hold plating until call," the runner had said. Not a suggestion. A leash.

Connor watched the pass without appearing to. He kept his eyes just high enough to take in motion, just low enough to look obedient. The kitchen was still moving, still breathing in tickets and exhaling plates, but the rhythm had a new tension to it. It wasn't the stress of a rush. It was the stress of being forced to perform restraint.

Time belonged to Renaud, Dumas had said. Tonight, time was being negotiated.

Connor could feel the negotiation in small things. Runners didn't linger in the aisle the same way; they hovered nearer the pass, ready to sprint on a signal that might come too late. Sofia moved in tighter arcs, orbiting Renaud and then breaking away to stations in short, surgical visits. She didn't correct with words as much now. She corrected with presence. The room adjusted around her like water around a blade.

Dumas didn't fill the silence. He used it.

"Do not touch anything," he murmured, not looking at Connor. "You warm it."

Connor nodded. "Heard."

"Don't nod," Dumas said quietly. "It's movement."

Connor stilled, embarrassed at the sudden awareness of his own body. Even agreement had to be invisible.

A runner approached the tape line again. Not the same runner as before. This one was older, hair shaved close, eyes empty in the way the kitchen liked them.

He didn't say table seven.

He said, "Black."

The word hit Connor as oddly as “hold” had. It didn’t belong to the call-and-response vocabulary of service. It sounded like code.

Dumas answered without hesitation. “Heard.”

The runner waited a beat longer than usual, then left without looking at Connor.

Connor’s throat tightened. He leaned a fraction toward Dumas, careful not to make it look like conversation. “Chef,” he whispered. “What does ‘black’ mean?”

Dumas didn’t turn. His hands continued resetting the station with slow, deliberate movements that looked like calm and were actually control. He aligned a container lid so precisely it could have been measured.

“It means you don’t speak,” Dumas said.

Connor’s skin cooled. “I didn’t speak to him.”

“You spoke to me,” Dumas replied. “In front of him.”

Connor forced his jaw to unclench. He stared at the stainless steel and tried to see what Dumas saw: the invisible lines, the rules that existed not because they were posted but because they were enforced.

Dumas’s voice lowered another degree. “There are tickets,” he said. “And there are patterns.”

Connor didn't respond. He waited. Waiting, he was learning, was the only way to get anything true out of anyone in this kitchen. Questions invited correction. Silence sometimes earned instruction.

Dumas tapped the edge of a container with one finger. A quiet, controlled sound. "You've been watching table seven," he said. "Because it's loud."

"It isn't loud," Connor said before he could stop himself, then immediately wished he could pull the words back into his mouth.

Dumas's eyes flicked to him, sharp. "Loud doesn't mean noise," he said. "Loud means it changes the room."

Connor swallowed. "Yes, Chef."

Dumas returned his gaze to the station. "Good. Now watch what else changes it."

Connor lifted his eyes again, careful, stealing the pass with peripheral vision. A plate came up under the heat lamps. Renaud's gaze swept it in a single pass. He didn't speak. He didn't have to. A runner wiped the rim. The plate moved.

Then another plate arrived, and the response was different.

Sofia stepped in immediately, not waiting for Renaud to signal. She checked the plate from two angles, rotated it a fraction, wiped nothing, then nodded to the runner. The plate left.

It looked identical to the others. Connor felt sure of it. And yet Sofia had treated it as if it carried a different weight.

The runner who carried it out was different too. Not one of the newer ones. Not the ones who moved like ghosts. This runner had posture like a soldier. He held the plate with an almost ceremonial steadiness, as if it were not food but an object that could break more than porcelain if mishandled.

Connor watched the runner disappear through the service corridor and tried to track the chain back. Plate. Pass. Sofia. A different runner. A different urgency that had nothing to do with ticket volume.

He turned his eyes slightly toward the rail. He couldn't see the writing clearly from garde manger, but he saw the placement of the tickets themselves. Most were clipped in a dense row, their corners aligned. One ticket sat separated by a finger's width, as if the rail itself had been instructed to keep it apart.

Sofia's hand had placed it there earlier, he realized. Not the runner. Sofia.

Unseen patterns.

A call came from the hot side. "Fire two, course three."

"Heard," someone answered.

Then Sofia's voice, low but distinct. "Not that table."

Two words, and the kitchen adjusted. A pan was moved off flame. A garnish held back. A runner stopped mid-step and redirected without protest.

Connor's pulse picked up. There was a layer of service happening beneath what he understood, a parallel choreography shaped by tables that were not treated equally. Not by preference. By instruction.

Dumas slid a container closer to Connor without looking at him. "Open," he said.

Connor obeyed, loosening the lid carefully so it didn't make a sound. Inside was a gel so smooth it looked untouched.

Dumas didn't say what it was. He didn't have to. Connor had learned that ingredients here were less about flavor than function. Gel meant hold. Gel meant control. Gel meant the plate could be made to behave.

"Smell it," Dumas said.

Connor hesitated. Smelling was human. It was sensory. It looked like enjoyment or uncertainty. Both were dangerous.

Dumas's eyes cut toward him. "Not like a tourist," he said. "Like a chemist."

Connor leaned in and inhaled once, shallow and controlled. Citrus, faint. Something bitter behind it. Not sweet. Not warm.

"Bergamot," he said quietly, then added, "or something close."

Dumas nodded once. "Good."

Connor waited for more. Dumas gave him a fraction.

"This goes on some plates," Dumas said. "Not all."

Connor's stomach tightened. "Why?"

Dumas didn't answer immediately. He closed the container with a soft seal and aligned it back into place. "Because the dining room isn't one room," he said. "It's compartments."

Connor kept his face blank, but his mind lit up. Compartments meant categories. Categories meant selection. Selection meant someone decided who received what, and it wasn't decided by taste alone.

Across the kitchen, Marcus Hale was still at the corridor mouth. He didn't move like staff. He didn't speak like staff. He existed like a clause in a contract.

Connor's eyes drifted to him for a split second and then back down. He remembered Dumas's warning: don't feed him. Attention was food.

Another runner appeared at garde manger. The older one again. His eyes met Dumas's, not Connor's.

"Table seven," the runner said. "Call in thirty."

Dumas answered, "Heard."

The runner added, almost as if reciting a memorized line, "No micro shiso. Replace with chervil."

Connor's throat tightened. "Why would table seven—"

Dumas cut him off with a look. Not angry. Corrective. Connor shut his mouth mid-sentence, the words dying behind his teeth.

The runner left.

Connor stared at the chervil container as if it might confess. Micro shiso was used on the cold course tonight. Connor had placed it earlier himself. It had a specific aroma, a specific shape, a clean graphic edge on the plate. Chervil was softer. More classic. Less aggressive.

A substitution wasn't just a tweak. It was a message.

Dumas began pulling plates from the chilled stack. "You're learning the first invisible rule," he said. "Menu is not fixed."

Connor reached for components automatically, hands steady. "I thought Michelin—"

Dumas's voice stayed quiet. "Michelin is a story people tell," he said. "This place is a system. Systems adjust."

Connor's fingers selected chervil sprigs, the smallest, the ones that wouldn't bend under their own weight. He plated in silence beside Dumas, movements precise, no wasted motion, no visible checking. He wiped the rim without making the wipe look like correction.

As he worked, he watched the plate become something slightly different than the one he had executed earlier. The geometry remained. The negative space remained. But the feel changed, the character of it, as if the dish had been dressed for a different audience.

“Who decides?” Connor asked softly, keeping his mouth barely open, letting the words leave without breath.

Dumas didn’t look at him. “Sometimes Sofia,” he said. “Sometimes Renaud.”

“And sometimes?” Connor pressed, then immediately regretted it.

Dumas’s hands didn’t stop moving. He placed a component, adjusted nothing, moved on. “Sometimes it arrives from the corridor,” he said.

Connor’s skin prickled. The corridor. Hale.

They finished plating and held the plates at the station edge, not releasing them to the runner yet. Held, as instructed, until call. The plates sat like frozen time.

Connor felt his legs aching again, but he didn’t shift his weight. He didn’t flex his fingers. Stillness was part of execution now.

The runner returned at exactly thirty seconds, as if the kitchen had timed him with a metronome.

“Walk,” he said.

Dumas slid the plates forward. The runner took them and vanished, moving fast without looking fast.

Connor watched the plates leave and felt something settle into place in his mind, cold and precise.

The patterns weren't random. They weren't chef's whims. They were consistent enough to be language. Certain tables triggered substitutions. Certain tickets were separated on the rail. Certain runners carried certain plates. Sofia rotated some dishes before they left, not correcting flaws but aligning them to an invisible expectation. Timing wasn't just about food dying under lamps; it was about pacing being used as a lever, bent to match someone else's appetite for control.

Connor looked toward the pass again. Renaud remained still, a fixed point, as if nothing in the kitchen could touch him. Sofia moved in his orbit, blade-bright, enforcing rules that weren't spoken. Hale watched from the border, a man who didn't plate and didn't cook and yet made the kitchen tighten as if he held the gas line in his fist.

Connor returned his eyes to his station and reset it to perfect stillness. Wipe. Align. Close. Fold.

"Chef," he said quietly to Dumas, careful now, asking as if he didn't care.

Dumas didn't look up. "What?"

Connor chose the words like garnish, placing them carefully so they wouldn't be seen as too much. "If the menu isn't fixed," he said, "how do we know what's correct?"

Dumas paused for the first time in several minutes. A pause that meant the question had struck the right place.

Then Dumas said, very softly, "Correct is what the watchers expect."

Connor's throat tightened.

Dumas resumed resetting, restoring the illusion that nothing had ever happened. "And the second invisible rule," he added, "is that you don't get told who the watchers are until it's too late to pretend you didn't see them."

Connor kept his hands moving, matching the grid, erasing his own presence. But his mind kept tracking the separated ticket, the coded word "black," the substitution for table seven, Sofia's silent rotations, the different runner, Hale at the threshold.

Unseen patterns were becoming visible to him.

And once you could see them, he realized, you were already implicated.

The kitchen kept moving, but Connor no longer believed in the simplicity of movement.

He reset his station again, not because anything had shifted, but because the act of resetting gave his hands somewhere to put the energy his mind couldn't spend. He aligned containers to the counter edge. He wiped stainless steel in one pass. He folded the towel into thirds as if the fold itself was a vow. In the reflection of the refrigerated counter he could see the pass in fragments, the bright spine of heat lamps and the blur of white jackets.

He could also see the corridor mouth, and the man occupying it.

Marcus Hale did not step into the kitchen. He didn't need to. He stayed at the border like a sentence you couldn't argue with, framed by shadow and the soft seal of the service door. Tonight he wore the same dark suit Connor had seen earlier, the fabric too clean for this heat, the cuffs too sharp for work. His presence had the wrong texture for stainless steel and flame. And yet the kitchen adjusted to him as if he belonged more than anyone.

A runner moved toward the pass and halted half a pace earlier than he would have otherwise. Sofia cut her orbit tighter. Even Dumas, who had been stone all night, angled his shoulder minutely, as if making sure garde manger's territory looked smaller, cleaner, more controlled under that gaze.

Connor felt a familiar instinct rise: impress. Perform. Prove. The instinct had gotten him here. It would get him erased if he fed it now.

Don't feed him, Dumas had said.

Connor kept his eyes down and worked, but his peripheral vision tracked Hale with a precision that felt like stealing.

Hale spoke to no one openly. When he did speak, it was close enough to Sofia that the words became part of her posture rather than sound. Sofia would listen, jaw tightening once, and then she would move, and the kitchen would change around her. The changes were small but immediate: a ticket separated by a finger's width, a substitution like the chervil swap for table seven, a pacing adjustment that made runners hover closer.

Hale controlled the room without lifting a pan.

A runner came down the aisle toward garde manger, stopped at the tape line, and looked past Connor to Dumas. "Stand by," he murmured. "Table seven is holding again."

Dumas answered without hesitation. "Heard."

The runner left, and Connor felt the impulse to speak, to ask what table seven wanted now. He swallowed it. Curiosity was blood in the water.

Dumas didn't need Connor's question. He spoke as if continuing a thought already in motion. "You know what people think keeps stars?" he said quietly, hands moving in a slow reset that looked like calm.

Connor kept wiping, aligning, refusing to make the conversation visible. "Consistency," he said.

Dumas made a sound that was almost a laugh, except laughter didn't exist here. "That's what they print," he replied. "Consistency. Vision. Hospitality. Words that fit in glossy articles."

Connor set a container lid down with deliberate softness. "What keeps them, then?"

Dumas paused for a fraction of a second, a risky pause, as if checking whether the air was safe for this truth. Then he said, "People."

Connor's throat tightened. "The brigade?"

Dumas's eyes flicked toward the corridor mouth. "Not just us."

Connor didn't look up. He didn't want to be caught looking at Hale as if he mattered. Hale mattered anyway. "Hale," Connor said softly, more a test of language than a question.

Dumas didn't correct him. That alone felt significant. "He's the reason you don't hear shouting," Dumas said. "He's the reason the dining room stays quiet. He's the reason the inspector doesn't get bored."

Connor's fingers tightened around the towel. "He works for Michelin?"

Dumas's mouth tightened, not in disapproval, but in caution. "No," he said. "Michelin doesn't employ men like him. Michelin measures. Hale shapes what gets measured."

Connor felt cold move through him, the way a refrigerator's breath could seep into bone. He tried to keep his voice neutral. "He's a fixer."

"Call him whatever helps you sleep," Dumas replied. "He's a keeper."

Connor's mind grabbed on the word because it matched Sofia's earlier phrase. He keeps the stars. Keeper. A man who didn't earn something, didn't create it, but prevented it from being taken away.

The service corridor door opened and closed softly. Another runner passed through, carrying nothing, eyes fixed forward. The kitchen's choreography continued, but Connor's attention narrowed to Hale in the shadows, to the way the room's pulse responded to him.

Sofia broke from the pass and moved toward the corridor mouth. She stopped just short of Hale's space, still inside the kitchen light, as if refusing to step into his shadow. Hale leaned in slightly, no more than a polite conversational distance. To anyone watching, it could have been a simple exchange between a manager and a staff member.

Connor watched the shape of it in the reflection.

Sofia's posture stayed rigid. Hale's stayed relaxed. He didn't need tension because he didn't need to move fast. He had consequences to do his work for him.

Sofia spoke first. Connor couldn't hear words, only cadence: short, controlled phrases. Hale listened, then answered with a tilt of his head and a slight movement of his hand, as if moving a piece on a board. Sofia's jaw tightened again, a single muscle jumping, then she turned away and returned to the pass.

Hale didn't follow. He didn't need to.

He stayed at the border, and for the first time his eyes swept the line not as an audit of plates but as an audit of people. Connor felt the gaze reach garde manger like a cold draft. He didn't lift his head. He focused on the alignment of a label, the straightness of a container, the fold of a towel.

The gaze lingered anyway.

Dumas spoke without looking at Connor. "Still," he murmured.

Connor obeyed. His hands stopped moving mid-reset. He stood with fingers lightly touching the counter edge, not gripping, not fidgeting. He made himself an object.

Hale's footsteps were silent on the kitchen floor, but Connor sensed the approach because the air changed. Pressure near the station. Space being occupied by someone who did not belong to it.

Hale stopped just outside the tape line, respecting the border in the way a man respects rules when breaking them isn't necessary. Connor kept his eyes down.

"Chef Dumas," Hale said.

Hearing Hale's voice in the kitchen was like hearing a phone ring in a chapel. Not loud, but wrong enough that the whole room registered it. Dumas didn't flinch.

"Mr. Hale," Dumas answered.

A beat of silence. Connor felt the temptation to look up like a physical itch.

Hale's tone remained mild. "Your new commis," he said, as if Connor were a product being discussed. "Felwick."

Connor's stomach tightened at the sound of his name spoken by that voice. Dumas didn't answer immediately.

"He's executing," Dumas said at last.

Hale made a small sound of acknowledgment. "Executing is basic," he replied. "Everyone can execute when the machine is strong."

Connor felt something rise in him, a defensive heat, and crushed it instantly. Defensive was loud. Defensive got you removed.

Hale continued, still speaking to Dumas, not to Connor. "Tell me what he does when the machine is weak."

Dumas's gaze did not move to Connor. He kept his focus on the station, the containers, the illusion of stillness. "He discards," Dumas said. "Before he hesitates."

Hale was quiet for a moment. Connor's mind flashed back to the refired spoon, the discarded garnish, the willingness to waste rather than risk visibility. It had felt like adaptation. Now he heard it described as a trait being measured.

Hale spoke again. "Table seven," he said.

Dumas answered, "Yes."

Hale's voice stayed calm. "He likes control," Hale said, as if discussing a known allergy. "We give him the illusion, but we don't surrender the pacing. Understood?"

Dumas didn't hesitate. "Understood."

Hale's gaze, though Connor couldn't see it directly, felt like it shifted onto Connor. "Does he understand?" Hale asked.

For the first time, the question angled toward Connor without addressing him. Dumas didn't look up when he replied. "He will."

Hale gave a small, polite hum. "He will," he repeated, like a verdict that sounded like agreement.

Connor remained still. He did not speak. He did not nod. He did not acknowledge that he had been discussed as if present and absent at the same time.

Hale took a half step back, and the pressure near the station eased. "Keep him clean," he said to Dumas. "No noise. No stories."

"Heard," Dumas replied, and the word sounded strange in his mouth when aimed at Hale, as if the kitchen's language had been forced to serve someone else.

Hale left as quietly as he'd approached, returning to the corridor mouth where shadow waited like a tailored coat. The kitchen resumed its earlier pulse, but Connor felt as if something had been pressed into him, a fingerprint that couldn't be wiped.

He exhaled carefully, the smallest release of air.

Dumas spoke, still not looking at him. "Now you know why your questions are dangerous."

Connor's voice came out low, controlled. "Because he hears them."

"Because he uses them," Dumas corrected.

Connor stared at the edge of his cutting board as if it were a horizon. "What does he want?"

Dumas's hands moved again, slow and exact, resetting the station not because it needed it, but because the ritual kept his face from betraying anything. "He wants the restaurant to be untouchable," Dumas said. "Not just in reviews. In reality."

Connor swallowed. "And if it isn't?"

Dumas's pause this time was heavier. "Then he makes it untouchable anyway," he said softly. "By removing what threatens it."

Blank lockers. A corridor swallowing footsteps. Julien Morel's raised hand. The word remove delivered like a menu change.

Connor felt the cold station's chill under his skin. "He can fire people."

Dumas's eyes flicked toward the corridor mouth for a fraction of a second. "Firing is messy," he replied. “People talk. People sue. People become interviews.”

Connor’s mouth went dry. “So, what does he do?”

Dumas looked at Connor then, fully, tired steel eyes pinning him in place. “He makes them disappear from the story,” Dumas said. “Sometimes they still walk out the door. Sometimes they don’t walk out the same way they came in. Either way, the restaurant stays clean.”

A runner appeared at the tape line before Connor could respond, and the interruption felt like a mercy.

“Garde manger,” the runner murmured. “Table seven. Call in one.”

Dumas’s face returned to blank function. “Heard.”

Connor’s hands moved again, reaching for chilled plates, for components, for tweezers. He built the course with the same precise geometry as before, using chervil instead of micro shiso because a message had been delivered from the corridor and the kitchen had complied.

But as he plated, Connor understood something he hadn’t understood when he first heard Sofia’s phrase.

He keeps the stars didn't mean Hale protected the restaurant from critics.

It meant he protected the restaurant from consequence by relocating consequence onto people.

Connor finished the plates and held them at the station edge, waiting for the call, hands steady, breath invisible. He could feel his own pulse trying to make him human, trying to remind him he was alive and afraid.

He couldn't afford either.

Because now that Hale had said his name, Connor knew he had been filed somewhere beyond the kitchen's hierarchy, beyond Dumas and Sofia and even Renaud.

Filed in the ledger of the man who kept the stars.

And Connor had the sinking certainty that once you were in that ledger, you were no longer just trying to be good.

You were trying to remain real.

The runner returned at the count of one the way a metronome returned to its mark, as if the kitchen had built him and set him loose.

"Walk," he murmured.

Dumas slid the plates forward without looking at them again. The inspection had already happened in his head. Connor watched the runner lift the two chilled dishes, palms under porcelain, thumbs kept off the rims and vanish toward the pass with the same careful speed that made haste look like grace.

Only after the plates were gone did Connor allow his hands to move. He closed containers with soft seals, aligned labels outward, returned tweezers to their parallel line, folded his towel into its obedient thirds, and wiped stainless steel in one pass that erased the idea of hands.

Dumas didn't speak until the station looked like it had never produced anything.

"Performance," he said quietly.

Connor kept his eyes on the counter edge. "Yes, Chef?"

Dumas's mouth tightened at the question. Not anger. Correction. "Not a topic you ask about," he said. "A topic you observe."

Connor nodded once, then stilled, remembering Dumas's earlier reprimand. Even nodding was movement. He kept his face blank and let his peripheral vision do the work.

The pass had become a narrow stage under the heat lamps. Plates arrived and left in clean arcs.

Renaud stood at center as he always did, fixed point, hands near stainless steel, eyes traveling with the measured cruelty of a ruler. Sofia moved in and out of that light, her corrections smaller than breaths. Marcus Hale remained at the corridor mouth, a border drawn in human form.

From garde manger Connor couldn't see the dining room, but he could feel it. The kitchen did not serve a room. It served a mood. A room could forgive an error. A mood could not.

A ticket slid onto the rail, clipped by Sofia rather than a runner. Connor watched the paper's placement: separated by a finger's width from the others, its corner aligned with unnatural care. An unseen pattern made visible again.

Sofia spoke, low. "Hold fire on eight. Delay two minutes."

"Heard," came answers from stations without questions.

Two minutes didn't sound like much until Connor imagined what it meant. It meant someone in the dining room needed the illusion of being unrushed. It meant a table's conversation had to feel private and unbothered by service. It meant the kitchen would bend time without letting time bend it back.

Dumas leaned a fraction closer to Connor, still not looking at him. "You think cooking is the performance," he murmured. "It's not."

Connor didn't speak. The words were bait for curiosity. Curiosity was blood.

Dumas continued anyway, as if deciding Connor needed the rule more than he needed silence. "The performance is control that looks like hospitality," he said. "And protection is control that looks like nothing."

A runner appeared at the tape line, waiting. Not speaking yet. The waiting itself was instruction: stand by, do not guess.

Connor stared at the chilled plates stacked at his station. The porcelain was perfect, but he could feel how fragile perfection was here. Not fragile like it broke. Fragile like it required constant guarding from human reality.

Across the line, a plate approached the pass. Sofia rotated it a fraction, not correcting a mistake, but aligning it to an axis that existed only in the mind of whoever would receive it. The runner took it and left.

Then Sofia's gaze flicked toward the corridor mouth. It wasn't a look of fear. It was a check. A confirmation that the watcher remained where he wanted to be.

Connor felt his stomach tighten. Renaud dominated with stillness. Hale dominated with consequence. Sofia was the translation between them, the person who made stillness and consequence usable at speed.

The runner at garde manger finally spoke. “Table seven,” he murmured. “Hold. He’s speaking to the maître d’.”

Dumas answered without any outward reaction. “Heard.”

Connor kept his hands behind his back. Waiting made his calves ache. Waiting made his mind race. He watched the aisle, the runners’ paths, the way bodies tightened when Hale’s gaze drifted. He watched how often Sofia separated tickets. He watched how often table numbers repeated.

Table seven was not the only table the kitchen obeyed differently, Connor realized. It was just the loudest.

A small disruption occurred at the pass, subtle enough that no diner would ever know it existed. A runner arrived a half-beat early with two plates that should have landed together. The second runner was missing.

Renaud's eyes shifted. Not a frown. Not a glare. Just attention.

Sofia stepped in instantly and took one plate, holding it just outside the heat lamp's brightest circle so its surface wouldn't tighten, so its sheen wouldn't change. She didn't say anything. She didn't need to. The plate waited in her hand like a secret.

The missing runner appeared seconds later, moving fast without looking fast. He carried the second plate, face blank, breath hidden. He had been delayed by something invisible to the kitchen, a door that didn't open on time, a guest who asked a question, a corridor moment that stole seconds.

Sofia released the first plate at the precise moment the second arrived. The two moved forward together as if nothing had happened.

That was protection. Not preventing delay. Erasing evidence of it.

Connor's mouth went dry. He understood then why Renaud didn't tolerate visible drift. Drift was not just a flaw. It was a crack in the story. The dining room needed to believe the experience was effortless. Effortlessness was the product. Food was only the medium.

Dumas spoke again, quiet enough that it stayed inside the station's border. "You saw that."

Connor kept his eyes forward. "Sofia held the plate."

Dumas didn't let him keep it simple. "Why?"

Connor searched for the answer that mattered. "So, they arrive together," he said. "So, the table thinks it's intentional."

Dumas nodded once. "Not thinks," he corrected. "Knows. They know because everything in that room trains them to know."

Connor tried to imagine the dining room. Low light. Quiet wealth. The kind of stillness that signaled power. People who expected reality to bend.

A voice came from near the pass, not Renaud's, but a front-of-house voice that didn't belong in the kitchen. The maître d', Connor realized, had crossed the threshold just enough to speak to Sofia. He didn't step deep in. He stayed near the entrance, respectful of borders, posture careful.

"Madame Alvarez," he said softly. "Table seven requests a pause before the next course."

Sofia didn't look at him the way front-of-house wanted to be looked at. She looked at him like a component that had arrived without being ordered. "How long?"

"A few minutes," the maître d' said. "He's receiving a call."

A call. In the dining room. During service. Connor felt the absurdity rise and crushed it. Absurdity was opinion. Opinion was noise.

Sofia's gaze flicked to Hale, as if the information belonged to him more than to her. Hale's expression didn't change. But he made a small gesture with two fingers, not pointing, not commanding, simply deciding.

Sofia turned back to the maître d'. "Tell him we will pace it," she said. "No gaps. No waiting."

"Yes, madame."

The maître d' withdrew immediately, as if his presence could contaminate the line.

Connor watched Sofia return to the pass. She leaned toward Renaud and spoke close enough that her words became part of his stillness. Renaud didn't nod. He didn't answer. He shifted his posture by a fraction, and the kitchen adjusted.

Saucier pulled a pan off heat. Poisson tightened timing. Runners hovered closer. Garde manger held.

The performance was not only for diners. It was for the kitchen itself. Everyone had to believe the kitchen was choosing the pause, not obeying it. The moment obedience became visible, dominance weakened.

Dumas breathed out through his nose, barely audible. “Protection,” he said.

Connor didn’t trust himself to speak. He kept his posture and listened.

Dumas continued, voice flat. “Protection is why the dining room never sees confusion. Why the maître d’ never looks uncertain. Why the plates arrive like choreography.”

Connor’s pulse thudded in his throat. “And the cost?”

Dumas’s eyes flicked toward the corridor. “The cost is carried somewhere else,” he said. “By someone you won’t see.”

The words landed in Connor like cold water. Someone you won’t see. The blank lockers. The corridor swallowing sound. The erased names. He understood that protection didn’t always mean saving. Sometimes it meant relocating damage until it disappeared from view.

A runner returned to garde manger, older eyes, empty face. “Stand by. Table seven in ninety seconds.”

Dumas answered, “Heard,” and then, without looking at Connor, added, “You will plate at sixty.”

Connor’s stomach tightened. “Yes, Chef.”

He didn’t move yet. Moving early would warm the components. Moving late would create delay. The timing wasn’t about readiness. It was about discipline.

The seconds stretched. Connor counted without counting, feeling the kitchen’s pulse. He watched Sofia’s shoulders near the pass. He watched Hale’s stillness at the border. He watched Renaud’s hands, the way they didn’t need to move for the room to obey.

At sixty seconds, Dumas’s fingers twitched once, the smallest signal.

Connor moved.

He pulled chilled plates, aligned them, opened containers with soft seals, placed lids in the same corner, labels facing outward. His hands worked quickly and cleanly. Chervil, not micro shiso. A substitution as message. A plate dressed for a different audience.

He plated without hesitation, no hovering, no rehearsals. The garnish went down like a decision. The rim wipe was invisible. The plates looked untouched by human need.

At thirty seconds, the runner arrived and waited at the tape line, posture rigid, hands behind his back.

Dumas inspected with a single sweep. He slid the plates forward.

“Walk,” the runner murmured.

The plates left. The story remained intact.

Connor reset immediately. Wipe. Align. Close. Fold. Erase.

As he worked, he realized the most frightening part wasn’t that the kitchen could bend itself around a table like seven.

It was that the bending had become elegant.

The performance made obedience look like choice. The protection made correction look like perfection. And the people who made it possible had trained themselves to vanish from their own work until only the result existed.

Connor’s hands kept moving, restoring stillness. But inside him something shifted again, a quiet recalibration.

He had come here to learn how to cook at the highest level. He was learning something else: how to build an experience that could not be questioned, and how to guard that experience by absorbing every crack before anyone else could see it.

A kitchen could make food.

L'Étoile Noire made reality.

And as Connor stood at garde manger, station immaculate, pulse hidden, he understood the final part of Dumas's lesson without needing it spoken.

If you could perform control, you could rise.

If you failed to protect the story, you didn't just fail service.

You became the thing the restaurant removed to keep the stars clean.

Chapter 6

Pressure Test

The pause for table seven ended the way everything ended here: without acknowledgement.

The plates left garde manger, and the kitchen swallowed the moment so cleanly it was as if the maître d' had never crossed the threshold, as if no one had asked for time to bend. Connor reset his station again, wiping stainless steel in one pass, aligning container edges to the counter seam, refolding his towel into thirds until the fold felt less like fabric and more like a rule.

He could still feel the shape of that pause in his body, the way waiting had made his calves tremble with restrained motion, the way holding still had been harder than plating. The kitchen demanded action with discipline. It demanded stillness with cruelty.

Dumas didn't speak until the station was immaculate enough to look unused.

“Drink,” he murmured.

Connor turned his head a fraction. Dumas had slid a small paper cup of water to the back edge of the station, out of sight from the aisle. Not a break. A concession to physics.

Connor lifted the cup, kept it low, swallowed without sound. The water felt like it fell through him without touching anything on the way down. He set the cup back exactly where he’d found it, as if the cup had never existed.

Dumas’s eyes moved once over Connor’s face. Not concern. Assessment. “How long since you slept?”

Connor’s mind did the count automatically, as if numbers were the only honest language left. “Three hours,” he said, then corrected himself before the correction could become a stutter. “Two and a half.”

Dumas nodded, as if confirming a schedule. “Good,” he said. Not good as in healthy. Good as in expected.

Connor felt a quick, stupid flare of pride, and then hated himself for it. Pride was heat. Heat left fingerprints.

Across the kitchen, the pass continued to glow under the heat lamps, a narrow bright spine. Renaud remained fixed at its center, stillness made human. Sofia cut across stations in short arcs, a blade moving through bodies that parted without being asked. Hale stayed at the corridor mouth, half in shadow, as if his job was to remain exactly where consequences entered.

The tickets kept coming. They always did. The dining room exhaled demand, the kitchen inhaled and returned it as plates that looked untouched by effort.

But the rhythm had shifted. Not into panic. Into endurance.

Connor began to understand what pressure test meant in this place. It wasn't a single brutal service. It was a long, controlled narrowing of margin until every action became a choice between being correct and being alive.

A runner approached the tape line. Older eyes, empty face.

"Black," he said.

Dumas answered without hesitation. "Heard."

Connor's stomach tightened at the code, at the way it flattened conversation into obedience. Dumas didn't look at him, but his voice tightened slightly, as if the kitchen had drawn the leash shorter.

"Today," Dumas murmured, "you don't speak unless spoken to."

Connor kept his eyes down. "Heard."

Dumas's head angled a fraction toward him. "Not that word," he said quietly. "Not today."

Connor felt a cold prickle. The word heard belonged to the brigade. The brigade's language was safe. If Dumas was removing even that, it meant the room was listening differently.

Connor made his face blank and said nothing.

The runner remained at the tape line half a beat longer than usual, then left without looking at Connor.

Dumas slid a tray of components out of the refrigerator and set it down with care that looked like reverence. The labels were new. The dates were today. The weights were precise to a tenth of a gram.

Connor's eyes tracked them, and his hunger for pattern woke up again. New labels meant a new sequence. A shift in menu. Or something else.

"Special lunch," Dumas said, as if reading Connor's thought without granting him the dignity of a question. "Private room."

Connor remembered the dining room compartments. The separated tickets. The different runner who carried certain plates like they were volatile.

“Who?” Connor asked before he could stop it, and the word left his mouth like a dropped spoon.

Silence tightened around the station.

Dumas didn’t turn fully. He didn’t need to. The correction arrived in the stillness of his posture; in the way he let the question hang long enough that Connor could feel it poisoning the air.

Then Dumas said, very softly, “You’re tired.”

It wasn’t sympathy. It was diagnosis. Fatigue was a liability because it loosened impulse. It made you curious. It made you human.

Connor swallowed. “Yes, Chef.”

Dumas’s eyes finally flicked to him. “No,” he said. “Not that either.”

Connor’s throat went dry. He nodded once, realized nodding was movement, froze mid-motion, corrected himself by becoming still. His heart beat too hard in his chest. He made it quieter by slowing his breath until his ribs hurt.

Dumas began arranging the station for the new sequence, moving containers like pieces on a board.

"Pressure test," he said quietly, not to Connor exactly, more like naming the weather.

Connor's hands followed without being invited. He aligned chilled plates. He set tweezers parallel. He placed the towel folded into thirds. He read labels and committed numbers to memory because numbers could be defended. Opinions could not.

The first ticket for the private room arrived. Sofia herself clipped it to the rail, separated by that finger's width that Connor had learned to see. A runner did not call it out loud. The call moved through the kitchen without sound, carried by the sudden tightening of posture at the pass.

Renaud spoke one sentence, low enough that it shouldn't have carried as far as garde manger.

"Nothing returns."

The words didn't sound like ambition. They sounded like threat.

Connor's fingers tightened on the chilled plate edge, then relaxed. Fingerprints. Warmth. Evidence. He adjusted his grip to the towel instead, touching porcelain only where it could be wiped without being seen.

Dumas slid a small container toward him. The bergamot gel. The same smooth surface, untouched. Connor's mouth went dry. The gel went on some plates, not all. A message. A marker.

Dumas didn't tell him why. He didn't need to. The private room was a different dining room, a different audience, a different story.

"Portion," Dumas said.

Connor took the scale, weighed without breathing too loud, adjusted with tweezers until the number matched the label. He didn't say the number. He held it in his head like a weapon he might need to show.

The runner arrived at the tape line, posture rigid. Not the older one. The soldier-runner. The one who carried the separated plates as if they were evidence.

He didn't say table number.

He said, "Now."

The word hit Connor's nervous system like an electric pulse.

Dumas answered, "Heard," then corrected himself without changing his face. "Go."

Connor understood. Different vocabulary. Different ears.

They built two plates. Then two more. The pattern was familiar in geometry but different in scent, a cold course dressed like a signal. The bergamot gel was laid with a precision that made it look printed, not placed. The garnish was softer than the standard dining room, more classic. Not shiso. Not chervil either. Something else, fine and flat, designed to look inevitable.

Connor's hands began to ache from the tweezers, a constant pinch at the base of his thumb. He ignored it. Pain was noise. Noise got you noticed.

As the fourth plate neared completion, the kitchen shifted again.

Sofia appeared at garde manger, half a step inside the station boundary, close enough that Connor felt her presence like a hand on the back of his neck.

Her eyes scanned the plates. Not the food first. The rims. Always the rims. The proof of human contact.

Connor didn't breathe.

Sofia leaned closer to the nearest plate and spoke to Dumas without looking away from the porcelain. "He's behind," she said.

Connor didn't know who she meant at first. Then he felt his body react before his mind could stop it. She meant Connor. The machine had measured him and found a fraction of delay.

Dumas's voice stayed flat. "He's tired."

Sofia's gaze flicked to Connor, quick and cutting. "So is everyone," she said. Her tone wasn't angry. It was factual. "Tired isn't an excuse. It's the condition."

Connor felt a thin heat of shame rise and crushed it into stillness. He adjusted his pace, not by moving faster wildly, but by removing micro-pauses. No rehearsals. No hovering. No checking that looked like checking.

Sofia's attention stayed on the plates. "Private room wants it tight," she said. "No holds. No pacing games."

Connor's mind flashed to table seven's call, the pause request, Hale's gesture, the way obedience had been made to look like choice. Private room meant something different. No illusion. No negotiation. Just delivery.

Sofia's voice lowered another degree. "If you miss a moment," she said to Dumas, "you refire without being told. If anything looks handled, you remake it. If anything returns, you will know before I tell you."

Dumas gave a single nod.

Sofia's eyes moved over Connor again. "Felwick," she said.

Connor's stomach tightened. His name in her mouth meant visibility.

He didn't answer. He remembered: today, don't speak unless spoken to. But she had spoken to him. He had to respond, and response itself was a trap.

Sofia waited, expression unreadable.

Connor chose the smallest possible sound. "Yes."

Sofia's eyes narrowed slightly. "Don't give me yes," she said. "Give me function."

Connor's throat tightened. He forced his voice into neutrality, stripped of student apology. "Understood," he said.

Sofia held his gaze half a second too long, then turned away as if satisfied not by the word but by the way he'd said it. She left the station without another sound, returning to the pass, to Renaud's orbit.

The runner at the tape line leaned in. "Walk," he murmured, and for the first time Connor heard something close to impatience in the hush. Not anger. Expectation.

Dumas slid the plates forward. The soldier-runner took them and vanished toward the pass.

Connor reset the station immediately, but his hands felt slower now, heavier, as if fatigue had coated his joints in glue. He wiped stainless steel, aligned lids, refolded towel edges. The ritual kept him from shaking. It gave the illusion that he was unchanged.

But the pressure kept tightening.

Tickets came faster. Not louder. Denser. Lunch bled into prep for dinner without a true break, only a shift in lighting, a shift in temperature, a change in the smell of reductions beginning on the hot side. Connor's body began to lose track of time. The kitchen didn't mark hours. It marked sequences.

At some point, Dumas handed him a new tray of components without looking at him. The labels were different again. The weights tighter. The tolerances smaller. Connor read them, committed numbers, adjusted portions with tweezers until the scale agreed.

His eyes burned. Not from tears. From refusing to blink too often, as if blinking might be counted.

Another runner approached. Older eyes. Empty face.

"Black," he said again.

Dumas answered, "Heard," and the air felt colder after it.

Connor's hands paused a fraction over the plates, then resumed. The code meant silence, but it also meant something else now. It meant attention had narrowed. It meant the watchers were closer.

Across the kitchen, Hale remained at the corridor mouth. Not moving. Not speaking. Yet the kitchen's posture kept tightening around him, as if everyone could feel the distance between doing well and becoming a problem was shrinking.

Connor plated through it anyway, removing hesitation, turning fatigue into function. Each garnish landed like a decision. Each rim wipe disappeared into motion. Each plate left the station looking as if it had assembled itself, untouched by sweating hands and aching joints.

But inside Connor, something began to fray.

Not skill. Not discipline.

Margin.

He could feel how little room remained between his thoughts and his hands. A half second of drift and the kitchen would see it. A moment of curiosity, a flash of irritation, a need to breathe too loudly, and he would become visible as human.

And the machine did not tolerate visible humanity.

Dumas leaned close, still not looking at him. "This is the test," he murmured, voice nearly lost under refrigeration hum.

Connor kept his eyes on the plates. "I know," he said, then instantly regretted speaking at all.

Dumas didn't correct him this time. He only said, "No. You don't."

Another ticket slid onto the rail, separated by Sofia's hand. Another private-room call traveled without sound.

Dumas's hands moved faster, and Connor matched him, but he could feel his body fighting to slow down, to protect itself. The kitchen demanded the opposite. It demanded he spend himself without leaving proof that he was spent.

Connor reached for garnish, and his fingers tremored, small enough that no one across the aisle would see. But he saw it. He felt it. The tremor was a confession.

He steadied himself by changing grip, letting tweezers become an extension of bone rather than muscle. He placed the garnish in one clean motion. No hover. No rehearsal. No visible correction.

The plate looked perfect.

Connor's pulse kept pounding anyway.

Because he understood now what being pushed to the limit meant here.

It wasn't being busy. It wasn't being tired. It wasn't even being afraid.

It was being forced to remain invisible as you broke.

Dumas's "No. You don't," hung in the cold air like condensation that refused to fall.

Connor kept plating anyway.

The next sequence arrived without a call. Not a shouted order, not even the runner's usual murmur. The signal was in the way bodies tightened near the pass, in the way Sofia's orbit narrowed until she was almost shoulder-to-shoulder with Renaud, translating his stillness into movement before he had to spend a word.

Dumas slid another tray from the refrigerator. Fresh labels. Today's date. Initials Connor didn't recognize. The weights were tighter than the last set, the margins reduced until the numbers looked less like portions and more like tolerances.

Connor read them once and let the information settle into his hands.

He stopped trying to feel awake.

Awake was a feeling. Feelings were unreliable.

Instead, he did what the kitchen demanded: he converted everything into function.

Plate. Align. Open. Place lids in the same corner. Labels outward. Towel folded into thirds. Tweezers parallel. Scale at the exact position that kept his body from drifting into wasted movement.

Dumas watched him without watching, his gaze angled toward the station the way a pilot watched instruments.

"Again," Dumas murmured, and Connor understood he didn't mean refire. He meant the sequence. Repeat it until repetition replaced fatigue.

A runner appeared at the tape line, the soldier-runner, posture too rigid to be natural. He didn't say a table. He didn't say "walk."

He said, "Now."

Connor didn't answer. Dumas didn't either. Dumas's hands moved, and Connor moved with him, building two plates, then two more, their motions overlapping without collision. It wasn't teamwork in the friendly sense. It was two people operating inside the same grid, two sets of hands trying not to reveal the existence of breath.

Connor placed the bergamot gel in a line that looked printed, not placed. He used the edge of a spoon, then removed the spoon without leaving a trace of the spoon's passage. He hated how much he liked the precision of it. Liking was also a feeling, and it had no place here.

His fingers tremored once as he picked up a garnish. The tremor was small, but it was a betrayal, and he corrected without drama: he changed the angle of his wrist, transferred the burden from muscle to bone, let the tweezers become a hinge instead of a grip. The garnish landed exactly where it needed to, at an angle that matched the negative space like a threat.

Dumas's voice came low, close enough that it didn't travel. "No rehearsals."

Connor heard the command in his body rather than his mind. He stopped hovering. Stopped checking in a way that looked like checking. Verification became part of the motion: his eyes confirmed spacing on the way in, his fingers confirmed alignment on the way out. Nothing lingered.

The plates left the station.

He reset.

The reset used to feel like cleaning. Now it felt like disappearing. Wiping stainless steel wasn't sanitation; it was erasure. Folding the towel wasn't tidiness; it was obedience. Aligning containers to the counter seam wasn't organization; it was making sure nothing on the station suggested a human had ever panicked there.

A new runner arrived, older eyes, empty face.

"Black," he said.

Dumas answered immediately. "Heard."

Connor felt his shoulders tighten, then forced them down. Black meant don't speak. Black meant the watchers were close enough that even the brigade's language could be overheard and interpreted.

The kitchen's hum deepened, not louder, but heavier. Connor sensed rather than saw Marcus Hale at the corridor mouth. He didn't turn to confirm. Confirmation was attention. Attention fed him.

The next ticket for the private room came through Sofia's hand, clipped to the rail with that finger's width of separation. Connor couldn't read it from garde manger, but he could read the room. The pass stiffened. Runners stopped hovering and began waiting with an almost ceremonial stillness.

Renaud spoke again, low.

"Nothing returns."

The words were not for the brigade. They were for the story. A reminder that tonight was being recorded by people who didn't write with pens.

Connor took chilled plates from the stack and felt how easily his hands wanted to warm them. Warmth was proof. He held porcelain only with the towel, touching edges that could be wiped without leaving a smear. The old part of him, the student who had wanted to be noticed for skill, would have called it obsessive.

Here it was basic.

Dumas placed components in front of him in a sequence that made the station feel like an operating table. Connor didn't ask what any of it was. Names were for menus and guests. In this kitchen, ingredients were behaviors. Gel held. Pickle cut. Crisp snapped. A single leaf changed the tone of an entire plate.

Connor portioned without staring at the scale. Staring looked uncertain. He glanced once, corrected with tweezers, and moved on. The number lived in his head in case Sofia demanded proof, but he didn't carry it on his face.

They plated four.

Then the kitchen shifted sideways.

Not a rush. Not a stack. A sideways shift, like a door opening somewhere you couldn't see.

A front-of-house presence crossed the threshold just enough to speak near the pass. Connor didn't hear the words, but he saw Sofia's posture change: her shoulders drew in, her head angled a fraction as if listening to something unpleasant but expected.

Sofia's gaze flicked down the line.

It landed on garde manger.

Connor felt his chest tighten. Not because he was doing anything wrong. Because being looked at was risk.

Sofia moved toward them, quiet as a decision. She stopped half a step inside the station border, close enough that the cold air around the refrigerator seemed to shift.

Her eyes went to the plates first. Then the rims. Always the rims.

Connor kept breathing shallow, controlled. He didn't blink too often.

Sofia reached out and rotated one plate a fraction, not correcting the food, correcting the axis. The rotation was so slight it looked like nothing. It was everything. It aligned the plate to the story the private room expected to receive.

Connor felt a hard flash of irritation and crushed it instantly, not by denying it, but by translating it.

Rotation was data. If Sofia rotated, that meant there was a preferred orientation that wasn't written on the ticket. It was an invisible rule. Now Connor knew it existed.

Sofia leaned closer, voice low enough that it stayed inside the station. "Private room wants the second plate delayed by thirty seconds," she said to Dumas.

Delayed. The word would have sounded obscene yesterday. Today it sounded like code.

Dumas didn't ask why. "Heard."

Sofia's eyes cut to Connor. "Can you hold it without it dying?" she asked.

The question wasn't about cold food warming. It was about Connor. Could he hold tension without showing it? Could he keep the plate in a state of readiness without touching it too much, without re-wiping so often it looked handled, without checking so often it confessed doubt?

Connor didn't say yes. Sofia had told him not to give her yes.

He answered like function. “I can hold it,” he said, voice stripped clean.

Sofia watched him a beat longer, then nodded once, not approval, confirmation. She disappeared back toward the pass.

Dumas slid two of the plates forward to the runner who had been waiting at the tape line like a statue.

“Walk,” the runner murmured, and took them with careful speed.

Two plates remained on the station.

Connor held them in time.

He didn’t touch the rims again. He didn’t wipe what didn’t need wiping. He stood with his hands behind his back, body still, eyes forward, counting seconds without moving his lips. Thirty seconds was a long time when you were forbidden from looking like you were waiting.

His calves burned.

His mind tried to drift into thought, into story: who was in the private room, why they wanted a staggered delivery, what was being negotiated beyond the kitchen. Connor cut the thoughts off by giving his brain a task it could survive: inventory. Plate edges clean. Garnish unchanged. Condensation minimal.

Lighting consistent. If he had to defend it, he could defend it with facts.

At the exact count, Dumas slid the remaining plates forward.

The runner took them and left.

No one commented on the hold. No one praised the timing. The absence of correction was the only signal that Connor hadn't failed.

The next sequence came fast. Another four plates. Another set of portions with margins too small for comfort. Another "black" murmured at the tape line, as if the kitchen needed periodic reminders that it was being listened to from the corridor.

Connor's hands began to move without friction. Not because he had energy, but because he had removed everything that wasted it. He stopped shifting his weight. Stopped swallowing too loudly. Stopped lifting his shoulders in anticipation. Even his breathing became part of the grid: inhale while reaching, exhale while withdrawing. A rhythm no one could see.

He executed.

A garnish leaf was slightly larger than the others. He discarded it instantly without pausing. The motion didn't register as a mistake because he didn't allow it to become one.

A smear appeared on a rim, not from his fingers, from the invisible oil that lived in the air of a working kitchen. He wiped once, invisibly, then moved on. Not twice. Twice would look like panic.

A lid stuck on a container the way one had earlier, threatening to cost him a second. Connor didn't force. He adjusted, broke the seal with controlled pressure, and continued without speed changing. No spike. No flinch. No evidence.

Dumas's voice came again, quiet. "That's it," he murmured.

Connor didn't ask what he meant. He could feel it too: the moment the work stopped feeling like a series of tasks and became a continuous state. Not flow the way chefs bragged about it in interviews. This was something colder.

This was the machine's rhythm entering his nervous system.

Tickets stacked. Plates moved. Runners flowed like blood. Sofia cut in tight arcs. Renaud stayed still. Hale remained at the border where consequences lived.

And Connor, exhausted enough that his personality should have been leaking through, instead became more invisible.

He executed with a calm he didn't feel, and because the kitchen only cared about what could be seen, the calm became real.

At some point, Connor realized his hands had stopped trembling. Not because he was rested, but because there was no room left for tremor. The body either obeyed or broke.

He didn't want to break.

A runner arrived for another private-room call, soldier-runner again, eyes forward.

"Now," he said.

Dumas slid the plates forward, then paused just long enough to scan Connor's station, the lids, the towel, the alignment. He didn't look at Connor's face. He looked at the evidence of his mind.

"Reset," Dumas said.

Connor reset in one pass, stainless steel returning to a mirror that reflected nothing human.

He lifted his eyes a fraction, just enough to catch the pass.

Chef Renaud's gaze was moving over plates as they arrived beneath the heat lamps, as it always did, surgical and indifferent. For a brief moment, the gaze drifted beyond the plates, beyond the runners, beyond Sofia's orbit.

It cut down the line.

It landed on garde manger.

Connor felt it like a hand closing around his throat. Not because it was hostile. Because it was precise.

Renaud didn't nod. He didn't frown. He didn't acknowledge Connor as a person. The gaze held for less than a second, then returned to the plates as if Connor had never existed.

But Connor knew what it meant to be measured by that stillness.

Flawless execution wasn't perfection that earned praise.

It was perfection that drew attention.

And attention, here, was never free.

Renaud's gaze moved away as if it had never paused.

The pass returned to being a bright spine of heat and porcelain, runners flowing in and out like blood. Sofia's orbit tightened and loosened in practiced arcs. Dumas's hands resumed their parallel work at garde manger with the same unhurried economy. The room did not acknowledge what Connor had felt.

But Connor did.

The glance hadn't contained anger or approval. It hadn't even contained recognition. It was measurement, clean and indifferent, and it left an afterimage behind his eyes the way a camera flash left darkness brighter for a moment. He stared at his station and saw it as Renaud would see it: not as a place where a person worked, but as a surface that either held the standard or contaminated it.

He reset again, though nothing needed resetting.

One pass of the towel. Containers aligned. Labels outward. Tweezers parallel. Fold into thirds, the crease sharp enough to cut. His hands moved with the compulsive precision of someone trying to erase evidence of thought.

Dumas's voice came quietly beside him, not looking at Connor. "Don't chase it."

Connor's throat tightened. He didn't ask what. He didn't need to.

Dumas continued, the words low enough to live inside refrigeration hum. "He looks at everyone. It means nothing."

It was a lie, and they both knew it. In this kitchen, nothing was wasted. Not motion. Not silence. Not a glance.

Connor kept his face blank. "He looked here," he said anyway, and immediately felt the risk of speaking, the small flare of humanity the word here contained.

Dumas didn't correct him. That was its own correction.

"He looked at the line," Dumas said. "If you make it about you, you become about you."

Connor swallowed. He forced his breathing smaller until it hurt, because pain was easier to manage than the desire to be seen and not punished for it. He returned to function. He returned to the grid.

A runner appeared at the tape line, older eyes, empty face. "Black."

Dumas answered without hesitation. "Heard."

The code landed like a clamp tightening around Connor's ribs. Black meant the watchers were close. Black meant the room was listening differently. It also meant, Connor realized, that his body would betray him faster. Fatigue pulled at the seams of discipline. Hunger made the mind loud. The desire to interpret the glance made him want to find meaning in everything, and meaning was a luxury.

The runner didn't call a table. He didn't call a count.

He only waited, posture rigid, like he was there to remind them that time belonged to someone else.

Dumas slid a fresh tray from the refrigerator and set it down with controlled care. New labels, tighter tolerances. Connor read the weights once and let the numbers sink into muscle memory without letting his eyes linger too long. Linger looked uncertain.

Across the kitchen, the pass tightened. Sofia moved closer to Renaud, her shoulders drawing in as if bracing against a change in pressure. Connor caught the shift in the reflection of stainless steel, not directly, because direct looking fed the wrong things.

The soldier-runner arrived next. He stopped at the tape line with an unnatural stillness.

"Now," he murmured.

Dumas moved. Connor moved.

Two plates. Then two more. Bergamot gel drawn in lines that looked printed. Garnish placed at an angle that made the negative space feel intentional rather than empty. Rim wipe invisible.

Hands behind back when waiting. No rehearsals. No hovering.

Connor felt the machine's rhythm holding him upright. He didn't feel calm, but he looked calm. In this room, looking was most of reality.

When the fourth plate was finished, Dumas's eyes swept them once. He didn't nod. He slid them forward.

The soldier-runner took them and vanished toward the pass.

Connor reset without being told. The station returned to stillness, immaculate enough to look unused.

And then, as if the kitchen had decided to test whether Connor had absorbed Dumas's warning, Sofia appeared at the edge of garde manger.

She didn't step deep into the station. She didn't need to. Her presence tightened the air anyway.

Her eyes moved over the counter, the lids, the alignment, the fold of the towel. She didn't look at Connor's face at first. That would have been too human.

"You were seen," she said.

It wasn't a question. It wasn't a comfort. It was a fact delivered like a temperature reading.

Connor kept his hands still behind his back. He didn't nod. "Yes," he said, then regretted the word because it sounded like the wrong kind of agreement, too personal, too eager to acknowledge the moment.

Sofia's gaze lifted to his eyes. Her own were unreadable, dark and steady. "Not yes," she said. "Not even that."

Connor felt the heat of shame rise and cut it off by emptying his expression. "Understood," he said, the word stripped of emotion.

Sofia's jaw tightened once, the muscle jumping near her cheekbone. "Good," she said, and it wasn't praise. It was confirmation that he had corrected the right thing.

She leaned a fraction closer, close enough that Connor caught the faint smell of citrus sanitizer and warm stainless steel on her jacket. "You think his glance is a reward," she said softly. "It is not."

Connor kept his eyes on hers without staring. Neutral. Functional. "What is it, Chef?"

Sofia's mouth didn't change shape, but something in the air sharpened. "It is weight," she said. "It means your margin got smaller."

Connor felt his stomach tighten. Margin had become his private word for survival. Dumas had said it was what frayed first. Sofia named it like a verdict.

She turned her eyes away from him and toward the pass, as if to show him what the glance belonged to. Renaud stood at center, fixed point, hands near stainless steel. He didn't move, but the line adjusted around him as if the floor tilted.

"Do you know what happens when he remembers you?" Sofia asked.

Connor kept his voice low. "You correct me."

Sofia's gaze snapped back to him. "No," she said. "I correct things that can be corrected."

Connor's throat went tight. He understood the distinction too well. Correction meant you were still part of the machine. Uncorrectable meant you were a problem the machine removed.

Sofia's voice dropped another degree, private inside the station border. "If he remembers you," she said, "it's because you were useful or you were dangerous. There is nothing else."

Connor held still, letting the words settle in him like cold metal. Useful or dangerous. Either way, visible.

Sofia looked down at his hands, as if checking whether they tremored. Connor willed them into stillness. The urge to prove he was steady made him want to move. He refused. Stillness was proof.

Sofia straightened. “Private room again,” she said, and then she was gone, cutting back toward the pass with the same silent decisiveness, leaving the station colder than before.

Dumas didn’t speak immediately. He waited until the air felt normal again, until Connor’s breathing stopped trying to announce itself.

Then Dumas said quietly, “She’s right.”

Connor’s mouth was dry. “I didn’t do anything.”

Dumas’s hands moved, aligning a container lid by a millimeter. “That’s what scares you,” he said. “You didn’t do anything and he still looked.”

Connor swallowed. The glance replayed again, and this time he noticed what he hadn’t allowed himself to notice before: it had landed on garde manger after the hold, after the staggered delivery, after Connor had kept the plates alive for thirty seconds without touching them. Flawless execution. Invisibility performed.

It had worked too well.

A runner appeared at the tape line, not older eyes this time. A newer one, but trained hard, face blank, posture rigid. He didn’t say black. He didn’t say now.

He said, “Chef wants four in two.”

Chef. Not Dumas. Not Sofia. The word in this kitchen meant one person unless specified.

Dumas’s posture didn’t change, but the air around him tightened. “Heard,” he said.

Connor’s body reacted before his mind could. Heat in the chest. A spike of adrenaline. Not fear of work. Fear of being late, of being seen failing under the weight of a glance.

Two minutes was nothing and everything.

Dumas slid four chilled plates out. Connor aligned them to the counter seam. Components out, lids placed in the same corner, labels outward. Tweezers in hand. Breath reduced to a quiet mechanical cycle.

Connor moved fast, but the speed didn’t flare. He removed micro-pauses, the tiny hesitations that fatigue snuck in. He didn’t hover over garnish. He didn’t check in a way that looked like checking. Verification happened in the motion: eyes confirmed as fingers placed. Rim wipe invisible, one pass, no second guessing.

On the second plate, his tweezers picked up a leaf that was almost correct and not quite. He discarded it instantly. The motion didn’t register as correction because it didn't cost time. It was part of the flow.

On the third plate, the bergamot gel line threatened to break, a slight inconsistency where the spoon lifted. Connor adjusted the angle of lift, smoothed it without touching the gel directly, and continued. No pause. No visible fix. The line remained printed-perfect.

Dumas's eyes swept the plates once, then again, faster than Connor liked. "Rims," Dumas murmured.

Connor wiped, one pass, towel folded into thirds, the wipe so smooth it looked like part of plating rather than cleanup. He set the towel back exactly where it belonged.

The runner's posture tightened. "Walk," he said, but the word came sharper than usual, as if someone behind him was already pulling the leash.

Dumas slid the plates forward.

Connor watched them leave and felt something in him strain, not relief, not pride, but the awareness that this was no longer just station work. It was response to attention. It was proving, in seconds and millimeters, that the glance hadn't broken him.

He reset on instinct, wiping stainless steel in one pass, aligning containers, restoring the illusion of stillness. His hands were steady, but his body felt hollowed out, as if every movement took something he wouldn't get back.

Dumas leaned in slightly without turning his head. "Do you feel it?" he murmured.

Connor didn't ask what. He said the truth. "Yes."

Dumas's voice stayed flat. "That's the weight. Not his eyes. What his eyes do to your time."

Connor stared at the clean counter edge and understood with a clarity that made him cold. The glance wasn't a moment. It was a new condition. It changed the way tickets landed. It changed the meaning of two minutes. It changed how Sofia spoke to him. It made his own mind louder, eager to interpret, eager to perform, eager to survive.

From across the kitchen, Renaud's voice carried, quiet but absolute.

"Again."

The word wasn't for garde manger. It wasn't even for a specific plate. It was a reminder that the standard refreshed itself constantly, that the room never arrived at perfection and rested. It only returned to perfection over and over, like a punishment.

Connor's throat tightened. He realized he was holding his breath again.

He released it carefully, silently, then reached for chilled plates as the next call arrived.

The kitchen kept moving. The pass stayed bright. The corridor remained a mouth that swallowed sound. Somewhere near that mouth, Hale's presence lingered like consequence waiting to be assigned.

And Connor, newly measured, newly visible in the smallest way that mattered, executed under the weight of a glance that had already moved on, as if it were still resting on his hands.

Chapter 7

The Inner Circle

The next call came before Connor's pulse had finished settling from the last one.

Not a runner at the tape line this time. Not the older eyes with "black" in their mouth. Sofia's shadow cut across the aisle and stopped at garde manger's border as if the boundary lines were hers to redraw.

"Felwick," she said.

Connor's hands went behind his back before his mind could decide. Stillness first. Control second. "Chef."

Sofia's eyes swept the station the way Renaud's had, as if the counter itself could confess. "You're moving," she said.

Connor didn't know what she meant until he felt it: the slight restless tightening in his shoulders, the micro-adjustments of posture he'd been making to keep his legs from locking. He stopped them. He became vertical and quiet.

Sofia held the silence long enough to make it hurt. Then she said, "You're coming up."

Up meant the pass. Closer to the bright spine. Closer to where plates either became story or became waste. Closer to Renaud's stillness, where time was owned.

Dumas didn't look surprised. That was what frightened Connor most. Dumas's calm was never casual. If he wasn't surprised, it meant this had been trending toward inevitability the moment Renaud's glance had landed.

Dumas spoke without turning his head fully, as if to keep the station from witnessing. "He's garde manger."

Sofia's gaze didn't move from Connor. "He can carry," she said. "And he can stand without shaking."

Connor kept his face blank. The urge to accept with gratitude rose and died in the same breath. Gratitude was emotion. Emotion was noise.

"Yes, Chef," he said.

Sofia's jaw tightened once, that familiar muscle jump. "Not yes," she replied. "You're not agreeing. You're receiving."

Connor recalibrated instantly. "Understood, Chef."

Sofia nodded, and the nod was not approval. It was confirmation that he could be corrected without fracturing.

"Apron clean," she said. "Towel. Tweezers."

Connor reached for a fresh towel and folded it into thirds without looking down, fingers finding the creases by memory. He slid his tweezers into his pocket with the careful economy of someone handling a blade. He didn't ask why. He didn't ask how long. He didn't ask what he'd be doing.

Sofia stepped away from garde manger and didn't look back to see if he followed. She moved as if the kitchen made room for her because it had learned not to resist.

Connor fell in behind her, staying half a pace back, careful not to crowd. The aisle between stations felt narrower than it had earlier, as if being invited to the pass changed the geometry of the room. He became aware of everybody he passed, every knife angle, every handle protruding from a lowboy. The kitchen didn't forgive collisions. Not because they made noise, but because they proved you existed as a clumsy thing.

They approached the pass from the side, where runners queued like sealed envelopes, waiting to be opened at the exact moment. Heat hit Connor's face, a wall of warmth that made his eyes sting after hours of cold station refrigeration hum. The pass was brighter than anywhere else, the light under the lamps flat and merciless. It made food look like evidence.

Renaud stood at the center, unchanged. The same white jacket, unwrinkled by effort. The same posture, anchored. Hands near stainless steel as if he'd been built there.

Marcus Hale was visible at the corridor mouth, half in shadow, as if the pass were a stage and he was the audience that mattered. Connor did not look at him directly. Not now. Not ever, if he could help it. Don't feed him.

Sofia stopped a fraction behind Renaud's shoulder, close enough to speak without moving her lips much. She said something too low for Connor to catch. Renaud didn't nod. He shifted his weight by a millimeter and the shift rippled through the runners' line as if they'd been tugged on a wire.

Sofia angled her head toward Connor, a small command. "Stand there," she said, indicating a spot at the pass's edge, not in the center light, but close enough that Connor could see plates arrive and leave.

Connor stepped into the position and locked himself into stillness. Heat made sweat want to appear. Sweat was proof. He slowed his breath until it became barely more than a mechanical exchange.

A runner came forward with two plates, hands steady, eyes forward. He stopped at the tape line, not crossing into the pass until invited. The plates hovered under the lamps for a beat.

Renaud's eyes moved over them. Not scanning like a person. Measuring like a machine that knew the correct answer before it inspected the work. His gaze went to the rims first, then to the negative space, then to the height of a garnish.

He didn't touch. He didn't taste. He looked, and looking was enough to turn a room's stomach inside out.

Sofia's hand appeared, wiped a rim once. Invisible wipe. Towel folded into thirds, the motion so fluid it looked like part of plating rather than correction. Then her hand withdrew.

Renaud's eyes moved to the runner. One fraction of a head tilt, and the runner stepped forward, delivered the plates to the waiting hands of another runner, and vanished toward the dining room.

The exchange was soundless. The pass did not clatter. It did not breathe loudly. It simply processed.

Connor watched and felt something in him sharpen. At garde manger, he'd believed the pass was a checkpoint. Standing here, he realized it was a nerve center. Everything converged here: timing, appearance, temperature, story. This wasn't where food was finished. It was where reality was approved.

A plate arrived next, a single dish, carried by the soldier-runner Connor recognized from the private room calls. The runner's posture was rigid enough to read as fear disguised as discipline.

Sofia's eyes flicked to the ticket on the rail, separated by a finger's width. Private room again. The hidden dining room behind the visible one.

Renaud inspected the dish without blinking. The lamp light caught a sheen in the sauce. For a moment Connor couldn't see anything wrong. The plate was immaculate, built like an object meant to be photographed.

Renaud's gaze paused at the edge of a component, a piece of crisp that cast a shadow. The shadow was a fraction longer than it should have been, which meant the component sat a fraction higher. Which meant it would snap differently. Which meant time or humidity or handling had changed it.

Renaud didn't speak.

Sofia leaned in, eyes narrowing, seeing what he saw. She didn't correct the component. She didn't touch the plate. She only turned her head slightly toward the runner holding it.

The runner froze, as if movement would be confession.

Renaud spoke at last, quiet enough that only those at the pass could hear. "Again."

The soldier-runner's face did not change. He didn't argue. He didn't flinch. He simply withdrew the plate by a clean inch and turned away, carrying it back toward the hot side as if returning a weapon to be rebuilt.

Connor's stomach tightened. Again. Not shouted. Not dramatic. Absolute. Here, the command wasn't a correction. It was a standard reasserting itself. A refusal to let a fraction become a story.

Sofia didn't look at Connor, but her voice reached him anyway. "You see it."

Connor chose his words carefully, keeping them minimal. "The shadow," he said.

Sofia's eyes cut toward him for half a second. "And what made it?"

Connor's mind raced through the variables: humidity from the pass heat, a plate held too long, a hand too warm, a runner's path delayed. He remembered the flinch earlier. He remembered table seven bending time. He remembered the private room demanding tight pacing.

"Time," Connor said.

Sofia's jaw tightened again. "Time is always the answer," she replied, and turned away as if that was enough instruction for now.

Another runner approached with a pair of plates, hot this time, steam rising in a controlled whisper. The pass heat wrapped around Connor's face and made his skin feel too alive. He wanted to wipe his upper lip. He didn't. Touching your face was a confession that you had a body.

Renaud's eyes swept the plates, then moved past them, down the line. For a fraction of a second, Connor thought the gaze might land on him again. It didn't. It cut through him anyway, a reminder that being near the pass meant being in the field of view even when you weren't the target.

Sofia shifted her stance slightly, creating a pocket of space at the pass edge. She spoke without looking at him. "When I tell you, you will carry."

Connor felt his throat tighten. Carrying meant crossing the tape line. Carrying meant being seen by front of house, by diners if a door opened wrong, by anyone whose money demanded perfection. Carrying meant that if his hand tremored, it would not tremor in the privacy of cold station light. It would tremor under the lamps, in the pass's bright spine, where mistakes became public.

"Understood," he said.

Sofia's head angled toward him. "Not that word," she murmured. "Less."

Connor recalibrated again, stripping language down. "Heard," he whispered, and immediately realized heard might be too much today, too brigade. But Sofia didn't correct him. She let it pass, which meant the word had fit the moment's required texture.

Plates continued arriving. The rhythm at the pass was different from garde manger. At garde manager, the work had been continuous and compressed. Here it was discrete and ceremonial. Each plate arrived as a proposition. Each plate left as a decision.

A runner came forward with a cold plate Connor recognized from his own station's geometry, though he couldn't be sure it was his. Chervil instead of micro shiso. The plate was dressed for a different audience.

Sofia's eyes tracked it. She rotated it a fraction. That invisible axis again. Renaud looked, approved without a word.

Sofia turned her head slightly. "Felwick."

Connor's hands went behind his back, then he remembered she'd said carry. He brought them forward, palms open, fingers relaxed enough not to grip too hard. Gripping meant fear. Fear translated into tremor.

"Take it," Sofia said, and the plate was suddenly in front of him, hovering under the lamp light.

Connor stepped forward and received it the way he'd seen runners do: palms supporting porcelain, thumbs kept clear of the rim, wrists locked into steadiness. The plate was cooler than he expected against the heat, and the temperature contrast made his body want to react. He did not.

For a moment the world narrowed to the weight of the dish and the distance to the corridor. Not far. Just a few steps. But every step was now a statement. The plate could not tilt. The garnish could not shift. The negative space could not be disturbed.

Sofia's voice came low, close enough that it felt like pressure against his ear. "Do not rush," she said. "Do not slow. You move like you were built for it."

Connor took one step, then another, matching the runner pace he'd studied for weeks. Fast without looking fast. Careful without looking careful. The kitchen behind him continued without acknowledging his departure, as if removing him from the line did not change the machine at all.

At the corridor threshold, the light changed. Shadows waited. The dining room's quiet wealth breathed behind the door.

Connor felt Marcus Hale's presence without seeing him, felt it like a pressure shift. A gaze that didn't need to be direct to be felt. He kept his eyes forward. He did not look toward the border.

A front-of-house hand appeared, gloved, precise. Connor transferred the plate without letting it dip, without letting his fingers brush the rim. The hand took it and vanished into the dining room.

Connor returned to the pass empty-handed, the sensation of carrying still in his wrists. The empty hands felt wrong, too light, as if weight had been the only thing keeping him anchored.

Sofia watched him re-enter his position. Not his face, not his expression. His hands. His steadiness. The absence of sweat on his palms.

Renaud did not look at him.

That was not relief. It was instruction. Being close to the pass did not mean being seen. It meant being used.

Connor stood in the heat and understood something Dumas had tried to warn him about.

At garde manger, he had been tested for precision.

Here, he was being tested for proximity.

The inner circle wasn't a group you joined with talent. It was a radius around power you were allowed to enter if you could keep your humanity from leaking through the seams.

Plates arrived again. Renaud's stillness held the room. Sofia translated, silent and sharp. Hale watched from the corridor mouth, consequence waiting to be assigned.

And Connor, closer to the pass now, felt the margin shrink further, not because he had failed, but because he had succeeded without breaking.

In this place, that was how the trap tightened.

You executed well.

They brought you closer.

Then they watched to see what you would become when the heat and the eyes and the story pressed right up against your skin.

The heat at the pass didn't fade just because Connor stepped back into position. It stayed on his face like a hand that refused to lift, forcing his skin to remember it. He stood at the edge of the lamps, empty-handed, wrists still carrying the ghost weight of porcelain.

Plates arrived. Plates left. Renaud's stillness held.

Connor thought he understood control from garde manger: the grid, the resets, the invisible rules that kept panic from ever becoming visible. But here, under the lamps, control wasn't an internal discipline. It was architecture. It was the entire kitchen being moved as if it were one body, with Renaud as the spine.

A runner stepped forward with a pair of hot plates, steam tight and disciplined, not billowing but contained. The runner's eyes stayed forward, his face neutral in that practiced way that made him look less like a person and more like a function.

Renaud didn't speak. His gaze traveled the plates in the order Connor had learned to recognize: rims, negative space, height, sheen. When his eyes paused, everyone paused. Not because he commanded them to stop, but because a pause from him was information, and information here was dangerous if you misread it.

Sofia leaned in, her towel already folded into thirds. She wiped nothing, then withdrew. The runner didn't move until Renaud's head made the smallest tilt.

The plates left. The runner vanished.

Connor's breathing stayed shallow. He tried to keep his eyes from lingering on the corridor mouth, but the corridor was part of the pass the way a blade was part of a knife. You couldn't ignore it and pretend you understood the weapon.

Marcus Hale stood there, half in shadow, exactly where he always stood when he wanted to be seen but not touched. Hale's gaze wasn't pinned to the plates the way Renaud's was. Hale's gaze moved through bodies. He tracked the passes of runners, the timing between plates, the micro-delays that were being erased before they could exist.

A small shift at the rail drew Connor's attention. Sofia reached out and moved a ticket. Not replacing it, not reorganizing for neatness. She slid it apart from the others by the width of a finger, the same separation Connor had learned to associate with compartments, with tables and rooms that weren't allowed to behave like normal guests.

The soldier-runner appeared immediately, as if the separation itself had summoned him. He didn't speak a table number.

He said, "Now."

Sofia answered without looking up. "Hold thirty."

The soldier-runner's jaw tightened once, then he went still again, receiving the instruction the way a machine received code.

Connor felt the internal flinch that went through the pass when someone said hold. Hold was not a kitchen word. Hold was what the dining room did to the kitchen. Hold was a hand around the throat of timing.

Renaud didn't react. That was the first sign of total control Connor had not understood before: Renaud didn't show strain when the system was forced to bend. The system bent. He remained.

He turned his head a fraction toward Sofia. He didn't move his hands. His voice was quiet enough that Connor had to lean on proximity to catch it.

"Not on the lamps," Renaud said.

Sofia replied in the same tone. "No, Chef."

Renaud's eyes returned to the rail. His gaze didn't ask why there was a thirty-second hold. Why belonged to people who believed they had choices. Here, only adjustment mattered.

Sofia pivoted toward the hot side. Not hurried. Exact. Her presence cut a path through the line without anyone looking like they were moving out of her way. She spoke low to a chef Connor didn't recognize by name, only by station posture and the quick flare of fear in his eyes.

"Refire garnish," she said.

The chef opened his mouth as if to answer, then closed it. He nodded once, then seemed to remember nodding was movement and converted it into a still, verbal response.

"Heard, Chef."

He moved instantly, hands precise, face blank.

Connor realized what Sofia had just done. A thirty-second hold in the dining room would kill certain elements. Not the whole plate. Not in a way diners would notice. In a way Renaud would notice, and in a way Hale would count.

So, Sofia didn't risk it. She removed the risk by refiring garnish, a correction hidden inside a hold, a way of making forced obedience look like chosen pacing.

Renaud spoke again, almost conversational, if conversation here meant something stripped of warmth.

"Table seven?" he asked.

Sofia's eyes flicked toward the corridor mouth, then back to the rail. "No, Chef. Private room."

Private room. Connor felt the words land in his body with a different weight than table seven. Table seven was a lever, loud because it changed the room through preference. The private room changed the room through authority.

Renaud's gaze didn't move to Hale. It didn't need to. Hale was part of the air now, like pressure. But Connor saw, in the reflection of the pass's stainless edge, that Hale's posture shifted slightly, as if he had heard his presence named and approved of the accuracy.

A runner returned with a dish from the hot side, presenting it at the tape line. The plate looked immaculate, but Connor had learned not to trust the surface. The surface was the story, and the story could be forged.

Sofia stepped in first this time. She rotated the plate a fraction, then looked toward Renaud.

Renaud didn't touch it. He didn't taste. He looked, and his eyes narrowed by a millimeter, the smallest sign of friction.

Connor held his breath.

Renaud's voice came, quiet and final. "Again."

No anger. No escalation. The runner withdrew as if pulled back by gravity, turning away with the plate still level, still perfect by every normal standard. The runner didn't show reaction. That was the point. Reaction would imply the decision had human emotion attached to it. Here, decisions were supposed to appear inevitable.

Sofia didn't follow the runner with her eyes. She tracked the timing instead, already patching the hole the refire would create.

"Two minutes," she murmured to someone Connor couldn't see.

A voice answered from the line. "Heard."

Renaud's stillness didn't change. He didn't fill the gap with explanation. The line would refire. The story would remain intact.

Connor felt something cold settle into his understanding. At garde manger, control had looked like discipline. At the pass, control looked like the removal of alternatives. There was never a debate because the outcome was predetermined: if the plate wasn't correct, it didn't exist. If time touched it wrong, it didn't exist. If the story threatened to crack, the evidence was destroyed and rebuilt without anyone admitting the crack had ever been there.

That was total control. Not perfection, but the refusal to let imperfection remain long enough to be witnessed.

A front-of-house hand appeared near the pass, gloved, precise. The maître d' didn't step fully into the kitchen. He hovered at the threshold like a man aware of borders and consequences. He spoke to Sofia, not to Renaud.

"Madame Alvarez," he said quietly. "Private room requests a pause."

Connor felt the word pause hit harder than hold. Pause implied the dining room believed it could stop the kitchen and the kitchen would remain obedient and smiling.

Sofia's face stayed composed. Her eyes moved once, not toward Renaud, but toward Hale at the corridor mouth.

Hale answered with barely a gesture. Two fingers, not pointing, not commanding, simply placing a decision into the air.

Sofia turned back to the maître d'. "We will pace it," she said. "No gaps."

The maître d' hesitated, a fraction of a second too long, then corrected himself by bowing his head slightly. "Yes, madame."

He retreated without turning his back too slowly, leaving the kitchen's air cleaner behind him, as if front-of-house language contaminated stainless steel.

Connor watched Renaud. He had not moved. He had not acknowledged the request. Yet the kitchen began to adjust.

That was the part that made Connor's throat tighten. Renaud didn't have to speak for the kitchen to comply. Sofia translated the request into a set of mechanical actions: pull a pan off heat, delay a garnish, hold a runner at the corner without making the hold visible. The machine complied while preserving the illusion that it was not.

Renaud's total control wasn't in forcing obedience. It was in making obedience disappear into workflow.

Sofia leaned close to Connor, her voice low enough that it stayed inside the pass's bright spine. "When the pace changes," she said, "you don't watch the dining room. You watch the rail."

Connor didn't speak. He felt the lesson settle in place: the rail was the throat of the kitchen. Whoever controlled the rail controlled time.

Sofia straightened and scanned the line. Her gaze was sharp, measuring people the way Renaud measured plates. Connor realized she wasn't only looking for flaws in food. She was looking for stress in bodies. A chef whose hands were too tight. A runner who swallowed too hard. A station whose movements became fractionally frantic.

The elite weren't immune to pressure. They were just trained to hide it better. And Sofia's job, Connor understood, was to keep that hiding intact.

The soldier-runner returned, appearing at the tape line with a stillness that looked ceremonial. "Now," he said again.

Sofia answered, "Walk."

But she didn't hand him plates. She held up one finger, a small command that didn't look like a command unless you knew how to read it. The soldier-runner froze.

Sofia's eyes moved to a plate coming up under the lamps. She waited until it arrived, until Renaud's gaze swept it once, until his head tilted the smallest degree.

Then Sofia released her finger.

The runner stepped forward and took the plate as if the timing had always been this way, as if no one had been held, as if the private room's demands were not shaping the flow.

Connor felt the hair rise on the back of his neck. Total control wasn't loud. It was seamless. It was the ability to make a forced adjustment look like the original plan.

Renaud's voice came again, so quiet it almost blended into the refrigeration hum Connor had left behind at garde manger.

"Felwick."

Connor's stomach tightened. He was being addressed directly by the fixed point of the room.

He stepped half a pace forward, careful not to move too much, careful not to look eager. "Chef."

Renaud didn't look at him the way Sofia did. Sofia's attention cut. Renaud's attention erased. His eyes stayed on the pass as he spoke, as if Connor were being integrated into the machine rather than acknowledged as a person.

"Carry the next," Renaud said.

Not a question. Not an opportunity. A function being assigned.

Connor's palms went faintly damp, then he forced the dampness out of his mind. Dampness was proof. Proof was dangerous. He made his hands ready, fingers relaxed, wrists steady.

Sofia's voice slid in, quiet and quick. "No rush," she said. "No hesitation."

Connor understood. The worst thing wasn't dropping a plate. The worst thing was making the pass look human.

A plate arrived. Cold, precise. One of his geometries, though he couldn't be sure. Sofia rotated it a fraction to the invisible axis. Renaud's gaze swept it, approved without a word.

Sofia lifted it and placed it into Connor's hands.

The porcelain's weight grounded him. He moved toward the corridor, fast without looking fast. Careful without looking careful. The dining room's quiet wealth waited behind the door, hungry not only for taste but for the sensation that the world would behave for them.

At the threshold, Connor felt Hale's presence like a hand at his shoulder. Not touching. Not needed. Hale didn't stop him. Hale didn't speak. Hale simply watched Connor's wrists, Connor's pace, Connor's ability to be nothing but a clean transfer of perfection.

A gloved hand received the plate. Connor released it without a tremor and returned to the pass.

When he stepped back into the light, Sofia's eyes flicked over him once. Not praise. Audit. She turned away immediately, already tracking the next adjustment.

Renaud didn't look at him again.

Connor stood at the pass and felt the shape of the inner circle more clearly now. It wasn't a group that welcomed you. It was a radius in which you were allowed to function under pressure without contaminating the illusion of effortlessness.

And the more flawlessly you functioned, the more closely you were watched.

The plates kept coming. The rail kept shifting. Holds became invisible. Refires happened without announcement. The dining room's demands were absorbed and translated into choreography so clean it looked like choice.

Connor understood, with a clarity that made his mouth go dry, that total control didn't mean nothing went wrong.

It meant nothing wrong was allowed to remain true long enough to become real.

Connor returned to his position at the pass with the same careful emptiness he'd used to carry the plate out. His hands went behind his back, fingers touching lightly, not clasped tight enough to show strain. The heat lamps pressed against his face; the kitchen's air smelled of butter, reduction, sanitizer, and the faint metallic edge of stainless steel warmed beyond comfort.

The plates kept coming. The rail kept shifting. Holds became invisible. Refires happened without anyone naming them too loudly.

And still, the thing Connor couldn't stop noticing was not the perfection.

It was the fear.

Not the obvious fear of a new commis who still had skin in the game. This fear lived deeper, in people who were supposed to have outgrown it. People who'd survived long enough to be considered untouchable inside the brigade. People who could make a dish look inevitable.

Fear among the elite didn't look like panic. It looked like cleanliness taken to the point of compulsion. It looked like hands that never stopped moving, not because there was more work, but because stillness gave the mind room to imagine consequence.

A senior chef from the hot side stepped up with two plates, posture controlled, eyes fixed on the pass as if the lamps might burn him if he looked away. His name was Luc, Connor thought, one of the sauciers who spoke in clipped syllables and never missed his times. Connor had watched him earlier refire without protest, his face unchanged.

Now Luc's jaw worked once, a small grinding movement, then stopped. A tick Connor wouldn't have seen from garde manger.

The plates hovered under the lamps. Renaud's gaze traveled them. Sofia stood half a step back, towel folded into thirds, waiting.

Renaud didn't speak. He didn't need to. His eyes paused on a point near the protein, where a glaze caught the light in a way that looked almost too perfect, as if it had been corrected.

Connor felt Luc's breath catch. Not a sound, just a pause in the rise of his shoulders that lasted half a beat too long.

Sofia's eyes narrowed slightly, her attention shifting from the plate to Luc's hands, then back. She didn't intervene yet.

Renaud tilted his head the smallest degree.

The runner reached forward to take the plates.

Luc's fingers twitched as if to reach out and re-center something that did not need re-centering. He stopped himself at the last instant, hand freezing midair for a fraction of a second before returning to his side.

Connor's stomach tightened. That twitch was confession. Not of a mistake, but of doubt. Doubt was the first visible crack.

The plates left. The runner vanished.

Luc stepped back and exhaled, controlled, through his nose. He did not look relieved. He looked like a man who had just walked past a ledge he'd pretended not to see.

Connor tracked the edge of the kitchen where Marcus Hale stood near the corridor mouth, half in shadow. Hale had not moved. Yet Connor felt, in the subtle tightening that followed Luc's twitch, that the room believed Hale had seen it.

A runner returned, older eyes, empty face, and stopped at the tape line near the pass. He didn't say "black" this time. He didn't need to. His stillness carried the code. It was the same message delivered without language: the air is recording.

Sofia spoke without turning her head. "Walk," she said.

The runner moved.

Renaud's posture never shifted.

Connor realized then that fear among the elite did not come from uncertainty about technique. Technique was the easy part. The fear came from the rules that couldn't be studied, only sensed: the invisible expectations that changed depending on who was behind a closed door, who was eating slowly at table seven, who was receiving a call mid-course, who was being kept satisfied not with flavor but with obedience.

Sofia made another adjustment at the rail, sliding a ticket apart by a finger's width. The separation was clean, deliberate. A private-room call again.

The soldier-runner appeared immediately, as if the separation had summoned him. He stood with his hands behind his back, posture so rigid it bordered on ceremonial.

"Now," he murmured.

Sofia's gaze flicked toward the corridor mouth, toward Hale's silhouette, then returned to the lamps. "Hold," she said. "Twenty."

The soldier-runner didn't react, but Connor saw his throat move as he swallowed. It wasn't dramatic. It was simply the body reminding itself it was alive.

Twenty seconds. Not much. Enough to ruin something if it sat in the wrong heat. Enough to expose a delay if anyone looked like they were waiting.

Sofia leaned close to Renaud's shoulder and spoke too low for Connor to hear. Renaud didn't answer. He shifted his weight by a millimeter. The pass adjusted around that millimeter as if it were a command.

Connor watched Sofia's jaw. The muscle jumped once, then stilled.

That was her fear, he realized. Sofia didn't fear failing at service. She feared being forced to comply in a way that made compliance visible. She feared the line between correction and submission.

The elite weren't immune. They were simply trained to keep the fear inside their bodies where it couldn't be used as evidence.

A plate came up that Connor recognized in a way he couldn't prove: the negative space, the angle of the garnish, the quiet aggression of the geometry. Garde manger's handwriting. Possibly his, possibly Dumas's. The distinction blurred here, because the station demanded the same hand no matter who held the tweezers.

Sofia rotated it a fraction to the invisible axis.

Renaud's gaze swept it.

He did not speak.

Sofia's hand lifted it and set it into the soldier-runner's palms at the exact moment the count reached twenty.

The runner left.

The hold disappeared.

That was total control. Not the prevention of interruption, but the eradication of its existence.

Connor's eyes returned to the line of chefs beyond the lamps. He watched the way the best of them held themselves. Not relaxed. Never relaxed. The word didn't belong here. They stood like people bracing against a storm no one admitted was weather.

On the far side of the pass, Dumas appeared briefly, crossing behind with a tray, face unreadable. He didn't come close, didn't look at Connor, but Connor caught the smallest sign of strain: Dumas's towel was folded into thirds with a sharpness that looked newly aggressive, the crease pressed hard enough to suggest his hands needed something to do.

Dumas had called Hale a keeper. He'd described disappearance as story editing. Dumas was not afraid of service. He was afraid of being included in that editing.

Connor felt the impulse to look at Hale again and stopped himself. Don't feed him. But the fear in the room fed Hale whether Connor looked or not. Hale didn't need attention. Hale was consequence. Consequence fed itself.

The maître d' hovered near the threshold again, speaking quietly to Sofia, not stepping fully into the kitchen. Connor couldn't hear the words, but he saw the effect: Sofia's shoulders tightened a fraction, then she smoothed them back into control as if pressing fear flat beneath her jacket.

Sofia answered with a short sentence and a hand gesture that meant leave. The maître d' withdrew immediately, and the kitchen swallowed the exchange.

For a moment, the pass was only plates and light and the soft whisper of runners' shoes.

Then Renaud spoke again. Quiet. Precise.

"Who fired that garnish?"

The question was not loud enough to carry down the line, but it didn't need to. It was asked at the center, and the center was where gravity lived. The hot side stiffened as if the air itself had been struck.

A junior chef stepped forward half a pace, stopped, then corrected his movement by freezing. He didn't raise his hand. Hands were too expressive. He simply said, "I did, Chef."

Renaud's eyes didn't go to him. They stayed on the plate beneath the lamp.

"How many seconds?" Renaud asked.

The junior chef hesitated. Hesitation was a visible thing. Sofia's head tilted slightly, a warning.

"Eight," the chef said. "Chef."

Renaud's gaze lifted at last, not fully to the chef's face, but to the space where his face existed, like acknowledging a fault line rather than a person.

"Again," Renaud said.

The plate was withdrawn without argument. The chef didn't protest. He didn't apologize. Apology was emotion, and emotion was noise. He simply took the plate away and vanished back into heat and flame.

Connor's chest tightened. Eight seconds. In another kitchen, it would be nothing. Here, it was a question asked out loud at the pass. A question that turned time into a blade.

Fear among the elite wasn't just fear of Renaud's standard. It was fear of being made an example in front of the watchers.

Connor saw the glance that followed, not from Renaud, but from Sofia toward the corridor mouth, as if measuring whether Hale had registered the exchange.

Hale's posture did not change.

That was the worst part. When Hale reacted, at least reaction could be mapped. A gesture. Two fingers. A decision placed into air.

When Hale stayed still, the room had to imagine what was being recorded.

A runner stepped up with a dish, then another. The pass processed. Renaud's stillness held. Sofia corrected the world in millimeters.

Connor stood where he'd been placed, close enough to the lamps that heat tried to pull sweat from his skin. He refused it. He made his breath a mechanical exchange, shallow and invisible.

He watched the elite around him and understood the ugly truth: the longer you survived here, the less margin you were given.

A new commis could be corrected because expectation for him was low. A senior chef could be refired, but he could also be marked. Being excellent didn't make you safe. It made your failures more interesting. It made your cracks more valuable to whoever needed to prove the system's purity.

Sofia shifted slightly and spoke to Connor without looking at him. "You see them?"

Connor kept his eyes forward, careful not to turn his head too much. "Yes, Chef."

Sofia's jaw tightened once. She let the word yes pass this time, as if she didn't have the patience to sculpt his language while the room compressed.

"You think they don't fear," she murmured. "Because they don't show it."

Connor swallowed. "They do."

Sofia's voice dropped lower. "They fear because they know," she said. "They know what gets erased. They've seen it happen. They've watched lockers go blank. They've watched names stop being said."

Connor felt cold slide through him despite the heat lamps. He thought of Julien Morel and the returned dish from the prologue story, the erasure delivered like a service correction.

Sofia's gaze flicked to him for half a second, dark and steady. "You're close now," she said. "Close enough to see the seams."

Connor didn't speak. The urge to ask what she meant pressed against his teeth. He held it back. Curiosity was blood.

Sofia turned away again as another private-room ticket was separated on the rail.

The soldier-runner appeared.

The kitchen tightened.

Connor felt the fear pass through the best of them like an electrical current, contained but undeniable.

And he understood that being invited closer to the pass did not mean being invited into safety.

It meant being invited into the place where fear was most carefully managed, most expertly hidden, and most brutally punished the moment it became visible.

The inner circle was not calm. It was controlled.

And control, Connor was learning, was only ever as strong as the terror underneath it.

Chapter 8

Collapse Point

The soldier-runner's "now" had become a kind of weather.

It didn't announce itself with volume, only with effect. Backs straightened along the line. Hands tightened around tongs, tweezers, spoons. Sofia's orbit narrowed until she was almost fused to the pass, and the rail became the throat of the kitchen again, swallowing tickets and spitting out decisions.

Connor stood where he'd been placed, close enough to feel the lamps, close enough to hear the micro-sounds people tried not to make: a swallow, a breath taken too deep, the soft click of a container lid reseated with more force than necessary. Fear disguised as precision.

The private-room ticket appeared, clipped by Sofia and separated by that finger's width. The separation looked calm. It never was.

The soldier-runner materialized at the tape line, hands behind his back, jaw set. He didn't look at anyone. He looked through the pass as if the air itself could be reprimanded.

"Now," he murmured.

Sofia didn't hand him anything. She held up one finger. A pause measured in muscle memory, not in seconds. The runner froze, obeying without movement, making obedience look like readiness.

Renaud stood centered, still and immaculate, his white jacket untouched by effort. He didn't ask why. The why belonged to people who still believed their stress mattered.

A plate arrived from hot side, carried by a runner with the blank face of someone trained to be forgettable. The dish was glossy, precise, built for lamp light. Connor could see the reflection of the lamps in the sauce like a clean mirror.

Renaud's eyes moved: rim, negative space, height, sheen.

They paused at the sheen.

Connor felt the smallest ripple go through the hot line behind him. Not visible as panic, only as a tightening of silence.

Luc stepped forward half a pace behind the runner, then caught himself and became still, as if movement itself could be counted as guilt. Luc was one of the senior sauciers, the one Connor had watched earlier with the jaw-tick, the man whose plates looked inevitable until you stood close enough to see how hard inevitability had to be manufactured.

Renaud said nothing.

Sofia leaned in, towel folded into thirds, ready to wipe if she could wipe without confessing. Her eyes tracked the plate and then, briefly, tracked Luc's hands.

Renaud's gaze returned to the sheen, and Connor understood what he was seeing, even if he couldn't have named it yesterday: the sauce had been touched. Not by fingers. By correction. A quick swipe, a back-of-spoon rescue to repair a break or a drag line. A fix that made the surface too perfect in a way only someone like Renaud would find offensive. In this kitchen, the only acceptable perfection was the kind that looked like it had never been pursued.

Renaud's head tilted by a fraction.

The runner began to step forward, interpreting the tilt as approval the way runners did, translating stillness into motion.

Renaud spoke, quiet and final. "Stop."

The word didn't rise. It dropped.

The runner froze mid-step, one foot half lifted, then set it down as if he'd never moved. The plate hovered under the lamps, and the heat began to work on it immediately, trying to change it in ways the dining room would never notice but the pass would.

Luc's throat moved. A swallow.

Sofia didn't look at Luc. She didn't need to. Her presence tightened around the pass like a bandage being pulled too hard.

Renaud's eyes stayed on the plate. "Who touched it?"

No one answered.

The kitchen did not go silent; it was already silent. What changed was the quality of it. It thickened. It became heavy enough to press against skin.

Luc's mouth opened as if to speak, closed again. Connor saw his fingers flex once, an involuntary motion, then go rigid.

Sofia's gaze flicked to Luc's hands again, a warning delivered without sound: if you make this messy, it becomes worse than a refire.

Luc's jaw worked. The tick returned, harder now, not just a muscle habit but the body trying to release pressure in the only way it knew.

Renaud repeated, softer. "Who touched it?"

Luc's voice came out like something forced through a narrow gap. "I did, Chef."

No apology. No explanation. Just a fact, offered like a blade's edge.

Renaud did not look up. "Why?"

Luc hesitated. The hesitation lasted too long. In that extra beat, Connor felt the entire brigade lean inward, not physically, but in attention. This was how fractures began. Not with explosions. With pauses.

Luc's lips parted. "The line broke," he said. "I corrected."

Corrected. The word sounded wrong in this room. Correction belonged to Sofia's towel, to invisible rim wipes and rotations that erased evidence. Correction didn't belong to a sauce, where correction left ghosts.

Renaud's gaze finally lifted, not to Luc's eyes, but to the space where Luc existed, as if acknowledging a structural flaw. "You corrected in sight of the lamps."

Luc's nostrils flared once. Connor saw the moment his control tried to hold and slipped.

"It was going to return," Luc said. The volume wasn't loud. The tone was. It carried something human: urgency, self-defense, the need to be understood.

Sofia's shoulders tightened. Hale's silhouette at the corridor mouth didn't move, but Connor felt the kitchen register the change anyway. Tone was noise. Noise was evidence.

Renaud's voice stayed level. "Nothing returns," he said, as if reading from a rule that never changed.

Luc's face drained of something. Not color. Certainty. He looked at the plate again, and Connor saw him see it the way Renaud saw it: not as a dish, but as a confession of struggle.

Luc's hands moved. Not toward the plate. Toward himself. He wiped his palms against his apron once, a quick, unconscious attempt to get rid of sweat.

Sofia's head snapped toward him, a sharp look. Touching yourself was humanity. Humanity was what the kitchen removed.

Luc seemed to feel her look like a slap. He pulled his hands back to his sides, fingers rigid, shoulders too square. His breathing changed.

Deeper. Faster. He tried to make it quiet and couldn't.

Renaud watched him for a beat that felt longer than it was. The pass lamps hummed. The plate sat under heat, aging, becoming more wrong by the second.

Renaud turned his gaze back to the plate. "Again," he said.

The runner withdrew it by a clean inch, turned away to carry it back to be rebuilt.

Luc didn't move.

At first Connor thought Luc was simply being still, absorbing correction the way everyone had been trained to. But then seconds passed and Luc remained in the same exact posture, not resetting, not returning to station, not doing the next thing that was always supposed to follow.

The line behind him kept working. The kitchen couldn't stop to accommodate one man's processing. Sofia's eyes cut past Luc to the rail, to the next ticket, to the timing that couldn't be allowed to show strain.

But Luc didn't go.

A runner brought up another plate, another pair, and the pass processed them, Renaud's gaze sweeping, Sofia's towel ready, the choreography continuing around a man who had become an obstacle simply by becoming human.

Connor saw it: Luc's eyes weren't tracking the pass anymore. They were unfocused, fixed on some point beyond the lamps, beyond the room. His jaw ticked in a rapid stutter now. His throat worked as if he were trying not to gag on his own breath.

Sofia leaned slightly toward Renaud, her lips barely moving. Connor couldn't hear the words, but he saw Renaud's posture shift by a millimeter, the smallest acknowledgment that something other than plating had entered his field.

Renaud didn't look at Luc yet. He approved another plate with a head tilt. The runner moved. Service continued.

Then, in the space between plates, Renaud spoke quietly. "Luc."

Luc didn't respond.

The name, spoken at the center of gravity, should have snapped him back into function. Instead, it seemed to pin him in place.

Sofia stepped half a pace toward him, still within the pass's light, her voice low and sharp. "Chef Renaud spoke to you."

Luc's eyes flickered, focusing for an instant. He looked at Sofia like she was speaking through glass. His lips parted, but nothing came out.

Another plate arrived. Another runner waited. Renaud did not look at it. Not yet. His attention had shifted, and Connor felt the room tighten in response. When Renaud's attention left food, it meant the threat was no longer on the plate.

Luc's hands rose slightly, then stopped midair, hovering at his waist as if he didn't know what to do with them. Fingers tremored. Not a small tremor like Connor's had been at garde manger. This tremor was visible. This tremor was an announcement.

Luc's breathing became audible. A wet inhale that he tried to swallow down and failed.

Sofia's eyes narrowed. "Luc," she said again, and this time there was something else in her tone, not kindness, not patience. A warning meant for the whole room: do not let this become a scene.

Luc's head shook once. Tiny. Involuntary.

Then his knees softened.

He didn't fall. He simply stopped holding himself up with the rigid discipline that had kept him functional for years. His shoulders sagged as if the jacket suddenly weighed too much. His hands drifted toward the counter edge like he needed something to grip.

Sofia moved instantly, not to catch him, but to block him from contaminating the pass. She stepped between Luc and the lamps, placing her body as a barrier so whatever happened next would be contained in the smallest possible footprint.

“Step back,” she said, and this time the command was to the space around him as much as to Luc himself. Runners shifted their paths by inches, avoiding proximity without looking like they were avoiding anything.

Renaud’s voice remained level. “Move,” he said.

Luc’s mouth worked. His eyes shone, not with tears yet, but with the threat of them. “I can’t,” he whispered.

The words were small. They were catastrophic.

A runner at the tape line stared forward, face blank, holding plates that were dying under lamp heat. The dining room didn’t care why time slipped; it only cared if it ever saw time slip.

Renaud looked at the plates waiting, then at Luc, as if comparing two problems. Connor felt his stomach tighten with the recognition: Luc was the bigger problem now. Food could be remade. A fracture could spread.

Renaud spoke without raising his voice. "Remove him."

No drama. No anger. Not even disappointment. Just execution, the same word delivered in the prologue as if it were a standard kitchen action.

Two senior chefs appeared from the hot side with the same calm efficiency Connor had seen before when a mistake had to be erased quickly. They approached Luc from either side, not grabbing, not violent, simply taking his elbows with practiced firmness, turning him away from the pass as if redirecting a cart.

Luc didn't resist. That was the worst part. His body went with them too easily, like something emptied.

As they guided him toward the corridor, Luc's eyes flicked once toward the pass lamps, toward the plates still arriving, toward Renaud's stillness. For a brief moment Connor saw something like pleading in his face, not for mercy, but for acknowledgment that he had been a person here.

Renaud had already turned back to the plates.

Sofia's towel moved. A rim was wiped. A plate rotated to the invisible axis. A runner was released at the exact second that made the delay disappear.

Service continued without pause.

Connor stood in the heat and watched Luc vanish into the corridor shadow, escorted with such quiet competence that it looked like Luc had simply been reassigned. The kitchen did not speak his name again. The air sealed over the absence as if the absence had never been created.

The soldier-runner returned to the tape line, rigid, waiting for the next private-room call.

"Now," he murmured.

And the word landed in Connor's body with a new meaning.

Now wasn't only about timing.

Now was about how quickly a person could become a problem, and how quickly the machine could erase that problem while keeping the story clean.

Connor's hands went behind his back again. His fingers touched lightly, not clasping, because clasping would mean he needed something to hold on to.

He stared at the rail, at the separated tickets, at Sofia's orbit, at Renaud's stillness, at the corridor mouth where Hale stood as consequence made human.

Fear among the elite had always been there, Sofia had said, hidden under control.

Now Connor had seen what happened when the fear broke containment.

It didn't become a scene.

It became an absence.

And the kitchen, immaculate and relentless, kept moving as if that absence had been part of the plan all along.

Luc was gone so quickly the kitchen barely had time to register the shape of his absence.

Two senior chefs guided him toward the corridor with hands that looked gentle until you understood gentleness here was just a way of keeping noise out of the story. One at each elbow, turning him with the same efficiency they used to turn a tray on a lowboy. Luc's jacket brushed the corner of the pass on the way out. The edge of fabric came too close to the lamps and Sofia moved, a small sidestep that blocked the brush from happening, as if even contact between collapse and the pass would leave residue.

The plates under the lamps did not wait for the moment to finish. They kept aging, heat changing surfaces by degrees no diner would name but Renaud could feel in his teeth without tasting.

A runner stood frozen at the tape line holding two dishes that were supposed to leave together. His arms trembled with the discipline of not letting them tremble. The runner's eyes stayed forward, blank as a wall.

Renaud looked at the plates, then at the runner, as if both were identical problems with different consequences.

"Walk," he said.

The runner stepped forward at once, relieved of waiting the way a prisoner was relieved of uncertainty. He moved fast without looking fast, the plates level, his wrists locked, his breath invisible. Sofia's towel hovered in her hand, already folded into thirds, not wiping now, just ready in case something threatened to show.

Connor watched the plates leave and felt the wrongness of it: a man had just fractured in front of everyone, and the kitchen's response had been to keep the timing clean.

That was what instant removal meant here. Not a decision made quickly. A decision that had been made long before, waiting like a trapdoor under the floorboards.

Luc's heels didn't scrape. He didn't plead. He didn't call out. The senior chefs did not speak to him as they guided him. They didn't have to. Conversation implied choice, and there was no choice in this. The corridor swallowed them with a soft seal of the door.

Connor's eyes flicked, against his will, toward Marcus Hale at the corridor mouth.

Hale hadn't moved from his place in shadow. He didn't step forward to meet Luc. He didn't step back to make space. He only watched the transfer the way he watched everything else: as a movement of assets across a boundary line. His face stayed mild, almost bored, as if he'd already seen this scene too many times to find it interesting.

Connor forced his eyes back to the pass.

Don't feed him.

But the knowledge of Hale's presence clung to Connor's skin anyway. It didn't matter where you looked. The corridor was the corridor. Consequence lived there whether you acknowledged it or not.

Sofia leaned close enough to Connor that her voice could hide beneath the hum of lamps and refrigeration, the machinery of control.

"Hands," she murmured.

Connor realized his fingers had tightened behind his back, clasping too hard. A grip like prayer. A grip like fear.

He released them into the lightest contact, fingertip to fingertip, nothing that could be read as needing. Stillness returned to his posture, but it took effort. He could feel his pulse in his wrists.

The space Luc had occupied at the pass was already being filled. Not by another person stepping into his exact spot, but by the re-expansion of workflow. The hot side tightened its line. A saucier leaned into the gap and covered the next plate as if Luc had never existed, as if station coverage was just a mathematical adjustment. The runners' queue smoothed out. Sofia slid a ticket forward with two fingers, resetting the sequence the way Dumas reset a station: erase evidence, restore grid.

Renaud didn't look toward the corridor again.

Connor wanted, with a sudden urgent need that felt like nausea, to know where Luc was being taken. Not out of curiosity, he told himself. Out of safety. Because safety depended on mapping exits.

But safety was another word that didn't belong here. There was only function and removal.

A new plate arrived under the lamps. Renaud's gaze swept it and paused at the rim. Sofia's towel moved once, a single wipe so smooth it looked like part of the plating. The plate left. The story stayed clean.

Connor felt the room's collective agreement settle into place: no one would say Luc's name.

Not now. Not later. Not in the quick private language of the walk-in. Not in the bathroom where steam and fluorescent light could make men feel briefly human. Names were how you kept people real. The kitchen's first act of violence was always the same: it edited you out of the mouth.

The soldier-runner appeared again, rigid at the tape line, eyes forward.

"Now," he murmured.

Sofia didn't even look at him. Her eyes were on the rail, on the finger-width separation that marked private-room gravity. She held up one finger.

Hold.

The soldier-runner froze.

Renaud's voice didn't change. "Not on the lamps," he said again, as if the rule needed to be reasserted after the contamination of a human moment.

"Yes, Chef," Sofia replied, then corrected herself without letting the correction show in her face. "Heard."

Language here was also a surface that could betray you. Too formal, too human. Too much.

A chef on hot side moved a plate back from the brightest heat circle by half an inch. Another plate was covered with a cloche for a breath, then uncovered at precisely the right second. The hold disappeared into choreography.

Connor watched, and the sickness in him sharpened into something colder. Luc's collapse hadn't stopped the system. It had proven the system. It had demonstrated, to anyone watching, that even a senior chef could be removed without causing a ripple in output.

Proof of power.

Sofia shifted, blocking Connor's line of sight to the corridor with her body for a moment, a subtle act that looked like nothing. When she spoke again, her voice was flat, functional.

"You didn't see him," she murmured.

Connor's throat tightened. The words were absurd on their face. Of course he had seen him. Everyone had.

But this wasn't about sight. It was about record.

Connor kept his gaze on the lamps. "Heard," he said, as softly as possible.

Sofia's jaw tightened once, then relaxed. Confirmation. Not approval.

From the hot side, one of the senior chefs who had escorted Luc returned alone. He didn't re-enter with urgency. He walked back into the line with the same calm pace as a man returning from a supply run. His hands were clean. His jacket was clean. The only evidence that he'd just removed a person was the faint flush at the base of his throat, a human detail that would fade.

He slid into position without greeting anyone.

Service continued.

Connor felt his mind trying to fill the gap Luc had left. His brain offered images like it wanted to make sense of the disappearance: Luc being sat down in an office, given water, spoken to quietly, told to go home. Another version: Luc being taken down a back stairwell, through a door that wasn't used by staff, into the city where no one would connect him to this kitchen again.

And the version Connor couldn't keep from forming, the one that made his stomach tighten: Luc being taken somewhere inside the building that wasn't on any floor plan he'd seen, somewhere the corridor swallowed and didn't return.

Dumas's words came back uninvited. Firing is messy. People talk. People sue. People become interviews.

So, Hale made them disappear from the story.

Sometimes they still walked out the door. Sometimes they didn't walk out the same way they came in.

Connor forced the images away by focusing on the only safe thing: plates. Timing. The rail. The grid that kept him from becoming a person with questions.

Renaud inspected another dish. His head tilted. "Walk."

The runner took it.

Then, in a thin gap between movements, Sofia spoke quietly to Renaud. Connor didn't hear the words, but he saw the exchange as posture: Sofia's body angled toward him, offering a fact; Renaud's stillness receiving and filing it without reaction.

Connor understood the fact without hearing it.

Coverage.

Station reassignment.

The machine had already redistributed Luc's labor like a resource.

Renaud's gaze drifted down the line, not to look for grief, not to look for shock, but to look for weakness that might spread. He wasn't measuring emotion. He was measuring performance degradation.

His eyes passed over Connor without pausing.

That should have felt like relief. Instead, it felt like something worse: proof that the removal had been clean enough to not require further attention.

A runner approached with a pair of plates that were supposed to leave together. One was present. The other was half a beat behind.

Sofia's hand lifted, not a full stop, just a small pause. She held the first plate just outside the brightest heat circle, exactly as she had before, erasing the timing slip without anyone naming it. When the second plate arrived, Sofia released the first at the precise moment that made the delay cease to exist.

Connor watched the act and realized he'd just seen a second removal.

Not of a person.

Of evidence.

That was the pattern. That was how the kitchen survived itself: remove the flaw, remove the proof, remove the memory. Restore the story. Keep the stars clean.

The soldier-runner returned at the tape line. "Now," he murmured again, as if the word was the only one he was permitted to have.

Sofia held up one finger again, then dropped it.

"Walk."

The soldier-runner stepped forward and plates moved out.

For a moment, Connor's mind did something dangerous: it tried to calculate how many seconds Luc had been unable to move before Renaud ordered removal. How long the fracture had lasted. How quickly the senior chefs had appeared. How quickly the corridor had sealed.

Instant.

Not impulsive. Not emotional.

Instant because it was practiced.

Connor felt the cold clarity settle deeper. This wasn't a kitchen that occasionally erased people. It was a system built to do it smoothly. The same way it was built to refire without drama, to hold without showing, to rotate plates to an invisible axis, to translate dining room demands into seamless choreography.

Instant removal wasn't punishment. It was maintenance.

Sofia leaned toward Connor again, her voice low and sharp. "Breathe," she murmured.

Connor realized he hadn't been, not fully. He released a controlled exhale and took in air in a shallow, quiet mechanical draw.

Sofia's eyes stayed on the lamps. "You keep working," she said. "You keep your face clean. You keep your hands steady. You do not carry what you saw."

Connor kept his gaze forward. "Yes, Chef."

Sofia's head angled a fraction, the smallest correction. "Less."

Connor swallowed. "Heard."

Sofia didn't answer. She didn't need to. The pass filled with plates again. Renaud's gaze measured. Sofia's towel erased. Runners flowed.

And somewhere behind the corridor door, Luc had become an absence so complete that the kitchen could pretend he'd never stood under these lamps at all.

Connor stood close enough to the pass to feel the heat and the pressure and the tight, controlled fear among the best of them, and he understood the part that mattered most.

If collapse happened to him, it would not be dramatic.

It would be handled.

Quickly. Quietly. Efficiently.

Instantly.

The pass filled again as if it had been starving for plates.

Connor stood where Sofia had placed him, close enough to feel the lamps on his face, far enough to not cast a shadow into Renaud's light. The kitchen moved with the same deliberate precision it had before Luc fractured, but the air carried a new brittleness, like stainless steel under too much cold.

Sofia's words stayed lodged behind Connor's ribs. You do not carry what you saw.

He tried. He kept his face blank. He kept his hands behind his back with the lightest contact at the fingertips. He forced his breath into shallow, quiet exchange. But the absence had weight. It shifted the room's geometry in a way no towel wipe could erase.

A runner approached, eyes forward, holding two plates that looked identical in the lamp light. Connor watched the runner's wrists, the tension locked into them, the effort required to make effort invisible.

Renaud's gaze swept the plates. Rim. Negative space. Height. Sheen.

A head tilt.

"Walk."

The plates left.

The kitchen did not pause to remember Luc. It did not pause to grieve him. It did not pause to wonder where the corridor door led. It did what it had been designed to do: replace the missing piece with motion so continuous the gap became theoretical.

Connor felt, more than heard, Marcus Hale at the corridor mouth. The way the air seemed to tighten when bodies drifted too close to the border. The way front-of-house voices softened even further when they approached the threshold. Hale did not have to step forward. He didn't have to speak. He was present in the way everyone kept their shoulders from rising, the way runners swallowed without making it visible.

The soldier-runner appeared again, rigid at the tape line. "Now," he murmured.

Sofia held up one finger.

Hold.

Connor watched the count happen in Sofia's body rather than in time. A stillness that looked like readiness. A pause that had been trained to not resemble waiting.

A plate came up from the hot side, carried by a different saucier than before. The sauce shone under the lamps. Too perfect, Connor thought, and then hated himself for thinking in words. Words made patterns. Patterns made stories. Stories got people erased.

Sofia's towel hovered, folded into thirds, ready to remove a rim smear before it could become proof of handling. Renaud didn't blink as he inspected.

He didn't say again.

He didn't say stop.

His head tilted.

Sofia dropped her finger.

"Walk."

The soldier-runner took the plate and vanished toward the corridor like he had been summoned by the separation on the rail and dismissed by a gesture no diner would ever know existed.

Connor's stomach stayed tight. He kept expecting the room to fail, for the removal to cause some stutter in output, some friction that would confirm the obvious truth: a senior chef had broken in front of them. But the machine refused the truth by refusing evidence.

That was when Connor understood the first part of it.

The system did not punish collapse. It planned for it.

A hand-off at the rail. A quiet coverage adjustment. A man returning alone from the corridor with clean hands and a clean jacket. The station absorbed. The pass processed. The dining room remained unaware.

No one would ever see the seam.

Sofia leaned slightly toward Renaud, lips barely moving, and Renaud shifted his posture by a millimeter. The millimeter traveled down the line, the way a signal traveled down a wire. A pan moved off flame. A garnish was refired. A runner's path changed by inches. The machine compensated without announcing that it was compensating.

Connor felt the compensation land on people.

He saw it in the hot line's faces, not expression exactly, because expression was forbidden, but in the tightness around eyes, in the compulsive cleanliness of movements. A chef wiped a spoon handle twice, then caught himself and stopped at one. Another chef re-aligned containers that were already aligned, needing the ritual because ritual was the only permitted outlet.

Fear among the elite, Sofia had said.

Now fear had a name, even if no one spoke it.

Luc.

Or rather, the space where Luc had been.

Renaud's voice cut through the lamp hum. Not loud. Precise. "Where is his replacement?"

No one answered immediately, because the question wasn't simple. Replacement implied a void could be filled by a body the way a container could be filled by gel. A person could be moved into the gap, yes, but the gap wasn't only labor. It was knowledge, muscle memory, timing. It was the part of the line that had been trained around Luc's hands.

Sofia answered for the kitchen. “Covered, Chef.”

Renaud didn’t look at her. “Names.”

Sofia’s jaw tightened once. She gave them anyway, each syllable clipped clean. “Antoine has sauce. Malik has garnish. I’m watching plating.”

Connor’s pulse bumped at Antoine’s name. The warning from earlier returned uninvited: don’t try to stand out. That’s how you get noticed.

Antoine had warned him, and now Antoine was being moved closer to the heat, closer to blame, closer to a place where a pause could turn into a fracture.

Renaud’s head tilted. Not approval. Filing.

The kitchen kept moving.

Connor watched the rail, watched Sofia’s fingers separate another ticket by a finger’s width, watched the soldier-runner appear as if the paper itself had authority. The private room’s gravity did not change because Luc had broken. If anything, it intensified. The demand stayed constant. The people adjusted or were removed.

A front-of-house hand appeared near the pass, gloved, hovering at the threshold. Not the maître d’ this time. A manager Connor didn’t recognize, hair slicked back, face too smooth.

"Madame Alvarez," the manager said softly, voice barely present. "Table seven is requesting—"

Sofia didn't let him finish. She turned her head just enough to cut him with her eyes. "Not here," she said.

The manager's mouth tightened, then he stepped back, withdrawing so quickly it looked like obedience rather than correction.

Connor felt a sudden, sharp insight: even front-of-house could be erased from this space. The pass didn't belong to the restaurant as a whole. It belonged to Renaud's standard and Hale's consequence. Everyone else borrowed access.

Sofia returned her attention to the lamps, to the plates, to the story.

But Connor saw the manager's hands as he retreated. They tremored slightly, as if he'd just brushed against something dangerous and couldn't admit it.

No one is safe, Connor thought, and then forced the thought into a colder shape. Not thought. Rule.

He watched Renaud inspect another plate. A microscopic pause at the rim.

Sofia's towel moved once, wiping a smear that might have been nothing, might have been oil in the air, might have been a fingerprint no one would ever claim. The wipe was invisible, a gesture designed to erase the idea that erasure had occurred.

The plate left.

Renaud didn't speak.

And yet Connor's mind ran a different rail beneath the visible one, clipping new tickets into place.

If Luc could be removed, then everyone could.

Luc had been senior. Luc had been consistent. Luc had been, by normal standards, excellent.

Excellence had not protected him. It had only made his failure more interesting.

Connor's skin prickled with the urge to look toward the corridor mouth.

Don't feed him.

He didn't turn his head. He used reflection. Stainless steel held a ghost image of the border, the shadow there that did not need to move to be present.

Hale remained where he always remained, half in darkness, watching the machine prove itself.

The next private-room plate arrived, carried by the soldier-runner. Sofia rotated it to the invisible axis. Renaud approved without a word.

Sofia's voice came low beside Connor, not looking at him. "Carry."

Connor stepped forward and received the plate into his palms with wrists locked, thumbs clear of the rim. The porcelain was cool, controlled, too perfect in his hands. He felt the same narrowness of the corridor approach, the shift in light at the threshold, the sense of the dining room waiting behind the door like an open mouth.

At the border, a gloved hand reached out to take the plate.

As Connor transferred it, he realized the hand belonged to one of the senior chefs who had escorted Luc away. Not front-of-house. Not a runner.

A kitchen hand.

The chef's face was blank, eyes lowered. He took the plate and disappeared into the corridor without meeting Connor's gaze.

A simple transfer. An adjustment no one in the dining room would question.

But Connor's stomach tightened.

The corridor wasn't only an exit. It was a network. People moved through it who weren't supposed to be visible. If the kitchen could send plates through it, it could send anything through it.

Including a person.

Connor returned to the pass empty-handed. His palms felt damp, and he hated it. Dampness was evidence. He dried them against his towel with a single controlled press, not a wipe, not something that looked like nerves.

Sofia's eyes swept him once. Audit. Then away.

Renaud didn't acknowledge the carry. He didn't need to. Connor was function.

Service rolled forward until time became meaningless. Lunch bled into dinner the way fatigue bled into discipline, the way hunger became a distant sensation that only mattered if it made you slow. Connor watched the line for signs of fracture, because now he knew what fracture looked like.

It wasn't yelling. It wasn't drama.

It was a pause that lasted too long.

A swallow that became visible.

Hands that touched apron fabric as if seeking something to grip.

Eyes that lost the rail and stared through it.

He saw small versions of those signs everywhere, quickly corrected, quickly hidden. A junior chef's breath hitched; he turned it into a controlled exhale and moved faster without looking faster. A runner's fingers tightened; he released them and adjusted his grip to look effortless. People were managing themselves harder now, because they had seen what happened when management failed.

The machine had shown them.

The machine had shown Connor.

When the last major push of service finally eased, it didn't end with relief. It ended with reset. Stations scrubbed. Lids aligned. Labels faced outward. Towel folds pressed sharp. The kitchen erased its own labor so thoroughly it could pretend it had never struggled.

Connor moved with them, wiping stainless in one pass, restoring stillness the way he'd been trained to.

And still, the absence stayed.

At some point, Connor drifted toward the lockers in the back corridor, not because anyone told him to, but because his body needed proof of something normal: a name on a door, a bag where it belonged, a life that continued outside the lamps.

The locker area smelled different from the kitchen. Damp concrete, detergent, stale heat trapped in fabric. It should have felt like release.

It didn't.

The row of lockers stood in harsh fluorescent light. Metal doors with scuffed paint. Small nameplates. Some handwritten, some printed, some blank.

Connor's eyes moved without permission, scanning for what he knew would be there.

Luc's nameplate was gone.

Not crossed out. Not removed with obvious violence. Just absent, as if it had never been attached. The metal where it should have been was cleaner than the surrounding paint, a faint rectangle of difference that would fade with time, the way a bruise faded.

Connor stared at the clean rectangle until his throat tightened.

He wasn't sure what he expected. A note. A warning. An explanation.

There was nothing.

That was the point.

Behind him, footsteps approached, calm and unhurried. Connor forced his gaze away from the locker and down to his hands, making them still at his sides.

Dumas appeared in the corner of Connor's vision, jacket slightly rumpled now, the first sign all night that he had a body under the uniform. His eyes went to the lockers, then to Connor's face, then away.

Dumas didn't ask what Connor was doing back here. Questions were for people who had the right to answers.

He only said, very softly, "You understand now."

Connor's mouth was dry. He didn't trust himself to say yes. He didn't trust himself to say anything that sounded human.

So he chose function. "No one is safe," he said.

Dumas held Connor's gaze for a beat longer than the kitchen usually allowed. In that beat Connor saw something like resignation, a truth too old to be dramatic.

Dumas nodded once, minimal movement, and didn't correct the nod because they weren't under the lamps now, because the locker corridor was still part of the building but not part of the performance.

"No," Dumas said. "No one."

Connor swallowed, controlled. "Even Sofia?"

Dumas's eyes flicked down the hall toward the corridor mouth, as if even here the walls might listen. "Especially her," he said.

Connor felt cold move through him. Sofia, who rotated plates on invisible axes. Sofia, who could hold time in her fingers. Sofia, who could block a collapsing chef from contaminating the pass and make it look like nothing happened.

If Sofia wasn't safe, then safety didn't exist at any altitude.

Dumas's voice stayed flat. "You think it's about mistakes," he said. "It's not. It's about cracks."

Connor looked back at the clean rectangle where Luc's name had been and felt something inside him settle into a harder shape.

Cracks didn't have to be large. They didn't have to be dramatic.

They only had to be visible to the wrong eyes.

Dumas stepped closer, lowered his voice until it barely carried. "You saw how fast it happens," he said.

Connor didn't answer.

Dumas continued, quiet as breath. "That speed is the protection. That speed is what keeps the dining room clean."

Connor's hands curled slightly, then he forced them open again. Stillness. Control. No proof.

In the distance, the corridor door opened and closed with a soft seal. A sound so normal it barely registered.

But Connor heard it as a reminder.

People went in.

Not everyone came out in the same way they entered.

Dumas turned as if to leave, then paused. "Go home," he said, and the words were strange in this place, almost indecent. Home implied a life outside the machine.

Connor managed a small nod.

Dumas didn't offer comfort. He didn't offer strategy. He only delivered the final truth with the calm of someone who had lived with it too long to pretend it would change.

"Keep your face clean," Dumas said. "Keep your hands steady. And never believe you've earned safety."

Then he walked away down the hall, steps quiet, leaving Connor with fluorescent light, metal doors, and the clean rectangle where a name had been erased.

Connor stood there for a long moment, not moving, because he didn't know what moving would mean.

Behind his eyes, the pass kept glowing. Renaud's stillness kept measuring. Sofia's towel kept erasing. Hale's shadow kept recording.

And Luc's locker, blank where a name should be, offered the only message the building was willing to give.

No one is safe.

Chapter 9

The Cost of Stars

Connor left the locker corridor with Luc's clean rectangle still burning behind his eyes.

The route out of L'Étoile Noire was designed to feel incidental. A back hallway that smelled of mop water and cooling fat. A door that opened onto an alley where the city sounded too loud, too ordinary, as if the restaurant's silence had been a sealed environment and he'd just broken through the membrane.

He should have gone home.

Dumas had said it like an instruction that could pass for mercy. Go home. Keep your face clean.

Connor made it as far as the service entrance.

The door was half-open, held by its own weight. Cold air slid in. He stepped toward it, and then he felt it: pressure shifting, a presence aligning behind him with the same inevitability as a ticket being separated on the rail.

"Felwick."

The voice was soft. It didn't need volume. It was placed precisely, the way Sofia placed her finger-width separations. The syllable landed at the back of Connor's neck.

He stopped without turning too quickly. He turned just enough.

Marcus Hale stood in the corridor behind him, coat on as if he'd been outside already, as if he could pass through borders without changing state. His face looked calm in a way that didn't read as relaxed. Calm like a locked door.

Connor kept his hands at his sides, fingers open, not making fists. "Sir."

Hale's eyes moved over Connor's jacket, the towel loop, the clean line of his apron as if he were reading a report. "You're learning," Hale said.

It wasn't praise. It wasn't even approval. It was an observation, like a banker noting a balance.

Connor didn't answer. The instinct to say yes rose and died. Yes was too human. Understood was too brigade. Heard belonged to the kitchen's internal language. None of them felt safe in this corridor.

Hale angled his head toward the alley door, then away. "Not out there," he said.

Connor felt the smallest tightening in his chest. The city was safety only by contrast. Here, safety didn't exist.

Hale turned and began walking deeper into the building without looking back to see if Connor followed.

The corridor swallowed light in segments. A turn that hid the kitchen's glow. Another that cut off the locker area's fluorescent harshness. The sound changed too, as if the building absorbed footfalls. Connor followed half a step behind, keeping his pace even, neither rushing to close distance nor lagging like resistance.

Hale stopped at a door Connor had never noticed. It wasn't marked. No sign. No keypad. Just a plain door in a plain wall, the kind you didn't look at twice because looking was curiosity and curiosity was blood.

Hale opened it with a key.

Inside was a narrow room that felt more like a private office than anything belonging to a restaurant. No stainless. No tile. Dark wood, muted light, a single table with two chairs, a shelf lined with folders that looked too clean to have been handled often. The air smelled faintly of paper and something citrus, the same sanitizer note Sofia carried, but softened, civilized.

Hale closed the door behind them with a quiet finality.

Connor stayed standing.

Hale sat. He didn't invite Connor to sit. The chair opposite remained empty like a test.

On the table sat a thin folder and a small object that caught the low light: a star pin, silver, no larger than a thumbnail. It looked innocuous. It looked expensive. It looked like something people would kill for without ever admitting they had.

Hale rested two fingers near the pin without touching it. Connor's eyes went there and then away, as if looking too long would leave fingerprints.

"You saw what happens when someone cracks," Hale said.

Connor felt the alley air he hadn't reached yet, the idea of escape pressed away by this door. He answered carefully. "Yes."

Hale's mouth curved slightly. Not a smile. A recognition of language being stripped down. "You were told you didn't see him."

Connor didn't flinch. "Yes."

Hale leaned back, studying Connor the way he studied movement at the corridor mouth: not for emotion, but for reaction. "Good," he said. "That's the first price."

Connor kept his face blank. The word price made his stomach tighten. The building loved transactions. Everything here was an exchange: sleep for function, hunger for speed, silence for survival.

Hale tapped the folder once. "People think the stars are earned on the plate," he said. "Flavor. Creativity. Discipline."

He paused, letting the expected myths fill the room, then cut through them with the same quiet efficiency the kitchen used to remove evidence.

"That's what we let them think."

Connor's throat went dry. He forced his breath into the shallow, mechanical exchange Sofia demanded at the pass.

Hale continued, voice calm. "A star is not a compliment. It's a lever. It moves reservations, investors, leases, suppliers, careers. It moves cities."

He glanced at the pin. "And because it moves cities, it attracts people who want to move it."

Connor thought of the private room, the separated tickets, the holds that weren't allowed to exist. “Table seven,” he said before he could stop himself.

Hale’s eyes flicked up. Not irritation. Interest, as if Connor had identified the correct thread.

“Table seven is one lever,” Hale said. “A loud one. Visible wealth. Visible demand. Useful, but crude.”

He lifted his hand slightly and Connor’s body tightened without permission, as if a gesture could become a sentence that changed his life. Hale’s hand settled again.

“The private room,” Hale said, “is the quiet lever.”

Connor didn’t ask who was in it. He didn’t ask what they wanted. He let the question remain inside him where it could rot silently without being spoken.

Hale watched him for a beat and then, as if rewarding restraint with information, said, “Inspectors don’t always sit in the dining room. Not the ones who matter.”

Connor’s mind flashed to the prologue story he’d heard in fragments when he first arrived, the returned dish, the erased chef. An anonymous diner among quiet wealth, unnoticed yet feared. The plate returned without comment.

Hale's voice dropped slightly, as if the walls enjoyed secrecy. "Sometimes they watch the kitchen through people like me."

Connor's mouth tasted metallic. He thought of the code word black and how it made the air colder. Not because of superstition. Because someone was listening.

Hale leaned forward just enough to change the room's gravity. "You believe Michelin is a church," he said. "Pure and blind and incorruptible."

Connor didn't respond. He didn't know what response wouldn't be used against him.

Hale's gaze held him. "It's an industry," he said. "Industries have costs. Costs are negotiated."

He reached for the folder and opened it. Inside were papers that looked like schedules, seating charts, supplier invoices. Ordinary. But Connor could feel the pattern in them without reading: timing grids, names, movements. The rail translated onto paper.

Hale slid one sheet across the table so Connor could see without being invited to touch.

It was a list of dates with notes in the margins, written in a hand as controlled as Sofia's. Some notes were simple: "Menu A," "Room closed,"

"Security." Others were stranger: "Black," written beside certain nights, and "No returns," beside others, as if someone had formalized the threats into administration.

Connor's eyes moved down the list and snagged on a line that turned his skin cold.

A name: Luc.

Not last name, just Luc. Next to it: "Risk. Monitor."

The date was weeks before tonight.

Connor felt his own face try to change, a flicker of horror or understanding, and he smoothed it back into blankness as fast as he could.

Hale watched him smooth it. He saw everything.

"You think tonight was sudden," Hale said. "It wasn't. Cracks show early. The ones who survive learn to seal them. The ones who don't…" He let the sentence die without finishing it, because finishing would be too honest.

Connor stared at Luc's name. "You knew," he said quietly.

Hale didn't correct the accusation. He accepted it like a fact that had been signed. "I knew he was approaching a threshold," he said. "Sofia knew.

Renaud knew. Luc knew, even if he pretended he didn't."

Connor's pulse thudded in his wrists. He kept his hands still at his sides. "And you let him stay on the line."

Hale's eyes narrowed by a millimeter. "We let him work," he corrected. "Staying is earned. Every service. Every plate. Every breath you keep quiet."

He closed the folder partway and rested his palm on it as if sealing a document. "L'Étoile Noire is not a restaurant," he said. "It's a promise. People pay for the promise that nothing will go wrong where they can see it."

Connor heard Renaud's voice in his head: Nothing returns.

Hale nodded slightly, as if he'd heard the echo too. "Exactly," he said. "And do you know what's more dangerous than a returned plate?"

Connor didn't answer.

"A visible struggle," Hale said. "A human moment. A story that suggests the machine is made of people."

Connor's stomach tightened, and for a flash he saw the pass again, the lamps, Luc's trembling hands, Sofia stepping in as a barrier to keep collapse from contaminating the light.

Hale's voice stayed calm. "You want to know the cost of stars," he said. "It's not the hours. It's not the bruises. It's not the marriages that die quietly. It's the agreements."

He tapped the star pin lightly with a fingernail. A soft click in the low-lit room, too loud because it was the only sound.

"We protect the promise," Hale said. "Renaud protects it with standards. Sofia protects it with choreography. I protect it with… clearance."

Connor forced himself to meet Hale's eyes. "Clearance," he repeated, keeping the word flat so it didn't sound like fear.

Hale's gaze held steady. "When an inspector is in play, when an investor is in the private room, when a guest at table seven believes the universe should pause for them, we adjust the world," he said. "And when the world cannot be adjusted cleanly, we remove what makes it messy."

Connor thought of Luc's locker. Not crossed out. Just absent.

Hale leaned back again, as if the core truth had been delivered and the rest was administration. "You did well tonight," he said. "You carried under pressure. You didn't make a face. You didn't let what you saw leak onto the pass."

Connor felt something twist in him. Being told he did well by Hale didn't feel like praise. It felt like being measured for a different kind of use.

Hale's eyes moved to Connor's hands, then back to his face. "That's why I'm telling you this," he said. "Not because you deserve to know. Because you're close enough now that you'll be forced to choose without being told you're choosing."

Connor didn't move. "What choice."

Hale's mouth curved again, almost amused, as if the question itself proved Connor was still human enough to ask. "Whether you want the stars," he said. "Or whether you want to sleep at night."

Connor felt the room tilt slightly, the way the kitchen tilted when a private-room ticket was separated on the rail. The question wasn't rhetorical. It was a gate.

Hale pushed the folder back toward himself and closed it, the sound soft but final. "You can leave," he said. "Tonight. Walk out that door. Pretend you never learned what the stars cost."

He paused, then added, quieter, "Or you can stay long enough to learn how to pay it without flinching."

Connor's mouth was dry. He thought of his first day, the exhilaration, the belief that greatness was discipline and sacrifice. He thought of Dumas's water cup hidden at the back edge of a station. He thought of Sofia's jaw tick when she held time in her finger. He thought of Renaud's glance, weight that changed your time. He thought of the clean rectangle where Luc's name had been.

And he realized Hale had not offered him a choice at all.

Hale stood, coat settling on his shoulders like he'd never sat. He opened the door and the corridor air slid in again, cooler, thinner.

As Connor stepped past him, Hale's voice followed like a final instruction delivered without heat.

"One more thing, Felwick," he said.

Connor stopped, turned just enough.

Hale's eyes were calm. "If you repeat anything you heard in this room, you won't be removed," he said. "You'll be corrected."

The word corrected landed differently here than it had on the line.

It didn't mean refire.

It meant erasure with paperwork.

Connor held Hale's gaze, made his face clean, made his hands steady, and gave the only answer that felt safe.

"Heard," he said softly.

Hale nodded once, minimal movement, as if confirming a transaction had been completed.

Connor walked back into the corridor toward the service entrance, the city waiting outside like an ordinary life he could still pretend to belong to.

But the building had already shifted him.

He could feel the star pin's tiny weight in his mind like a physical object, and he understood, with cold clarity, that the stars were not a reward.

They were a contract.

And now he had been shown the price list.

Connor stepped into the alley and let the city hit him the way a loud room hit you after hours of silence. Engines. A scooter whining past. A couple laughing too hard. The noise should have felt like freedom.

It felt like contamination.

He walked without choosing a direction at first, as if his body expected someone to stop him, to hold up one finger, to make time obey. The back door of L'Étoile Noire closed behind him with its soft, sealing finality, but the building's pressure followed. Hale's calm voice followed. The word "clearance" followed, hanging in Connor's head like a code that would never be called out loud.

He made it two blocks before he realized his hands were still held a certain way, fingers slightly spread, as if he was still carrying porcelain.

At a corner, he stopped beside a shuttered bakery and forced his hands into his coat pockets. Fabric. Warmth. Proof he had a body, a life outside the pass.

He should have gone home. Hale had said he could. The offer had been presented like mercy, and it had felt like a trap.

Connor kept walking anyway, cutting through side streets until he reached his building and climbed the stairs without turning on the hall light. Inside his apartment, he didn't undress right away. He stood in the dark and listened for a sound he couldn't name. The refrigerator hum. The distant city. His own breath. He waited for the moment his mind would stop replaying Luc's empty eyes, the clean rectangle on the locker, the star pin's soft click on Hale's table.

It didn't stop.

Sleep arrived late and thin. When it came, it wasn't rest. It was a temporary loss of vigilance.

By noon, he was back in the kitchen.

The dining room was empty, chairs perfectly aligned, glassware catching the muted light like small, obedient reflections. In the kitchen, the silence had returned to its usual form, controlled rather than bruised. The absence of Luc was not spoken. It was everywhere anyway, in the way bodies held themselves a fraction tighter, in the way eyes avoided the corridor mouth as if the shadow could be offended.

Dumas was already at garde manger, labels printed, lids aligned, towel folded into thirds so sharply it looked like the crease could draw blood. He didn't greet Connor. Greeting implied that time belonged to them.

Sofia crossed the line once, fast and clean, and stopped at Connor's station border long enough to deliver an instruction without giving it the dignity of conversation.

"Private room tonight," she said.

Connor kept his eyes down. "Understood."

Sofia didn't correct him this time. Her jaw ticked once and stopped. "Hale will be here early," she added, and then she was gone, already cutting arcs toward the pass, already controlling air.

Hale.

The name tightened Connor's throat. He remembered Hale's file on the table, the sheet with dates and notes, the word "black" written like administration. He remembered Luc's name on that page with the quiet phrase "Risk. Monitor." He remembered Hale saying the cracks show early.

Connor's hands moved through prep automatically. Chopped components. Measured portions. Plated test arrangements. His body returned to function, because function was the only language this place respected. But his mind kept tracking a different rail beneath the visible one, clipping questions into place the way Sofia clipped tickets.

If the stars were a lever, who was pulling it?

If the inspector wasn't always in the dining room, who were they performing for?

And if Hale controlled clearance, what did that mean in practice?

By late afternoon, Hale appeared without announcement.

There was no dramatic entrance, no shift in lighting, no moment that made people look up. He simply became present at the corridor mouth as if he had always been part of the architecture. Coat on, posture relaxed in a way that made relaxation look like a weapon. He watched the kitchen as if it were a balance sheet.

Connor didn't look at him directly. He used reflection, stainless steel giving him a ghost image of Hale's silhouette.

Sofia approached Hale briefly, head angled, mouth barely moving. A private exchange that looked like nothing. Hale's response was two fingers, a gesture so small it could have been a scratch on his knuckle. Sofia nodded once and returned to the pass without breaking her pace.

The kitchen adjusted around that gesture. Connor saw it in details that had no explanation attached: an extra tray of components brought out and relabeled; one dish removed from the prep plan without a word; a runner reassigned to hover closer to the pass even though service hadn't started.

Strategic manipulation, Connor thought, and hated the clarity of it. Not improvisation. Not crisis management. The sense that the night had already been decided and the kitchen was only executing the decision.

At five, Dumas slid a small paper cup of water to the back edge of the station, out of sight.

Connor drank without sound.

Dumas's voice came low, as if even the hum of refrigeration might repeat words. "You talked to him."

It wasn't a question.

Connor kept his eyes on his hands. "He spoke to me."

Dumas's gaze flicked once toward the corridor mouth. "Same thing," he murmured.

Connor didn't answer. Silence was safer, and yet Dumas had given him water. A concession to physics, yes, but also a signal that the rules could flex in places the pass didn't see.

Dumas continued, his tone flat but not unkind. "He'll start moving pieces tonight."

Connor placed the cup back exactly where it had been. "Why me."

Dumas's hands didn't pause. Labels outward. Lids aligned. "Because you carry," he said. "Because you don't flinch. Because you still look clean when you're scared."

Connor felt a thin line of anger rise and pressed it down. Anger was heat. Heat left fingerprints.

Service began without fanfare, as it always did. Tickets appeared. Runners lined at the tape. The pass lamps turned the counter into a strip of merciless light. Renaud stood at its center, fixed and immaculate, his stillness taking ownership of time.

Sofia rotated plates to invisible axes. Wiped rims in one pass, her towel folded into thirds like doctrine. The line moved in a rhythm that pretended it had never been trained to hide fear.

But tonight, the dining room's demands arrived already pre-shaped.

Table seven was in play again.

Connor didn't know it because someone said it. He knew it because the rail behaved differently. Sofia separated a ticket by a finger's width. A runner shifted his stance and swallowed without making sound. A hold was called without using the word hold.

"Pace," Sofia murmured, not to anyone in particular. A word that pretended control belonged to them.

Renaud replied without looking up. "No gaps."

The phrase had become their compromise. Bend time without showing the bend.

Hale remained at the corridor mouth, watching.

Connor watched him watch, and something cold settled into Connor's understanding: Hale wasn't reacting to the kitchen. The kitchen was reacting to Hale. His presence wasn't oversight. It was leverage placed in human form.

The first overt move happened mid-appetizers.

A runner approached Sofia with a quiet urgency that still tried to look like discipline. Sofia leaned in. Connor couldn't hear the words over the lamp hum, but he saw the effect: Sofia's posture tightened. Her jaw ticked once.

She looked toward Hale.

Hale lifted two fingers again, the same motion as earlier, and then added something else: a slight tilt of his head toward the dining room, as if indicating a location in space.

Sofia turned back to the rail and made an adjustment so subtle it could have passed for organization. She slid tickets into a different order. Not by course. By guest.

Connor watched the new sequence play out instantly. A dish that should have gone to table twelve left early. A dish destined for table seven was delayed by exactly the kind of invisible pause that didn't look like waiting. The pass choreography swallowed the manipulation so cleanly it appeared natural.

Renaud didn't speak. He didn't have to. Sofia translated. The line executed.

That was how it worked, Connor realized. The manipulation wasn't a separate layer. It was embedded in the kitchen's claim to perfection. The story of control included the ability to rewrite the order of reality.

A second move came through front of house.

The maître d' hovered at the threshold, eyes lowered, careful not to step fully into the kitchen's territory. He spoke to Sofia in a voice so soft it barely existed.

"Madame Alvarez, our guest has asked for…" His sentence died there, unfinished, as if finishing it would be an insult.

Sofia didn't look away from the rail. "No," she said quietly.

The maître d' blinked. A rare sign of human reaction. He recovered fast, as trained as any commis. "Yes, madame," he corrected himself automatically, turning no into compliance the way the kitchen turned holds into choreography.

He withdrew.

Connor's stomach tightened. It wasn't that Sofia had refused a request. It was that front of house had accepted refusal as if it were normal. The dining room's power ended at the pass's light. Beyond that light, different rules applied.

Hale's rules.

Minutes later, the same maître d' returned, this time not alone. A man Connor had never seen in the restaurant stepped into the threshold's edge as if he belonged there. He wore a dark suit with no tie and carried himself like someone used to doors opening for him.

He didn't look at the line. He looked toward Hale.

Hale stepped out of shadow by half a foot, enough to be seen.

The suited man spoke, low and smiling. Connor couldn't hear the words, but he saw Hale's expression: calm, mildly bored, as if this was not a negotiation but a scheduled maintenance check. Hale answered with a few syllables and the suited man's smile tightened, then returned.

The man glanced once toward the pass, toward Renaud's stillness, and then backed away as if the light itself could burn.

When he was gone, Sofia's hand separated another ticket. A private-room call. The soldier-runner appeared as if summoned by paper.

"Now," he murmured.

Sofia held up one finger.

Hold.

Connor watched her count in her body. The hold was not about food. It was about the suited man. About table seven. About a guest who wanted something at a moment that served their power rather than their appetite.

Renaud's voice came quiet, precise. "Not on the lamps."

Sofia answered, "No, Chef."

She moved the plate half an inch out of the brightest heat circle. Covered it briefly. Uncovered it at the exact second that made the hold disappear.

Then she dropped her finger.

"Walk."

The soldier-runner took the plate and vanished into the corridor, and Connor understood with a clarity that made him cold: the private room wasn't only about secrecy. It was about control of narrative. Plates going into that room were not just courses. They were signals, confirmations, payments delivered as food.

A third move happened behind Connor's station.

Dumas leaned in without looking at Connor directly. "Watch the runners," he murmured.

Connor's eyes tracked the flow. A familiar runner was suddenly absent. In his place was a new face, posture trained too quickly, eyes too blank. The new runner moved with careful precision, but there was something else in his pace, a slight stiffness that wasn't fear of Renaud.

It was fear of being watched by someone else.

Hale's gaze followed that runner more than the others.

Connor understood: Hale was not only managing diners. He was managing the people who moved between kitchen and dining room. He was selecting who carried what, who was seen, who was forgettable, who could be trusted not to talk.

Strategic manipulation wasn't bribery in a smoky back room. It was logistics. It was the control of contact points. The mapping of mouths that could leak story.

The realization made Connor's skin prickle. He had believed the kitchen was the machine. Now he saw the kitchen was only one component of a larger system that included money, access, schedules, bodies, and silence.

Hale wasn't keeping the stars with taste.

He was keeping them with choreography and threat.

At the pass, Renaud approved another plate with a head tilt.

Sofia rotated another dish to the invisible axis and wiped a rim in one pass.

Service moved on, flawless on the surface.

Connor executed at garde manger and felt his earlier belief crack quietly inside him. He had thought the stars were protected by standards, by discipline pushed into cruelty. That had been true, but it wasn't complete.

The stars were protected by manipulation so seamless it looked like reality.

And once you saw the seams, you couldn't unsee them.

Connor's hands kept moving. Portions exact. Garnish placed like printed lines. Rim wiped once, invisible. Station reset in one pass.

His face stayed clean.

But behind his ribs, something began to turn, slow and relentless, like a key being worked into a lock that had never been meant to open from the inside.

Connor's hands kept moving, but the new understanding made every motion feel borrowed.

He plated as if plating could drown thought. Portion. Place. Wipe once. Reset. The station returned to immaculate stillness after each run, stainless steel reflecting only light and discipline. But the reflection carried ghosts now: the corridor mouth in the distance, Hale's silhouette, the way two fingers could reorder an entire room without ever sounding like an order.

A plate left garde manger and Connor's eyes followed it for half a beat too long.

Dumas's voice came without looking at him. "Don't watch your work leave."

Connor cut his gaze back to the counter seam. Watching was attachment. Attachment was evidence of ego, and ego created the kind of heat that got measured.

"Understood," Connor said, then felt the wrongness of the word as soon as it left him.

Dumas didn't correct him. That was worse. Correction meant you were still inside the rules. Silence meant you'd said something too human to be worth sculpting.

The kitchen moved into its second rhythm of the night, the one that wasn't about the menu but about the people eating it. Connor could feel it in the rail's behavior even from cold station: tickets separated by a finger's width; a runner standing too still at the tape line; Sofia's orbit tightening around the pass like a belt being pulled one notch smaller.

Pace. No gaps. Not on the lamps.

They weren't just phrases. They were tools for hiding force.

A runner crossed in front of garde manger, not one of the usual faces. New. Too clean. Too disciplined in a way that looked learned fast, like someone rehearsing stillness rather than owning it. He moved with care, but his eyes flicked once toward the corridor mouth as if checking whether his leash was still held.

Connor felt something crawl at the base of his neck. He'd been watched all night. That wasn't new. What was new was realizing the watchers had layers.

Renaud's gaze was the standard.

Sofia's gaze was enforcement.

Hale's gaze was consequence.

And somewhere beyond Hale, unseen, there were people who could move the entire restaurant with a request spoken softly enough to seem like courtesy.

The private room again.

Connor didn't know it from the ticket itself. He knew it from the slight cold that passed through the line when the soldier-runner appeared. The soldier-runner didn't look at anyone. He didn't need to. His presence was already a message.

"Now," he murmured.

Sofia held up one finger.

Hold.

Connor felt his stomach tighten. Holds weren't just timing problems. Holds were negotiations.

He kept plating anyway, because the only safe response to unease was to become function. He measured the gel to the tenth of a gram. He placed garnish at the same angle, the same distance from negative space. He wiped a rim once and resisted the urge to wipe again. Twice was panic. Twice was admission that you believed there might be proof.

Across the aisle, a chef on hot side refired garnish without being told. Not because the dish was wrong, but because the air said it might become wrong if the dining room decided to bend time.

That was the part that hollowed Connor out. They were cooking for the possibility of manipulation, not the certainty of appetite.

A brief gap opened in movement near the pass, and Connor caught a glimpse of Hale in reflection. Half in shadow, coat still on, calm like a locked door. He wasn't watching plates. He was watching vectors: runners' paths, the distance between hands, the micro-delays that could be smoothed before anyone could call them delays.

He was watching the story stay clean.

Connor's fingers tightened on his tweezers, then relaxed. Fingerprints. Evidence. He shifted grip so metal rested in bone rather than muscle.

He tried to tell himself it didn't matter. He was a cook. A commis. His job was to execute.

But Hale had put a star pin on a table and called it a contract.

And Connor had heard the word clearance said like it belonged in an office, not a kitchen.

The thought returned, persistent as a tongue worrying a sore spot: Luc had been on a list.

Risk. Monitor.

Weeks before the night he collapsed, his name had already been filed as a problem.

Connor felt the unease turn sharper, no longer diffuse. If Luc could be monitored, anyone could. Monitoring meant prediction. Prediction meant planning. Planning meant that what had felt like sudden cruelty was actually procedure.

Connor's eyes flicked to the rail again, then away. Don't look. Looking was curiosity, and curiosity was blood.

But his mind did it anyway, mapping the kitchen like a diagram. If Hale could formalize "black" on paper, then the codes weren't superstition. They were infrastructure.

Who else was on those sheets?

Connor.

He felt the urge to find his own name the way you felt the urge to touch a bruise just to confirm it was real. He resisted. He kept plating. He kept his face clean.

Dumas moved beside him, setting down a fresh tray of components, labels outward. His towel fold was sharp, pressed hard enough to look angry.

Connor spoke without lifting his eyes. "Does it ever stop?"

Dumas paused a fraction, then continued aligning a container lid by a millimeter. "Does what stop."

The answer wasn't a question. It was a warning: define the thing you're asking about, and you give it a name.

Connor kept his voice low. "The… adjustment."

Dumas's mouth tightened, almost a smile but not quite. "You found a polite word."

Connor felt heat rise in his chest and smothered it. Polite meant weak. Weak meant visible.

Dumas's hands kept moving. "It doesn't stop," he said. "It just gets quieter."

Connor swallowed. "And if you don't play along."

Dumas didn't look at him. "Then you become noise."

Noise. Connor thought of Luc whispering "I can't." The smallest human sentence, catastrophic in this room.

A runner approached the tape line and murmured something Connor couldn't hear. Sofia answered with a gesture. Two fingers. Not Hale's two fingers, but her own, as if the vocabulary of control had leaked into everyone's hands.

Connor plated and felt the edges of something inside him begin to shift. He'd entered L'Étoile Noire believing discipline was a path upward.

Discipline was still the path, but it wasn't leading to greatness the way he'd imagined. It was leading to complicity.

Because the manipulation wasn't external to cooking. It was built into it. The ability to hold without showing, to refire without announcing, to reorder guests on the rail as if people were tickets and tickets were truth.

Connor's station sent out another set of plates. The geometry was perfect. The leaves identical. The gel line printed-clean.

He should have felt pride. He felt nothing.

The nothing scared him more than fear would have. Fear was at least honest. Nothing was adaptation.

A front-of-house voice drifted near the threshold, then stopped. Not entering. Respecting borders. Connor didn't look up, but he could feel the presence, the way the kitchen tightened slightly when the dining room tried to speak.

Sofia answered, quiet and final. A few syllables. A refusal disguised as a promise.

The presence withdrew.

The kitchen exhaled without making sound.

Connor's unease deepened into a new shape: the realization that the dining room wasn't in charge. The dining room was a stage. The real power lived in the corridor mouth, in whatever Hale represented.

And Hale wasn't a chef. Hale didn't have burns on his arms or calluses from knives. He didn't stand under lamps with sweat trying to betray him. Yet he controlled the outcome more than anyone on the line.

Connor had built his identity around craft. Around the idea that excellence was earned by suffering for the plate.

But Hale had made the plate feel like a bribe you could eat.

A subtle shift ran through the kitchen. Sofia moved down the line toward garde manger, not fast, not slow. Exact. She stopped at the border of Connor's station.

"Felwick," she said.

Connor's hands went behind his back by reflex. Stillness first. "Chef."

Her eyes scanned his counter, the alignment, the towel fold, the lids. Then, finally, his face.

"You're thinking," she said.

It wasn't an accusation. It was a diagnosis delivered like temperature.

Connor kept his expression empty. "Working."

Sofia's gaze held him for a beat. Her jaw ticked once, then stopped. "Thinking shows," she said softly.

Connor felt a thin panic try to rise. He crushed it into stillness. "How."

Sofia leaned closer, voice low enough to stay inside the station. "Your eyes follow plates," she said. "You count things you shouldn't count. You look for patterns that aren't yours."

Connor's throat tightened. "There are patterns."

Sofia's eyes didn't soften. "Yes," she said. "And they will kill you if you try to understand them out loud."

Connor wanted to ask her if she hated it. If she ever wished the kitchen was only about cooking. But wanting was human, and human was dangerous.

Sofia's gaze flicked once toward the corridor mouth, then back to Connor. "You're uneasy," she said. "That's normal."

Normal. The word didn't belong here, and hearing it from her made Connor feel the ground tilt.

Sofia continued, quieter. "What you do with it is what matters."

Connor's mouth was dry. "What do you do with it."

Sofia looked at his hands behind his back, the posture of restraint. "You put it where no one can see," she said. "Or you let it leak, and then you become a problem someone has to clean."

Clean. Another polite word for erasure.

Sofia straightened, voice returning to function. "Private room will want two carries tonight," she said. "You will not ask why."

Connor kept his face blank. "Heard."

Sofia didn't correct him. She nodded once and left, returning to the pass, back into Renaud's orbit where emotion was shaved off into choreography.

Connor stood at garde manger with the weight of her words pressing against his ribs. Put it where no one can see. Don't let it leak.

He understood the instruction. It was the same instruction the whole building ran on.

Hide the strain. Hide the bend in time. Hide the refire. Hide the removal.

Hide the cost.

Tickets continued to flow. Plates continued to leave. The dining room continued to believe it was being served perfection rather than controlled compliance.

Connor executed until his hands moved without friction. Until his face stayed clean without effort. Until unease became a steady background hum, not loud enough to interrupt function.

And in the quiet place beneath his discipline, a question kept forming and reforming, sharper each time it returned.

Not who was pulling the lever.

Who was going to be moved next.

He turned slightly to reset his station again, wiping stainless steel in one pass, folding his towel into thirds until the fold felt like a rule.

He didn't look toward the corridor mouth.

But he could feel it anyway, like a shadow that didn't need light to exist.

And he understood with a cold clarity that made him careful in a new way: the stars were not just something you earned.

They were something that earned you.

Once you were useful enough, the system would claim you.

And if you ever stopped being useful, it would clean you the same way it cleaned everything else.

Quietly. Efficiently.

As if you'd never been there at all.

Chapter 10

Transformation

The next morning, Connor woke before his alarm, eyes open in the dark as if someone had called “now” inside his skull.

For a moment, his body waited for a finger held up in the air. For permission to move. For the count that would make movement disappear into choreography. When nothing came, he swung his legs out of bed anyway and stood with his hands at his sides, fingers spread slightly, an empty-carry posture his muscles hadn’t forgotten.

In the bathroom mirror his face looked clean. Too clean. The exhaustion was there, but it had been organized, filed away behind his eyes the way Sofia filed tickets. He ran cold water over his wrists until sensation returned, then practiced stillness the way he practiced plating: shoulders low, jaw relaxed, breath shallow, no proof.

On the walk to L’Étoile Noire the city felt unreal, like a dining room that didn’t understand it was being managed. People laughed too loudly, stopped in doorways, spilled time without consequence. Connor moved through them with a narrow attention, watching hands, watching distances, watching for the soft violence of collision.

At the service entrance, he paused before the door. Dumas's voice returned from the locker corridor: never believe you've earned safety.

Connor pushed the door open.

Inside, the kitchen smelled of sanitizer and metal and the faint sourness of yesterday's fatigue. The lights were bright and indifferent. The counters were immaculate in that way that wasn't cleanliness, but denial. The building didn't admit it had been used.

Dumas was already there, as if he lived inside the refrigeration hum. He didn't look up when Connor stepped into garde manger, but his hands shifted, moving a container half an inch so its label faced perfectly outward.

"You're early," Dumas said.

It wasn't praise. It was a data point.

Connor tied his apron with the same tight, flat knot, ends aligned. "I woke up."

Dumas's mouth twitched, almost a smile. Almost. "That's one way to say it."

Connor washed his hands, dried them once, folded his towel into thirds until the edges looked sharp enough to cut. His station waited. The trays were lined. The tweezers rested where they were supposed to, not a millimeter out of place. Everything had a place, and everything was watched, even when no one looked.

He started prep without being told.

As he worked, he kept seeing Hale's table in his head, the folder, the star pin catching low light. Risk. Monitor. A word written beside a human name like it was an ingredient. Connor wondered, once, where his own name would fall on that list, and then he forced the thought away. Looking for your name was the fastest way to make it appear in the wrong column.

Sofia came in without sound, the way she always did, as if air moved around her before she arrived. She crossed the kitchen in a straight line that ignored obstacles by making them shift before she reached them.

She stopped at the edge of garde manger's territory and scanned Connor's counter. Lids. Labels. Knife angle. Towel fold.

Then his eyes.

"You slept?" she asked.

Connor didn't know what answer was safe. Yes implied softness. No implied weakness. He kept his face blank and gave her the simplest truth. "Some."

Sofia's jaw ticked once. "Some is better than none."

It was the closest thing Connor had heard to permission in days, and he hated that he felt it that way.

Sofia's gaze slipped past him toward the corridor mouth. Not because Hale was there, but because the corridor was always there, a border that never stopped meaning something.

"Private room tonight," she said again, as if the building had only one season now.

Connor kept plating components into clean rows. "Heard."

Sofia didn't correct him. She leaned closer, voice low enough to stay inside stainless steel. "Your unease," she said. "Put it away."

Connor's fingers tightened on his tweezers, then loosened. He didn't look at her. Looking at Sofia too directly felt like staring at a blade. "It's away."

Sofia paused, as if considering whether to argue. Then she said, "Good. Because you'll be asked to do more."

Connor looked up, just enough. "More carries?"

Sofia's eyes narrowed. Not anger. Calibration. "More visibility," she corrected. "Carries are nothing. Visibility is everything."

She left without another word, already moving back toward the pass where she belonged like a hinge belonged to a door.

Connor returned to his prep. He moved faster than he had last week, faster than he'd believed possible. Not rushed. Just reduced. Every action shaved down to the minimum. Open container, take portion, close container. Tweezers lift, place, release. Wipe once. Reset. He stopped thinking in full sentences and started thinking in distances.

If thinking showed, then he would become the kind of quiet problem someone had to clean.

By late afternoon, the kitchen tightened into its pre-service posture. The air itself seemed to fold into thirds. The rail waited for tickets like a mouth waiting for food.

Hale arrived before service, just as Sofia had said. He didn't announce himself. He simply became present at the corridor mouth, half in shadow, coat on, hands relaxed. His calm was not stillness like Renaud's. Renaud's stillness was discipline. Hale's calm was ownership.

Connor did not look at him directly. He used reflection. Stainless steel offered a ghost image that was safer than eye contact.

Renaud appeared at the pass with the same immaculate jacket, the same centered posture. The lamps came on, and the pass became a strip of merciless truth.

Service began.

The first tickets clipped onto the rail. Sofia separated one by a finger's width. The soldier-runner appeared as if summoned by paper.

"Now," he murmured.

Sofia held up one finger. Hold, without saying hold.

Connor plated without interruption. He could feel the shift in pacing even at garde manger, as if the private room pulled on the building like gravity. He watched runners adjust, watched the way their feet found the same silent rhythm, fast without looking fast, careful without looking careful.

The first cold plates from garde manger went up. Connor sent them with the same geometry as always, but something in him had changed. He no longer felt pride when the negative space looked perfect. Pride was attachment, and attachment made you watch your work leave.

He felt only relief that the plate would not return.

A junior commis at garde manger, new enough that his hands still betrayed him, reached for the herb tray and set it down a fraction off the station's invisible grid. It wasn't dramatic. It was nothing. But Connor saw it the way Sofia saw rims.

The commis started to work anyway, not noticing.

Connor didn't speak at first. He watched the misalignment create a cascade: the commis's elbow bumped the squeeze bottle. The bottle rotated slightly so the label faced inward. The tweezers lay at a wrong angle. Small wrongnesses breeding.

Connor felt irritation rise, clean and sharp. Not anger, not heat. A colder need: erase the wrongness before it became visible to someone who mattered.

He stepped in, moved the herb tray exactly one inch back to where it belonged. He rotated the squeeze bottle so the label faced outward. He placed the tweezers back at the correct angle.

The commis froze, startled, eyes flicking up to Connor's face.

Connor kept his voice flat. "Reset."

The commis swallowed. “Chef?”

Connor hated the word. He wasn’t a chef. He was just closer to the pass now, closer to consequence. But he didn’t correct it. Correcting it would be emotion. Emotion was noise.

“Reset,” Connor repeated, quieter. “Everything has a place.”

The commis nodded too fast. Too human. He started moving, hands suddenly clumsy with awareness.

Connor watched him for a beat, then turned back to his own station, heart steady. No satisfaction. No guilt. Only the clean click of order restored.

He realized, with a faint nausea, that the irritation had felt good.

Not pleasure. Control.

At the pass, Sofia’s voice cut through the lamp hum. “Felwick.”

Connor’s hands went behind his back by reflex, then he brought them forward again as he remembered visibility. He moved up without rushing, towel folded into thirds, tweezers in pocket. The heat hit his face and tried to pull sweat from him. He refused it.

A plate hovered under the lamps, a cold dish with quiet aggression in its geometry. Sofia rotated it a fraction to the invisible axis. Renaud's gaze swept it and tilted his head.

Sofia set the plate into Connor's hands.

"Private room," she said without looking at him.

Connor moved toward the corridor. At the threshold the light changed, dining room air pressing behind the door like a held breath. A gloved hand appeared to receive the plate.

As Connor transferred it, he felt eyes on his wrists. Hale's eyes, without needing to look directly. Connor kept the plate level, release clean, fingers clear of the rim.

He returned to the pass empty-handed and took his place at the edge of the lamps again.

Sofia leaned close. "Cleaner," she murmured.

Connor barely moved his lips. "Cleaner than what."

Sofia's jaw ticked once. "Cleaner than you," she said.

Then she straightened, and the moment was gone, folded back into work.

Connor stood in heat and understood what she meant. It wasn't about porcelain. It was about him.

About whether his humanity leaked into motion. About whether the private room's gravity changed his pace, whether carrying into that corridor made his breath audible, whether the knowledge of what happened to Luc made his hands tighten.

Cleaner meant less visible life.

The next hour of service pressed hard. Tickets stacked, then vanished. Holds arrived dressed up as pacing. Renaud's voice stayed quiet, final, a blade that never needed to swing wide.

"Again," he said once, and the plate disappeared without argument.

Connor watched the refire happen with the same clean efficiency as removal. The word again wasn't punishment. It was maintenance. It kept the story pure.

At garde manger, the junior commis made another small error, reaching across the counter and dragging the edge of his sleeve near an arranged line of microgreens. He didn't touch them, not quite, but close enough that Connor saw the air move.

The commis didn't notice. He kept working.

Connor stepped in and stopped his hand with two fingers, light contact on the wrist. Not rough. Just certain.

The commis's eyes widened.

Connor spoke without raising his voice. "Don't reach over finished work."

The commis flushed. "Sorry."

Connor felt something in his own face want to react, to soften or reassure. He didn't let it.

He released the wrist. "Do it again," he said, and hated how easily the words came out in Renaud's shape.

The commis stared, then nodded, blinking hard, and restarted the plating.

Connor went back to his station with his hands steady, towel sharp.

The edges in him were getting sharper too, honed by heat and watching and the knowledge that mistakes weren't corrected because someone cared. They were corrected because evidence couldn't be allowed to exist.

In the reflection of the pass's stainless, Connor saw Hale at the corridor mouth, still as consequence. He saw Sofia in her orbit, shaving seconds into invisibility. He saw Renaud centered under light, approving reality one plate at a time.

And he saw himself, not as the boy who'd arrived hungry for greatness, but as something being shaped by the same tools that shaped the kitchen: pressure, silence, removal.

The thought should have frightened him more than it did.

Instead, it settled into place like a knife sliding into its slot.

Sharper edges didn't announce themselves. They simply made the cuts cleaner.

The commis's second attempt came up cleaner, but Connor could see what the kid couldn't: the effort behind it. The microgreens sat where they were supposed to, the leaves aligned, the negative space preserved. Yet the commis's hands shook just enough to make the tweezers chatter against porcelain when he set them down.

Noise, tiny and sharp.

Connor's eyes lifted toward the pass without moving his head. The lamps made everything look like evidence. Renaud's stillness didn't shift, but Sofia's gaze traveled like a blade across stations, looking not only for errors but for strain that could become one.

The commis swallowed. Connor heard it.

Connor didn't say, "Relax." Relax was permission. Permission produced slack. Slack produced mistakes.

He said, "Again."

The word fell out of him with a calm that wasn't his own. It was a copy of Renaud's calm, lifted and worn like a jacket. The commis blinked.

"But it's—"

Connor didn't let him finish. "Again," he repeated, quiet and final. He reached over and slid the plate an inch away from the commis's hands, just far enough that the kid had to reset his posture. Far enough that he had to stop thinking about being watched and start thinking about mechanics.

The commis's cheeks flushed. He nodded too quickly, then forced himself to slow the nod down into something less human.

"Yes, Chef," he whispered.

Connor hated that too. Not the word. The need beneath it.

He watched the commis strip the plate down with tweezers, remove and re-place each component. The second build was faster, and the shaking diminished, not because the kid had gotten better, but because the kid was learning the only useful lesson here: fear had to be hidden inside motion.

Dumas crossed behind Connor with a tray, and as he passed, he murmured without looking at him, "You're teaching."

Connor kept his eyes on the plate. "He's slow."

Dumas made a sound that might have been agreement, might have been warning. "Slow is not the word," he said softly, and kept moving.

Connor didn't ask what word Dumas meant. He already knew. Weak. The subtext the kitchen never said out loud because speaking it turned it into a thing someone could argue with. But the kitchen did not argue with physics. Weak hands cost seconds. Weak minds cost timing. Weak faces cost the story.

The commis finished the third build. The plating was clean enough now that Connor could have sent it without worry. But Connor kept watching the kid's body.

The kid's shoulders were too high. His breathing was too deep. He was rehearsing control, and rehearsed control always cracked first under heat.

Connor leaned in, close enough that his voice stayed inside the station. "Drop your shoulders," he said.

The commis jerked as if touched. He tried, and failed, and tried again.

"Lower," Connor said.

The commis exhaled shakily through his nose and forced his shoulders down.

Connor watched his hands again. Still a tremor, smaller now. The tweezers were steadier.

"Reset your grip," Connor said.

The commis stared. "My grip?"

Connor took his own tweezers, held them up between thumb and forefinger. "Bone," he said. "Not muscle. Muscle shakes."

The commis copied him, awkwardly at first. His fingers trembled, then settled when the weight shifted into a different support. His eyes flicked up to Connor's face, searching for approval.

Connor gave him none. Approval was warmth. Warmth encouraged hope, and hope was the most dangerous drug in this building.

"Send," Connor said.

The commis slid the plate onto the tray for the runner. His hands didn't chatter this time when the tweezers met steel.

The runner took it and vanished toward the pass.

The commis stood very still, waiting for something.

Connor didn't look at him. "Next," he said, and turned back to his own work.

That was how correction worked here. You didn't comfort. You didn't explain feelings. You adjusted output until the human inside the body became irrelevant.

A half hour later, during the brief lull between tickets that were never allowed to look like lulls, Sofia appeared at garde manger's border.

She didn't say Connor's name. She didn't need to. Her presence was enough to make the commis's breath catch and to make Connor's spine straighten as if pulled by wire.

Sofia's eyes moved over the station. Not the food first. The order. The lids aligned. The labels outward. The towel fold sharp. The placement of tweezers. The absence of mess.

Then her gaze settled on the commis.

"How long have you been here?" she asked him.

The commis hesitated. Hesitation was a confession. "Three weeks, Chef."

Sofia's face didn't change. "And you still reach over finished work."

The commis's throat moved. "No, Chef."

Sofia didn't blink. "You did it tonight."

The commis looked toward Connor for half a beat before he caught himself. Looking for rescue was another confession.

Connor kept his face clean. He didn't give the kid anything to hold onto.

Sofia's eyes flicked to Connor, the smallest check. "Did he do it tonight?"

Connor answered with the same flat economy he'd learned at the pass. "Yes."

The commis's eyes widened, betrayed. Connor felt nothing. Betrayal implied a relationship. In this kitchen, there were only functions that intersected.

Sofia nodded once, not approval, not punishment. Filing.

She turned back to the commis. "If you create evidence," she said, "you become evidence."

The commis swallowed. "Yes, Chef."

Sofia's jaw ticked. She didn't correct his language. She corrected his understanding instead.

"Don't say yes," she said. "Show me you can adjust."

The commis nodded too fast again, then froze as if nodding was wrong too. His eyes watered. He blinked hard, trying to seal it in.

Sofia watched the blink, the moisture, the effort. She let the silence stretch until the commis's breathing threatened to become audible.

Then Sofia spoke again, quieter. "You want to stay?"

The commis's voice came out thin. "Yes, Chef."

Sofia's eyes narrowed slightly. "Less."

The commis tried again. "Heard, Chef."

Sofia held his gaze for a beat, then moved her eyes back to Connor. "You corrected him."

Connor didn't frame it as virtue. "He was going to contaminate finished work."

Sofia's mouth tightened, a fraction. "Good," she said, and the word didn't sound like praise. It sounded like confirmation that Connor was becoming useful in the way she needed.

She leaned slightly closer, voice low. "Correction is not anger," she said. "Correction is hygiene."

Connor understood immediately, and the understanding made him colder. Hygiene meant you didn't hesitate. Hygiene meant you didn't negotiate with a stain.

Sofia's gaze drifted past Connor, toward the corridor mouth. Hale stood there tonight, as always, half in shadow, coat on, calm like ownership. Sofia looked back at Connor.

"Be careful," she said.

Connor didn't ask of what. In this building, careful meant everything. Careful meant keep your face clean. Careful meant keep the story intact. Careful meant don't let your corrections become visible enough to draw the wrong attention.

Sofia left without another word, cutting back toward the pass where the next sequence of plates was already forming under the lamps.

The commis let out a small breath that sounded too much like relief.

Connor turned his head a fraction. "Don't," he said.

The commis startled. "Don't what?"

"Relieve," Connor said. The word came out wrong, too clinical, but the meaning held. "You're still in service."

The commis stared at him as if trying to locate the person Connor had been five weeks ago, the new arrival who'd been humiliated and exhilarated and desperate to belong.

Connor didn't give him that person. That person had been a liability.

A ticket came in. Another cold plate needed to be built. Connor's hands moved with practiced speed, reduced and clean. The commis reached for components, slower, careful, trying not to create evidence.

Halfway through, the commis placed an element a millimeter off the pattern. It wasn't enough that a diner would notice. It was enough that Connor did.

Connor didn't speak.

He lifted his tweezers and moved the element into place with one precise motion, no flourish. Then he set the tweezers back at their exact angle on the counter.

The commis flinched as if struck. "Chef—"

Connor cut him off with a single look, not angry, not loud. Just empty. A look that said: you don't get to fill the air with justification.

The commis swallowed the rest of his sentence and resumed work.

Dumas appeared again at the edge of the station, refilling a tray. His eyes lingered for a moment on Connor's hands, then on the commis's face.

Dumas spoke low, for Connor only. "You're wearing him down."

Connor kept his voice flat. "He needs to learn."

Dumas's mouth twitched in a way that didn't become a smile. "He needs to survive," he corrected. Then he added, almost too quiet to hear, "So do you."

Connor's fingers tightened around the towel, then released. He remembered Sofia's line: correction is hygiene. Hygiene didn't care about comfort.

Yet Dumas's warning sat in Connor's ribs like a splinter. Wearing someone down could look like weakness too, if it became messy. If the commis broke the way Luc had broken.

And if a commis broke at garde manger, the fracture might not reach the pass, but Hale's shadow still recorded the building. Weakness was currency here. Someone always collected it.

Connor made a decision as clean as a rim wipe. He shifted his correction from pressure to structure.

He leaned toward the commis and spoke in a tone that didn't invite emotion. "You're going to do three things," he said. "You will stop reaching over finished work. You will stop talking when you make an error. And you will reset before someone else has to reset for you."

The commis nodded once, carefully. "Heard."

Connor watched the kid's hands. Still trembling, but quieter now. The kid built the plate again. This time the pattern held.

The runner took it.

For a moment, Connor felt something that might once have been satisfaction. Not pride. Not warmth. The colder satisfaction of a system working as intended.

Then a voice cut through from the pass, Sofia calling, "Felwick."

Connor moved immediately, towel folded into thirds, hands ready. As he stepped away, he saw the commis watching him with a mixture of fear and something like awe. The look made Connor's stomach tighten with a distant disgust. Awe was another form of hope, and hope got people erased.

At the pass, the heat hit Connor's face like an open hand. Renaud stood centered, immaculate. Sofia rotated a plate to the invisible axis. Renaud's gaze swept it, approved with the smallest tilt.

Sofia placed the plate into Connor's hands. "Carry."

Connor moved toward the corridor, fast without looking fast, careful without looking careful. At the threshold, the light changed, and Hale's presence pressed against the air like pressure in a sealed room.

A gloved hand appeared to receive the plate.

Connor transferred it cleanly, without tremor, without touch on the rim, without a single visible sign that he was a human being moving through consequence.

He returned to the pass empty-handed, and in the stainless reflection he caught a brief glimpse of himself: face clean, posture controlled, hands steady.

He looked like he belonged.

And somewhere behind him, back at garde manger, a commis was learning the same lesson Connor had learned in the hardest way.

Weakness didn't get sympathy.

Weakness got corrected.

If you survived the correction, you stayed.

If you didn't, you became an absence so clean the building could pretend you'd never stood under its lights at all.

Connor returned from the corridor with the same empty hands and the same precise lack of expression he'd used all night. He stepped back into the pass's light as if the light belonged to him, as if carrying into the private room's shadow had not tightened something in his chest.

Sofia didn't look at his face. She watched his wrists for tremor, his fingers for sweat, his breathing for sound. Audit, not affection.

Renaud's gaze stayed on the next plate coming up, the center of gravity refusing to acknowledge anything that wasn't food or failure.

Connor took his place at the pass edge, hands behind his back, fingertips barely touching. He felt the heat lamps trying to pull moisture from his skin. He refused it. He made his body behave the way the kitchen demanded: a clean instrument, no visible life.

In the stainless reflection, the corridor mouth remained occupied. Marcus Hale stood half in shadow, coat on, calm like ownership. The calm wasn't stillness, not like Renaud. It was the casual certainty of a man who didn't need to prove he could ruin you because everyone already lived as if he could.

A runner approached the tape line with two plates. The runner's eyes stayed forward. His jaw worked once, then froze. Connor recognized the movement now the way he recognized a smear of oil on a rim. Fear had tells. The longer you worked here, the more you learned to see them in other people, and the more you hated them, because they threatened the illusion.

Renaud inspected. Rim. Negative space. Height. Sheen.

A pause.

Connor felt the pass stiffen.

Sofia's towel was already folded, already ready, but she didn't move. There was nothing she could wipe without admitting there was something to wipe. This wasn't a rim. This was the plate's story.

Renaud spoke, quiet and final. "Again."

The runner withdrew without visible reaction. The plates vanished back into heat and fire and remaking.

The word again didn't strike Connor the way it once had. In his first weeks, again had felt like cruelty. Now it felt like maintenance. An erasure of evidence. A reset of reality. It was almost comforting in its predictability, and the comfort scared him more than the refires ever had.

He realized he was no longer calculating cost in money or waste. He was calculating cost in visibility. If the plate left imperfect, it could return. If it returned, it became public. If it became public, it attracted the wrong eyes.

And the wrong eyes did not correct plates. They corrected people.

At garde manger, the commis Connor had been correcting worked a new ticket. Connor could see him from the pass edge when the line shifted: shoulders lower now, grip adjusted the way Connor had ordered, breathing pulled shallow into the body. The kid's movements looked less like a person cooking and more like a person trying not to exist.

Good, Connor thought, and the thought landed cold. Not good because the commis was learning craft, but good because the commis was learning disappearance.

Dumas slid into view behind Connor with a tray, moving in the quiet lanes between stations. His jacket was clean, but his eyes held the dull flatness of someone who'd watched too many clean rectangles appear on locker doors.

He didn't speak at first. Speech drew attention. Attention drew watching. Watching drew consequence.

But as he passed Connor, Dumas murmured, almost inaudible, "You're getting faster."

Connor kept his eyes forward. "I'm not slowing the machine."

Dumas paused half a beat, the smallest hesitation, then continued moving. "That's not what I meant," he said softly, and was gone.

The words stayed in Connor's body like a splinter. Faster, yes. But also faster in a different way. Faster to correct. Faster to cut someone off. Faster to decide a person was a liability.

Faster to remove.

The kitchen surged into another sequence, tickets arriving with the relentless calm of an assembly line. A private-room separation appeared on the rail. The soldier-runner materialized.

"Now," he murmured.

Sofia held up one finger.

Hold, without naming it.

Connor watched the hold happen inside Sofia's posture rather than in time. She had become the keeper of the rail's throat, and the throat was where the restaurant could be strangled without anyone in the dining room seeing a hand.

Renaud didn't look up. "Not on the lamps," he said, as if the rule had to be spoken any time the building bent.

Sofia answered, "Heard."

Connor noticed how the language had changed. Sofia no longer allowed herself yes in moments like this. Heard was cleaner. Heard meant you received the command without adding anything human.

Connor felt a quiet satisfaction at that cleanliness, and it made him nauseous for a heartbeat before he filed the nausea away. Feelings were distractions. Distractions were delays. Delays were stories.

A cold plate came up under the lamps. Connor's station's handwriting, the quiet aggression of the geometry. Sofia rotated it to the invisible axis. Renaud approved with a head tilt.

Sofia didn't hand it to a runner. She handed it to Connor.

"Carry," she said.

He moved toward the corridor with the practiced pace that had become muscle memory. Fast without looking fast. Careful without looking careful. At the threshold the air changed, cooler, less saturated with butter and flame, more saturated with money and silence.

A gloved hand appeared to receive the plate. The hand belonged to front of house this time, clean cuff, perfect stillness. Connor transferred the plate without touching rim, without dip, without tremor, and watched the plate vanish into the private room's network as if it had never been in his hands at all.

On his return, as he crossed back into the kitchen's light, he caught himself expecting a look from Hale. A sign. Two fingers. A tilt of approval.

He did not get one.

He realized, with an unpleasant clarity, that he wanted one anyway.

That was the transformation. Not the speed, not the precision, not the quiet. Those were skills. The real change was needing the eyes that terrified everyone to register him as useful.

He stepped back into position at the pass edge and forced the need down, flattening it the way Sofia flattened holds into choreography. Need was human. Need was loud.

But it remained, silent and persistent.

Service pushed on. The commis at garde manger sent up two plates in a row without visible tremor. Connor watched them arrive at the pass in the corner of his vision and felt nothing like pride for the kid. He felt only the cold relief that the plates did not create new work.

Then the commis made a mistake.

It wasn't dramatic. It wasn't even a visible mistake to anyone not trained to see ghosts. A herb sprig placed a fraction too close to the protein, narrowing negative space. The plate arrived under the lamps and Sofia's hand hovered, towel folded, ready to erase.

But Sofia didn't move.

Renaud's eyes paused.

Connor saw the exact moment the commis's life became dangerous. Not because the plate was wrong enough to return. Because it was wrong enough to suggest someone had been shaky. Someone had been thinking. Someone had been human.

Sofia's gaze flicked back along the line, searching for the origin.

Connor stepped forward without being told. Not into the center light, but close enough that his voice could stay private.

"Chef," he said to Sofia, quiet.

Sofia didn't look at him. "Speak," she murmured.

Connor's mouth was dry. He made himself say it cleanly, with no apology woven in. "It's garde manger. New commis. His spacing is off."

Sofia's eyes cut to him, sharp. There was no gratitude in them. Only calculation, as if she were measuring whether this information helped protect the story or threatened it.

Renaud's voice came, still quiet. "Again," he said.

The plate withdrew. The pass resumed.

But Connor felt the shift. He had just named the weakness. He had just pointed to the origin of the flaw. He had done it the way the kitchen did everything: without emotion, without warmth, without hesitation.

He told himself he'd done it to protect service.

He did not let himself admit that he'd done it to protect the pass's illusion from being contaminated by someone else's tremor.

Sofia leaned close enough that her words could hide in the lamp hum. "Go back," she said. "Fix it."

Connor returned to garde manger with the heat still on his face, carrying the instruction like a blade. The commis stood stiffly at the station, eyes wide, trying to read the air for whether he was about to be erased.

Connor looked at the kid's hands first. Slight tremor. Too much breath.

He kept his voice flat. “You sent that plate.”

The commis swallowed. “Yes, Chef.”

Connor’s eyes narrowed. “Less.”

The commis blinked fast, then corrected himself. “Heard.”

Connor reached for a plate and placed it on the counter between them with a controlled, quiet tap. “Build it,” he said. “Same dish. Now.”

The commis’s hands moved quickly, too quickly. Speed without control. A new kind of mistake. Connor watched the tweezers chatter once against porcelain.

“Stop,” Connor said.

The commis froze, eyes snapping up.

Connor pointed to the counter. “Reset your tools. Reset your breath. Then build.”

The commis’s throat worked. “Chef, I—”

Connor cut him off with a look that held no anger and no comfort. Empty. A look that said words were noise.

The commis swallowed the sentence and did what he was told. Tweezers angled correctly. Herb tray aligned. Towel folded. Breath pulled shallow.

He began again, slower, cleaner, more careful.

Connor watched the spacing. A millimeter off.

He corrected it without speaking, moving the herb sprig with tweezers so precisely it looked like it had always been there.

The commis flinched as if struck.

Connor leaned in, voice low. "You don't get to make the pass think you were nervous," he said. The sentence was colder than he intended. It was also true in the only way truth mattered here.

The commis's eyes watered. He blinked hard.

Connor felt a flicker of something old in his chest, a memory of being new and terrified and desperate to belong. It tried to rise into his face.

He killed it before it reached the surface.

"Again," he said.

The commis rebuilt the plate a third time. The tweezers didn't chatter now. The spacing held. The negative space looked clean enough to be believed.

Connor took the plate from him without ceremony and sent it up.

As the commis reached for the next ticket, hands steadier now, Connor realized he had not given the kid a single human word. No reassurance. No explanation that would make him feel safe.

Because safety didn't exist.

Connor walked back toward the pass, and as he crossed the aisle he caught his reflection in the stainless of a lowboy door. The jacket, the apron, the towel fold, the posture. The face clean enough to be used in the dining room without frightening anyone.

His own eyes looked different.

Not harder, exactly. Narrower. As if his vision had learned to exclude anything that wasn't function.

Unrecognizable, he thought, and the thought didn't come with panic the way it should have. It came with a kind of quiet acceptance, like realizing your knife hand had developed a callus you could no longer feel.

At the pass edge, Sofia was rotating a plate to the invisible axis. Renaud approved without looking up. Hale stood in shadow, watching vectors and silence.

Sofia glanced at Connor for half a second, her eyes doing what they always did: measuring for leak. For humanity on the surface.

Whatever she saw must have satisfied her. She didn't correct him. She didn't speak. She simply turned back to the rail and lifted one finger, holding time again.

Connor took his place, hands behind his back, fingertips barely touching, and felt something settle into him with frightening smoothness.

He had entered this kitchen believing greatness would make him visible.

Now he understood the real requirement.

To survive, he had to become invisible in the right way. Not overlooked. Not ignored.

Invisible like a rule.

Invisible like a system.

Invisible like a man who could say again without heat in his voice, and mean it the way Renaud meant it.

Plates arrived. Plates left. Holds vanished into choreography. Refires erased evidence. The dining room remained clean, unaware of the human cost being paid in the kitchen's shadows.

And Connor, standing close enough to the pass to feel heat on his skin and consequence in the corridor, realized with cold clarity that he could no longer remember the exact shape of his own fear.

He could only remember what fear looked like in someone else.

And how to correct it before it became visible.

Chapter 11

The Watchers

Connor learned the watchers first as absence.

Not the dramatic absence of Luc, not the clean rectangle on a locker door, but the smaller kind: the way conversations died before they became sentences, the way people stopped themselves mid-motion as if a thought had touched the surface of their face and had to be wiped away.

He stood at garde manger the next afternoon with his towel folded into thirds and his station aligned so precisely it looked untouched, and he felt the kitchen watching him back.

Not Renaud's watching. That was simple. Brutal, clean, centered at the pass like gravity.

Not Sofia's watching either. Hers moved. A blade traveling across surfaces, correcting without leaving fingerprints.

This was different. This was peripheral. Not aimed at plates, but at people. The kind of attention that didn't feel like critique. It felt like inventory.

He noticed it in the reflections first. Stainless steel didn't only reflect light; it reflected movement. A runner pausing at the wrong place. A commis turning his head as if someone had spoken when no one had. Dumas's eyes lifting for half a beat toward the corridor mouth, then returning to his labels as if he hadn't looked at all.

Connor adjusted his breathing to match the hum of refrigeration, shallow and quiet, and focused on the safe things: portion weights, angles, distances.

It didn't stop the feeling.

Near the corridor mouth, Marcus Hale stood half in shadow, coat on, calm like ownership. Connor didn't look at him directly. He used the lowboy's brushed steel, a ghost image. Hale didn't move much. That was his skill. Movement invited interpretation. Stillness didn't.

But Hale's stillness carried instructions anyway. People routed around it. Front of house drifted closer, then stopped short of the threshold like dogs trained not to cross an invisible line. Runners tightened their grips. Someone on hot side wiped a spoon handle once, then set it down, clean and final, as if the spoon itself was being audited.

A new face appeared at family meal.

Not in a chef coat. Not a commis. A man in dark slacks and a plain button-down, no visible logo, carrying a small paper cup of coffee as if it belonged to him. He stood near the wall by the dry storage door, out of traffic, out of light. He didn't speak to anyone. Yet the room's volume dropped around him anyway, like sound recognized danger and stepped back.

Connor ate without tasting. He kept his eyes on his tray, posture controlled, hands not clasping, nothing that could be read as need. In his peripheral vision, the man's gaze skimmed the room the way Renaud's gaze skimmed a plate: not looking for beauty, looking for deviation.

When Sofia entered, the man straightened slightly, not as a sign of respect, but as a signal that his attention had locked onto the correct axis.

Sofia took her coffee, didn't sit, didn't relax. Her jaw ticked once and stopped. She didn't look at the man directly, but she angled her body so she could see him without appearing to see him.

The man nodded, minimal.

Sofia nodded back, even smaller.

A transaction completed without words.

Dumas leaned past Connor to take a container of salt and murmured, "Don't stare."

Connor didn't move his eyes. "Who is he."

Dumas didn't answer immediately. Silence was still a kind of answer here, the kind that kept you alive. Then, quietly, as if he were speaking to a shelf rather than to Connor, he said, "Another set of eyes."

Connor's throat tightened. "For Hale?"

Dumas's mouth tightened too, not quite a smile, not quite a warning. "For the building," he said, and carried the salt away as if the conversation hadn't happened.

The man in the button-down left before the plates were cleared. No goodbyes. No explanation. He slipped through the corridor mouth like he belonged to the corridor's network, the same way plates slipped through to the private room without being seen by diners. Connor watched the empty space he left behind and felt the kitchen exhale without making sound.

Service started early, the way it always did when something important was in play. Tickets came with a steadier pressure, not rushed, just relentless. Sofia's orbit tightened toward the pass, and the rail became a throat again, swallowing paper and spitting out decisions.

Connor executed at garde manger, faster than he used to be, less like a person making food and more like a set of hands translating a grid into porcelain. He didn't watch his work leave. He didn't let his eyes follow runners. He kept his face clean.

Still, he sensed the watchers multiplying.

It wasn't only Hale at the corridor mouth. It was also the way the corridor itself seemed more occupied than usual. Shadows shifting. A door sealing softly and too often. A runner he didn't recognize appearing at the tape line, posture too correct, eyes too blank. The runner murmured "now" with the same controlled tone as the soldier-runner, but it wasn't the soldier-runner. This was a different mouth using the same word.

Sofia held up one finger.

Hold.

The runner froze, obedient without movement. That obedience was not training. It was fear delivered as posture.

Connor's stomach tightened. He kept working.

A plate came up from hot side and paused under the lamps. Renaud's gaze swept it: rim, negative space, height, sheen. No pause this time. A head tilt.

"Walk."

The runner moved.

Nothing looked wrong. That was the problem. The kitchen's surface had become too smooth, like a pond that didn't ripple because something heavy was moving beneath it.

Halfway through the first push, Sofia appeared at garde manger's border. Not a full stop, just a pivot, a glance across Connor's station to confirm it was clean and would stay clean without her.

"You," she said quietly, without using his name.

Connor's hands went behind his back by reflex, then returned to function. "Chef."

Sofia's eyes held his face for a beat longer than usual. Not audit for plating. Audit for leak. "After service," she said.

It wasn't a request. It was scheduling.

Connor felt a cold pulse behind his ribs and forced it down into stillness. "Heard."

Sofia left, already returning to the pass's light.

Connor's mind tried to build stories. Stories were dangerous. He cut them off the way he cut off commis excuses. He returned to mechanics. Portion. Place. Wipe once. Reset.

But the kitchen kept offering evidence that this wasn't a normal night.

Front of house came to the threshold twice and withdrew both times as if they'd been reminded of their place. A manager Connor recognized, the slick-haired one from before, hovered with a question on his face and then erased it before anyone could hear it spoken. Hale didn't move, didn't speak, but his presence acted like a silent hand at the back of the manager's neck, guiding him away.

At the pass, Renaud's voice stayed quiet and final. No drama. No outbursts. The cruelty remained in restraint.

"Again," he said once.

Not because a plate was visibly flawed, but because something in its story had shown. Connor couldn't see it from garde manger, but he felt the line stiffen. Sofia's towel stayed still, not wiping, because there was nothing safe to erase without confessing. The plate withdrew. Refire happened. The dining room stayed clean.

The watchers, Connor realized, weren't only looking for mistakes.

They were looking for the kind of correction that revealed weakness.

A chef on hot side hesitated before answering a call, a fraction too long. Not even a full second. Connor saw Sofia's head turn, the smallest angle, and then turn away again.

The chef's hands moved faster immediately, as if his body had felt the look land like a touch.

No words exchanged. Correction delivered through the air.

Connor felt a thin, unfamiliar sensation: not fear, not exactly. A kind of irritation at the watchers for being so everywhere, and at himself for noticing. Noticing was thinking. Thinking showed.

He forced his attention back to his station.

A runner came in close to garde manger, too close, as if he'd been sent to pass through Connor's peripheral vision on purpose. He carried two plates and moved with careful precision, but his eyes flicked once toward Connor's hands.

Checking for tremor. Checking for sweat. Checking for humanity.

Connor kept his face blank, hands steady, and didn't react.

The runner vanished toward the corridor mouth.

Dumas appeared at Connor's side with a tray refill, labels outward, lids aligned. His movements were calm, but his voice dropped low enough to hide under the refrigerators.

"You feel it," Dumas murmured.

Connor didn't look up. "What."

Dumas placed the tray down with a controlled, quiet tap. "Them," he said. "More eyes."

Connor's throat tightened. "Why tonight."

Dumas hesitated half a beat, then answered in the only safe currency: function. "Because there's pressure upstairs," he said. "And when pressure goes up, watching goes up."

Connor's mind flashed to Hale's folder, dates and notes, the word black written like administration. He wanted to ask if tonight was black. He didn't. He kept his mouth shut.

Dumas leaned in closer, a whisper that barely moved his lips. "You don't talk about what you notice," he said. "You don't ask why you're being watched. You just get cleaner."

Cleaner than you.

Sofia's line returned like a hand at the back of Connor's neck.

He swallowed, controlled. "Heard."

Dumas's eyes flicked to him for the briefest moment. In that glance Connor saw something rare:

fatigue that wasn't physical. The old resignation of someone who'd watched too many people learn the same lesson and pretend it was new.

Then Dumas moved away.

Service continued, relentless. Plates left and never returned. Holds vanished into choreography. The pass lamps kept their merciless light, turning every surface into potential evidence.

Near the end of the push, Connor glanced into stainless steel and saw something that made his stomach tighten.

The man in the button-down had returned. He wasn't at family meal now. He was closer, near the corridor mouth but not in it, standing just outside Hale's shadow as if the shadow belonged to Hale alone. The man's hands were in his pockets. His face was blank. His eyes moved constantly, not darting, just scanning. Recording.

Hale didn't look at him. Didn't acknowledge him. But the space between them felt coordinated, a quiet partnership of consequence and documentation.

Connor felt a sudden clarity: Hale was not the top of this. Hale was the visible edge. The man in the button-down looked like someone who reported upward.

Connor's hands kept moving, but a different part of him ran its own rail beneath the visible one.

If there were reports, there were files.

If there were files, there were names.

He felt the urge to locate himself inside that system the way he'd once felt the urge to locate his place in the brigade hierarchy. The difference was that this hierarchy didn't end in stations.

It ended in erasure.

The final tickets of the push thinned. Not a lull, never allowed to be a lull, but a controlled easing. Stations cleaned as they worked. Evidence erased as it was created. The kitchen restored its immaculate denial.

Connor was wiping his counter in one pass when Sofia's voice came again, close behind him.

"Now," she said, using the word the runners used, but aimed at him.

Connor turned without turning too fast.

Sofia stood at the edge of his station, face clean, eyes sharp. Behind her, the corridor mouth waited, and Hale's shadow still occupied it.

Sofia didn't look toward the corridor. She didn't need to. "Walk with me," she said quietly.

It wasn't an invitation. It was a route.

Connor set his towel down at the correct angle, aligned his tools, and stepped out from garde manger as if he were leaving nothing behind. As if nothing of him remained on the counter. As if he could move through the kitchen without leaving a trace that someone might read later.

As they approached the corridor, the air changed. Cooler. Thinner. Less butter and flame, more sanitizer and money.

Sofia didn't slow. Connor matched her pace, fast without looking fast.

They passed Hale without looking at him.

Connor felt Hale's attention anyway, like heat on the side of his face.

And then Connor felt something else: the man in the button-down watching them both, his gaze sliding over Sofia's posture and then over Connor's, as if he were comparing them to a standard on paper.

Sofia reached a door Connor hadn't noticed before, plain, unmarked. She didn't use a key. She knocked once, a soft, controlled sound that barely existed.

From inside, a voice answered, low.

"Enter."

Sofia's hand rested on the knob. She didn't open it yet. She angled her head slightly toward Connor, close enough that her words stayed private.

"Keep your face clean," she murmured. "In there, more than anywhere."

Connor's mouth was dry. He nodded once, careful, minimal.

Sofia opened the door.

The room beyond was dimmer than the corridor, the light softened, made administrative. Not a kitchen space. A space for decisions. Connor stepped over the threshold and understood, with cold certainty, that the watchers weren't only in the shadows of the corridor.

They were in rooms like this, writing the shadows down.

The room smelled like paper that had never been allowed to soften with age.

No stainless. No tile. The walls were a muted gray that absorbed sound. A single desk lamp cast a narrow cone of light across a table that was too clean to feel human. Two chairs faced the table, and behind it sat the man in the button-down.

Up close, he looked even less like staff. No flour under the nails. No faint burns on the forearms. His sleeves were rolled with deliberate casualness, and his posture was the kind that suggested he could sit anywhere and make it feel like his office. A paper cup of coffee sat near his hand, untouched, as if it existed only to make him seem ordinary.

His eyes went to Sofia first, then to Connor, and Connor felt the assessment like a hand flattening his chest.

Sofia closed the door behind them with a soft click that sounded too final for a restaurant.

The man nodded once. "Alvarez."

Sofia didn't offer a greeting. She stepped to the chair nearest the table and sat without being invited. She did not relax into it. She sat like she was still under the pass lamps, spine straight, hands still, face clean.

Connor remained standing until Sofia spoke without looking at him. "Sit."

He took the second chair and lowered himself carefully, as if sound could be measured here the way timing was measured at the rail. The chair didn't squeak. That felt intentional too.

The man watched Connor's hands settle on his thighs. Not clasped. Not fidgeting. Fingertips still.

"Felwick," the man said, testing the name like it was a label on a container. "Connor Felwick."

Connor did not answer with yes. He nodded once, minimal, the smallest confirmation that didn't sound like personality.

The man's gaze flicked to Sofia. "You brought him."

"I did," Sofia said.

"And you're sure."

Sofia's jaw ticked once and stopped. "If I wasn't sure, he wouldn't be in this room."

Connor kept his face clean, but his stomach tightened. The room wasn't an office. It was a filter. People were either brought here, or they weren't. Luc had not been brought here. Luc had been escorted somewhere else.

The man opened a thin folder on the table. The motion was quiet, practiced, the same economy as Sofia's towel wipe. He didn't slide it toward them. He kept it within his own cone of light and looked down as if reading was a form of control.

"Your service output has improved," he said, eyes still on the page. "Your errors have decreased. Your ability to carry has been noted."

Connor heard the word noted and felt something cold tighten under his ribs. Not praised. Not encouraged. Recorded.

The man turned a page. "You were present for the incident involving Luc."

The word incident landed with administrative weight, the way Hale had used clearance. Not collapse. Not removal. Incident. A term designed to keep mess from becoming story.

Connor didn't speak.

Sofia did. "He handled it."

The man's eyes lifted to Connor. "Did you discuss it."

"No," Connor said, and made the word as flat as possible.

The man watched for a beat, then nodded as if satisfied or bored. He turned his attention back to Sofia. "Why now."

Sofia's gaze didn't move. "Because the watchers are getting closer."

The man's mouth curved slightly, not a smile, more a recognition that Sofia was naming what didn't usually get named. "They've been close for a long time."

"They're multiplying," Sofia said. "And they're nervous."

At the table, the man tapped the folder once. "What makes you think they're nervous."

Sofia's eyes held his, calm in a way that didn't read as peace. "Because they're watching me."

The room's quiet sharpened. Connor felt it like the pause before Renaud said again.

The man didn't react, at least not visibly. "They always watch you."

Sofia leaned forward a fraction, and Connor saw the pass Sofia in that movement, the one who could tighten her orbit and pull the line with her. "Not like this," she said. "This is audit behavior. They're looking for cracks."

The man's eyes slid, briefly, to Connor. Connor kept his face empty. He let Sofia do the talking, because Sofia's voice sounded like it belonged in rooms where decisions happened.

Sofia continued, "There's pressure upstairs. Private room pressure. Table pressure. Investor pressure. And pressure makes them impatient. Impatience makes them sloppy."

The man's fingers rested on the folder. "Who is them."

Sofia held the silence for a beat longer than Connor expected, as if measuring the room for risk. Then she said, "People who don't stand under the lamps but still want the light."

The man nodded once, small. "Names are useful."

Sofia's jaw ticked again, and this time it didn't feel like habit. It felt like the body trying to release tension it wasn't allowed to show. "Names aren't safe."

The man didn't argue. He let that hang, then said, "And yet you're here."

Sofia's eyes didn't flicker. "Because you're one of the few rooms that still understands the difference between performance and infrastructure."

Connor felt his throat tighten. Sofia wasn't pleading. She was negotiating. Not for herself, Connor realized, but for the kitchen's ability to keep the story clean without breaking the people who kept it clean.

The man looked down at his folder again. "You asked for Felwick specifically."

Sofia didn't look at Connor when she answered. "He's becoming visible."

Connor's stomach tightened. Visibility was everything, Sofia had said. Not in a good way.

The man's eyes lifted. "Explain."

Sofia's voice stayed controlled. "He doesn't leak. He carries without tremor. He corrects without noise. He's doing what the system wants."

"And that's a problem?" the man asked.

Sofia's gaze narrowed slightly. "It can be. If he becomes useful to the wrong leverage."

Connor felt the room tilt. Useful to Hale, he thought. But Sofia didn't say Hale's name. She didn't need to. Hale lived in the corridor mouth like consequence given a coat.

The man studied Sofia for a long moment. "You're protective," he said, as if making an observation about a tool.

Sofia's mouth tightened. "I'm practical."

The man's fingers shifted on the folder. "Practical would be letting the machine use him."

Sofia leaned back in her chair, still straight. "Practical is keeping the machine from eating its own parts too fast."

Connor kept his eyes forward, but he could feel the exchange like heat. Sofia was saying something in the only language that might matter to this kind of room: longevity. Output. Loss rates. Not grief.

The man looked at Connor again. "Do you know why she brought you here."

Connor wanted to choose a safe answer. Safe answers were usually small. “To keep my face clean,” he said.

Sofia’s eyes flicked to him, sharp. Not approval. Check.

The man’s mouth curved again. “He learns quickly.”

“He learns because he’s afraid,” Sofia said.

Connor felt something in his chest tighten, the smallest flare of irritation at being described that way. He crushed it immediately. Emotion was noise. Noise was evidence.

The man didn’t seem interested in Connor’s internal reaction. He closed the folder and folded his hands. “Alvarez,” he said, “you know the rules.”

Sofia answered without hesitation. “I know them better than most.”

“And yet you’re speaking as if you want different ones.”

Sofia’s eyes held steady. “I want the existing ones applied consistently. If you’re going to monitor, then monitor. If you’re going to remove, then remove. But don’t let them play games with the line.”

The man’s gaze sharpened. “Games.”

Sofia's jaw ticked. "Moves meant to test control. To see if they can make Renaud bend. To see if they can make me miss a hold. To see if the pass can be made to show effort."

Connor's pulse bumped in his wrists. He'd felt it, the subtle adjustments, the way the night seemed pre-shaped. Sofia was putting words to it now.

The man was silent for a beat, then said, "They've been testing for a while."

"Yes," Sofia replied. "And Luc was part of it."

The room's air tightened again. The name, spoken here, sounded strange, like bringing a ghost into a lit room.

The man didn't flinch. "Luc cracked on his own."

Sofia's eyes hardened by a fraction. "Luc was pushed. Not by Renaud. By pressure that didn't belong in the kitchen."

Connor felt his stomach go cold. Sofia had known Luc was being monitored. She had seen the threshold. She had watched him work anyway.

The man's tone remained even. "You're careful how you say that."

Sofia's voice dropped slightly. "Because you're not the only one who keeps records."

The man's gaze held hers. For the first time, Connor saw something like respect flicker in the space between them. Not warmth. Recognition of competence.

The man turned his head a fraction, as if listening. Connor realized then there was a faint hum under the room's quiet. Not refrigeration. Something electronic. Too steady.

A recorder, Connor thought.

Sofia must have thought it too, because she shifted her eyes, briefly, toward the corner where the shadow was thickest. Then her gaze returned to the man.

"So," she said, carefully now, "this is what I'm saying. Felwick is on a path. He will become a lever if someone decides to use him as one. And if he becomes a lever, he becomes vulnerable."

The man's eyes moved to Connor again, inventory gaze. "Vulnerable how."

Sofia didn't answer immediately. She chose her words with the same precision she chose timing. "To believing he has choices when he doesn't."

Connor's throat tightened. Hale's offer returned in his mind: you can leave tonight. Or you can stay long enough to learn how to pay it.

Sofia continued, "To thinking approval is safety. To thinking usefulness is protection."

The man sat very still. "And you want what."

Sofia's voice stayed calm. "I want him trained correctly. Not just in food. In silence."

Connor felt a chill. He had thought silence was the absence of speech. Sofia was talking about a deeper silence. Silence as discipline. Silence as survival.

The man nodded once. "He already has it."

Sofia's eyes didn't soften. "Not enough. Not for what's coming."

Connor's skin prickled at that phrase. What's coming. The kitchen had been feeling like a pond with something heavy beneath it. Sofia was confirming the weight.

The man's gaze went distant for a moment, as if checking something internal. Then he leaned forward and finally spoke the first thing that sounded like a decision.

"There are two kinds of secrets, Alvarez," he said quietly. "The kind you keep because you're loyal. And the kind you keep because you're scared."

Sofia didn't blink. "Both can be useful."

"And which are yours."

Sofia held his gaze. "Mine are the kind that keep the line alive."

The man's eyes flicked to Connor's hands again, still and clean. "And his."

Sofia answered without looking at Connor. "He doesn't have secrets yet. He has questions."

The man's mouth tightened. "Questions become leaks."

Sofia's jaw ticked once, then stopped. "Not if they're given a place to go."

The man studied her, then sat back. "You're asking for containment."

"I'm asking for structure," Sofia said. "Structure keeps people from cracking."

Connor felt the word crack land in his chest like a dull impact. Dumas had said it wasn't about mistakes. It was about cracks.

The man reached for the folder again but didn't open it this time. He slid it to the side, as if the paper could wait.

"Felwick," he said, addressing Connor directly now. "Look at me."

Connor lifted his eyes. The man's gaze was neutral, but it held the weight of paperwork.

"What do you want," the man asked.

Connor knew the wrong answer was ambition spoken out loud. The wrong answer was anything that sounded like hunger. Hunger made you easy to move.

He kept his face clean and told the truth that sounded least like desire. "To not become noise."

The man watched him for a long beat, then nodded once, minimal. "Good."

Sofia's posture did not change, but Connor felt the slightest easing in the air around her, as if one part of her calculation had landed where she wanted.

The man stood, a smooth motion, and the chair barely made a sound. He moved toward the door and opened it a crack, glancing out as if checking the corridor's temperature.

When he looked back, his eyes were on Sofia. "You'll get your structure," he said. "But understand this. Structure is not protection. It's just cleaner consequence."

Sofia's face stayed composed. "Consequence is always there."

The man's gaze shifted to Connor. "And now," he said, "so are you."

He stepped aside, indicating the door.

Sofia rose immediately. Connor rose with her, careful, no rush.

As Sofia reached for the knob, the man spoke one last time, quietly, almost conversational.

"You're right about one thing, Alvarez," he said. "They are getting sloppy."

Sofia didn't turn her head. "Then they'll make a mess."

"They already have," the man said.

Connor felt the blood cool in his veins.

Sofia opened the door and stepped back into the corridor without looking left or right. Connor followed, and the colder air hit his face. The corridor mouth waited ahead, and beyond it, the kitchen's light glowed like a controlled fire.

They walked in silence for several steps before Sofia spoke, low enough to stay inside their moving bodies.

"You don't talk about that room," she said.

Connor kept his eyes forward. "Heard."

Sofia's jaw ticked. "And you don't talk about what I said in it."

Connor's throat tightened. Sofia had just admitted things that could get her erased if they were repeated to the wrong ears.

He answered carefully. "Heard."

Sofia finally turned her head a fraction, just enough that he could see her eyes. For the first time since Connor had met her, her gaze held something that wasn't only audit.

It wasn't kindness. It wasn't comfort.

It was intent.

"Listen," she said, and the word sounded like an order more than a request. "Hale is not the only one who keeps the stars."

Connor felt the corridor narrow around them. He didn't ask, because asking was a way of begging for information.

Sofia continued anyway, as if she'd decided the question needed a place to go before it turned into a leak.

"There are people who don't eat here," she said. "They don't care about food. They care about what the restaurant allows them to do."

Connor kept walking beside her, matching her pace, fast without looking fast.

Sofia's voice stayed low. "They use the private room to trade. They use the dining room to signal. They use the kitchen to prove control."

Connor's stomach tightened. Plates as signals. Holds as negotiations. He'd felt it. Now Sofia was naming it.

"And if they can't control it cleanly," Sofia added, "they break it."

Connor thought of Luc's empty eyes, of the clean rectangle on the locker door.

Sofia's gaze flicked ahead toward the corridor mouth where Hale's shadow usually lived. "That's why the watchers are here," she said. "Not because of food."

Connor's mouth went dry. "Then why."

Sofia looked at him again, and this time her face was still clean, but her eyes carried a hard clarity that felt like a warning meant to stick.

"Because someone returned something," she said. "Not a dish."

Connor felt his pulse jump.

Sofia's jaw ticked once, then stopped. "A message," she finished. "And they don't know who sent it."

She turned away and kept walking toward the kitchen light, her posture already sealing itself back into the shape she wore under the lamps.

Connor followed, his face clean, his hands steady.

But inside him, the words rearranged the air.

A message had returned.

The watchers were nervous.

And somewhere in the building, or somewhere beyond it, someone had started a new kind of service.

One that didn't end with refires.

One that ended with names.

The kitchen light took them back the way a tide took back footprints.

Sofia stepped through the corridor mouth first, and the air changed around her immediately, warmer, louder in its quiet way. Stainless hummed. Refrigeration breathed. The pass lamps cast their strip of merciless light across the center of the room, turning everything into surface.

Connor followed half a step behind and let his face settle back into the shape the building required. Clean. Blank. Unremarkable. He felt as if the corridor had left a residue on his skin anyway, a thin film of administrative cold that the heat of the line couldn't burn off.

Sofia didn't look at him again. She crossed the kitchen with exact pace and slid back into her orbit around the pass as if nothing had happened. No one stopped her. No one asked why she'd vanished into an unmarked door with a commis at her heel. Questions were noise. Noise was evidence. Evidence invited cleaning.

Connor returned to garde manger and moved his tools the way Dumas had taught him to move his thoughts: quietly, deliberately, leaving no trace that anything had shifted.

But it had.

A message had returned. Not a dish. A message.

He kept hearing Sofia's voice in the corridor, low and controlled. They don't know who sent it.

The sentence had teeth. It implied an unknown actor, and unknown actors were the kind of thing Hale eliminated. Hale could erase a nameplate without leaving a smear. Hale could adjust the world until it stopped resisting. But an unknown sender meant someone had moved without permission. Someone had reached into the system and touched it.

Connor built cold plates and tried to anchor himself in mechanics. Portion. Place. Wipe once. Reset. He aligned lids outward. He folded towels into thirds until the folds felt like doctrine.

His eyes betrayed him anyway.

He began to watch the watchers.

Not directly, never directly. He used reflections, angles, the safe peripheral vision the kitchen trained you to use for timing and collision. Hale was where Hale always was, at the corridor mouth, coat on, stillness weaponized into ownership. But tonight there were edges around him. More shadow than the corridor normally held. Movement that didn't belong to runners.

The man in the button-down was gone, at least from view, but Connor felt his presence the way you felt a shift in barometric pressure. The building had been cataloged. Notes had been made. The room with paper-smell had been used.

And now everyone moved as if they knew it.

A runner crossed too close to garde manger and didn't take anything. No plates. No tray. Just a pass-by with eyes forward and posture perfect.

Too perfect.

Connor kept his hands steady and didn't react. But his mind clipped the moment onto a private rail.

Why walk that line if you weren't moving food?

Inventory, he thought. Not of components. Of bodies.

Dumas appeared beside him with a refill tray, labels already faced outward as if the tray itself had been prepared for inspection. He set it down with a quiet tap and didn't look at Connor.

"You're tight," Dumas murmured.

Connor didn't ask how he knew. Dumas had lived long enough in this building to read tension in the angle of a wrist. "Working," Connor said, the safest answer he had.

Dumas's mouth tightened, not a smile. "Working is what you do when you don't want anyone to ask you questions," he said softly. Then he slid away into the lanes between stations before the sentence could become a conversation.

Connor's stomach tightened. Dumas wasn't warning him about his output. He was warning him about his posture in the larger story.

Questions. Leaks. The room Sofia had taken him to.

Connor focused on the line of microgreens in front of him and made them identical the way soldiers were taught to stand identical. But he could feel his own attention roaming, searching for the thing Sofia had named without naming it: the returned message.

Service pushed forward with the strange calm that meant pressure was present but controlled. Tickets arrived and disappeared. Holds were called without being said. The soldier-runner appeared once, murmured "now," and froze when Sofia held up one finger.

But the soldier-runner wasn't the only mouth using that word anymore.

Another runner stepped to the tape line an hour later and said it the same way, as if the vocabulary had been distributed to more bodies. "Now."

Sofia's head turned by a fraction. Her eyes didn't leave the rail, but Connor saw her jaw tick once and stop. She held up one finger.

Hold.

The runner froze.

Connor watched the runner's hands. They were clean. Too clean for someone who carried hot plates all night. No redness at the knuckles. No faint sheen of sweat. His wrists were locked like a trained runner's, but his posture didn't have the kitchen's fatigue in it.

Not one of ours, Connor thought, and felt the thought sharpen into a dangerous shape.

A plant, his mind offered. A watcher in runner clothing.

He tried to kill the thought before it reached his face. Paranoia was a form of visibility. People who looked like they suspected things got noticed by the wrong eyes.

But suspicion kept crawling back. Sofia had said they were getting sloppy. Sloppy meant more movement in the open. More bodies. More eyes.

At the pass, Renaud's voice stayed quiet and final. "Again," he said once, and a plate vanished back into the line without argument. The refire happened so smoothly it looked like the plate had never existed.

Connor wondered if the refire was about food or about message. He hated that he couldn't tell anymore.

He sent another cold plate up and forced himself not to watch it leave. Don't watch your work leave. Dumas's rule. Attachment made your eyes travel. Eyes traveling betrayed interest. Interest betrayed thought. Thought betrayed questions.

Yet Connor felt himself counting movements anyway.

Hale spoke to no one. Hale didn't have to. His stillness made everyone adjust around him like water adjusting around a rock. Front of house approached the threshold twice and withdrew as if the air had spoken. A manager appeared, then disappeared. A door somewhere in the corridor sealed softly, and the sound raised the hairs on Connor's arms as if it were a whisper.

He remembered the file Hale had shown him, dates and notes, "Risk. Monitor." The administrative cold of it. The idea that you could be listed as an approaching threshold weeks before you broke.

He tried not to imagine similar notes being written now.

Connor Felwick. Useful. Carries. Clean face.

Or worse: Connor Felwick. Questions.

Sofia moved down the line once, not to correct a plate but to correct flow. She stopped at garde manger's border and spoke without looking directly at him.

"Two carries," she said quietly. "Private room."

Connor nodded once. "Heard."

Sofia's eyes flicked over his station, then his face. A fast audit for leak. "Less," she murmured, and left again, already back in the pass's gravity.

Less meant less expression. Less breath. Less human.

Connor washed his hands, dried them once, and stood ready.

When Sofia called him up, the pass heat struck his face, and he felt his body settle into the carry posture automatically. Wrists locked. Thumbs clear. No tremor. No sweat.

A plate waited under the lamps, a dish arranged with a severity that looked almost like code. Not a special menu item he recognized from the standard progression. The components were familiar, but their placement was different, as if someone had rearranged the grammar while keeping the same words.

Sofia rotated it to the invisible axis and wiped nothing, because wiping would confess.

Renaud's gaze passed over it and tilted, approval without language.

Sofia placed it into Connor's hands. Her voice was almost nonexistent. "Walk."

Connor moved toward the corridor, fast without looking fast, careful without looking careful. At the threshold the air cooled, and the corridor's silence pressed in. He didn't look toward Hale, but he felt

Hale's attention brush his wrists like a measurement.

Halfway down the corridor, a door opened that Connor had never seen opened during service. Not the unmarked door Sofia had taken him through earlier. Another one. It cracked just enough for a sliver of light and a hand to appear.

Not a gloved front-of-house hand.

A bare hand.

The fingers were clean, nails short. The wrist wore no watch, no cuff. The hand took the plate with a precision that looked practiced, then withdrew. The door sealed softly.

Connor stopped walking only in his mind. His body kept moving, because hesitation in the corridor was a kind of scream.

He returned to the pass empty-handed, face clean, but inside him something had shifted.

The private room wasn't the only destination, he realized. The corridor was a network with more doors than the kitchen admitted existed.

And someone inside that network could receive plates without being seen by diners, by servers, even by the line.

A message.

His mind stitched the pieces together with the ugly speed of a survival instinct: food as signal, doors as pathways, watchers multiplying because they didn't know who had used those pathways without authorization.

He went back to garde manger and forced his hands into prep again until the second carry was called.

On the second trip, the door stayed closed. A gloved hand took the plate at the threshold like normal. The sudden normality felt staged, as if the building had corrected itself after showing him too much.

Connor returned to his station and found Dumas waiting near the edge, wiping stainless in one pass. Dumas didn't look at him directly.

"You saw something," Dumas said softly.

Connor kept his eyes on his hands. "No."

Dumas's towel paused for a fraction, then moved again. "Good," he said. Not praise. A warning that denial was the correct tool.

Connor's throat tightened. "What did Sofia mean," he asked, barely moving his lips. "About a message."

Dumas didn't answer immediately. The kitchen's hum filled the gap like water filling a crack.

Then Dumas said, so quietly Connor almost didn't hear it, "If you feel it, you're already late."

Connor's fingers tightened on his tweezers, then relaxed. "Late for what."

Dumas finally glanced at him, a fast look with old fatigue in it. "Late for innocence," he said. Then his eyes slid away again as if even that sentence had been too much.

The rest of service passed with the same flawless surface, but Connor no longer believed the surface. Every clean movement felt like it might be hiding a second movement beneath it. Every runner looked like a possible watcher. Every unmarked door felt like a mouth.

When the push eased, stations scrubbed, reset, erased their own labor. The kitchen returned itself to immaculate denial.

Connor wiped his counter in one pass and aligned his tools as if alignment could quiet his thoughts. He tried to slow his breathing, to flatten his expression, to make himself less.

But paranoia didn't make you bigger. It made you sharper.

He caught himself scanning for cameras in corners. Listening for clicks that weren't part of refrigeration. Noticing who approached Hale and who didn't. Noticing that Sofia's orbit was tighter than usual, her movements more economical, as if she were trying to outrun scrutiny by becoming perfect.

Connor realized, with a cold clarity that made his stomach sink, that the watchers weren't only watching for a sender.

They were watching for who reacted.

Who flinched. Who looked toward the wrong door. Who asked questions. Who tried to understand the pattern out loud.

And once you knew that, every effort to appear calm became another kind of evidence.

Connor finished his reset and stood very still, hands at his sides, fingertips open. He kept his face clean.

In the stainless reflection of the lowboy door, he saw Hale at the corridor mouth, still and calm and unreadable. For a moment Connor thought he saw a faint shift beside Hale, a shadow that wasn't a runner, a presence that lingered just outside the pass's light.

The man in the button-down, perhaps. Or someone else.

Connor didn't turn to confirm. Confirming would mean admitting he'd seen.

He lowered his eyes back to his station, because a clean face was survival and a clean station was alibi.

But inside him, the paranoia kept growing in careful, quiet increments, like a crack spreading beneath paint.

Someone had sent a message through the corridor network.

The watchers didn't know who.

And until they did, everyone was suspect, including the ones who thought they were only cooking.

Chapter 12

Fault Lines

The next day didn't feel like a reset. It felt like the same service, stretched thinner, the way a sauce could be reduced past the point of gloss into something that threatened to split.

Connor arrived early enough that the street outside was still half-asleep, and the service entrance smelled of damp concrete and last night's garbage pickup. He paused at the door the way he always did now, listening for the building's mood through the metal.

Inside, the kitchen lights were already on. Not all of them, but enough to turn stainless into a pale mirror. The counters were spotless in that aggressive way the place preferred, as if cleanliness could overwrite memory. A mop bucket sat by the dish pit like an apology no one planned to make.

Dumas was at garde manger, of course. Labels outward. Lids aligned. Towel folded into thirds so sharply it looked pressed. He didn't look up when Connor tied his apron.

"You're here," Dumas said.

It wasn't greeting. It was inventory.

Connor washed his hands, dried them once, and moved his tools into the exact grid he'd left them in the night before. "I'm scheduled."

Dumas's mouth tightened. "We're all scheduled."

Connor heard what Dumas didn't say: and we can all be unscheduled.

They worked without conversation for a while, the air filled with the small sounds the kitchen allowed. Knife on board. Container lid snapping shut. Printer paper feeding and tearing. The refrigerator hum that never changed, steady enough to be mistaken for safety.

But the tension was there in the lanes between stations, in the way people moved as if the floor had become narrower. A commis on hot side stopped mid-reach and looked toward the corridor mouth for half a beat too long before catching himself and returning to his mise en place. A runner entered, paused as if waiting for an instruction that didn't come, then left again without carrying anything.

Connor's eyes tried to follow the runner. He stopped them. Curiosity was blood.

Still, he couldn't stop himself from mapping the room. Not the stations. The pressure points.

The corridor mouth looked normal at first glance. Empty shadow. A border. But Connor had learned that empty didn't mean unoccupied. Empty meant someone wanted it to look unoccupied.

Sofia arrived with the same silent economy she always carried, and the room tightened around her. She didn't say good morning. She didn't need to. Her presence was a directive to remove anything unnecessary from your posture.

She crossed behind Connor and stopped at his station border long enough to scan the alignment. Her eyes moved the way they moved under the pass lamps: quick, precise, finding error without emotion.

"Today," she said quietly.

It wasn't a full sentence. It wasn't supposed to be.

Connor kept his gaze on his hands. "Yes, Chef."

Sofia's jaw ticked once. "Less," she said.

Connor recalibrated without thinking. His shoulders lowered by a fraction. His breathing flattened. His face became cleaner.

Sofia continued toward the pass, and the room took a small, silent breath as she went.

Dumas leaned in just enough that his voice could hide under the refrigeration hum. "She didn't sleep."

Connor didn't ask how Dumas knew. He simply said, "Neither did we."

Dumas's towel moved in one pass across steel, erasing a smear that hadn't existed. "There's strain," he murmured. "Under everything."

Connor thought of Sofia's words from last night: someone returned a message. Not a dish. A message. And they don't know who sent it.

He didn't repeat it. He didn't even shape the words in his mouth. Instead he measured out portions with a precision that didn't require thought. Thought was where the strain lived.

By midday, it became clear the building had made adjustments.

A new clipboard appeared by the service entrance with sign-in sheets for vendors and maintenance that no one had ever bothered with before. The camera above the back hallway door had been replaced, a sleeker model with a small blue indicator light that felt too modern for the rest of the space. A lock on a storage room had been changed. Connor could tell because the keyhole was new metal, unscuffed.

Small changes, administrative changes. The kind that said someone outside the kitchen had begun to treat the restaurant as a site, not a place.

At family meal, the volume was lower than usual, and it had been low already. People ate fast, eyes down, shoulders tight. No one spoke about Luc. No one spoke about the room Sofia had taken Connor into. No one spoke about the unmarked door in the corridor that had opened for a bare hand.

But Connor felt the fact of it in the way people watched each other's reactions more than they watched the food.

A new face sat near the wall, not in chef whites, not in front-of-house black. Dark slacks, plain shirt. Another set of eyes. The man didn't eat. He drank coffee and looked at the room as if counting exits.

Connor kept his eyes on his tray and chewed without tasting.

Dumas didn't touch the salt. It sat in the center of the table untouched, as if seasoning implied comfort.

Service prep began earlier than usual. Not because there were more reservations, but because the kitchen moved as if time had become unstable. As if a hold could be demanded without warning and everyone needed a buffer to hide the bend.

At four-thirty, Renaud appeared.

Connor always noticed him, even when he didn't look. The room aligned itself to Renaud's presence the way metal aligned to a magnet. His jacket was immaculate. His posture centered. His face unreadable, not blank, but controlled in a way that made emotion look like a hygiene problem.

He didn't speak. He walked the line slowly, eyes scanning stations. His gaze passed over Connor once, and Connor felt it like a hand pressing flat on his chest.

Renaud stopped briefly at garde manger. Not long. Just long enough to confirm the station was clean, the hands were steady, the output would not embarrass the pass.

Then he moved on.

Connor exhaled without making sound.

Dumas murmured, "He's counting."

Connor kept his eyes down. "Counting what."

Dumas's mouth tightened. "Cracks."

The word sat in Connor's ribs.

At five, Hale arrived.

He didn't enter like a manager. He didn't announce himself like an owner. He became present at the corridor mouth as if the building had grown him there, coat on, hands relaxed, calm like a locked door.

The room's posture changed immediately. Not in a dramatic way. In the way a dog goes still when it senses something behind it.

Sofia approached Hale for a brief exchange. Connor watched in reflection, never directly. Sofia's mouth barely moved. Hale's response was minimal: a slight tilt of his head and two fingers lifted and lowered.

The kitchen adjusted.

A dish disappeared from the prep list. A runner was reassigned without explanation. A tray of components was moved closer to the pass as if anticipating a sequence that hadn't been called yet.

Connor felt the adjustments like pressure on his skin. Strategic manipulation, embedded in the choreography. But tonight the manipulation carried an edge it hadn't before. Not smooth. Not confident.

Impatience, Sofia had said. Pressure makes them impatient. Impatience makes them sloppy.

He saw the sloppiness in small things.

A runner whispered too close to the pass and Sofia's eyes snapped toward him, sharp enough to cut. The runner backed away too quickly, nearly colliding with a commis. A front-of-house manager entered the threshold with a question on his face and left again without asking it, his jaw tight like he'd swallowed something hot.

The building was tightening its grip, and the tighter it gripped, the more the seams showed.

Service started.

Tickets appeared on the rail, and the pass lamps turned the counter into merciless evidence again. Sofia's orbit tightened. Renaud stood centered. The line moved.

At first, it was flawless. The kind of flawless that was more frightening now because Connor knew how much it concealed.

Then, mid-first course, an anomaly.

Not a plate. Not a call.

A runner Connor didn't recognize stepped to the tape line and murmured, "Now," with the same controlled tone the soldier-runner used.

Sofia held up one finger without looking up.

Hold.

The runner froze, obedient.

Nothing about it should have been notable. It was the system working. But Connor felt Sofia's posture tighten by a fraction, and he understood: the runner wasn't supposed to have that word. The vocabulary was being shared too widely.

Hale's gaze tracked the runner, and for the first time Connor saw something shift in Hale's face. Not anger. Not fear. Calculation disturbed.

The runner didn't move. The hold lasted two beats too long, and then Sofia dropped her finger.

"Walk."

The runner left.

As the plates continued to move, Connor's station sent up cold dishes with printed-clean geometry. He didn't watch them leave. He didn't allow pride. He allowed only the relief that nothing returned.

But beneath the rhythm, the fault lines widened.

On hot side, a senior chef snapped a container lid shut harder than necessary. The sound was small, but in this kitchen, small sounds were sirens. Two heads turned. The chef froze, then forced his hands into slower, cleaner motion as if sound could be rewound.

At garde manger, the junior commis Connor had been correcting reached for a tray and stopped halfway, eyes flicking toward Connor for permission he didn't have the right to need.

Connor didn't speak. He shifted his own body slightly, a silent instruction. The commis followed it, moving the tray along the correct path, not crossing finished work, not touching the rim.

The commis's gratitude showed for half a second on his face.

Connor crushed it with a look that held no comfort. Gratitude was attachment. Attachment was weakness.

The commis's face went blank again, and he worked.

Connor felt something cold and unpleasant settle in him: the awareness that he had become the thing that scared people into compliance. Not through volume. Through absence of warmth.

He didn't have time to think about it.

A private-room separation appeared on the rail. Connor couldn't see the ticket from garde manger, but he felt it anyway. The building changed its breathing. Sofia's posture tightened. The corridor mouth became heavier.

Hale lifted two fingers.

Sofia adjusted the sequence.

Connor's stomach tightened as he remembered the bare hand in the corridor door, the plate disappearing into a network he wasn't supposed to know existed. He kept his face clean. He kept his hands steady.

Another ticket came. Another sequence. Another hold that wasn't called hold.

The line executed, but the strain beneath it began to surface in human places.

A commis on pastry dropped a spoon. It clattered once on tile, a bright sound that made the entire kitchen flinch as one organism. The commis froze, eyes wide, breath audible for a fraction.

Renaud didn't look toward pastry. He didn't need to. Sofia's head turned, and her eyes landed on the commis like a temperature check.

The commis bent slowly, picked up the spoon, and placed it on his counter with exaggerated care. He wiped the spot where it had fallen as if cleaning could erase the sound.

Service continued.

But the clatter left a residue. A reminder that humans were still inside the machine, and humans made noise when they were scared.

Connor felt eyes on him and didn't know which layer they belonged to. Sofia's audit. Hale's consequence. The new watchers' inventory. The unseen people who "didn't eat here" but used the restaurant as a lever.

He focused on what he could control: his station, his posture, his silence.

Halfway through the push, Antoine passed behind garde manger carrying a tray toward hot side. Antoine's face was always controlled, but tonight his jaw was tight, and his eyes didn't look at the food. They looked past it, as if tracking a second service running underneath the visible one.

As he passed Connor, Antoine's shoulder brushed close enough that it could have been accidental.

It wasn't.

Antoine didn't stop. His mouth barely moved, but the words landed anyway, tucked into the noise of fans and refrigeration like contraband.

"Don't let them make you choose too soon," Antoine murmured.

Then he walked on as if he'd never spoken.

Connor's hands didn't pause. Portion. Place. Wipe once. Reset.

But inside him, the sentence caught and held.

Don't let them.

Them was a dangerous word. It suggested multiple hands on the lever. Multiple watchers. Multiple pressures.

Connor kept his face clean, because clean was survival.

Yet beneath the stainless and the silence, beneath the flawless plates and the controlled holds, the kitchen's fault lines were widening.

And Antoine, who rarely wasted words, had just confirmed what Sofia had implied.

Whatever was happening wasn't contained to returned dishes or secret doors anymore.

It was moving into people. Into choices. Into the kind of tension that didn't explode loudly.

It split quietly, and then everything above it collapsed without warning.

Antoine's words stayed lodged under Connor's ribs like a fishbone.

Don't let them make you choose too soon.

Connor didn't turn to watch Antoine disappear into hot side traffic. Turning would have been acknowledgment. Acknowledgment was attachment. Attachment made you visible in the wrong way. He kept his hands moving at garde manger, portioning and placing with the same clean economy, as if the sentence hadn't cut through the fan noise and sunk into him.

But the kitchen had changed since last night, and Connor could feel the change the way you felt humidity in the air before a storm. The fault lines weren't just in timing anymore. They were in people. In the way stations held their breath when Hale shifted his weight at the corridor mouth. In the way Sofia's orbit tightened and tightened, as if she could compress the entire restaurant into a single strip of light and keep it from spilling.

Connor forced his eyes down, and still he saw too much in reflection.

The runner who shouldn't have had the word now. The hold that lasted two beats too long. Hale's face, the smallest disturbance passing over it like a shadow crossing glass.

Something was moving under the choreography. Something impatient.

He wanted to find Antoine's eyes again, to pull the warning into clearer shape, to understand what choice Antoine meant. Connor hated the want as soon as it formed. Want was hunger, and hunger was leverage. Hale had said it like a gate: whether you want the stars, or whether you want to sleep at night. Sofia had said it like instruction: put your unease away. Train your silence. Not for food. For what's coming.

And now Antoine had added a third line, quiet as contraband, implying that the choice could be forced early.

Connor reset his towel fold into sharper thirds than necessary and corrected himself immediately, loosening the crease by a fraction. Too sharp looked like effort. Effort looked like strain. Strain was what the watchers cataloged.

Tickets kept feeding. Plates kept leaving. The dining room stayed clean.

Then the private-room separation appeared again, sensed more than seen. The air in the kitchen changed, a subtle pressure shift. Sofia's hand lifted, one finger, holding time without naming it. The soldier-runner waited at the tape line with the controlled stillness of someone who had been trained not by kitchens but by consequences.

Connor didn't get called to carry this time. That, too, felt like a decision. Visibility was rationed now. Given and withheld like an ingredient.

He felt eyes on him anyway.

Not Renaud's. Renaud's attention was a blade that cut plates, not people, until a person became a plate. Not Sofia's either, though Sofia's audit passed over him in quick sweeps, checking alignment, checking breath, checking for leak.

This was different. Peripheral inventory. The same kind of gaze Connor had felt from the man in the button-down. The kind that didn't care if the microgreens were perfect. The kind that cared if Connor's pupils widened when a corridor door clicked.

Connor kept his face clean and did not look toward the corridor.

But the paranoia had trained him too. He caught the movement anyway in stainless: Antoine, crossing behind hot side, tray in hand, jaw locked. The older chef's pace was controlled, but it carried a different tension than the kitchen's usual cruelty. Not fear of Renaud. Not fear of a returned dish. Fear of something outside the pass's light.

A choice.

Too soon.

A plate returned to garde manger for adjustment. Not a return from the dining room. Nothing ever returned from the dining room. This was a runner bringing back a cold component with a silent gesture that meant, change this, erase this, make it match the story.

Connor adjusted without comment, moving an element a millimeter, wiping the rim once, sending it back. The runner didn't meet his eyes.

No one met anyone's eyes anymore unless they had to.

Service pressed forward until the push eased into that controlled thinning where everyone cleaned as they moved, erasing evidence of strain. The rails held fewer tickets. The fan noise seemed louder because there was less motion to absorb it.

And then Sofia's voice, clipped and low, came from the pass.

"Alvarez," a runner murmured at the tape line, and Connor felt his stomach tighten at hearing Sofia addressed by her own name instead of Chef. The runner corrected himself instantly. "Chef."

Sofia didn't look at him. "Speak."

The runner leaned in, mouth barely moving. Connor couldn't hear the words, but he saw Sofia's jaw tick once. A harder tick than usual, like restraint under pressure.

Sofia's eyes flicked toward the corridor mouth.

Hale lifted two fingers.

Sofia didn't respond with a nod. She simply shifted tickets with a precision that made the adjustment disappear into normality. But Connor felt it in the rhythm. Something had been moved. Something had been covered.

A few minutes later, Antoine appeared at garde manger's border as if he'd been routed there by accident. He did not step into Connor's station. Station borders were treaties. Antoine hovered at the edge, hands occupied with a tray, posture careful.

Connor did not look up. He kept his hands moving.

Antoine spoke without turning his head. "You heard me."

It wasn't a question.

Connor's fingers placed garnish with tweezers, then set the tweezers down at the correct angle. "I heard words."

Antoine exhaled through his nose, a sound so small it might have been fan noise. "Good," he murmured. "That's the safe part."

Connor's throat tightened. "What's the unsafe part."

Antoine's eyes stayed forward, as if he were looking at food. His mouth barely moved. "Asking."

Connor felt a thin flare of irritation, quickly smothered. He understood the rule. He lived by the rule. But Antoine had chosen to speak first, which meant Antoine wanted something said, even if he pretended he didn't.

Connor kept his voice flat and low. "Then why warn me."

Antoine's grip tightened slightly on the tray edge. "Because you're new enough to believe you can wait until it's obvious," he said. "And you can't."

Connor's pulse bumped once in his wrists. He kept it out of his hands.

Antoine continued, still not looking at him. "They don't force choices when you're ready. They force them when it benefits them. When it's cleanest."

Cleanest. Connor thought of Sofia calling correction hygiene. Hale calling it clearance. The man in the button-down calling it structure, cleaner consequence.

Connor asked, carefully, "Who is they."

Antoine's jaw tightened. He didn't answer the question directly, which was answer enough. He shifted the tray a fraction, as if adjusting his posture gave him cover to speak.

"People who don't sweat," Antoine said. "People who don't stand under the lamps and still believe they own the light."

Sofia's phrasing, almost exactly. Connor felt cold settle deeper in his stomach. The language was spreading because the truth underneath it was shared.

Antoine's voice dropped another degree. "Hale is one hand," he said. "He's the one you can see. He makes everyone stare at him so they don't notice what moves around him."

Connor's eyes flicked, almost involuntarily, toward stainless reflection. Hale at the corridor mouth, coat on, still as a locked door. A presence designed to feel like the top of the hierarchy even if he wasn't.

Connor kept his face blank. "So what do they want."

Antoine hesitated a beat too long. Connor felt the risk in that hesitation. Antoine was measuring the danger of the words against the danger of silence.

Finally, Antoine said, "Control. Always control." His mouth tightened. "But lately it's not enough that the plates are perfect. They want proof."

"Proof of what," Connor asked.

Antoine's gaze slid briefly toward the pass. Renaud stood centered, immaculate, approving reality one plate at a time. Sofia moved like a hinge, holding time, erasing holds into choreography. The line ran cleaner than any human line had the right to run.

"Proof that Renaud is still the center," Antoine said. "Or proof that he isn't."

Connor felt the sentence land heavy. It reframed the tension Connor had been sensing all day: the subtle tests, the holds that stretched too long, the vocabulary distributed too widely, the runners who didn't look like kitchen.

They weren't just protecting stars.

They were checking who held the kitchen.

Antoine's voice stayed low. "If they can make him bend, they'll own him," he said. "If they can't, they'll replace the leverage. They'll find another center."

Connor's skin prickled. Another center. The thought rose unwanted: Sofia. Or someone else. Or…

Connor felt the room narrow around him. He did not let his expression shift. "And where do I fit."

Antoine's mouth curved in something that wasn't humor. It was recognition of a trap being seen. "That's the choice," Antoine said. "Not stars. Not sleep. Not the romantic lie." He paused, then added, "You're already being shaped into an answer."

Connor's throat went dry. He thought of Hale's calm voice in the paper-smelling room: you can leave tonight. Or you can stay long enough to learn how to pay it without flinching. He thought of Sofia telling him he was becoming visible, that he could become a lever for the wrong leverage. He thought of the bare hand taking a plate through an unmarked corridor door.

A message returned.

A message that made watchers multiply.

Connor kept his hands still for a fraction, then resumed plating. Stillness itself could look like reaction if it lasted too long.

Antoine shifted, readying to move away as if the conversation had never happened. But Connor caught one more question before Antoine disappeared back into the machine.

"How do they force it," Connor asked, voice barely there.

Antoine's eyes lifted for the first time, not meeting Connor's directly but landing near his shoulder, as if eye contact was too intimate for what he had to say.

"They create a situation where silence becomes complicity," Antoine murmured. "Or where speaking becomes betrayal." His jaw tightened. "And they do it when everyone's watching."

Connor felt his pulse thud once, heavy. Silence becomes complicity. Speaking becomes betrayal. Two doors, both leading to consequence.

Antoine started to turn away, then stopped himself just long enough to drop the last piece like a knife set down without sound.

"When it comes," he said, "don't look at Hale. Don't look at Renaud. Look at who benefits."

Then he moved, tray in hand, back into hot side lanes, disappearing into stainless reflections and fan noise as if he'd never stepped near garde manger at all.

Connor kept plating, hands steady, face clean.

But the warning had already done its damage. It had given his paranoia a shape. It wasn't just that someone had sent a message through the corridor network. It was that the message had shifted the balance, and now the restaurant was being tested, audited, prodded for a weak point that could be exploited in public without looking public.

A choice forced too soon.

Connor heard the spoon clatter from earlier in his mind like a replayed mistake, and he understood with cold clarity that the next sound might not be an accident.

It might be engineered.

And when it happened, the kitchen would do what it always did.

It would keep moving.

The only question was what it would have to erase to keep the story clean.

Connor kept plating as if Antoine's words hadn't entered his body, as if they were just fan noise. His hands moved with the shaved-down economy the kitchen demanded: portion, place, wipe once, reset. The plate in front of him accepted the geometry without argument. Microgreens aligned like a printed line. Gel placed as if it had been measured by a machine.

But his mind had changed channels.

Don't look at Hale. Don't look at Renaud. Look at who benefits.

Benefit implied intent, and intent implied that what felt like pressure was actually design. The kitchen had taught Connor to read design in tiny things: a towel fold too sharp, a tray moved a fraction off-grid, a ticket separated by a finger's width. Now he was reading it in people.

Across the aisle, the junior commis kept his shoulders low the way Connor had ordered. His grip held on bone, not muscle. He was learning to disappear. Good. The cold satisfaction returned, and Connor shut it down. Satisfaction was a kind of pride, and pride was a flag.

A runner crossed near garde manger, not taking anything, just moving through the lane too smoothly, too clean. Inventory, Connor thought again. He didn't turn his head. He used stainless reflection and saw the runner's eyes skim his hands, then his face, then slide away as if recording had been completed.

Hale remained a still point at the corridor mouth. He was where he always was, coat on, calm like a locked door. But the stillness no longer felt like the top of the system. It felt like a mask designed to take blame.

Connor built another plate, and the printer chattered out a new ticket. Sofia's orbit tightened at the pass. Renaud stayed centered under the lamps, immaculate and unreadable, approving reality one plate at a time.

The machine moved. It always moved.

And then, for the first time in days, the machine hesitated.

It was small, barely visible. A fraction of a second where the rail did not advance and the line did not fill the gap instantly. Connor felt the hesitation like a pressure change in his ears.

At the pass, a runner leaned in, mouth barely moving. Sofia held her posture, one finger already half-lifted as if the air itself had asked for a hold. Renaud did not look up.

Hale shifted his weight.

Not much. Just enough.

The kitchen tightened.

Sofia dropped her finger without holding it fully. No hold. Not allowed to be seen. She snapped the sequence forward with a movement that looked like efficiency but carried the edge of correction.

"Walk," she said.

A plate moved out. Another replaced it.

Connor's station sent two cold plates up in quick succession. The runner took them without meeting his eyes. The plates disappeared into the pass light and then into the dining room, leaving no trace except the absence of porcelain in his hands.

He tried to focus on the safe work. He tried to keep his attention on distances, on weights. But the hesitation at the pass repeated in his mind, replaying like a dropped spoon.

Engineered, he thought.

A few minutes later, Sofia's voice cut through the kitchen's controlled silence.

"Felwick."

Connor's hands went behind his back by reflex, then returned forward because Sofia had told him visibility was a different kind of danger. He moved toward the pass without rushing, towel folded into thirds, face clean.

Heat struck his skin as he reached the lamp line. The pass was a strip of merciless truth. Under it, a plate waited that Connor did not recognize as part of any standard progression.

The components were familiar, but the arrangement was wrong in a way that felt intentional, like language rearranged to carry a secondary meaning. A slice set at an angle that drew the eye to negative space. A dot pattern that suggested a number. A garnish placed with the severity of code.

Sofia rotated the plate to the invisible axis. She did not wipe the rim. Wiping would confess.

Renaud's eyes swept the dish. For the first time Connor saw a pause in that gaze that was not about food.

A beat.

Renaud's head tilted, but not in approval. In recognition.

His eyes flicked, just once, toward the corridor mouth.

Hale did not move.

Renaud's gaze returned to the plate and he spoke quietly, as if the word belonged only to the pass.

"Carry."

Sofia's eyes snapped to him. A fraction of surprise, immediately smothered. She recovered in the same breath and placed the plate into Connor's hands.

"Walk," she murmured, and her voice carried something else underneath function. A warning that was too disciplined to sound like one.

Connor turned and moved toward the corridor, fast without looking fast, careful without looking careful. His wrists locked. Thumbs clear. No tremor, no sweat. He made himself a clean instrument.

At the threshold, the air cooled. The corridor's silence pressed in like a held breath. He felt Hale's attention graze his hands as if measuring steadiness. He did not look at Hale.

Halfway down the corridor, the unmarked door opened again.

Not the private room door with the gloved hand. The other door. The one that had shown him too much the night before.

A sliver of light. A bare hand, clean nails, no watch, no cuff.

The hand took the plate with practiced precision.

This time, Connor allowed himself one microsecond of observation: the fingertips did not touch the rim. They knew the rules. Whoever was behind that door understood pass protocol as well as any chef.

The door sealed softly.

Connor kept walking. The corridor did not permit hesitation. He returned toward the kitchen with empty hands and a face so clean it could have belonged to someone else.

When he stepped back into the pass heat, Sofia was waiting at the edge of the lamps. She did not ask what he had seen. Asking made story. Story made noise.

She leaned close enough that her words hid inside the fan hum.

“Not a word,” she said.

Connor kept his eyes forward. “Heard.”

Sofia’s jaw ticked once. “That plate wasn’t for a guest,” she murmured.

Connor’s throat tightened. “It was a message.”

Sofia’s eyes cut toward him, sharp enough to stop the sentence from turning into conversation. “Don’t name it,” she said. “Naming makes it real.”

Renaud’s voice came again, quiet and final, without looking at them. “Back.”

Sofia straightened instantly, the moment erased. Connor moved away from the pass, returning to garde manger as if he had never left.

But the message sat in him like a foreign object.

Someone inside the corridor network was receiving plates as signals. And tonight, Renaud himself had ordered Connor to be the one to deliver it.

Connor's hands resumed work. Portion. Place. Wipe once. Reset. Yet his mind was tracking benefits now, the way Antoine had told him to.

Who benefited from showing Renaud that the corridor network still existed?

Who benefited from proving that plates could bypass the dining room entirely?

Hale would benefit if the message reinforced his control. But Hale hadn't moved. Hale had been still.

Renaud had paused.

Sofia had looked surprised.

That meant the move had not come from them. Or it had come from a layer above them, using them like tools.

The next sequence of tickets came fast. Sofia held time without naming holds. Plates walked. The dining room stayed clean. But Connor could feel a second service running beneath the first, quieter, more dangerous.

Near the end of the push, front of house approached the threshold in the careful way they always did, and this time they brought someone with them.

Not the slick-haired manager from before. Someone older, suit without shine, posture carrying the kind of authority that didn't need volume. He stopped at the threshold like the light itself had rules.

He didn't look at the line. He looked at Hale.

Hale stepped out of shadow by a fraction, enough to be seen.

The suited man spoke with a smile that didn't reach his eyes. Connor couldn't hear the words, but he saw the rhythm of the exchange: the suited man speaking longer than Hale, Hale answering in short, precise phrases. The suited man's smile tightening, then smoothing again like a napkin being refolded.

Sofia's posture tightened at the pass. Not fear. Calculation.

Renaud did not look toward the threshold. He stayed centered, refusing to acknowledge that the dining room and whatever lived behind it were trying to enter his light.

The suited man's gaze drifted, just once, toward Renaud. Then toward Sofia. Then, unexpectedly, toward Connor's station.

Connor kept his face clean and did not stop moving.

The suited man said something to Hale, and Hale finally moved his hand.

Two fingers.

A gesture Connor had come to associate with adjustments, with the world being rewritten without anyone admitting it had been rewritten.

Immediately, Sofia separated a ticket by a finger's width. A private-room sequence reshuffled. A runner who should have been on another lane appeared at the tape line, too clean, too blank.

"Now," the runner murmured.

Sofia held up one finger.

Hold.

The hold lasted longer than it should have. Two beats too long. Three.

Renaud's gaze snapped up, not to the dining room, not to Hale, but to Sofia's finger in the air.

Sofia dropped it.

"Walk," she said quickly.

The runner moved, and the plates went, and the hold disappeared into choreography. But the moment had been visible to the wrong eyes.

Connor felt it. The kitchen felt it. A ripple of strain that no one spoke.

After the plate walked, Sofia moved off the pass line for half a second and came to the border of garde manger. She did not look at Connor's food. She looked at his face.

"Ambition," she said quietly.

It was not an accusation. It was a word placed like a blade on a table.

Connor kept his hands moving. "Chef?"

Sofia's eyes held his. "That's what they buy," she said. "That's what they use. Not money. Ambition."

Connor's throat went dry. He thought of Hale's star pin. The contract. The price list.

Sofia leaned closer. "They'll offer you visibility," she murmured. "They'll make you think you're moving up because you earned it. But what they're really doing is placing you somewhere you can be pulled."

Connor heard Antoine again: you're already being shaped into an answer.

He forced his voice to stay flat. "What's the price."

Sofia's jaw ticked once, hard, then stopped. "The same as always," she said. "You'll pay in people. You'll pay in silence. And you'll pay in the moment you realize you don't know which part of you is still yours."

She straightened, her face sealing back into function. "Send clean," she said, as if that was all she had ever come to say.

Then she returned to the pass, and Connor remained at garde manger with his hands moving and his mind splitting cleanly into two rails.

One rail kept the plates perfect.

The other counted who had been at the threshold, who had exchanged smiles with Hale, who had made Sofia hold too long, who had prompted Renaud's pause, who had received a coded plate through an unmarked door.

Look at who benefits, Antoine had said.

Connor understood now why the warning had come with the phrase too soon. The choice wasn't a distant philosophical one about stars or sleep.

It was immediate and practical.

If he stayed clean and useful, he would be pulled closer, given carries, given visibility. He would be made into a lever because levers were what this building produced when pressure rose.

And the more visible he became, the more the system could charge him for it.

Service continued. Plates walked. Holds vanished. The dining room remained unaware that a different kind of transaction had taken place in the corridor.

Connor sent out another cold plate with flawless negative space, and for a brief moment he saw his own reflection in stainless: face clean, eyes narrowed, hands steady.

He looked like someone worth using.

He hated that a part of him, small and cold, felt something like satisfaction anyway.

The price of ambition, Connor realized, wasn't that it made you ruthless.

It was that it made you available.

And once you were available to the wrong hands, the kitchen was no longer the most dangerous place you could be watched.

It was the safest. Because under the lamps, at least, the rules were honest.

In the corridor, the rules could change without warning.

And tonight, someone had proven they could make even Renaud pause.

Chapter 13

Beneath the Stars

Connor left the building after close the way he'd learned to do everything lately: without looking like he was leaving.

The kitchen had erased itself back into immaculate denial. Stations scrubbed. Lids aligned. Labels faced outward. The pass lamps went dark, but the heat they'd made still lived in his skin as he changed in the locker corridor under fluorescent light that made everyone's face look guilty.

No one spoke.

Not because there was nothing to say, but because words created edges. Edges could be grabbed.

He washed his hands even though he'd already washed them a dozen times. Soap. Rinse. Dry once. He stared at the mirror and tried to find some sign that he'd carried a message into a door that wasn't supposed to exist. His face gave him nothing back. Clean enough to pass.

In the corridor outside, Hale was gone. The shadow at the mouth had emptied, or had decided to look empty. Connor couldn't tell the difference anymore.

He stepped into the night and found the city louder than he remembered. Car doors. Laughter spilling out of bars. People leaning into each other with the careless closeness of bodies that didn't know what it cost to be precise.

He walked fast without looking fast, hands loose at his sides, posture controlled. He didn't take the most direct route home. He didn't take the same route twice. It was a habit he didn't remember deciding to build, and the fact that it existed made his stomach tighten.

At his apartment, he turned the lock softly and stood still in the entryway with his shoes still on, listening.

Nothing.

No refrigeration hum. No fans. No printer. The silence should have been relief. Instead it felt like a room where someone had just stopped speaking because you'd entered.

He set his phone on the counter and didn't check it. He didn't trust himself not to search for signals that weren't there. Searching turned you into the kind of person who could be baited.

He poured a glass of water and drank without tasting.

Then, without planning to, he remembered the plate under the lamps. Not the food. The arrangement. The way the familiar components had been re-ordered into grammar that didn't belong to the menu. Sofia had told him not to name it, and in the same breath had confirmed what it was.

A message.

And tonight, Renaud had seen it. Renaud had paused.

Renaud did not pause for food.

Connor lay in bed and stared at the ceiling until his eyes burned. When he finally slept, he dreamed of the corridor: doors without handles, opening for hands that weren't gloved, closing without sound. He woke before his alarm with the same internal command he'd felt before, as if someone had said now inside his skull.

In the morning he arrived at L'Étoile Noire early enough that the service entrance was still wet from a late-night rinse. Inside, the kitchen lights were on in that partial way that made steel look tired. The counters were clean in the aggressive way the building preferred, as if cleanliness could scrub out the memory of a held finger in the air.

Dumas was already at garde manger. Of course he was. His hands moved like he'd been switched on hours ago.

"You're early," Dumas said without looking up.

"It's what we do," Connor answered, and heard the dryness in his own voice. A joke shaped like a fact. Dumas didn't respond. Jokes were noise.

Connor washed his hands, dried them once, and set his tools into the grid he'd left behind. His towel folded into thirds as if his fingers had been taught by someone else.

A new camera sat above the back hallway door. He had noticed it yesterday, but today he noticed the angle. Slightly lower. It covered more of the corridor mouth than the old one had. The blue indicator light blinked once, steady as a heartbeat.

Containment, Sofia had called it. Structure.

Cleaner consequence.

He kept his eyes on his station and began prep.

By late morning, Sofia arrived. She moved through the kitchen with the same silent economy, but Connor saw the strain in her anyway. Not in her hands. In the fractionally tighter set of her jaw. In the way her eyes checked the corridor mouth more often than they needed to.

She stopped at garde manger's border, scanned alignment, lids, labels. Then she looked at Connor's face.

"Sleep," she said.

It wasn't a question. It wasn't concern. It was data.

"Some," Connor replied, the same answer he'd learned to give when any truth could be used against him.

Sofia's jaw ticked once. "Keep it that way."

Connor wanted to ask what she meant. He didn't. Asking was blood.

Sofia's gaze shifted past him, toward the dry storage door, toward the corridor beyond it. "No carries today unless I call you," she said.

Connor's throat tightened. Visibility rationed. He kept his face clean. "Heard."

Sofia didn't soften. "And if you see a door open that shouldn't open," she continued, voice low enough to stay inside stainless, "you didn't."

Connor's fingers paused for a fraction, then resumed cutting with measured speed. "Heard."

Sofia leaned closer, just a little. The kind of closeness that meant this wasn't only about kitchen rules. "They want you curious," she said. "Curiosity makes you move wrong."

Connor kept his eyes down. "Who."

Sofia's gaze snapped to him. Sharp. A correction delivered through air. "Less," she said again, and the word contained everything: less speech, less shape, less interest.

Then she walked away, back toward the pass, leaving Connor with a mouth full of questions he couldn't spit out.

Family meal was quieter than usual, which meant it was nearly silent. People ate fast. Eyes down. No one reached for salt. The new man in a plain shirt sat near the wall again, coffee in hand, not eating, watching the room as if counting exits.

Inventory.

Connor didn't look at him directly. He used the reflection in a metal water pitcher. The man's gaze moved across faces the way Renaud's gaze moved across rims. Finding deviation. Recording.

When Sofia entered, the man's posture adjusted. A minimal straightening. A signal. Sofia didn't acknowledge it. She took her coffee and didn't sit.

Dumas leaned close enough to hide his voice under the scrape of trays. "That's not front of house," he murmured.

Connor didn't respond. Response would be a conversation, and conversation would be visible.

Dumas continued anyway, as if he couldn't hold it alone. "They rotate," he said. "So no one gets used to a face."

Connor's throat went dry. "Who rotates."

Dumas's eyes stayed on his food. "Eyes," he said simply. "People who only do eyes."

Service prep began earlier than it needed to. Not because of reservations. Because time had become another lever: stretch it, compress it, see who cracks. Connor focused on the only thing that didn't lie. The work. He built rows, measured portions, aligned trays until they looked untouched.

At four-thirty, Renaud arrived. Centered. Immaculate. His presence made the room straighten without anyone admitting they'd bent. He walked the line slowly, eyes scanning for deviation.

When his gaze passed over Connor, it didn't linger. It didn't need to. Connor's station was clean enough to be believed.

Renaud continued to the pass without a word.

At five, Hale returned to the corridor mouth like consequence taking its assigned place. Coat on. Hands relaxed. The stillness that made everyone route around him. But tonight there was someone with him.

Not the suited man from yesterday. A different one. Younger. Sharper haircut. Same kind of posture, authority without shine. He stood half a step behind Hale, close enough to be included, far enough to imply hierarchy.

Hale spoke to him with minimal movement of his mouth. The suited man nodded once, then his eyes drifted across the kitchen.

Connor felt the gaze land on him like a fingertip on skin.

He did not react.

He kept cutting.

The suited man's eyes moved on.

Dumas appeared beside Connor with a tray refill and set it down with a controlled tap. His voice was low. "Don't take it personally," he murmured.

Connor's lips barely moved. "What."

Dumas wiped steel in one pass as if cleaning a sentence. "The looking," he said. "It's not about you. It's about who you connect to."

Connect. The word tightened something in Connor's chest. He thought of the bare hand receiving the plate. The unmarked door. The fact that whoever took it knew pass protocol. No rim touch. No wobble. Someone trained.

A chef wouldn't do that. A server wouldn't do that.

Someone who understood the rules well enough to use them.

Service began with the same controlled precision, but the air had changed. The kitchen felt crowded without being crowded. Not with bodies. With attention.

Tickets fed. Sofia held time with her finger without naming holds. Renaud's voice stayed quiet and final. "Again," once, and a plate disappeared as if it had never existed.

Connor executed at garde manger. Fast without looking fast. Careful without looking careful. He tried to stay inside the safe channel of function.

But function was no longer the only channel running.

Halfway through the first push, a runner Connor hadn't seen before stepped to the tape line and murmured, "Now."

The word had spread. The vocabulary being distributed like a uniform.

Sofia held up one finger.

Hold.

The runner froze, obedient.

The hold lasted two beats too long.

Connor watched in reflection and saw Hale tilt his head a fraction, as if listening to something no one else could hear. The suited man behind him didn't move, but his gaze sharpened.

Sofia dropped her finger.

"Walk."

The runner moved.

The hold vanished into choreography, but the fact of it remained: someone was testing how long Sofia could hold the throat of the rail without Renaud turning his head. Someone was testing what could be made visible under the lamps without looking like sabotage.

Connor felt Antoine's warning press up through his work like a bruise. Silence becomes complicity. Speaking becomes betrayal.

He kept his mouth shut and his hands moving.

Then Sofia called him, sharp and low, from the pass.

"Felwick."

Connor's stomach tightened. Visibility.

He moved up, towel folded, face clean. Heat hit his skin as he reached the lamp line. Under the lamps sat a cold plate from garde manger. His station's components, but arranged wrong. Not sloppy. Intentional. The same severe grammar of code.

Sofia rotated it to the invisible axis. Her eyes flicked to Connor, and in that brief look he felt something he couldn't name: not warning, not instruction. A question that wasn't allowed to be spoken.

Renaud's gaze swept the plate and paused. Again, not about food. Recognition.

He didn't say carry this time.

He said, very quietly, to Sofia, "Not him."

The words were small, but they landed like a door slamming in Connor's head.

Sofia's jaw ticked once. She didn't argue. "Heard," she said, and took the plate away from the lamp line herself.

Connor stood at the edge of the pass and felt something cold move through him. Not him. Renaud had made a correction that wasn't about plating.

He was moving Connor out of a path.

Or out of a trap.

Sofia handed the plate to a runner Connor recognized: the soldier-runner, posture trained, eyes blank. The runner took it and moved toward the corridor without hesitation.

Hale did not move.

The suited man behind Hale watched the runner go with a focus that felt too sharp for a plate.

Connor returned to garde manger with his hands empty and his face clean, but inside him the rails rearranged. The hidden agendas were no longer theoretical. They were operational, running in parallel with service.

Someone was sending messages through plates.

Someone was testing Sofia's holds.

Someone was watching Renaud for a pause.

And now Renaud had begun to intervene, quietly, by changing who carried what through the corridor network.

Connor focused on his station to keep his expression from shifting. Portion. Place. Wipe once. Reset. He sent plates up and tried to be nothing but output.

But he could not stop the one thought that cut through everything else, clean and unwanted.

If Renaud was protecting him, then the agenda wasn't only about stars.

It was about succession.

And if it was about succession, then Connor wasn't just being watched.

He was being positioned.

Connor didn't leave right after close.

He did the right things first, the things that made him less noticeable on paper and in memory. He scrubbed his station until the steel stopped reflecting fingerprints and started reflecting only light. He aligned lids so their labels faced outward like they were presenting themselves for inspection. He folded his towel into thirds and then unfolded it and refolded it, softer, because too sharp looked like effort.

Effort was a symptom.

When he finally stripped off his apron, the air in the locker corridor felt thinner than it should have, a utilitarian cold that made every sound seem too loud. The fluorescent lights made his skin look wrong, like he belonged to a different building.

A rectangle of clean metal stared back at him from the locker door where Luc's nameplate used to be. Connor caught himself looking for it, then corrected his eyes away. Looking was a kind of attachment.

He changed quickly, shirt over head, no lingering. He didn't check his phone until he was outside, and even then he only glanced at the lock screen to confirm there were no missed calls from numbers he didn't recognize. Nothing.

The street behind L'Étoile Noire had the damp smell of late-night cleanup: wet concrete, a hint of bleach, the sourness of garbage that had been moved but not erased. The city beyond it kept living, louder than the kitchen ever allowed itself to be.

Connor stood for a moment with his hands at his sides, fingers slightly spread, the empty-carry posture still in his muscles. He could feel the building behind him like a pressure at his back, as if the corridor mouth and its network of doors extended through the wall and into the night.

He forced himself to move.

He didn't take the most direct route home. He hadn't for weeks. He cut toward the main avenue, then doubled back through a smaller street lined with closed boutiques and dark windows that reflected him in fragments. He used the reflections the way he used stainless: not to admire, to verify.

Half a block behind him, a pair of headlights lingered at a corner longer than necessary. Connor didn't turn his head. He watched the white smear of light in a storefront window. The car rolled forward and turned away.

Maybe nothing, he told himself. Maybe the city was just a city.

But the kitchen had trained him out of maybe.

At the end of the street he reached a busier road, where noise and bodies made it easier to disappear. A late crowd spilled out of a bar. Laughter cracked the air like glass. Someone bumped someone else and apologized with a grin, as if contact didn't cost anything.

Connor kept his shoulders low, his pace even. Fast without looking fast.

At the next intersection he stopped at the crosswalk and let himself look back, casually, like any person might. No one was close enough to be following him. No faces repeated. No runner-clean posture, no blank-eyed stillness.

Still, his skin stayed awake.

He could go home, lock the door, stand in the quiet and feel the quiet press against him like a room where someone had stopped speaking. Or he could keep moving until the noise of the city drowned the hum in his head.

He chose movement.

He walked toward the center, past the restaurants that stayed open late for people who ate because they could. He passed a brasserie with fogged windows and saw chefs inside laughing, loud, careless with their hands. It looked obscene, like watching someone bleed without fear of consequence.

He kept going.

Two blocks later he saw a black sedan pull up to the curb outside a private club whose sign was small and unlit. The kind of place you didn't notice unless you were looking for it. The sidewalk out front was clean, free of smokers, free of loiterers, as if the city itself had been instructed to keep a perimeter.

The rear door opened and a man stepped out.

Marcus Hale.

Coat on, posture relaxed, calm like he owned the air around him. In the kitchen he was shadow at the corridor mouth. Out here, he was the same shadow, just stretched taller by streetlights.

A younger man followed, sharp haircut, suit without shine. The one Connor had seen half a step behind Hale at the corridor earlier.

They didn't look around the way cautious people looked around. They moved as if caution was for other people.

Hale said something to the younger man, too far for Connor to hear. The younger man nodded once. No smiles. No wasted expression.

Then they walked into the club without breaking pace.

Connor felt his body slow on its own, a reflex he hated. Curiosity made you move wrong, Sofia had said. And yet Renaud had said not him, as if protecting him from a path he hadn't known he was on. The soldier-runner had carried the coded plate into the corridor network. Hale had watched the runner go with the kind of focus that wasn't about food.

Connor stepped closer to the corner and stopped beneath the pretense of checking his phone. The screen reflected his face, clean and pale in the dark.

He could see the club door in the glass. A man in black stood at the entrance, not a bouncer in the usual sense. Too still. Too neat. A watcher wearing security.

Connor didn't approach. He wasn't stupid enough to press his face against the glass. He stayed where the city could swallow him.

A woman in a long coat walked up to the door, spoke to the man, and was waved in. Behind her, another couple arrived, laughing too loud, and were stopped. The man in black said something. The laughter died. They turned away.

Access controlled. Stories curated. Just like a dining room.

Connor backed off, letting the crowd carry him. His mind tried to build a narrative: Hale inside, the suited man beside him, private rooms above private rooms, deals made in whispers instead of tickets. But narratives were dangerous. Narratives made you think you understood. Thinking made you visible.

He walked on.

He turned down a side street, narrower, quieter. The kind of street that held service entrances and delivery bays. His feet knew these streets now, the hidden veins behind the city's face. He passed a loading dock where a man in a kitchen jacket smoked, leaning against a wall, phone pressed to his ear. The man's laugh was tired, not joyful.

Connor reached a small square with a fountain that had been shut off for the season. A few late-night pedestrians cut across it, heads down. Connor slowed, then stopped near a bench as if he belonged there.

He listened.

No kitchen hum. No pass lamps. Just distant traffic and the occasional shout from a bar.

His body didn't relax. It didn't know how anymore.

A shadow moved at the edge of the square. Connor's eyes caught it in the dark glass of a parked car. A figure approaching, not fast, not slow, controlled.

Antoine.

He wasn't in his chef whites now. He wore a dark jacket, collar up, hands in pockets. In the kitchen, Antoine's control had been about not wasting motion. Out here, it looked like something else: a man trying not to be seen by anyone who knew how to see.

Antoine didn't come straight to Connor. He walked past him first, as if they were strangers.

Then he stopped a few feet beyond, turned back, and sat on the bench with his gaze forward.

Connor waited, because approaching first was a kind of admission. He let Antoine set the rhythm.

After a beat, Antoine spoke without looking at him.

"You followed them."

Connor didn't answer the accusation. He kept his voice flat. "I saw them."

Antoine's jaw tightened. "And you kept moving in the same direction."

Connor could have lied. He didn't. Lies were another kind of leverage once they were known. "Yes."

Antoine exhaled through his nose, a small sound. Not quite frustration. Not quite warning. "You're learning fast," he said. "Fast enough to get yourself killed for something you don't understand."

Connor's throat tightened. "Is that what this is now."

Antoine's eyes stayed forward. "It always was. The kitchen just made it feel like it was about plates."

Connor felt the square tilt subtly. The city noise seemed farther away. He made himself breathe shallow, quiet. “You told me to look at who benefits.”

Antoine’s mouth moved once, a grim acknowledgment. “Yes.”

“And,” Connor continued, careful, “I saw Hale. I saw the suited man. I saw where they went.”

Antoine’s gaze flicked, brief, toward Connor’s hands. Checking for tremor. Checking for reaction. Then he looked forward again. “You think that’s proof,” he said.

Connor didn’t say yes. He didn’t say heard. He waited.

Antoine leaned back slightly, still not relaxed. “Hale wants you to see him,” he said. “That’s his job. Even out here. Especially out here.”

Connor felt cold settle in his stomach. “Then what am I supposed to look at.”

Antoine’s jaw tightened. “Patterns,” he said. “Who’s suddenly close to the corridor. Who gets vocabulary they didn’t earn. Who holds Sofia’s finger in the air too long. Who makes Renaud pause.”

Connor remembered the plate's coded grammar. The unmarked door. The bare hand that knew not to touch the rim.

"Someone inside the network," Connor said quietly.

Antoine didn't look at him, but Connor felt the confirmation in the way Antoine's shoulders held. "Yes," Antoine said. "And someone using it to test the kitchen."

Connor's mouth went dry. "To test Renaud."

"To test control," Antoine corrected. "Renaud is just the most obvious place to see it break."

Connor stared at the dead fountain, the empty basin like a mouth that couldn't speak. "Why tell me this," he asked.

Antoine finally turned his head a fraction, not quite meeting Connor's eyes. "Because you're being positioned," he said, using Sofia's word like it was already known fact. "And because you're the kind of person who mistakes position for power."

The sentence landed hard, not because it was cruel, but because it felt accurate in the way the pass lamps were accurate.

Connor kept his face clean. "What do you want from me."

Antoine's mouth tightened, then softened by a fraction into something that wasn't kindness, just exhaustion. "I want you to last long enough to choose when it matters," he said. "Not when they force it."

Connor felt his pulse bump once. "How."

Antoine reached into his pocket and pulled out something small, dark. He didn't hold it out like a gift. He set it on the bench between them like a tool.

A cheap phone. Burner-clean. No case. No visible branding.

Connor didn't touch it.

Antoine spoke quietly. "If you get a message," he said, and the word message made the air tighten, "it won't come through the kitchen. Not always. Sometimes it comes through the city."

Connor's eyes stayed on the phone. "From who."

Antoine's jaw ticked, the same restrained tell Connor had seen in Sofia. "From whoever wants to use you," Antoine said. "Or whoever wants to warn you. The problem is, you won't know which is which."

Connor swallowed, careful. "And you."

Antoine's gaze finally met his, brief and hard. "I'm not clean," he said. "Not anymore. I'm just still here."

Connor felt the weight of that. Still here meant Antoine had survived by making compromises that didn't show on plates.

Antoine looked away again, scanning the square's edges. "Take it," he said.

Connor waited one more beat, then picked up the phone. It felt too light to be dangerous, which meant it was.

Antoine stood. "Don't go home the same way," he said, then paused, as if deciding whether to add one more piece of contraband.

"Renaud told Sofia 'not him' for a reason," Antoine murmured. "He's trying to keep you out of the corridor's story."

Connor's throat tightened. "Why."

Antoine's mouth curved in that humorless way again. "Because if you go too deep too fast, you become useful in a way you can't come back from."

He stepped back into motion, the city swallowing him as cleanly as a refire.

Connor stood alone by the dead fountain with the phone in his hand. The night felt suddenly less like noise and more like a second dining room: curated access, quiet power, watchers in plain clothes.

He didn't turn back toward the club. He didn't go straight home.

He walked, fast without looking fast, careful without looking careful, and felt the shape of the kitchen follow him through the city's streets like a shadow that had learned his name.

Connor didn't turn the burner on until he'd walked three neighborhoods away.

He kept moving because stopping felt like presenting himself. The city had too many reflective surfaces, too many windows that could show him whether someone was behind him. He used them the way he used stainless, quick checks without a full turn of the head. He crossed at lights even when there were no cars, because predictability made him look like anyone else. He avoided the quietest streets, because quiet gave footsteps meaning.

When he finally ducked into a late-night laundromat, the warmth and detergent smell hit him like something almost domestic, almost safe. Machines churned behind glass. A tired man slept in a plastic chair with his arms folded, mouth open, as if exhaustion could still knock someone unconscious without consequence.

Connor sat at the far end of a row of molded chairs and looked at the phone in his palm.

Cheap. Too light. A tool that could turn him into a lever faster than any carry ever could.

Antoine's words played back in the same low tone they'd been delivered. If you get a message, it won't come through the kitchen. Sometimes it comes through the city.

Connor's thumb hovered over the power button. He remembered Sofia at garde manger, eyes cutting into him as if curiosity had a scent. They want you curious. Curiosity makes you move wrong.

He pressed the button anyway.

The screen lit with a basic setup prompt. The phone vibrated once, a dry insect buzz against his skin. No notifications. No missed calls. Just a blank home screen and a signal indicator that promised him he was connected to something.

He didn't put in a SIM. He didn't have one. Antoine must have. The thought tightened Connor's stomach. Antoine wasn't clean, he'd said. Still here. Still here meant he'd learned which pockets could hide which tools.

Connor went into settings and turned off anything that looked like location. He didn't trust the icons to be honest, but he did it anyway because control mattered even when it was cosmetic. Then he stared at the screen as if it might confess.

Nothing.

He slipped the phone into his jacket pocket and sat very still, listening. The laundromat's noises were steady and mechanical, a kind of service rhythm without the cruelty. Wash cycles, spin cycles, the soft beep of a completed load. The sleeping man didn't wake.

Connor stood and left without turning back.

Outside, the air was colder. Streetlights made puddles look like black glass. He walked again, fast without looking fast, careful without looking careful, and tried to decide whether he'd already made his mistake by switching the phone on at all.

By the time he reached his apartment building, he had looped twice, doubling back through a bus stop and a convenience store, checking reflections, checking repetition. No one had stayed with him. Or if someone had, they were better at invisibility than he was at noticing.

He climbed the stairs quietly and let himself in.

The apartment greeted him with the same dead silence as the night before. No hum. No fans. No printer. The quiet didn't feel like peace. It felt like a room waiting to be used.

He locked the door and stood with his back to it for a moment, listening for the soft click of an adjacent lock, the subtle shift of air that meant another presence. Nothing.

Connor moved through the space without turning on all the lights. He set the burner on the kitchen counter and stared at it again as if it could bite.

This was the temptation, he realized. Not the phone itself. The possibility that there was an underside to the restaurant he could finally see. The corridor network, the coded plates, the watchers who rotated so no one got used to a face. Hale standing at the mouth like a visible threat, while something else moved around him.

And now a direct line into that underside, something that could bring the message to him instead of making him chase it.

He washed his hands out of habit. Soap, rinse, dry once. The motion steadied him. Then he poured water and drank without tasting, the way he'd been doing lately, as if taste itself was a distraction.

He picked up his own phone and checked it. No messages. No missed calls. Nothing that could be read as unusual.

Then he picked up the burner again and turned it over in his hands. No contacts saved. No photos. No history. Just a blank tool, waiting to be used.

His mind tried to be useful in the way the kitchen had trained it: build a system, reduce variables, create a clean plan. He could keep the phone off until something came. He could leave it at home, safe and silent. He could pretend Antoine hadn't put it on the bench between them.

But the kitchen had already changed him. He could feel it in the way his thoughts kept tilting toward action. Correction is hygiene, Sofia had said. Don't let wrongness exist. Erase it before it becomes visible.

Curiosity was wrongness in this world. But so was ignorance.

Connor set the phone down, went to his bedroom, and sat on the edge of the bed without taking his shoes off. His body didn't know how to settle. His shoulders held tension like a tray held weight.

He closed his eyes and saw the plate under the lamps, grammar rearranged to say something without words. He saw Renaud's pause, the smallest fracture in centered control. He saw Sofia's surprise, quickly cleaned away. He saw the bare hand taking the plate through an unmarked door, fingers disciplined enough not to touch the rim.

Someone had learned the kitchen's rules to use them as a language.

And now Connor had been given a way to receive that language without having to carry it himself.

He opened his eyes and went back to the counter.

He turned the burner on again and waited.

Minutes passed. Then ten. Then fifteen. The screen dimmed and brightened with his touch. Nothing.

He felt stupid, which made him angry, and the anger made him colder. Emotion meant he was being moved by something he didn't control. He shut the phone off and slid it into a drawer beneath the silverware.

He stood there with his hand on the drawer handle, breathing shallow, and realized that even hiding it was a choice. He was already participating. Already holding contraband in the same place he kept forks and knives.

He left the drawer closed and went to shower, letting hot water hammer his shoulders until his skin turned red. The heat didn't remove the kitchen. It only reminded him what it felt like to have sensation again.

He dressed and tried to sleep.

His body refused for a long time, then slipped under without warning the way exhaustion sometimes took him: abruptly, without comfort.

When he woke, it was still dark. Not early morning dark. Middle-of-the-night dark. The kind of dark that meant his body had heard a sound his mind hadn't registered.

He sat up, listening.

Nothing. No footsteps. No neighbor's television. No sirens outside. Just the building's own quiet.

Then, from the kitchen, a soft vibration.

Connor was out of bed before he thought about it. He moved down the short hallway without turning on lights, bare feet silent on the floor, and reached the drawer.

The vibration came again, faint but insistent.

He opened the drawer and the burner's screen lit his hand an artificial blue. One notification. No sender name, just a number he didn't recognize.

A single line of text.

You looked.

Connor stared at the message until the letters lost meaning.

His pulse started in his throat and traveled down into his wrists, threatening to become visible. He forced it down, breathing shallow. The kitchen had taught him how to keep fear inside.

He read it again.

You looked.

Not a question. Not an accusation. Confirmation. Whoever sent it knew he had watched Hale enter the club. Knew he had lingered near the door. Knew he had turned the burner on. Knew he had crossed into the underside even if he hadn't touched it yet.

The temptation tightened into something sharper: the need to answer. To ask how. To demand proof. To let his anger have a mouth.

Connor held the phone in both hands and let himself do the one thing he almost never did anymore.

He hesitated.

Antoine's warning returned with new weight. The problem is, you won't know which is which.

A lever, or a warning.

He set the burner down on the counter as if it were hot. He walked to the window and lifted the blind a fraction, checking the street below. Parked cars. Wet asphalt. A streetlight that flickered once, then steadied. No one standing in the open. No obvious watcher leaning on a lamppost.

But he knew better than to look for obvious.

He went back to the counter and picked up the burner again. The message waited, calm and still, the way Hale's presence waited in the corridor mouth. The same kind of calm that suggested ownership.

Connor's thumb hovered over the reply field. If he answered, he existed to whoever was on the other end. If he didn't, he might already exist anyway.

He thought of Renaud saying, "Not him," redirecting the coded plate away from Connor's hands. Protecting him, or protecting the kitchen's story from being contaminated by his visibility. He thought of Sofia's face as she told him not to name it. Naming makes it real.

This message had already named him without using his name.

He typed two words before he could stop himself.

Who are you.

He stared at the question, felt how it made him smaller. It sounded like need. It sounded like hunger. It sounded like exactly what Sofia had warned him they bought and used.

He deleted it.

He typed something else, slower, colder.

What do you want.

He didn't send it yet. He held the phone and looked at the blank field as if the space could reveal the trap.

What did they want from him? Visibility. Compliance. A mistake. A confession. A reaction they could record and later call evidence.

His finger hovered.

Then he remembered Antoine's last instruction in the square, delivered like a habit of survival. Don't go home the same way. Keep moving.

Connor lowered the phone without answering and turned it off.

In the dark kitchen, the screen went black. His reflection returned in the window, faint and fractured, a face without expression, eyes narrowed like he was already under the lamps.

He set the burner back in the drawer and closed it carefully, making no sound.

The temptation didn't go away. It only changed shape.

He understood now that someone had seen him looking, and they had decided to let him know.

Not as punishment.

As an invitation.

Chapter 14

The Secret Menu

Connor arrived before the sun had fully decided whether to show itself.

The service entrance was damp again, rinsed clean of last night's evidence, and the alley smelled of bleach and stale citrus from the trash bins. He paused with his hand on the metal door and listened, the way he always did now, as if the building had a pulse you could hear if you tried hard enough.

Inside, the kitchen lights were on in their partial state, bright enough to make stainless look accusing, dim enough to keep corners alive. Dumas was already at garde manger, his station set to a grid so exact it felt like an insult to human hands.

Connor washed. Soap, rinse, dry once. He kept his face blank as he tied his apron.

Dumas didn't look up. "You're early."

"It's what we do," Connor said, because function was safer than truth.

Dumas's towel moved in one pass across steel. "It's what they like," he corrected quietly.

Connor didn't ask who. Asking was a way of admitting you didn't already know.

He set his tools down, aligned them, and started prep. His hands moved with the shaved-down economy the place demanded, but his attention kept drifting toward the back hallway camera. The new one was still there, its blue indicator blinking steadily, a small mechanical heartbeat that said someone could watch later even if they weren't watching now.

He thought of the burner in his drawer and the message that had lit the dark like a match.

You looked.

He had not replied. He had turned it off. He had tried to seal the moment back into denial the way the kitchen sealed everything back into denial. But the message had changed the air inside him. It had confirmed that the city was part of the corridor network, and that someone could reach him in his own apartment without raising their voice.

At ten thirty, front of house began moving differently.

Not the usual glide of staff preparing for service, but a tighter pattern, like a floor plan had been rewritten overnight. Tables in the dining room were reset twice. Glassware was replaced even though it looked identical to Connor. Linen was steamed again. A manager Connor recognized, slick hair and smooth smile, entered the kitchen threshold and stopped as if the heat itself had rules.

Sofia arrived a few minutes later. She moved with her usual silent authority, but Connor saw the strain anyway, not in her hands, in the fractionally more frequent checks toward the corridor mouth. She didn't greet anyone. She crossed behind garde manger and paused at Connor's border long enough to scan alignment and his face.

"Less," she said, as if it were his name.

"Heard," Connor replied.

Her eyes held his for a beat longer than normal, an audit that wasn't about food. Then she continued toward the pass.

Dumas leaned in, voice low enough to hide under refrigeration. "They're setting for upstairs."

Connor kept his gaze on his knife. "Private room."

Dumas didn't answer directly. He didn't have to. The building itself was answering with the way it tightened.

Around noon, the first sign appeared that this wasn't just a VIP reservation. It was an event.

Renaud walked in earlier than usual, jacket immaculate, hair precise, face centered the way a blade was centered in its sheath. He said nothing. He didn't need to. The line straightened around him without anyone admitting they'd bent.

He walked the stations slowly, eyes scanning for deviation. When he reached garde manger, his gaze passed over Connor, not lingering, but stopping just long enough to feel like weight.

Then he moved on.

The only word he spoke before disappearing into the corridor was quiet and final, aimed at Sofia.

"Specials."

Sofia's jaw ticked once. "Oui, Chef."

Connor continued cutting, portioning, placing. He made himself a machine because machines did not flinch.

But "specials" in this kitchen did not mean seasonal. It meant selective. It meant code.

At family meal, no one spoke, which was normal now, but the silence had a different density to it. Front of house didn't sit. They hovered, ate quickly, left. Near the wall, a man in a plain shirt drank coffee and didn't eat. Another set of eyes, rotating, as Dumas had said. His gaze skimmed faces and hands, counting exits in his head.

Connor used the reflection in a water pitcher to check him and then forced his attention back down to his tray. Being seen noticing was worse than being seen.

Sofia entered, took coffee, didn't sit. The man in the plain shirt straightened a fraction, then went still again.

A transaction without words.

Service prep began early, not for volume but for control. Stations built redundancy the way people built alibis. Connor filled containers and faced labels outward, as if orientation could prove innocence later. He could feel the kitchen preparing not just to cook, but to perform.

At four forty-five, Hale appeared at the corridor mouth, coat on, calm like ownership. He wasn't alone.

Two men came with him, both in suits without shine, both wearing the same controlled posture as the one Connor had seen at the club. One older, one younger. They did not enter the kitchen fully. They didn't need to. Their presence at the edge rewrote the room.

Hale spoke to the slick-haired manager at the threshold. The manager nodded too quickly and left as if pulled by an invisible leash.

Sofia approached Hale for a brief exchange. Connor watched in stainless reflection, never directly. Sofia's mouth barely moved. Hale lifted two fingers, lowered them. Sofia nodded once, then returned to the pass.

The kitchen adjusted instantly.

A component list on a clipboard changed. A tray of something dark and glossy Connor didn't recognize was moved from dry storage into the pass's orbit. A runner was reassigned without explanation, replaced by another runner whose hands were too clean, whose posture had no kitchen fatigue in it.

Connor felt the building holding its breath.

At five thirty, the first VIP arrived.

Not through the dining room's main entrance, not with the usual whisper of expensive perfume and laughter. Connor saw it through behavior, not sight: front of house moved like they were carrying something fragile that wasn't a plate. The corridor mouth became heavier. Hale's stillness sharpened into a weapon.

A private-room separation appeared on the rail. Sofia's orbit tightened. Renaud stepped into position under the lamps, centered and unreadable, and the pass became the throat again.

Tickets fed. The line moved. It was flawless in a way that felt staged, like the kitchen was trying to convince itself as much as the diners.

Then Sofia stepped off the pass for the briefest moment and came to the border of garde manger.

"Felwick," she said quietly.

Connor's hands went behind his back by reflex. He brought them forward again because he had learned that submission could be read as weakness. "Chef."

Sofia didn't look at his station. She looked at his face. "You're on cold specials."

The phrase landed like a hand closing around his wrist.

Connor kept his expression flat. "Heard."

Sofia's jaw ticked once. "Listen," she murmured, so low it disappeared into the fan noise. "This is not menu."

Connor didn't respond with a question. Questions were hunger.

Sofia continued anyway, as if she were placing the words somewhere safe before they leaked. "There's the dining room menu," she said. "There's the kitchen menu. And then there's what gets ordered when people don't want to be seen asking."

She straightened as a runner passed too close, eyes skimming them. Sofia's face stayed clean.

When the runner was gone, she leaned in again by a fraction. "Special orders will come in without tickets," she said. "They'll come through me."

Connor's throat tightened. "Like the plates."

Sofia's eyes cut to him, sharp. "Don't name it."

"Heard," Connor said.

She held his gaze for one beat longer than a normal correction. "If you feel your curiosity rise," she added, "kill it. Curiosity makes you move wrong."

Then she turned and returned to the pass as if she had never left it.

Connor's station suddenly felt smaller, like the stainless around him had moved in. He kept working. He made his hands clean and steady. He waited for what came next.

It arrived ten minutes later in Sofia's hands.

Not a printed ticket. A folded slip of paper with no printer tear on it, placed on the corner of his station like contraband. Sofia's fingers didn't linger. She did not slide it toward him like an instruction. She placed it down and removed her hand as if the paper itself could be traced through touch.

Connor glanced at it without moving his head too much.

Three words, written in block letters.

BLACK STAR TABLE.

Beneath it, a list of components, not dishes. Temperature notes. A timing note. And one line that made his stomach go cold.

No garnish variation.

Connor looked up, and Sofia was already gone, back into the pass's gravity. He understood then what this paper was. It wasn't a recipe. It was a constraint. A demand for consistency so strict it became a signal: no deviation, no personality, no hidden grammar.

Someone had ordered silence on a plate.

Connor began assembling, hands moving faster than thought, but not rushed. He treated each component like evidence. He measured. He placed. He wiped the rim once and only once. He reset his towel fold because it had softened.

A runner approached, the soldier-runner, posture trained, eyes blank. He stopped at Connor's station border and waited without speaking.

Sofia's voice called from the pass, quiet and final. "Now."

The soldier-runner didn't flinch at being addressed. Obedience was built into him.

Connor lifted the plate carefully, wrists locked, thumbs clear. The dish was cold, but his palms felt hot with the awareness of being part of something he wasn't supposed to understand.

He held the plate out.

The soldier-runner took it without touching the rim, the same rule as the bare hand behind the unmarked door. The same discipline. The same language.

As the runner turned toward the corridor, Connor caught Hale in reflection. Hale's gaze followed the plate, not with hunger, with ownership. One of the suited men leaned slightly toward Hale, as if receiving confirmation. The other didn't move, but his eyes sharpened, recording.

The plate disappeared into the corridor network, toward the upstairs room where diners with names didn't need menus.

Connor kept his face clean, but inside him a pattern formed.

There was a menu beneath the menu, not written, not printed, not spoken out loud. A secret menu built of constraints and component lists, of timing notes and forbidden variations, of plates that meant something other than pleasure.

VIPs didn't just eat differently.

They ordered control.

And the kitchen, for all its discipline, was being used to serve it.

Another folded slip appeared a few minutes later, delivered the same way, left and abandoned to avoid fingerprints.

This one had no table name. Just a phrase.

OFF MENU. NO RECORD.

Connor's mouth went dry.

Sofia's warning echoed in his head: people don't want to be seen asking.

He looked at the component list and understood, with cold clarity, that the secret menu wasn't about indulgence.

It was about deniability.

And tonight, L'Étoile Noire wasn't just cooking for VIPs.

It was making their requests disappear.

Connor held the slip between two fingers as if paper could stain.

OFF MENU. NO RECORD.

The handwriting was the same blocky restraint as the BLACK STAR TABLE order, letters squared off like they'd been practiced. Not rushed. Not emotional. Whoever wrote it understood the kitchen's language: anything that looked improvised could be questioned later.

A runner waited at the edge of his station, not the soldier-runner this time. Another one with too-clean hands and a posture that didn't carry fatigue. He stood perfectly still, eyes forward, as if he'd been taught that stillness was the safest place to hide.

Connor didn't look at him directly. He read the component list again.

Not a dish. Components. Temperatures. A timing note that didn't align with any course on the printed menu. And a constraint line that made his throat tighten, because it wasn't culinary.

No rim marks.

Not wipe once. Not keep it clean. No rim marks. As if the rim itself was the boundary of evidence.

He set the paper down on the stainless without sliding it, then reached for a chilled plate and cooled it further with the back-of-house freezer air. He didn't ask what it was for. Sofia had told him where special orders came from. Through her. Without tickets. Without trace.

He began building.

Cold protein, sliced thinner than any guest would notice, arranged in a fan that wasn't decorative. The angle was too exact for beauty. It aimed the eye. It created a line. Next, a gel, placed in three dots, evenly spaced, but not in the standard pattern he'd drilled for weeks. This was a different grammar. A different punctuation.

He hesitated for half a beat, then corrected himself. Hesitation could be read.

He placed the dots again, aligning them to the plate's invisible axis the way Sofia aligned every dish under the pass lamps. He added a smear of something dark, glossy, almost black, but kept it contained, as if the darkness itself had to be controlled.

A message in color. In restraint.

Connor's hands moved as if he were assembling evidence rather than food. He kept his towel folded into thirds, but he didn't wipe the rim at all, not once, because the instruction wasn't cleanliness. It was absence.

No rim marks.

He held his breath and lifted the plate to eye level, checking for any accidental touch, any faint print where skin had kissed porcelain. He saw none. His fingers hadn't crossed the line. He could feel the runner watching the plate, not the way a runner watched timing, but the way someone watched a document being signed.

Sofia's voice, quiet and final, cut across the fan hum.

"Now."

Not from the pass this time. From somewhere closer, just behind him.

Connor didn't turn too quickly. He pivoted with controlled economy and found Sofia at his station border, face clean, eyes sharper than the knives on his board. She didn't glance at the plate the way she would have glanced at any normal output. She looked at Connor's hands.

"Carry posture," she murmured, not unkind. Just precise.

Connor adjusted without thinking. Wrists locked. Thumbs clear. Fingers under the plate, never on the rim. He held it out to her because she had called now.

Sofia didn't take it.

The runner did.

The too-clean runner stepped forward and accepted the plate with the same disciplined grip Connor had seen in the bare hand behind the unmarked door. No rim touch. No wobble. The plate moved from Connor's hands into the runner's as if it were passing through a checkpoint.

The runner turned toward the corridor without looking at Sofia for permission.

Sofia watched him go, and Connor saw her jaw tick once, a hard little movement that she usually erased. She didn't say hold. She didn't say walk. She let it happen as if denying it had been ordered.

When the runner disappeared into the corridor network, Sofia finally looked at Connor's face.

"Less," she said.

Connor forced his expression flatter. "Heard."

Sofia stayed one second longer than she should have, long enough for her presence to be noticed if someone wanted to notice. Then she leaned in by a fraction, close enough that her words could hide in the refrigerator breath.

"You felt it," she said.

It wasn't a question. It was an inventory statement, like Dumas saying you're here.

Connor didn't look toward the corridor. "Felt what."

Sofia's eyes narrowed, warning without volume. "Don't play clean with me," she murmured. "Not tonight."

Connor swallowed. The slip of paper lay on his stainless like a small, silent witness.

Sofia continued, voice steady. "They're not ordering food," she said. "They're ordering alignment."

Connor's throat tightened. "Messages."

Sofia's eyes snapped to him, sharp correction, but she didn't tell him not to name it this time. She only said, "Careful."

Then she straightened, her face sealing back into function, and moved away toward the pass as if she'd never stepped into his orbit at all.

Connor stared at his station and felt the kitchen's two services running at once: the visible one, with tickets, courses, timing, diners. And the hidden one, with folded slips, component lists, constraints designed to erase personality.

He kept working because work was the only thing in the room that didn't lie.

A third slip appeared not from Sofia's hand, but from a runner who moved like he belonged to front of house. He approached the station border, stopped, and placed the paper down with careful fingertips that still didn't touch the stainless longer than necessary. Then he withdrew without a word.

Connor waited until the runner was gone before he looked.

No table name. No components list. Just four numbers written in a vertical line.

3 1 7 2

His stomach tightened. Not a recipe. Not even a constraint. A code that didn't pretend to be culinary.

He lifted his eyes and used stainless reflection to see the pass. Renaud stood centered under the lamps, unreadable. Sofia moved around him in tight orbit, correcting time, erasing strain. Hale occupied the corridor mouth like a shadow given shape.

One of the suited men stood half a step behind Hale, posture perfect, gaze roaming. Recording.

Connor's attention returned to the numbers. 3 1 7 2.

Course sequence? Timing? A room number? A floor? He didn't have enough information, and that was the point. The message wasn't for him.

He was the medium.

A plate arrived at his station a minute later, empty and chilled, delivered by the soldier-runner. The runner didn't speak. He didn't need to. The plate itself was the instruction: build something that carries the numbers without printing them, build something that can be seen and understood by the right eyes and dismissed as art by everyone else.

Connor looked at his mise. Elements he could use: three dots of gel, one slice angled, seven micro leaves, two smears. He felt the temptation to become clever, to prove he could speak the language.

Ambition is what they buy, Sofia had said.

Connor crushed the urge and reached for the safest tool he had: replication. Not invention.

He built the plate with a cold, measured hand. Three gel dots in a line. One slice of protein offset. Seven micro leaves placed with tweezers, identical spacing. Two dark smears anchoring the negative space.

It looked, to a diner, like modern plating. Intentional. Severe. Expensive.

To someone waiting for a code, it would be a clear sentence.

Connor didn't wipe. No rim marks.

He checked the rim by tilting the plate under his station light. Clean porcelain. Nothing to read.

Sofia appeared again, fast, silent, as if she'd been summoned by the plate's existence rather than by a call.

Her gaze swept the plate, not tasting, not evaluating beauty. She counted.

Her eyes flicked to the numbers slip, still on Connor's steel. Her jaw ticked once, then stopped.

"You didn't invent," she murmured.

It sounded like approval and warning at the same time.

Connor kept his voice flat. "I executed."

Sofia's eyes held his for half a beat longer. Then she lifted the plate with her own hands, careful not to touch the rim, and carried it toward the pass.

She didn't hand it to a runner.

She placed it under the pass lamps directly, in the strip of merciless light where nothing could hide.

Renaud's gaze dropped to it immediately. He paused.

Not the long pause of hesitation. The small pause of recognition, the same fracture Connor had seen before, the tiny moment where food became something else.

Renaud's eyes moved across the plate in a pattern that looked like inspection until Connor realized it was reading. Count, angle, spacing, placement. A message extracted through geometry.

Renaud's face didn't change, but the air around the pass tightened. Sofia held perfectly still at his side. The line continued moving, because the machine never stopped, but Connor felt the strain like a thin wire pulled tighter.

Renaud lifted his gaze, not to Sofia.

To the corridor mouth.

Hale did not move. Stillness as a weapon. Stillness as denial.

The suited man behind Hale shifted his weight a fraction, as if reacting to something he understood.

Renaud looked back down at the plate and said one word, quiet enough that it belonged only to the pass.

"Again."

Sofia's head turned sharply toward him, surprise breaking the surface for a breath, then cleaned away. "Chef," she began, but Renaud didn't look at her.

"Again," he repeated, softer, more final.

The plate vanished from under the lamps, pulled back into the kitchen's throat as if it had never existed. The refire wasn't a punishment for a flaw. It was an erasure.

Connor stood at garde manger and felt the message collapse into absence. If someone had been watching for it, they'd seen it. And if someone wanted it un-seen, it had been killed under the only authority that could do it cleanly.

Sofia returned to Connor's station border, posture controlled, face clean again. She didn't look at him as if he were a person. She looked at him as if he were a point of failure that had just been tested.

"That wasn't for upstairs," she murmured.

Connor's mouth went dry. "Then who."

Sofia's eyes sharpened. "Less."

Connor forced his jaw to stillness. "Heard."

Sofia didn't soften. "Someone is sending messages through my kitchen," she said, voice low. "And they're doing it loud enough that Renaud can see it."

Connor's pulse started to climb into his throat. He pressed it down, pushed it into his hands and made his hands steadier, cleaner. "And he erased it."

Sofia's jaw ticked once. "He's buying time."

"For what," Connor asked before he could stop himself.

Sofia's gaze snapped to him hard enough to make his stomach drop. For a second she looked like she might cut him out of the machine right there, not violently, calmly, efficiently.

Then she exhaled through her nose, controlled.

"For the moment they stop using plates," she said. "And start using people."

She straightened. Her voice returned to function. "Back to specials," she said. "No variation. No rim marks. No questions."

Connor nodded once. "Heard."

Sofia walked away, returning to the pass's gravity, leaving Connor at garde manger with his hands moving and his mind colder than the plates.

The secret menu had rules. The secret messages had grammar. And tonight, Renaud had acknowledged the language by refusing to let one sentence stand.

Connor kept assembling, clean and silent, while the kitchen continued to serve diners who thought they were here for food.

Above them, behind unmarked doors, someone was reading what the plates were really saying.

And now Connor understood the most dangerous part.

Even a refire could be a reply.

Connor went back to work because the alternative was to stand still and listen to his own thoughts.

He built the next cold special exactly as instructed: no variation, no rim marks, no flourish that could be interpreted as personality. His station became a factory line that produced beautiful deniability. Every component placed with the same severity. Every plate identical enough to make memory unreliable.

The slips kept arriving.

Some came from Sofia, placed and abandoned like contraband. Some came from runners who didn't belong to the kitchen, their hands too clean, their posture too trained. Once, a slip appeared at the very edge of his stainless without Connor seeing who left it. He only noticed it when his tweezers brushed paper instead of steel.

He didn't pick it up immediately. He let it sit there, a test. If someone was watching for reaction, he would give them none.

When he finally glanced down, it was another vertical number list.

5 0 2

Not even pretending to be culinary now. Connor kept his face clean, but inside his mind began laying the numbers beside the first set.

3 1 7 2. 5 0 2.

Course counts? Timing codes? A sequence? It felt like the kind of thing that would mean nothing to anyone in the dining room and everything to someone who already had the key.

He built the next plate the way he'd built the first coded one: replication, not invention. Counted elements. Controlled angles. Negative space used like silence.

The soldier-runner appeared at his border and waited.

Sofia's voice drifted from the pass without turning her head. "Now."

The runner took the plate and vanished into the corridor network.

Connor watched the empty lane where the runner had been and forced himself not to look toward the corridor mouth. He could feel Hale there anyway, the same calm gravity that turned the threshold into a border.

Behind Hale, the suited men rotated positions with small, deliberate shifts. Never blocking each other's view. Never leaving a gap. Connor saw it in reflection: eyes moving, recording, not tasting.

A plate left Connor's hands and became something else the moment it crossed the tape line. Not dinner. Not art. A unit of communication.

Dumas drifted into Connor's orbit with a refill tray, lids aligned, labels faced outward. He set it down with a quiet tap and wiped a smear on the counter that hadn't existed.

"You're getting paper," Dumas murmured without looking at Connor.

Connor didn't answer in a way that could be called confirmation. "I'm executing specials."

Dumas's towel moved once more, slow. "Special doesn't mean food," he said. "Special means outside the printer."

Connor's throat tightened. The printer was the official truth. Anything outside it belonged to another system.

Dumas leaned a fraction closer, voice buried under refrigeration breath. "Don't keep them," he added. "Don't fold them. Don't pocket them. Paper has fingerprints."

Connor kept his eyes on his hands. "Then why give them to me."

Dumas didn't answer the question directly. He never did. "Because you're clean," he said. "And because they're not stupid."

The sentence landed like a cold spoon against teeth. Clean meant trusted. Clean also meant usable.

Connor continued plating, his movements shaved down to necessity. His mind, meanwhile, started counting not components but pathways.

The corridor network. The unmarked door. The bare hand that knew the rules. The runners who didn't sweat. The slips that didn't come from the printer. The way Sofia's finger could hold time, and how someone had made that hold stretch long enough to be seen. How Renaud had read the plate under the lamps and erased it with a refire, not because it was wrong, but because it spoke too loudly.

What kind of restaurant needed a second language that could be destroyed on command?

A runner returned to garde manger carrying nothing and stopped just inside the lane as if waiting for permission to exist. He didn't ask for anything. He didn't speak. His eyes skimmed Connor's stainless as if searching for a slip of paper left behind.

Inventory, Connor thought. Not of food. Of evidence.

Connor didn't give him any. The slips were already gone, dropped into the trash under a layer of damp paper towels the moment he'd read them, the way Dumas disposed of anything that could be recovered. He kept his station immaculate and uninteresting.

The runner moved on, empty-handed.

Sofia appeared at his border again, quick enough that her arrival felt like timing rather than footsteps. She didn't look at the food. She looked past him, toward the back hallway camera and the corridor mouth beyond it. Her jaw ticked once, hard, then stopped.

"They're pushing," she murmured.

Connor kept his hands moving. "Who."

Sofia's gaze snapped to him like a blade. "Less," she said. Then, softer, because softness could hide inside the command: "You don't ask that in here."

Connor swallowed. "Heard."

Sofia stayed one beat longer. "They want consistency," she said, and her voice carried a restrained disgust. "No variation. That's not for quality. That's for proof."

Proof. Antoine's word. Proof that Renaud was still center. Or proof that he wasn't.

Connor's next plate went out with counted elements and controlled negative space. The soldier-runner took it. The plate vanished upstairs.

Time passed in a series of carries Connor didn't make and slips he didn't keep. The visible service remained flawless, but the hidden one thickened. The kitchen felt like it was running two rails: one for diners, one for watchers.

Then something changed.

It wasn't a new slip. It wasn't a hold. It was an interruption in the flow that didn't belong to kitchen logic.

A front-of-house manager entered the threshold with a tray he wasn't supposed to be carrying. Not plates. Not wine. A slim black case, rectangular, handled like something fragile.

He stopped just inside the kitchen border as if he didn't dare bring it further. Hale didn't turn his head, but the manager's posture bent toward him anyway, seeking permission.

Hale lifted two fingers.

Sofia's head turned by a fraction. She moved off the pass line without breaking rhythm, crossed to the threshold, and took the black case without looking inside. Her face stayed clean, but Connor saw something in her eyes: not fear. Recognition.

Sofia carried the case not toward the corridor mouth, not upstairs. She carried it to the unmarked administrative door Connor had entered days earlier, the paper-smell room. She didn't knock this time. She opened it and disappeared inside for only a few seconds.

When she returned, her hands were empty.

The manager was gone.

Hale was still.

Connor's skin prickled. The case hadn't been food. It hadn't even tried to disguise itself as restaurant business. It was a delivery into the system behind the system.

A quiet transfer.

The kitchen never paused. But Connor felt a new clarity settle under his ribs: the secret menu wasn't only about messages on plates. It was a logistics channel. A pipeline.

Food as cover. Service as timing. Holds as control. Cameras as enforcement. Runners as couriers. And somewhere behind unmarked doors, an administrative layer that processed what moved through.

The conspiracy wasn't metaphorical. It had equipment.

Dumas returned, refilling a container, his eyes never lifting. "You saw a case," he murmured.

Connor kept his expression flat. "No."

Dumas's mouth tightened. "Good," he said again, the way he'd said it before when Connor denied seeing the bare hand. Then, after a beat: "That wasn't for the kitchen."

Connor's fingers tightened on his tweezers and relaxed. "Then what is it."

Dumas paused his towel for the smallest fraction, a rare break in his economy. He didn't look at Connor, but his voice lowered further, as if even the refrigerators could listen.

"It's why the stars matter," Dumas said.

Connor felt his throat go dry. "Money."

Dumas's towel resumed moving. "Not just money," he said. "Access. People come here because they can be seen here, and because they can't be seen doing what they do upstairs."

Connor's mind flashed to OFF MENU. NO RECORD.

Dumas continued, careful, each word measured. "A good restaurant is cover. A great one is a shield. Everyone assumes the worst thing that happens in a kitchen is a meltdown." His mouth tightened. "That's convenient."

Connor wanted to ask about Luc. About erasure. About where people went when they were removed but not fired. He didn't ask. The questions burned anyway, contained behind his teeth.

Dumas shifted the tray and moved away, then added one more sentence without turning back. "If you're smart," he murmured, "you'll keep thinking it's about plates."

Connor kept working, but his attention sharpened into something colder than paranoia. Paranoia was scattered. This felt like pattern recognition clicking into place.

He watched the next sequence with new eyes.

A runner arrived at the tape line and murmured "Now" without being taught by the kitchen. Sofia held up one finger. The hold lasted exactly long enough for a suited man behind Hale to glance toward the pass and then toward his own watch. Not a kitchen watch-check. A synchronization.

Sofia dropped her finger. "Walk."

A plate moved.

Connor felt it then: timing wasn't only about food. It was about aligning multiple rooms. Multiple transactions. Holds weren't just culinary control. They were schedule control. They created gaps, windows, moments where doors could open and close without colliding with visible service.

A courier system hidden inside a Michelin choreography.

Another black case appeared an hour later, carried by someone Connor didn't recognize at all, not front of house, not back of house. Plain clothes, calm posture, eyes that didn't linger on food. He didn't come past the threshold. He handed the case to the slick-haired manager, who handed it to Sofia, who carried it again to the administrative door.

The building swallowed it.

Connor's stomach tightened. Two cases in one night meant volume. Not a one-off. Not an anomaly. A schedule.

And the plates, coded and counted, were the language that signaled when the schedule moved.

Connor's own phone buzzed in his pocket. Not the burner, which he'd left at home, off. His real phone, set to silent. The vibration felt obscene, a human interruption in a room built to erase noise.

He didn't pull it out. He didn't look.

But the vibration came again, then stopped.

A message waiting. A temptation offered.

He kept his face clean and his hands moving, but his mind opened a new folder labeled with a cold internal word: leverage.

Someone had already shown they could reach him at home. You looked.

Now, with cases moving through unmarked doors and coded plates controlling timing, Connor could see the shape of the trap.

If he responded, he'd be pulled into the underside willingly.

If he didn't, he was still in it, because he could now recognize what he was watching.

Sofia returned to his border near the end of the push. Her face was clean, but her eyes were sharper than before, as if she'd made a decision she didn't like.

"They're going to ask for a plate that isn't food," she murmured.

Connor's pulse jumped, then flattened under discipline. "A message."

Sofia didn't correct him this time. She only said, "And this time, it won't be for upstairs."

Connor felt cold spread in his chest. "Then who."

Sofia looked past him, toward the pass lamps, toward Renaud's centered stillness, toward the corridor mouth where Hale stood like a visible answer.

"Someone wants to prove," she said quietly, "that they can make the kitchen carry anything."

Connor's throat tightened. "And if we refuse."

Sofia's jaw ticked once. "Then they'll find the weak part and call it an accident."

She stepped back, already sealing her expression into function again. “Send clean,” she said, louder now, for the room. “No variation.”

Connor nodded once. “Heard.”

He returned to his plates, but the world had shifted. The secret menu had become more than rumor and coded dots. It was a machine inside the machine, using Michelin perfection as camouflage for movement that had nothing to do with dinner.

And Connor understood the most dangerous thing about uncovering it.

Once you saw the system clearly, you weren’t just a cook anymore.

You were a witness.

Chapter 15

Ghosts in the Kitchen

The next morning, the kitchen smelled too clean.

Bleach and citrus clung to the air as if someone had tried to disinfect a memory. Connor arrived early enough that the alley behind L'Étoile Noire was still dim, the city not yet loud enough to hide footsteps. He paused at the service door with his palm against cold metal, listening for the building's mood the way he always did now.

Inside, stainless reflected the overhead lights in tired bands. The camera above the back hallway door blinked its small blue heartbeat. Someone could watch later even if they weren't watching now. That thought lived in Connor's body like a second spine.

Garde manger was already set. Dumas's grid was in place: containers squared, labels outward, towels folded into thirds with a precision that looked less like pride and more like a ritual meant to keep panic from leaking through fingertips.

Connor washed his hands. Soap, rinse, dry once. He tied his apron and arranged his tools into the exact order he'd left them.

Dumas didn't look up. "You're early."

"It's what we do," Connor said.

Dumas's towel moved once across steel, erasing a mark that hadn't been there. "It's what they like," he replied, the same correction as before.

They worked in silence for a stretch that could have been calm if it weren't so deliberate. Knife on board. Plastic lids snapping. The refrigerator hum steady enough to pretend it was safety.

Connor kept seeing last night in fragments: black cases moving through the administrative door; holds that weren't culinary; a suited man's watch-check timed to Sofia's finger; the phrase OFF MENU. NO RECORD; Sofia's quiet warning that someone wanted a plate that wasn't food.

And underneath it all, something else, older than last night's operations. The words Dumas had dropped like a coin into water: If you're smart, you'll keep thinking it's about plates.

Connor had tried to keep thinking that. He had failed.

At ten, Sofia arrived. She moved through the kitchen with her usual economy, but the strain showed in the way her eyes checked the corridor mouth more often than necessary, as if the shadow there had started to move even when Hale wasn't standing inside it. She scanned stations without stopping until she reached garde manger's border.

Her gaze flicked over Connor's alignment, then lingered on his face.

"Sleep," she said.

"Some," Connor replied.

"Keep it that way." Then, quieter, "No carries unless I call you."

"Heard."

Sofia left without another word, her presence tightening the room as it always did. But today there was a current of something else too, something Connor couldn't categorize at first because it didn't feel like pressure. Pressure was immediate. This felt like history.

It surfaced at family meal.

The room was nearly silent, as it had been for weeks, but the silence had changed texture. People ate with their eyes down and their shoulders slightly raised, as if waiting for an impact that never came. Near the wall, a rotating pair of watchers sat with coffee. They didn't eat. Their gaze moved across faces, hands, exits.

Connor kept his focus on his tray, chewing without tasting.

A commis at the far end of the table whispered something to another commis. Not loud enough to carry. Not meant for anyone outside their small orbit. But in this kitchen, whispering was a flare.

The second commis's eyes darted toward the corridor mouth, then snapped back down. His fingers tightened around a plastic fork.

Connor heard it anyway, not the words, but the change in breath. He tracked it the way he tracked timing: a deviation.

Dumas leaned in slightly, still facing his food. "They're talking about Luc again," he murmured.

Connor didn't let his expression change. The name still did something, even now, even after he'd learned to walk past the blank rectangle of metal where Luc's nameplate used to be without looking for it.

"Who," Connor asked, careful. Not curious. Functional.

Dumas's mouth tightened. "Kids," he said. "People who weren't here long enough to learn the right fear."

Connor kept his gaze down. "What are they saying."

Dumas paused a beat. “They’re saying he didn’t quit.”

Connor’s throat tightened as if the words had edges. Luc had been spoken about in absence the way a cut was spoken about in a kitchen: not directly, only in consequence.

“He was erased,” Connor said, quiet.

Dumas’s towel moved once, slow, like a sentence being wiped from a board. “That’s what everyone says,” he replied. “Erased sounds tidy. Makes it feel like there’s a system and the system is predictable.”

Connor didn’t like the cold that settled under his ribs. Predictability was the only thing that made this place survivable.

Dumas continued, still not looking at him. “You know why they call it a brigade,” he said.

Connor didn’t answer. The word brigade had already revealed itself as something more than a kitchen metaphor.

“Because people disappear in brigades,” Dumas said. “And the work continues.”

Connor’s jaw tightened. He kept it still.

Across the table, one of the whispering commis laughed once, too small and nervous to be joy. The other commis didn't laugh back. He went pale.

Dumas set his fork down. "Listen," he murmured. "Don't ask them. Don't correct them. Don't be seen hearing it."

Connor's eyes stayed on his tray. "Why bring it up."

Dumas's mouth moved in a way that wasn't quite a smile. "Because rumors are how kitchens talk to themselves," he said. "When they're not allowed to speak."

Service prep began, and with it, the building's denial returned: grids, labels, wiped steel, an immaculate performance built to convince everyone that nothing had ever happened here that couldn't be explained by heat and discipline.

But once Dumas had named it, Connor started hearing the past in places he hadn't before.

A dishwasher avoided a certain corner near the dish pit, rerouting his steps without thinking, like there was an invisible spill he didn't want to step through. A runner hesitated at the corridor mouth, then corrected himself with a stiffening of posture that looked less like deference and more like memory. Even on hot side, Antoine moved with a tightness that didn't belong only to last week's tension. He looked like a man carrying something that never got lighter.

Connor kept to his station, hands busy, face clean.

Still, the rumors threaded their way into the kitchen's permitted language: fragments passed in stainless reflections, in two-word exchanges that looked like function.

"He went downstairs."

"No, upstairs."

"They took his knives."

"He left them."

"They didn't let him leave."

Each fragment disappeared as soon as it was spoken, erased by the next call, the next wipe, the next lid snapped shut.

Connor didn't participate. He didn't ask. But the building had trained him to read patterns, and rumors had patterns too. The same names floated through them, always the same gravitational centers: Luc, Renaud, Hale.

And another name, said less often, in voices that dropped lower when it surfaced.

Marcus.

Not Hale. Marcus. Like a person, not a title. Like the shadow at the corridor mouth had once had edges you could touch.

At four-thirty, Renaud arrived.

Centered. Immaculate. Unreadable. He moved along the line with quiet authority, his gaze cutting across stations, finding deviation without emotion. When his eyes passed over Connor, Connor felt the familiar weight, but there was something else today too: not softness, not concern, but calculation. Like a man deciding which pieces on a board could be moved without revealing the hand that moved them.

Renaud said nothing and went to the pass.

At five, Hale appeared at the corridor mouth. Coat on. Calm like ownership. A suited man stood half a step behind him, posture perfect, eyes roaming. The kitchen's posture shifted around them the way metal shifted around a magnet.

Connor watched in reflection only, the safe way.

The rumor of Luc didn't fit cleanly with the operational facts Connor had seen: coded plates, secret slips, black cases, administrative rooms. Those were mechanisms. Luc was a person. People didn't disappear neatly unless the mechanism was built to handle people.

And this kitchen was built for erasure.

He thought of the prologue story he'd heard in fragments when he first arrived, the myth that the kitchen told itself like a prayer: a dish returned, silence like oxygen removed, a young chef escorted out with his apron still on.

Not fired.

Erased.

Connor had believed then that erasure meant career death. Reputation. Blacklisting. A vanishing from the industry.

Now he wasn't sure.

Service began, and the visible rail rolled out its usual perfection. Tickets fed. Sofia held time without naming holds. Plates walked.

But under the visible choreography, the past kept pressing its fingerprints against the present.

Mid-first push, a junior commis at garde manger reached for a tray and then froze, eyes flicking toward Connor for confirmation he shouldn't need.

Connor gave him none. He shifted his body a fraction, an instruction without words. The commis moved.

Then, so quietly Connor almost missed it, the commis whispered, "Did you hear what happened to Luc?"

Connor's hands didn't stop. He didn't turn his head. He kept placing elements with tweezers, his posture the same blank economy Sofia demanded.

"No," Connor said.

The commis swallowed. "They said he tried to leave with something."

Connor's grip on the tweezers tightened for a fraction, then loosened. "Focus," he said, flat.

The commis nodded too quickly and returned to his work, his face flushing with fear at having spoken at all.

Connor kept plating, but the sentence lodged in him.

He tried to leave with something.

A black case. A slip. A message. Proof. Or maybe just a memory.

Connor remembered Sofia's word from last night: proof. Consistency wasn't for quality. It was for proof.

Proof of what, Antoine had asked earlier in the week, and answered with that cold clarity: proof that Renaud is still the center. Or proof that he isn't.

Connor's mind connected the rumor to the mechanism with a click that felt like a lock turning.

If Luc had tried to leave with something, then the system had responded the only way it knew how: remove the variable. Erase the person. Keep the service moving so the dining room never noticed a human consequence.

Connor looked toward the corridor mouth in stainless reflection and saw Hale's stillness, the suited man's watchful eyes. A clean perimeter around an unclean history.

And suddenly the rumors didn't feel like idle kitchen fear.

They felt like a warning the building couldn't say out loud.

People didn't just get removed for mistakes here.

They got removed for knowing.

A few minutes later, Sofia appeared at Connor's border, her face sealed into function. She didn't look at his plates. She looked into his eyes as if checking for a leak.

"Less," she said.

Connor flattened his expression further. "Heard."

Sofia held his gaze one beat too long, and Connor saw something in it that wasn't instruction. It was a question she couldn't ask: What have you heard?

He gave her nothing. That was the only safe answer.

Sofia's jaw ticked once, hard, then stopped. She leaned closer by a fraction, just enough that her words could hide under refrigeration hum.

"Rumors are how they bait you," she murmured.

Connor's throat tightened. "They."

Sofia's eyes sharpened, a blade unsheathed and immediately put away. "Less," she said again, but quieter now, and the repetition carried urgency. "If you hear Luc's name, you didn't."

Connor nodded once. "Heard."

Sofia straightened and moved away, pulled back into the pass's gravity.

Connor returned to his plates, hands steady, face clean.

But the kitchen had already changed around him. Not in layout. Not in rhythm.

In the way the past had begun to move again, not as a story people told to scare new hires into compliance, but as something active. Something that had unfinished business.

Ghosts in this kitchen weren't metaphors. They were the residue of people who had been erased so completely that only rumors remained.

And if Luc had tried to take something out, Connor realized, then the most dangerous thing he could do now wasn't to ask questions.

It was to become someone who might be tempted to carry proof past the service door.

The whispering commis was named Jules. Connor learned it the way he learned most things in this kitchen: not from introductions, but from necessity.

Jules worked two spots down from him at garde manger, young enough that his whites still looked too crisp at the seams, as if they hadn't yet been broken in by repetition. He had fast hands, good instinct for balance, and a habit of glancing sideways when he thought no one was watching. A few hours earlier he'd asked about Luc with a voice that tried to sound casual and failed.

Now he tried to disappear into his station, shoulders lowered, jaw set, as if he could retract the question back into his own throat.

Connor didn't acknowledge him. Acknowledgment was a rope. Rope could be pulled.

Service moved into its first real push with that clean, merciless glide the dining room paid for. Tickets fed. The pass lamps carved the world into a strip of truth. Sofia held time with her finger without ever naming holds. Renaud stayed centered, immaculate, his silence a kind of gravity that kept the entire room in orbit.

And still, the kitchen felt haunted. Not by sounds, but by absences. The way people avoided the dish pit corner. The way runners stiffened at the corridor mouth before remembering to smooth their faces. The way the rotating watchers near the wall didn't eat, didn't smile, didn't belong.

Jules reached for a tray of herbs and his hand hesitated a fraction too long.

Not a mistake. Not even a delay anyone would notice. Just the smallest stutter, as if his body had heard a word his mind was trying not to hear.

Connor caught it anyway. He shifted his own body a fraction, an instruction without looking like one. Move. Keep the rhythm. Don't let yourself become visible.

Jules corrected. His fingers closed on the tray. His posture flattened back into function.

For three minutes, he held it.

Then a runner approached the tape line. Not one Connor recognized as front of house or back of house. Plain black, too-clean hands, posture that didn't show kitchen fatigue. He stopped just outside the stations, not stepping into anyone's territory, and waited.

He didn't speak to Sofia. He didn't look at Renaud. His eyes went directly to Jules.

The runner's mouth barely moved. Connor couldn't hear the words, but he saw Jules's shoulders tighten. A flinch almost, quickly swallowed.

Jules glanced once, instinctively, toward Connor.

It wasn't asking for permission. It was asking whether this was real.

Connor didn't react. He kept his hands moving, portion, place, reset. He made his face blank, cleaner than blank. He refused to be a mirror Jules could read.

The runner lifted two fingers, not like Hale's gesture, but like a smaller imitation of authority. A directive given without raising a voice.

Jules swallowed. He set down the tray with exaggerated care, as if he were trying to prove his hands were steady. He wiped his fingertips on his towel once. Then he stepped back from his station border.

No one spoke. No one looked directly. The kitchen's silence didn't change because of it. Silence here wasn't an absence; it was policy.

Jules walked after the runner down the lane toward the corridor, moving quickly without looking like he was hurrying. His apron was still tied. His towel was still tucked into his waistband. He looked like someone going to fetch an ingredient.

That was the point, Connor realized. Make it look normal. Make it look like function. If it looked like function, the dining room would never feel the ripple. If it looked like function, the rest of the brigade could pretend it wasn't happening.

Sofia's eyes flicked once in Jules's direction, a glance as sharp as a knife tip. Not surprise. Not curiosity. Inventory.

Then her gaze returned to the rail. "Walk," she said quietly, and a plate left the pass as if nothing had changed.

Renaud did not look up.

The line continued.

Connor plated through it, keeping his station clean enough to be believed. He did not turn his head toward the corridor mouth, not fully. He used stainless reflection the way he'd trained himself to: quick, peripheral, deniable.

In the reflection, the runner and Jules reached the corridor threshold. Hale was there, of course, coat on, calm as a locked door. A suited man stood half a step behind him, gaze moving like a camera.

Jules stopped at the threshold as if the air there had weight. The runner murmured again, low, controlled.

Hale didn't speak. He didn't have to. He shifted his gaze from Jules's face to Jules's hands, as if checking for something the way Renaud checked rims.

Then Hale lifted his own two fingers.

Permission. Or selection.

The suited man behind him watched Jules like he was reading a receipt.

Jules's face went paler, but his posture stayed careful. He nodded once, too small to be a refusal, too stiff to be agreement. Then he stepped into the corridor.

The runner followed.

The corridor swallowed them.

The door did not close loudly. It did not need to. The corridor didn't make noise when it ate people.

Connor's hands kept moving. They had to. If his hands hesitated, the machine would notice. If the machine noticed, the machine would record. If the watchers recorded, someone would replay his reaction later and call it a choice.

He plated a cold dish with severe geometry, wiped no rim marks, reset his towel. He sent the plate up. A runner took it without meeting his eyes.

Time passed in a blur of clean actions. Plates left. Plates replaced. The visible service stayed flawless.

But Jules did not come back.

At first, that meant nothing. People left stations all the time. To run upstairs. To fetch something. To be corrected by Sofia in the dry storage corridor. To be pulled into the administrative room for a quiet warning that never officially happened.

Fifteen minutes became thirty.

A ticket rail advanced. A hold appeared without being named and vanished into choreography. Sofia's finger lifted and fell. Renaud's voice said, "Again," once, and a plate disappeared as if it had never existed.

Jules's station remained empty.

No one filled it.

That was what made Connor's stomach tighten. In a kitchen this disciplined, nothing stayed unassigned. An empty station was a wound left open.

Yet no one moved to cover. No commis slid over. No senior chef barked an order. The machine adjusted around the absence as if the absence had been planned.

Connor found himself compensating without being told. His own output increased by small degrees. He didn't rush. He shaved seconds from movements, cut corners out of corners, created time from nothing.

The kitchen accepted it without acknowledgment.

That was how it worked. The brigade didn't mourn. It redistributed load.

At the end of the push, when the rail thinned and people began that mid-service wipe-down that erased strain before it could become visible, Dumas drifted into Connor's orbit with a tray refill. He set it down with his usual quiet precision.

His eyes never lifted. His voice was low, hidden under the refrigeration hum. "Stop looking for him."

Connor kept his gaze on his hands. "I'm not."

Dumas's towel moved once across steel. "Good," he said, and the word carried no comfort. Only instruction. "Because he's not lost."

Connor's pulse bumped once. He pressed it flat. "Where did he go."

Dumas paused for the smallest fraction. In this kitchen, any pause was a confession. He resumed wiping. "He got taken off the board," he said.

"Fired," Connor asked, careful. A neutral word.

Dumas's mouth tightened. "No," he replied. "Firing leaves paper."

Connor felt cold settle under his ribs. "Then what."

Dumas didn't answer directly. He never did. He moved a container a millimeter, corrected an alignment that hadn't been wrong, then leaned in enough that his voice could hide inside the fan noise.

"He asked the wrong question to the wrong person," Dumas murmured. "And he did it loud enough that someone decided to make an example quietly."

Connor's throat tightened. "He asked about Luc."

Dumas's towel stilled. Not for long. Just long enough that Connor knew he'd hit a nerve.

"Less," Dumas said, echoing Sofia without meaning to. Then he corrected his own tone, making it flatter. "You didn't hear him ask anything."

Connor's fingers tightened on his tweezers and loosened. "I didn't."

Dumas continued wiping, one pass, erase, one pass, erase. "That's how it happens," he said. "No yelling. No scene. Just… reassignment."

Reassignment. A clean word for something dirty.

Connor kept his eyes down. "Where."

Dumas's breath came out controlled. "Not upstairs," he said. "Not the dining room. Somewhere the cameras already know how to forget."

Connor's skin prickled. The administrative room. The corridor network. Unmarked doors. Black cases. "The paper room."

Dumas didn't confirm. He didn't deny. He simply said, "Back to work."

Sofia's voice cut across the line. "Garde manger, two on twelve."

Connor responded automatically. "Oui, Chef."

He executed the next plates with even more care, as if perfect food could protect him from imperfect consequences. His mind, however, had begun to map a new kind of system.

In the prologue myth, the young chef had been escorted out with his apron still on. Not fired. Erased.

He had thought it meant career death.

Now he had watched Jules walk away in an apron and not return, and the kitchen had kept moving with the same indifferent precision it used to refire a dish.

A quiet disappearance wasn't an interruption here. It was part of the choreography.

Near the end of service, when the dining room's noise softened into that expensive afterglow and the kitchen began to thin its motion again, Connor caught sight of the corridor mouth in stainless reflection.

Hale was still there.

The suited man had rotated out. Another had taken his place, half a step behind, same posture, different face. Eyes that didn't eat.

Hale's gaze drifted across the line, and for a brief moment it landed in Connor's direction. Not warmly. Not even directly. More like a sensor passing over a surface.

Connor kept his face clean.

Hale's gaze moved on.

In the space Jules had occupied, a new commis appeared without announcement, sliding into the empty station as if he'd been there all along. He didn't introduce himself. He didn't look around. He placed his tools into a grid and began working with the same disciplined silence, like a replacement part installed in a machine that couldn't afford to remember what it had removed.

Connor realized then what Sofia had meant when she'd warned him about rumors.

Rumors weren't just bait.

They were a test. A way to see who flinched, who asked, who looked too hard at an empty space.

Jules had looked.

And someone had decided to let the kitchen know, without ever saying it out loud, that looking had a cost.

Connor kept plating until the last ticket cleared, until the pass lamps went dark, until the stainless could pretend it had never reflected fear.

But as he cleaned his station, aligning lids and facing labels outward like a ritual against chaos, he couldn't stop seeing Jules's back disappearing into the corridor.

Apron tied. Hands empty.

The kind of disappearance that left no record.

The kind that turned a person into a rumor fast enough that tomorrow, someone at family meal would whisper his name the way they whispered Luc's.

And the kitchen would do what it always did.

It would keep moving.

Connor left after close with the kitchen's routines still clinging to him like a smell that wouldn't wash out.

Stations were scrubbed into denial. Lids aligned. Labels faced outward. The pass lamps went dark, but the strip of heat they'd carved into the night still lived under his skin. When he untied his apron, he did it carefully, as if the knot itself could be read later.

He didn't look toward the space where Jules had worked.

Looking was how people became stories.

In the locker corridor, fluorescent light flattened faces into the same exhausted mask. Connor changed without lingering. His hands moved with the same economy he used at garde manger: remove jacket, fold, stow. No wasted motion. No pauses that could look like thought.

He caught himself turning his head toward the blank rectangle on the locker door where Luc's nameplate used to be. The metal looked newer there, as if the rest of the surface had aged around an absence. Connor corrected his gaze away, quickly enough to feel like a mistake.

The absence was the point. Not to erase a person entirely, because that was impossible. To erase them from the place where proof lived.

He stepped out into the alley, and the night air hit him with damp concrete and bleach. Even outside, the building felt like it watched. He walked fast without looking fast and didn't take the most direct route home.

Halfway down the block, he used a dark shop window to check his reflection and the street behind him. No one close. No face repeated. No suit without shine. The city offered its normal noise: a car door, a laugh, distant traffic. The normal noise didn't soothe him. It felt like cover.

He reached his apartment, locked the door softly, and stood in the entryway with his shoes still on, listening.

Nothing.

The silence pressed against him like a room waiting to be used.

He went straight to the kitchen drawer and stared at it for a beat too long before opening it. The burner phone sat where he'd left it, inert and harmless-looking among forks and spoons, as if it belonged there.

You looked.

The message hadn't changed, but he had. The text now felt less like a taunt and more like an operating principle. In this world, attention was a form of trespassing. It didn't matter if you acted. Looking was enough.

He closed the drawer and washed his hands. Soap, rinse, dry once. Then again, as if repetition could remove an idea. When he finally lay down, sleep came in thin strips, interrupted by the sensation that something had moved in the dark, not in the room but in the system.

In the morning he arrived early enough that the alley was still quiet. The service entrance smelled freshly rinsed, citrus trying to pretend it was cleanliness. Connor paused with his palm on the metal door and listened for the building's mood.

Inside, the kitchen lights were on in their partial state. Stainless looked tired. The new camera above the back hallway door blinked its blue heartbeat steadily.

Garde manger was set, but the station two spots down from Connor's was different.

Jules's grid was gone.

Not messy, not abandoned. Gone in the same way a knife disappeared from a magnet strip when someone wanted it to look like it had never been there. No towel folded into thirds at his edge. No container labeled in his handwriting. No tiny idiosyncrasies that marked a person's habits. The steel at that border was too clean, as if someone had wiped it more than necessary.

A new commis stood there already, shoulders lowered, posture cautious, hands moving with practiced silence. He didn't look around. He didn't look at Connor. He kept his eyes on his prep as if eye contact could be considered a claim.

Connor didn't ask his name.

Names were attachments.

Dumas was at the far end, of course, towel moving in single passes, erasing marks that hadn't existed. He glanced up once, and his eyes flicked toward the new commis, then to Connor, and then away again.

Inventory complete.

Connor washed his hands. Soap, rinse, dry once. He set his tools into his grid and began prep. Knife on board, precise. Portion, align, reset.

The new commis moved well, maybe too well. The hands were trained. The station looked like it had always belonged to him. That was the point too. Replace the part and let the machine claim continuity.

At family meal, the silence had turned thicker. People ate fast, eyes down. Salt remained untouched in the center of the table, a small unused comfort.

The rotating watchers sat near the wall with coffee, not eating. Different face from yesterday. Same posture. Eyes that counted exits as if exits were the only real menu.

Connor kept his gaze on his tray. Across from him, a pastry commis started to speak, then stopped and swallowed the words. A runner's fork paused halfway to his mouth, then continued as if nothing had happened. The whole room seemed to practice not having thoughts.

Dumas sat beside Connor and didn't touch the salt. His voice, when it came, was low enough to hide under the scrape of plastic trays.

"His locker's empty," Dumas murmured.

Connor chewed without tasting. He didn't look up. "Whose."

Dumas's towel wasn't with him at the table, but his fingers still made wiping motions against his thigh, a muscle memory of erasure. "Don't," he said, and the word came out sharper than usual.

Connor kept his face clean. "Heard."

Dumas exhaled through his nose and lowered his voice further. "They moved his name already," he murmured. "Off the list."

"What list," Connor asked, carefully neutral, as if he were asking about inventory.

Dumas didn't answer directly. He never did. "The one that matters," he said. "Schedules. Vendor sign-in. Staff meal headcount. The things that make you exist on paper."

Connor felt a coldness slide down his spine. Existence as a column in a spreadsheet. A name on a clipboard by the service entrance. The camera's blue heartbeat recording a hallway, not for safety, for verification.

If your name came off the list, what were you.

A rumor.

Dumas leaned in just enough that his words could disappear into the refrigerator hum. "You saw him go," he said. "So your head wants to keep him alive. That's a trap."

Connor's jaw tightened. "A trap for who."

Dumas's eyes stayed on his tray. "For you," he said. "Because you'll want to prove it. Proving it is the first step to carrying something out."

Carrying something out. Like Luc, if the rumors were true.

Connor set his fork down, then picked it back up because stopping looked like reaction. "Did he steal," Connor asked. A functional word for a dirty question.

Dumas's mouth tightened. "He talked," he said. "He asked." Then, after a beat, "And he looked like he wanted to be brave."

Connor felt the kitchen around them, the whole brigade pretending to be only a brigade. "Brave," Connor said quietly.

Dumas's fingers pressed into his thigh, wiping a nonexistent smear. "Brave is what people call it when they want to die for something," he murmured. "In here, it's just sloppy."

The word landed hard. Sloppy. The same insult reserved for a sauce that had split or a rim with a fingerprint.

Connor swallowed. “So what happens to him.”

Dumas didn’t look at him. “He becomes a lesson,” he said. “Or he becomes nothing. Depends on what they need.”

Who needed. Who benefited. Antoine’s instruction surfaced again, cold and steady.

Connor forced his voice to stay flat. “Do people come back.”

Dumas’s pause was small, but it was a pause, and that made it loud.

“Sometimes,” Dumas said finally. “Not to the line.”

Connor pictured a door opening in the corridor network, a bare hand taking something without touching the rim. The administrative room smelling like paper. Black cases carried through without tickets. A logistics channel disguised as service.

People didn’t come back to the line because the line was where witnesses stood under lamps.

Dumas pushed his tray away as if he’d eaten enough. He hadn’t. Hunger didn’t matter. “Don’t say his name," he murmured. "Don't think his name where it can change your face."

Connor knew what Dumas meant. The watchers didn't need your words. They needed your microreactions. Your pupils. The fraction of a second where you flinched when an empty space was mentioned.

Service prep began, and with it, the kitchen resumed its routine performance of normality. Sofia arrived midmorning, moving with her usual silent economy, but Connor saw her eyes scan the room the way you scanned a plate for contamination.

She stopped at garde manger's border. Her gaze flicked over Connor's alignment, then moved, quick and clinical, to the station where Jules had been.

No change in her face. No pause.

That was what made Connor's stomach tighten. Sofia had seen the absence and refused to acknowledge it, which meant she had been aware before Connor was. Either because she'd authorized it, or because she was forced to pretend she had..

Her eyes returned to Connor.

"Less," she said, as if the word could compress him into safety.

"Heard," Connor replied.

Sofia leaned closer by a fraction, close enough that the refrigerators could swallow her words. "Don't let the empty space pull your eyes," she murmured. "That's how they measure you."

Connor kept his gaze on his hands. "They," he said, barely moving his mouth.

Sofia's jaw ticked once. A hard, controlled tell. "You don't need a pronoun," she said. "You need discipline."

Connor nodded once. "Yes, Chef."

She straightened and moved away, her orbit tightening around the pass even though service was still hours away. As she went, Connor felt the building's attention settle. A kitchen wasn't only a room. It was an organism with senses.

By afternoon, the proof of Jules's erasure spread the way heat spread: quietly, inevitable.

A clipboard by the service entrance held a staff list. Connor had never cared about it before. Now he saw it the way he saw a rail of tickets. Names in clean blocks. Stations. Times.

Jules's name wasn't there.

No blank line. No strike-through. Not even a corrected typo.

He had been removed as if he'd never been assigned.

A runner he recognized from front of house passed by and stopped near garde manger as if to ask for something. Instead, in a voice too casual to be true, he said, "We're down one today?"

Connor didn't look up. He didn't answer. He continued cutting.

The runner lingered for a beat, then moved on, as if he'd gotten what he came for: confirmation that the question could exist without consequence, or that it couldn't.

Connor understood then that erasure wasn't only about making someone disappear. It was about making everyone else complicit in the disappearance by forcing them to behave as if nothing had changed.

If you acknowledged the absence, you became a problem. If you didn't, you became part of the mechanism.

Service started. Renaud arrived centered and immaculate. Hale took his place at the corridor mouth like a shadow with a title. A suited man stood half a step behind him, eyes roaming, recording.

Tickets fed. Sofia held time with her finger. Plates walked.

The machine moved, as it always did.

Connor executed at garde manger with the cold precision that kept him off the radar. Portion, place, no rim marks, reset. He didn't look at the empty space where Jules had stood yesterday, because it wasn't empty anymore. It held a replacement part, working silently, as if he'd always belonged.

That was the fear of erasure, Connor realized. Not death. Not dismissal. Something cleaner.

To be removed so thoroughly that the system didn't even have to lie about it.

It simply stopped including you in the version of reality it printed.

Mid-service, a runner approached the tape line and murmured, "Now." Sofia held up one finger. Hold. Two beats. Then: "Walk."

The suited man behind Hale glanced at his watch.

Synchronization.

Connor felt the kitchen's hidden rail running beneath the visible one, and he understood how erasure fit into it. A person could become a package. A name could become a variable to be removed. A witness could become a liability.

And in a place built on perfect control, liability didn't get argued with.

It got edited out.

As Connor sent a plate up, he caught Hale's gaze in stainless reflection. Not directly at him. Not warm. Not even interested.

Just a sensor passing over a surface, checking for movement that didn't belong.

Connor kept his face clean, his hands steady, and his attention narrowed to the only safe thing left: execution.

But inside him, a new calculation formed with cold clarity.

If Jules could vanish overnight, and Luc could become a rumor, then the only thing keeping Connor on the list was usefulness.

Not talent. Not effort.

Usefulness to the right hands.

And the moment his usefulness conflicted with someone else's control, the kitchen wouldn't yell.

It wouldn't argue.

It would simply keep moving, and Connor would become an empty space someone was trained not to look at.

Chapter 16

Breaking Point

The sabotage began the way everything here began: as something small enough to deny.

Connor felt it before he saw it, a subtle drag in the kitchen's rhythm, like a heartbeat catching on the wrong beat. The line was set, stations aligned, labels facing outward, towels folded into thirds. The visible service should have been clean.

But the air had teeth.

At four-fifteen, Sofia did her walk-through without stopping to correct anything obvious. That meant there was nothing obvious to correct, or she was spending her attention elsewhere. Her gaze kept cutting toward the corridor mouth as if it might open on its own. Hale wasn't there yet, but the threshold still felt occupied, as if the building remembered him.

"Felwick," Sofia said when she reached garde manger's border.

Connor's hands stilled for half a fraction and resumed, because even stillness was a tell. "Chef."

"Your mise," she said.

It wasn't a compliment. It was a check for anomalies, for additions that didn't belong. Connor lifted container lids in the order he always did. Herbs. Micro leaves. Chilled garnishes. Acid gel. Proteins pre-sliced to exact weight. Everything looked right.

Sofia's eyes tracked the sequence. Inventory, not admiration.

"Keep it boring," she murmured.

"Heard."

Her jaw ticked, then went still again. "Tonight, boring keeps you on the list."

She left without another word. Connor watched her move away in stainless reflection and caught the way she avoided the station two spots down, the one that had belonged to Jules. The replacement commis worked with his head down, too smooth, too ready. A part installed cleanly.

At five, the corridor mouth gained weight. Hale appeared as if the building had called him. Coat on, posture relaxed, calm that rewrote the room. Behind him, a suited man stood half a step back, eyes moving in slow, methodical sweeps. Rotating watchers, rotating faces. The same gaze.

Renaud arrived a minute later, centered and immaculate, jacket crisp, expression unreadable. He moved to the pass without acknowledging anyone, and the kitchen tightened around him, the way it always did. When he glanced toward garde manger, Connor felt the weight land and move on.

Service began.

Tickets fed. Plates walked. The dining room's hum stayed behind the wall like something expensive being kept alive. Connor executed with the drilled precision that had become his bloodstream: portion, place, no rim marks, reset. He didn't speak unless spoken to. He didn't look toward the corridor mouth directly. He used reflections the way he used knives.

The first sign of sabotage was scent.

Not smoke, not burning. Something sharper. Metallic and wrong, like electricity or pennies. It cut through the usual palette of cold station aromas: citrus, herbs, chilled cream. Connor's nose flared once before he forced it neutral.

He checked his station again, slow enough to look normal, fast enough not to look like panic. No spilled sanitizer. No open chemical container. No stray towel soaked in something it shouldn't be. The smell wasn't from him.

A runner crossed behind garde manger and Connor caught it again, stronger as the runner passed. The runner's hands were too clean, posture too controlled. Not front of house, not kitchen. Another courier-body in restaurant clothing. The runner didn't look at Connor, but the air around him carried that metallic bite.

Sofia's voice cut across the line. "Hold."

One finger raised at the pass.

The hold lasted two beats too long.

Connor's eyes flicked, in reflection, to the suited man behind Hale. Watch-check, precise. Synchronization.

Then Sofia dropped her finger. "Walk."

The hold vanished into choreography, but Connor felt the pressure in his teeth. Holds weren't for food tonight. Holds were for timing something else.

On the next push, a ticket printed for garde manger that didn't fit the menu.

Table twelve, allergy note: no citrus.

Connor paused internally. Citrus was everywhere on his station. Citrus was how the kitchen kept brightness controlled, how it made precision taste like relief. But allergy notes were normal.

What wasn't normal was that the note was in a different font weight, as if the printer had hesitated. As if the system had been touched.

Connor didn't look up. "Heard," he said to no one, because he couldn't say what he was hearing. He rebuilt the dish with substitutions he knew were safe: herb oil instead of citrus acid, a different gel, a cut of protein dressed in salt and controlled fat. No rim marks. He sent it.

Two minutes later, the plate came back.

Not returned from the dining room in the dramatic way the kitchen mythologized. It didn't come with a server holding it like guilt. It came through the pass, slid back into the lamp strip by a runner Connor didn't recognize. The runner's face was blank, but his eyes were alert in a way that belonged to people who watched consequences for sport.

The plate was untouched.

Renaud didn't raise his voice. He didn't need to. He stared down at the dish as if it were a crime scene. Sofia's posture tightened beside him, her hands still.

Connor watched in stainless reflection. He felt the entire kitchen's oxygen thin.

Renaud didn't ask who plated it, not yet. He looked at the allergy note, then at the dish, then at the rim.

His eyes narrowed by a fraction.

Then he said, quiet and flat, "Citrus."

Sofia's head turned sharply toward the plate. The rim was clean. No smears. No obvious mistake. But under the lamp heat, the dish gave off a faint brightness that didn't belong to herb oil.

Connor's stomach dropped with cold clarity.

Someone had dosed something.

Not enough to leave a mark. Enough to trigger a reaction in someone who knew what citrus did to their own mouth. Or enough to make a diner claim it. Or enough to let the kitchen's secret rail label the dish compromised.

Renaud's gaze lifted, not to Sofia, not to Connor. To the runner who had brought it back.

"What table," Renaud asked.

The runner answered instantly, as if rehearsed. "Twelve, Chef."

Sofia's voice stayed controlled. "We have the allergy note."

Renaud didn't move. "Do we."

It wasn't a question. It was an accusation aimed at the system itself.

The printer spit again. Another ticket for table twelve, same dish, no allergy note this time. Clean. Official. As if the first had never existed.

Connor felt the shape of it, the way he'd felt coded plates being erased by refires. Evidence could be edited. Paper could be made to disappear. The kitchen was a place where the truth could be printed and unprinted.

Sofia stepped closer to the rail and plucked the new ticket with fingers that didn't tremble. She stared at it for one beat too long.

Then she said, softly, "Again."

Renaud's eyes cut to her. A correction with no volume.

"Again," Sofia repeated, the word turning into obedience. She slid the returned plate off the lamp strip as if removing a body.

Connor's hands kept moving at his station, but his pulse tried to climb into his throat. He forced it down. He couldn't be seen reacting. Not by the watchers. Not by Hale.

A new ticket came for garde manger, different table. Allergy note: no nuts.

Nuts weren't on that dish.

Connor's fingers tightened around his tweezers and loosened. He scanned his station again. No nuts. No nut oil. Nothing.

Unless someone had put it there.

He lifted the lid on his herb oil and smelled it. Green, clean. He lifted the lid on his neutral oil and smelled it.

A faint sweetness, wrong.

He didn't know if it was nut or if his fear had given his senses imagination, but imagination could get you killed in a room that punished deviation.

He didn't look up. He reached under the counter and pulled a fresh bottle, sealed, one he hadn't opened yet. He broke the seal with controlled hands, poured into a clean container, labeled it in block letters without shaking.

Sofia appeared at his border as if summoned by the motion.

"What," she murmured, eyes on his hands.

Connor kept his voice flat. "Replacing oil."

Sofia's gaze flicked to the open container, to the sealed bottle, to his label. Her jaw ticked.

"Why."

The word carried danger. A why made a story.

Connor chose function. "Contamination risk."

Sofia's eyes sharpened. In another world, that answer would have been prudence. Here, it was a claim.

She leaned in by a fraction, voice low enough to live under refrigeration. "Don't start cleaning things that don't look dirty," she murmured. "That's how they frame you."

Connor's stomach tightened. "Chef, I—"

"Less," Sofia snapped, not loud, but the tone cut. Then, softer again, "Execute. Don't investigate."

The phrase landed like a cuff.

Connor nodded once. "Heard."

Sofia returned to the pass. Connor kept building plates, now with the fresh oil, now double-checking every component without looking like he was double-checking. He moved carefully enough that he felt slow, but he knew he wasn't. He was just aware.

Then the sabotage stopped being subtle.

A runner miscalled a table at the pass. Not by one number. By a different course entirely. A hot dish walked with a cold garnish. A cold dish walked with a sauce that belonged elsewhere. The kind of mismatch that didn't happen in a kitchen like this unless the machine had been fed bad input.

Renaud's head turned by a fraction. His eyes went to Sofia.

Sofia held her posture. "Refire," she said immediately.

Renaud didn't answer. His gaze moved past her to the corridor mouth.

Hale stood still, calm as ownership. The suited man behind him watched the pass like a scoreboard.

Sofia's finger rose. "Hold."

The hold was longer this time, and it wasn't culinary. It was damage control. It was Sofia trying to build a wall out of seconds.

Renaud said, very quietly, "Who touched the rail."

No one answered. The kitchen didn't breathe.

Connor felt the temptation to look at the replacement commis, the one installed where Jules had been. He didn't. Looking was how they measured you.

Sofia dropped her finger. "Walk," she said, too smooth, too fast.

The line moved again, but the machine had been wounded. Not in food. In trust.

A server appeared with a plate in his hands and his face too pale. He hovered at the threshold like he'd been taught to fear the pass. He didn't step in. He held the plate as if it might explode.

Sofia went to him, took the plate, brought it under the lamps.

Untouched. Again.

Renaud stared at it. The dish was correct. It was perfect. It was exactly what it should be, down to negative space.

And still it had been returned.

No complaint. No words. Just rejection.

Renaud's eyes moved across the rim. Clean. No rim marks. No fingerprints.

He lifted his gaze, and this time he looked down the line, slow and surgical, as if searching for the single point where a system could be made to fail without leaving a visible handprint.

His eyes passed over Connor.

Connor kept his face clean. He kept his hands moving. He made himself boring.

But he could feel the room's attention tighten around him anyway, not because he had done something wrong, but because sabotage didn't need guilt.

It needed a target.

Sofia's voice came, quiet and controlled, at the edge of the pass. "Chef, we can refire."

Renaud didn't blink. "We can," he agreed.

Then, softer, so soft it felt like a knife sliding into a seam, "Or we can stop pretending it's an accident."

The silence that followed was absolute. Not kitchen silence. Something heavier.

Hale didn't move.

The suited man behind him didn't look away.

And Connor understood, with cold certainty, what Sofia had warned him about weeks ago, when the secret menu stopped being plates and started being people.

Tonight, someone was proving they could make the kitchen carry anything.

Including blame.

Renaud's last sentence didn't float in the air. It sank.

Or we can stop pretending it's an accident.

The line kept moving because it had to, because motion was the only acceptable answer in this kitchen. But the motion had changed. It wasn't just execution now. It was theater under threat, hands performing normality while everyone listened for the next deviation like it might be a gunshot.

Sofia pulled the returned plate off the lamps with controlled fingers and slid it onto the refire stack without letting her eyes meet anyone's for too long. She spoke into the rail with the same tone she used for timing: flat, functional.

"Refire, table seventeen. Full course. Now."

A chorus of "Oui" moved through the line like a rehearsed confession.

Connor didn't look at the dining room. He didn't look at Hale. He kept his hands at garde manger and rebuilt what he'd already built, component by component, as if repetition could turn suspicion into math.

But suspicion wasn't math. Suspicion was a shape that looked for a body to fit.

The first refire went out. Then another ticket printed, then another. It should have stabilized. It didn't.

A second plate came back, this one from a table that hadn't ordered an allergy restriction. It returned untouched, no note, no explanation. A third returned with a single word scribbled by front of house in a tight, irritated hand: “Off.”

Off what, Connor thought. Off by a grain of salt? Off by a degree? Or off in the way a message was off, a code misread by someone who didn’t read it the way the kitchen did?

Renaud took the third returned plate and stared at it under the lamps until the heat began to dull the edges of the cold components.

He didn’t ask, “Who plated this?”

Not yet.

That was what made everyone’s throats tighten. The question was ritual. The question was a blade. If he wasn’t using it, it meant he was using something else.

He turned his head slightly toward Sofia. His voice was quiet enough to belong only to the pass.

“Call front,” he said.

Sofia didn’t move at first. For half a beat she held her posture as if she hadn’t heard him, as if her body was trying to decide whether obeying would be safer than resisting. Then she nodded once.

“Heard.”

She stepped away from the pass and walked toward the threshold where front of house hovered like it didn't want to be contaminated by heat. The slick-haired manager appeared as if summoned. His smile was gone. His face looked thin, stretched.

Sofia spoke to him without warmth. Connor couldn't hear the words, but he saw the manager's eyes flick once toward Hale at the corridor mouth before returning to Sofia. A reflex. Permission-seeking.

Sofia's jaw tightened. She leaned closer, her mouth moving in short sentences that looked like commands. The manager nodded too quickly, then turned and vanished toward the dining room.

Sofia came back to the pass, her steps controlled. She didn't look at Connor. She didn't look at anyone. She looked at the rail like it was the only thing in the room that hadn't been compromised.

Renaud's gaze drifted again toward the corridor mouth.

Hale stood in the same place he always stood, coat on, hands relaxed, calm like a room that belonged to him. Behind him, the suited man's eyes moved in slow sweeps, not following plates, following faces. Not timing, attention.

Connor felt the gaze skim past him and tried to make himself smaller without looking like he was making himself smaller. Boring, Sofia had told him. Keep it boring.

Another ticket printed. Allergy note again. This time it wasn't even plausible: "No herbs."

Connor's station was herbs. Micro leaves. Oils. Green precision. The note was absurd, like a joke, except jokes didn't exist here. Absurdity was how sabotage tested your willingness to panic.

Connor didn't say anything. He built a version stripped down to bare structure. Protein, neutral fat, controlled salt, no greenery. A plate that looked like a punishment.

He sent it.

It came back.

Untouched.

Renaud's hand moved once, a small gesture, and the plate slid under the lamps. He examined it the way he examined a rim: not for taste, for violation.

Sofia's finger rose. Hold. The line froze at the edge of motion.

Renaud didn't speak for two beats. Then he said, very quietly, "There's nothing wrong with this."

It wasn't reassurance. It was an indictment. If nothing was wrong with the plate, the wrongness was somewhere else.

The manager returned at a near-run, trying not to look like he was running. He stopped at the threshold, breath controlled, and spoke quickly to Sofia. Sofia listened without letting her face move. Only her eyes sharpened.

Then Sofia turned slightly to Renaud. "Chef," she said.

Renaud didn't look at her. "Speak."

Sofia's voice stayed low. "Table seventeen says the dish tastes like… almonds."

Connor's blood went cold.

Sofia's jaw ticked once as if she'd bitten down on her own anger. "They're claiming contamination."

Renaud finally turned his head, slow, toward Sofia. His eyes weren't angry. They were surgical.

"Claiming," he repeated.

Sofia nodded. "Yes, Chef."

Renaud's gaze returned to the plate. Then to the rail. Then to the ticket printer, which sat there like an innocent mouth.

The suited man behind Hale shifted his weight a fraction, and Connor saw it in reflection: not surprise, not discomfort. Interest. Like someone watching a scenario reach its intended beat.

Renaud's voice cut through the hold. "Walk," he said, and Sofia dropped her finger immediately, obedient even to a word that wasn't hers.

The kitchen resumed motion, but the air had changed again. Almonds. Nuts. Contamination. The word carried legal weight, health weight, reputation weight. The kind of weight that didn't belong to a simple mistake.

Connor thought of the faint sweetness he'd smelled in the neutral oil, wrong. He thought of Sofia warning him not to clean things that didn't look dirty because that's how they frame you. He thought of the way the first citrus allergy note had printed, then vanished as if it had never existed.

Sabotage wasn't just in the food. It was in the record.

Sofia moved off the pass and came straight to garde manger, stopping at Connor's border. She didn't look at his face first. She looked at his containers. His oils. His labels faced outward. His towel folded into thirds.

"What have you replaced," she asked quietly.

Connor kept his voice flat. "Neutral oil. Earlier."

Sofia's eyes narrowed. Not suspicion. Assessment. "Did you tell anyone."

"No, Chef."

Sofia's jaw ticked. "Good," she said, then caught herself and flattened the word into something less comforting. "Fine."

Connor's hands stayed still for half a fraction. He resumed plating. "They're saying almonds."

Sofia's gaze flicked to the corridor mouth, then back. "I heard."

Connor kept his mouth barely moving. "My station doesn't have nuts."

Sofia didn't answer directly. She leaned closer, voice low enough to be eaten by refrigeration. "It doesn't need to," she murmured.

Connor felt his throat tighten. "Then where."

Sofia's eyes snapped to him, sharp. "Less," she said, but the urgency in it wasn't about etiquette. It was about survival. "You don't ask that out loud."

Connor swallowed. "Heard."

Sofia straightened, but she didn't step away yet. Her gaze held on his hands, as if she were trying to memorize whether they shook.

"Someone wants a body," she said softly, and the word body did not mean a person. It meant a target.

Connor's pulse bumped once. "Why me."

Sofia's eyes didn't soften. "Because you're visible," she replied. "Because you've been on specials. Because you've touched the underside and didn't bleed."

Connor forced his face to stay clean. "I didn't carry."

"You were near it," Sofia said. "That's enough."

She stepped back and returned to the pass, sealing her expression into function again.

Connor's station suddenly felt like a stage.

He kept executing. He kept the rims clean. He kept the components aligned. But his mind began running in a different direction, cold and fast. If someone could introduce allergens without leaving obvious marks, then the contamination wasn't accidental. It was injected. And if it was injected, it could be injected anywhere.

Including into a narrative.

Another plate returned. This time, the server actually spoke, voice trembling as if he knew how dangerous words were near the pass.

"They're asking who made it," he said.

The kitchen's motion didn't stop, but it stuttered internally. That question belonged to the kitchen's ritual. Diners didn't ask it unless someone had coached them.

Renaud's gaze lifted. "No one asks that," he said, quiet.

The server swallowed. "They did, Chef."

Renaud's eyes moved, not to the dining room, to Hale. To the suited man behind Hale. To the corridor mouth that held more authority than any table.

Hale didn't move. But his stillness felt like an answer.

Renaud turned back to the server. "What table."

The server hesitated, then said, "Seventeen. And… and twelve."

Twelve again. The table where the citrus allergy note had appeared and then disappeared. A pattern.

Sofia's voice cut in, tight and controlled. "Chef, we can comp," she said, using the front-of-house solution as a shield.

Renaud didn't blink. "No," he said.

The word was small. It landed huge. No comp meant no quiet fix. It meant this was being treated as something that couldn't be paid away.

Renaud looked down the line, slow. His gaze passed each station the way it passed each rim, searching for the invisible.

When his eyes reached garde manger, they held for a fraction longer than usual.

Not accusation. Calculation.

Connor felt the weight settle on him, pin him to stainless. He didn't flinch. He didn't blink too fast. He kept his hands moving in measured economy, because anything else would become evidence.

Renaud finally spoke.

"Freeze service," he said, not loud, but absolute.

Sofia's finger rose. Hold.

The kitchen stopped.

Not fully. Refrigeration hummed. Flames on hot side stayed alive. But hands froze mid-motion, knives held above boards, squeeze bottles hovering like suspended decisions. The room became a still photograph.

Renaud's voice stayed calm. "Who plated seventeen."

No one answered.

Not because they didn't know. Because knowing was a liability.

Sofia's eyes flicked toward the rail, toward the tickets, toward the timeline that had already been rewritten once tonight. A record that could be altered wasn't a record. It was a weapon.

The slick-haired manager appeared again at the threshold, face pale. He opened his mouth, then closed it, as if words had become dangerous even to him.

Renaud didn't look at the manager. He looked at the line again.

"Who plated seventeen," he repeated, softer.

The silence that followed was not the kitchen's normal silence. This one had a new edge: fear of being named without proof.

Connor realized then what the sabotage had accomplished. It hadn't only compromised plates. It had compromised certainty. If tickets could change, if allergy notes could appear and vanish, if runners could return plates untouched without explanation, then anyone could be blamed.

Blame without proof. The cleanest kind.

Sofia's finger remained raised. Hold.

Connor stood at garde manger with his towel folded into thirds and his hands held still, and he understood with a cold clarity that made his stomach drop:

Tonight, someone had built a situation where the kitchen's most sacred ritual could be used against it.

Not "Who did this?" as a path to truth.

But "Who can we remove?" as a path to control.

Sofia's finger stayed raised. Hold.

The kitchen did not move, but it did not relax either. It held itself in a posture that looked like control and felt like a trap. Connor stood with his hands still in front of him, towel folded into thirds, eyes down, as if stillness could be mistaken for innocence.

Renaud waited.

He did not fill the silence with anger. He let it thicken until it became its own kind of pressure, a substance you could choke on without making a sound.

"Who plated seventeen," he repeated, softer, as if the answer might be coaxed out by lowering the temperature.

No one spoke.

Connor felt every chef calculate the same thing at once. If you spoke, you created a record. If you created a record, you could be edited out.

The slick-haired manager hovered at the threshold, face pale under the kitchen's light, hands half-raised like he wanted to show they were empty. He looked from Renaud to Sofia, then toward the corridor mouth with a reflex that betrayed him.

Hale stood there, coat on, calm as if he had all night. Behind him, the suited man's posture remained perfect, gaze sliding across faces with a patient, almost bored attention. The gaze did not read food. It read reactions.

Sofia's jaw tightened. Her finger did not drop.

Renaud's eyes moved, slow and surgical, from the manager to Sofia. "Answer," he said.

Sofia didn't speak immediately. Connor saw the calculation in her stillness. Anything she said could be used as confirmation that the rail had truth. Tonight, the rail had already been proven capable of lying.

She lowered her finger an inch, then raised it again, as if she had corrected herself. A small movement. A signal without words.

Renaud's gaze cut toward Connor's end of the line, not stopping on him yet. "Front of house," Renaud said, voice flat. "Who did you tell them made it."

The manager swallowed. "Chef, they asked who prepared it," he said, the words spilling too quickly. "They asked very specifically."

Renaud's eyes didn't change. "And you answered."

The manager's lips parted, then closed again. He looked at Sofia as if hoping she would rescue him. Sofia did not move.

"Who," Renaud asked.

The manager's throat bobbed. "I didn't give a name," he said. "I said the kitchen. I said we would refire."

Renaud's gaze held him in place. "You're lying," he said, quiet, and the certainty in it was worse than shouting.

The manager's face flushed with fear. His eyes flicked toward Hale again, and this time the flick was almost pleading.

Sofia's voice cut in, low and controlled. "Speak," she said to the manager, not loud, but sharp enough to be felt. "Now."

The manager's mouth worked. "They said… they said it came from cold," he admitted. "They said it was the cold course. They said the person on cold has been doing the off-menu orders."

Connor felt the sentence land in his body like a hand closing around his wrist.

Visible, Sofia had said. You've been on specials.

Renaud's gaze shifted, finally, and settled on Connor.

Not accusation. Not anger.

Inventory.

The suited man behind Hale leaned his head a fraction, as if receiving something through an earpiece. Hale did not react. He didn't need to. The kitchen could do the work for him.

Renaud spoke again, still calm. "Which person."

The manager's eyes dropped. "Chef, I don't know names. I don't—"

Sofia made a small sound through her nose, a controlled exhale that was almost contempt. "You know," she said. "You just don't want to say it."

The manager's hands tightened around nothing. "Felwick," he said finally, barely audible, as if whispering the name could lessen the damage.

Connor did not move. He didn't lift his chin. He didn't deny it. Denial was useless in a room built on discipline and hierarchy. You didn't defend yourself unless invited. Defense was emotion. Emotion was deviation.

Renaud looked at Connor for a beat that felt too long to survive.

Then he said, "Step up."

Not loudly. Not dramatically. Just an instruction, the same tone he used for "again," the same tone he used for "walk." It was the tone of a man moving a piece across a board.

Connor's feet carried him forward before his mind could protest. He walked fast without looking fast, stopped at the border of the pass, hands behind his back out of habit, then brought them forward again because he had learned the pass punished postures as much as it punished mistakes.

Sofia's finger remained raised. Hold.

The entire kitchen watched without looking like it was watching. Eyes down, hands frozen, bodies trained to pretend their attention belonged only to their own stations. Connor could feel them anyway, the way he could feel the heat lamps even without touching them.

Renaud did not ask him what happened. He did not ask him why. He did not ask him whether he had used nuts, citrus, or anything else. Those questions belonged to a world where facts mattered more than control.

He asked, "Did you plate seventeen."

Connor kept his voice flat. "I plated cold, Chef."

That was not an answer. That was function. It was also a refusal to claim a record that could be altered.

Renaud's eyes narrowed by a fraction. Sofia's jaw ticked once, hard.

Renaud asked again, softer. "Did you plate seventeen."

Connor felt the trap in the repetition. If he said yes, he became the body they wanted. If he said no, he contradicted the manager, and contradiction was a crack that could be widened into insubordination.

He chose the smallest truth that did not give them a clean sentence to weaponize.

"I executed what was called," he said.

The line stayed silent. Even the refrigerators sounded too loud.

Renaud held Connor's gaze, and in that moment Connor understood the most dangerous part of

Renaud's control. He could decide what counted as truth simply by choosing which words to accept.

Renaud looked past Connor to Sofia. "Tickets."

Sofia didn't move. "Chef," she began, and Connor heard the warning inside her tone.

"Tickets," Renaud repeated.

Sofia's eyes flicked toward the printer, then toward the rail where the tickets sat clipped in a clean line, official and therefore suspect. She stepped to the pass, lifted the clip, and pulled the stack with careful fingers.

She placed them on the stainless beside Renaud as if laying down evidence she did not trust.

Renaud flipped through them without hurry. The motion was precise, like turning pages in a book that could get someone killed. He stopped on table seventeen.

Connor saw it from the angle of the pass lamps: the ticket was clean. No allergy note. No void. No reprint stamp. It looked like it had always been that way.

Renaud looked at Sofia. "And earlier," he said.

Sofia's face stayed sealed. "It printed different," she admitted quietly.

The manager flinched at the admission, as if he had just heard something forbidden.

Renaud's gaze shifted to the manager. "Did it," he asked.

The manager's lips parted. "Chef, I don't—"

Renaud's voice stayed flat. "Did the ticket print differently earlier."

The manager swallowed hard. His eyes flicked to Hale. A reflex. A permission check.

Hale remained still.

The suited man behind him did not blink.

The manager nodded once, small and broken. "Yes."

Renaud turned back to Connor. "So," he said, almost conversational, "we have a plate returned untouched, a claim of contamination, and a ticket that changes."

Connor said nothing. Any response could be labeled defensive. Defensive could be labeled guilty.

Renaud's eyes moved across Connor's face, searching for a flinch. Connor gave him none. The kitchen had trained him well enough to hold his fear inside, to keep it from showing in his mouth, his pupils, his hands.

Renaud looked toward the corridor mouth again.

Hale did not move.

Sofia's finger was still raised. Hold. The line's stillness was beginning to strain, the way a long hold strained timing until the entire service threatened to break. But Sofia did not drop it. She held the kitchen in suspension as if she were protecting it from something worse than a delayed course.

Renaud said, "We can remove him."

The sentence was quiet. It did not sound like an execution order. That was what made it more terrifying. It sounded like a clean operational choice.

Connor felt his stomach go cold.

Remove him. The phrase did not mean fired. It meant erased. It meant Jules. It meant Luc. It meant an empty locker and a name lifted off a list so completely it looked like it had never existed.

Sofia's jaw ticked once, then stopped. Her eyes did not widen. She did not plead. Pleading was emotion. Emotion was weakness. Instead, she spoke in the same controlled tone she used for timing.

"If you remove him tonight," she said, "you give them what they're asking for."

Renaud didn't look at her. "They," he repeated, as if tasting the pronoun.

Sofia held still. "The ones making the rail lie," she said, and the words were a knife sliding under a door. Not loud enough for the dining room. Loud enough for the corridor mouth.

The suited man behind Hale shifted his weight a fraction. A microreaction. Connor saw it in stainless reflection and felt his skin tighten.

Renaud's gaze returned to Sofia. "And if I keep him," Renaud asked, "I keep risk."

Sofia's finger trembled for the smallest fraction and steadied. "You keep control," she corrected. "Because you show you decide who goes. Not them."

Silence.

Renaud's eyes moved back to Connor. "Do you understand what you are," he asked.

Connor's throat tightened. He chose obedience, the safest language. "A station, Chef."

Renaud's mouth moved, not quite a smile, not quite contempt. "No," he said. "You are a point."

Connor stayed still.

Renaud continued, voice low, almost instructional. "A point they can push."

Sofia's eyes cut to Connor, sharp, and in them he saw what she couldn't say: do not speak. Do not react. Do not offer them anything they can replay later.

Renaud looked at the manager again. "Tell the table we refire," he said. "And we do not discuss names again."

The manager nodded too quickly. "Yes, Chef."

"And," Renaud added, voice tightening by a fraction, "if they ask who prepared it, you tell them the kitchen. If they ask again, you tell them nothing."

The manager backed away as if he had been released from a chokehold and fled toward the dining room.

Renaud turned to Sofia. "Walk," he said.

Sofia's finger dropped immediately.

The kitchen exhaled without making a sound. Hands resumed motion in a controlled snap, knives returning to boards, squeeze bottles finishing the movement they had been trapped inside. Service surged forward again as if the hold had been part of choreography, not a near-fatal fracture.

Renaud didn't say Connor's name again. That was not mercy. It was strategy. Naming created a record.

He leaned closer to Connor, just enough that his words could hide under fan noise and the sudden clatter of resumed work.

"Do not change your prep," Renaud murmured. "Do not improvise. Do not clean like you are afraid."

Connor's pulse jumped at the echo of Sofia's earlier warning.

Renaud's eyes held his. "If you look guilty," Renaud continued, "you become useful to someone else."

Connor swallowed. "Yes, Chef."

Renaud straightened, and his voice returned to the room. "Again," he said, and plates began to refire, the brigade snapping into the familiar cruelty of perfection.

Connor stepped back from the pass and returned to garde manger with his hands steady and his face clean, but inside him something had shifted. Renaud had not removed him. Not because Connor was innocent. Not because Renaud trusted him.

Because removing him would have proven the kitchen could be steered by an outside hand.

At his station, Connor rebuilt the cold course for table seventeen with the same severe geometry, the same measured placement, the same absence of rim marks. He used sealed product. Fresh oil. Clean tweezers. He treated each component like evidence that could not be allowed to speak.

As he plated, Sofia appeared beside him for half a breath, eyes on his hands.

"You're on the edge," she murmured.

Connor didn't look up. "Of what."

Sofia's jaw ticked once. "Dismissal," she said. "Erasure. Whatever word you like."

Connor felt the burner phone in his drawer at home like a weight he could suddenly feel through distance. You looked. An invitation. A warning. The city was part of the corridor network. Tonight the kitchen had been used as a weapon. Tomorrow it could be used as a grave.

Sofia leaned closer, her voice lower. "They tried to hand you to Renaud," she said. "And he didn't take it."

Connor's throat tightened. "Why."

Sofia's eyes sharpened. "Less," she breathed, then softened the edge without removing it. "Because if he takes it, he admits the stars aren't his anymore."

Connor's hands did not stop. Portion, place, reset.

Sofia straightened, already sealing her face back into function. Before she moved away, she gave him one last sentence, quiet enough to be mistaken for nothing.

"Be boring," she said. "Boring is the only thing that can't be edited."

Then she was gone, pulled back to the pass, leaving Connor with a plate that had to taste perfect and mean nothing.

The refire went out. The line kept moving. The dining room would never know how close a person had come to being removed like a smudge on steel.

Connor kept his face clean and his hands precise, but inside him the understanding hardened into something cold and final.

He wasn't being judged tonight.

He was being measured for how easily he could be erased.

Chapter 17

The Final Service

The next morning, the kitchen moved as if it had learned to hold its breath for longer.

Connor arrived before most of the line, not because he wanted to, but because waiting at home had become its own kind of exposure. The alley behind L'Étoile Noire had been rinsed again. Bleach and citrus clung to the wet stone like an alibi. He paused with his palm on the service door and listened, the way he always did now, for the building's mood.

Inside, the lights were half-on, stainless bright enough to accuse and dull enough to let corners keep secrets. The camera above the back hallway blinked its blue heartbeat. Someone could watch later, even if they weren't watching now.

Dumas was already there, grid set, towel folded into thirds, wiping steel in single passes. He did not greet Connor. He didn't need to.

Connor washed his hands. Soap, rinse, dry once. He tied his apron, aligned his tools, and began prep with the same shaved-down economy the kitchen demanded.

Sofia arrived just after ten, not hurried but tight around the eyes. She did a walk-through that looked like routine until Connor noticed what she didn't correct. Normally she would shift a container a millimeter, square a label, erase any human drift. Today she mostly watched. Not the food. The room.

When she reached garde manger's border, her gaze flicked over Connor's station and then settled on his face.

"Boring," she said.

"Heard," Connor replied.

Her jaw ticked once. "No specials unless I call," she added. "Nothing outside the printer."

Connor kept his eyes down. "Understood."

She held her gaze on him for a fraction longer than normal, then moved away toward the pass as if pulled by gravity.

By noon, front of house began to shift. It was the same tell as the night of the private room: tables reset twice even though nothing looked wrong, glassware swapped for identical glassware, linen steamed again until the air tasted faintly of heat and detergent. The slick-haired manager appeared at the kitchen threshold, smile too practiced, eyes too alert. He didn't step fully into the heat. He hovered as if the air inside the kitchen had jurisdiction.

Hale was not yet at the corridor mouth, but the threshold still felt occupied. The building remembered him. Connor felt it in the way runners moved a little tighter, in the way the corridor door seemed to hold more weight than its hinges should allow.

At family meal, no one spoke. Silence was normal. Today it had a different density, like everyone had put their fear into the same container and sealed it.

The rotating watchers sat near the wall with coffee and empty hands. Connor did not recognize their faces. Their posture was always the same. Eyes that counted exits. Eyes that didn't belong to hunger.

Dumas ate without tasting, gaze down. After a few minutes, he set his fork down and didn't pick it up again.

Connor kept his own eyes on his tray. "Something's coming," he said quietly, careful to keep it functional.

Dumas's mouth tightened. His fingers made a small wiping motion against his thigh, muscle memory that never stopped. "It always is," he murmured.

Connor waited. Dumas never gave information directly. He left it on the counter and walked away.

After a beat, Dumas added, still not looking up, "They wiped last night clean."

Connor felt cold settle behind his ribs. Wiped clean meant no record, no proof, no way to point at what had happened and call it real. Jules's name had been lifted off the list. Tickets had changed. Allergy notes had appeared and vanished. Last night would become a rumor the same way Luc had become a rumor: something you could feel but couldn't touch.

"Who's 'they'," Connor asked before he could stop himself.

Dumas's eyes flicked toward him, quick and sharp. "Less," he said, echoing Sofia as if the word belonged to the building, not to her.

Connor nodded once. "Heard."

Dumas resumed eating as if nothing had been said.

At four-thirty, Sofia tightened the entire kitchen with her presence. She moved around the pass, checking the heat lamps, checking the rail, checking the printer as if it might lie again. She pulled the ticket stack, ran her fingers through it with clinical precision, then clipped it back on.

Renaud arrived at five on the dot, jacket immaculate, hair precise, face centered the way a blade was centered in its sheath. He did not greet the brigade. He didn't need to. The room aligned around him automatically, bodies straightening, voices tightening into function.

His gaze passed over the stations in a slow scan. When it reached garde manger, it paused a fraction on Connor, the weight of it like a fingertip pressing a bruise. Then it moved on.

Renaud said one word to Sofia, quiet enough to belong only to the pass.

"Tonight," he said.

Sofia answered, equally quiet. "Oui, Chef."

At five-thirty, Hale appeared at the corridor mouth as if summoned by the word. Coat on, calm like ownership. Two suited men stood half a step behind him. Different faces than yesterday. Same controlled posture. Same eyes that didn't eat.

The kitchen tightened around the threshold the way metal tightened around a magnet.

Connor watched in stainless reflection, never directly. Being seen noticing was worse than being seen.

The dining room filled in the usual expensive way: controlled laughter, low voices, the clink of glass that sounded like money. Service began with the machine's familiar glide. Tickets fed. Calls were clipped. Plates walked.

For the first half hour, nothing deviated.

That was what made it worse. After last night's sabotage, normality felt like a trap laid too neatly.

At six-ten, the slick-haired manager stepped into the kitchen threshold again. He didn't speak. He simply lifted his hand and made a small, tight gesture toward Sofia.

Sofia didn't respond immediately. She kept her eyes on the rail as if she hadn't seen him. Then she moved, controlled and quick, to the threshold. The manager leaned in and murmured something Connor couldn't hear.

Sofia's face didn't change. Only her eyes sharpened.

She returned to the pass without rushing and took her position beside Renaud as if nothing had happened.

Then she did something she almost never did.

She held up one finger.

Hold.

There was no culinary reason. No plate hanging. No timing issue that required a pause. The hold landed on the line like a hand on a throat.

Connor froze with tweezers above a plate, careful not to let his stillness look like surprise. Around him, hands stopped mid-motion. The room became a still photograph.

Renaud did not look at Sofia's raised finger. His gaze was fixed on the corridor mouth. Hale's stillness did not change.

The suited man behind Hale glanced at his watch.

Synchronization.

Sofia dropped her finger. "Walk," she said, and plates moved as if the hold had been planned. As if it had been choreography.

Connor's pulse tried to climb into his throat. He pushed it down. Boring, he reminded himself. Be boring.

A minute later, a runner appeared at garde manger's tape line. Not a kitchen runner. Too-clean hands. No fatigue. The soldier-runner posture without the uniform.

He didn't speak to Connor. He placed a folded slip of paper on the very edge of the stainless, then withdrew without a word.

Connor did not touch it immediately. He let it sit, a test. He kept plating, eyes down, hands precise. When he finally glanced at it, he read two words written in the same block letters as before.

GUIDE PRESENT.

Beneath it, one more line.

NO VARIATION. NO RIM MARKS.

Connor felt his mouth go dry.

The inspector.

The myth that hovered over the kitchen like a god that didn't need to be seen. The anonymous diner among wealth, unnoticed yet deeply feared. The returned dish that had triggered erasure in silence. The story that had been told so often it had become doctrine.

Connor kept his face clean. Inside, something tightened into clarity. Last night's sabotage had pushed the kitchen to the edge of erasure. Tonight, the inspector's presence meant every edge would be tested under a different kind of light.

Not the pass lamps.

A human eye trained to see what the dining room didn't know how to name.

Connor glanced, in stainless reflection, toward the dining room doors. He couldn't see the guests, only the movement of front of house, the way they smoothed their expressions into warmth and kept their hands too still. He caught a glimpse of the manager's posture as he passed, a quick bend of deference aimed at a table Connor couldn't see.

Sofia's voice cut across the line, calm and sharp. "Reset your towels," she said, a command that sounded like routine and felt like a warning.

The brigade obeyed instantly. Towels were refolded into thirds, corners aligned, stained cloth replaced. It wasn't about cleanliness. It was about looking controlled.

Renaud spoke for the first time since the hold, voice quiet, without drama. "No improvisation," he said. "No heroics."

"Oui, Chef," the line answered, a single controlled breath.

Connor's hands moved with cold precision. He built plates that meant nothing. He executed geometry, not art. He kept his thumbs clear, his fingers under porcelain, his touch absent from the rim.

The first course went.

The second course went.

Nothing returned.

That should have eased him. It didn't. The absence of a returned plate felt like the pause before impact.

At seven, Hale shifted his stance by a fraction at the corridor mouth. It was nothing. It was also a signal. One of the suited men leaned closer to him, murmured something. Hale's gaze slid toward the pass, then back toward the corridor network as if tracking two rail lines at once: the dining room performance and whatever moved behind the unmarked doors.

Sofia raised one finger again.

Hold.

Two beats. Three.

Renaud's jaw tightened by a fraction. He didn't look at Sofia, but Connor saw it anyway, a microfracture in a face built for control. The hold stretched one beat too long, like last night.

The suited man behind Hale checked his watch again.

Sofia dropped her finger. "Walk."

Plates moved.

Connor's stomach went cold. The inspector was not just present. The inspector was being used as timing. Another alignment. Another window.

Food as cover. Service as choreography. Holds as control.

The kitchen was running two services again, visible and hidden, and tonight the visible one had a silent judge sitting inside it.

Connor kept plating, but he felt the room tilt slightly, as if the building itself had shifted its weight to accommodate something heavy at one table.

Then, from the pass, Renaud said, very softly, "Eyes."

It wasn't a call. It was an instruction to the room.

Connor understood it immediately.

Not eyes on plates.

Eyes on everything.

Because the inspector had returned, and with him came the one thing the kitchen could not refire.

A first impression.

And somewhere in the machinery behind the corridor mouth, someone was counting on that impression to break in exactly the right way.

The word "Eyes" didn't change the volume of the kitchen. It changed the direction of attention.

Connor felt it in the way bodies angled without moving their feet, the way hands became even more economical, as if every unnecessary motion might be noticed and saved somewhere. The pass lamps carved the room into a narrow strip of truth, but the inspector in the dining room was a different kind of light. Not heat. Judgment.

Renaud stood centered, face sealed. Yet Connor saw the smallest deviation: a blink that came a fraction too fast, the kind of involuntary reset a body made when it was forcing itself not to look.

Sofia tightened her orbit around him. She called timing in clipped syllables, held and released in beats that felt less culinary than controlled. She was building walls out of seconds again. Connor could feel the hidden rail under the visible one, running in parallel, never quite touching, always threatening to cross.

"Two on eight," Sofia said.

"Heard," the line answered, in the same rehearsed breath.

Connor plated cold with severe geometry and absence. No rim marks. No variation. He kept his thumbs clear, hands under porcelain, as if the plate itself could carry fingerprints in a way a camera would understand later.

A runner crossed behind him and the air shifted with that metallic bite again, faint but present, like a coin held in the mouth too long. Connor's stomach tightened. He didn't look. Looking was a kind of answer.

At the corridor mouth, Hale stood calm as a locked door. One suited man watched the pass. The other's gaze moved across stations, faces, wrists. Not food. Reaction.

Sofia lifted one finger.

Hold.

The line froze mid-motion. Connor's tweezers hovered above a micro leaf, perfectly still, his breath shallow and controlled. He used stainless reflection to watch, because direct sight was too honest.

Renaud didn't look at Sofia. His gaze stayed fixed on the corridor mouth, as if waiting for a cue no one else could hear.

Hale's stillness did not change, but one of the suited men checked his watch and then lowered his wrist in the exact same controlled way as before. Synchronization.

Sofia dropped her finger. "Walk."

The kitchen resumed motion as if the hold had been planned, as if the pause hadn't been a throat-grip. Plates moved. Tickets advanced. The dining room remained a hum behind the wall.

Connor thought, briefly, that maybe this was how the night would go: two services running, two powers pulling, and the brigade forced to pretend it was only dinner.

Then the printer stuttered.

It wasn't loud. The sound was small and ordinary, but in this kitchen the ordinary had become suspicious. Sofia's head angled toward it. Not reaction, inventory.

A ticket printed and did not feed cleanly. It hung half-caught under the plastic lip, paper bent in a way that looked like an accident.

Sofia stepped to the rail and tore it free with two fingers, careful, as if the paper could be contaminated. Her eyes scanned. Her jaw ticked once, hard, then stilled.

She didn't call it.

That was what made Connor's skin tighten.

Sofia looked at Renaud. "Chef," she said, quiet enough that the word belonged only to the pass.

Renaud's eyes cut down to the ticket. He took it from her without touching her fingers. His gaze moved across it slowly, like reading a sentence in a language he hated.

The line kept moving because it was not allowed to stop unless ordered. But Connor felt the pass become a gravity well. Even the flames on hot side seemed to narrow.

Renaud's face did not change. Yet something did, a microscopic shift around the eyes, the same fracture Connor had seen the night coded plates had been erased with a refire. Recognition. Not of food.

Sofia leaned closer, her voice low. "No table," she murmured.

Renaud looked up for the first time in minutes and turned his head slightly toward the corridor mouth.

Hale was still there. Calm. Waiting.

One of the suited men leaned in and murmured something into Hale's ear. Hale didn't nod. He didn't need to. His gaze remained steady, and somehow that steadiness read like instruction.

Renaud looked back down at the ticket.

Connor couldn't see the words from garde manger, but he could see behavior. The way Sofia's posture tightened as if she had swallowed something sharp. The way Renaud's fingers held the paper without flexing, as if he refused to leave even a crease that could be interpreted.

Sofia called, into the room, too normal. "Continue."

No one had paused. No one had stopped. It was not a command. It was a cover.

Renaud stepped off center by half a foot.

The movement was tiny. In another kitchen it would have meant nothing. Here it was a rupture.

He leaned closer to Sofia. Connor watched their mouths in reflection, not the words, only the shapes of them.

Sofia said, "No record," barely moving her lips.

Renaud's answer was shorter. "No."

Sofia's jaw ticked again, faster this time, like a tell she couldn't fully erase. She said something else, longer, a sentence with weight.

Renaud's eyes narrowed. He didn't look angry. He looked cornered.

Then he did something Connor had never seen him do during service.

Renaud swallowed.

Not a theatrical swallow. A real one, the kind the body did when it was trying to force down something it couldn't digest.

Sofia's eyes flicked down the line, fast, clinical, and landed on Connor's station. Not for his food. For his presence.

Connor kept his hands moving. He refused to meet her gaze directly. He gave her nothing to replay.

Renaud returned to the center of the pass, but his centering looked forced now, like a man placing himself back into a role that had begun to slip. He held the ticket in his hand for another beat, then placed it facedown on the stainless.

Facedown meant concealment. Facedown meant denial.

He lifted his chin slightly and spoke, not loudly, but to the whole brigade. "Tighten."

The command was familiar. The tone was not. The word came with a thinness, an edge that suggested effort rather than effortless authority.

The line responded in a controlled breath. "Oui, Chef."

Connor tightened. Everyone tightened. Towels were refolded. Containers squared. A lid aligned.

The machine improved itself by increments because that was what it did when it was afraid.

Minutes passed. Plates walked. Nothing returned. The inspector remained a rumor made flesh somewhere beyond the wall, unseen yet shaping every movement.

Then a runner appeared at the pass who did not belong to the kitchen.

Too-clean hands. No fatigue. Eyes that didn't taste.

He did not carry a plate. He carried a small black case.

Connor's stomach went cold. Another delivery. Another piece of equipment swallowed by the administrative door. But the runner didn't turn toward that door.

He stopped at the pass.

Sofia's posture went rigid for half a fraction and then smoothed. Her face remained clean. She did not reach for the case.

The runner set it down on the stainless beside the lamps with careful fingertips and withdrew one step, waiting.

The case sat there like an accusation.

Renaud looked at it without moving. The pass lamps lit the black surface with a thin sheen that made it look less like an object and more like a void.

Sofia leaned in again, her voice too low to carry. Connor couldn't hear, but he caught the shape of the words in her mouth.

Not here.

Renaud's reply was a single syllable, clipped.

The runner waited, motionless. The suited man behind Hale shifted his weight. Interest.

From the corridor mouth, Hale lifted two fingers.

Not a big gesture. Not dramatic. The same efficient signal Connor had seen used to move people and plates and time.

Renaud's gaze flicked up, caught the gesture, and came back down to the case. For the first time tonight, Connor saw something that looked like emotion cross his face.

Not fear.

Anger, contained so tightly it became brittle.

Renaud reached for the case.

His hand hovered above it for a beat that felt too long in a room built on decisive motion. His fingers then closed on the edge, and he pulled it closer, into the strip of light beneath the lamps.

Sofia's mouth tightened as if she had bitten the inside of her cheek. Her eyes cut toward the dining room wall, as if she could feel the inspector's presence through stone.

Renaud opened the case.

Not fully. Just enough to see inside.

Connor couldn't see the contents, but he saw Renaud's reaction: a slight widening of the eyes, immediately corrected; a blink, slower now, like the mind was forcing itself to process.

Sofia whispered something that looked like a warning.

Renaud closed the case again, slow.

He stood very still with both hands resting on either side of it, as if holding something down.

Then, for the first time in weeks, Renaud's control cracked in a way the room could register.

A small tremor moved through his right hand.

Not much. A fraction. But the pass lamps were merciless, and this kitchen was trained to read fractions.

Sofia saw it. Her eyes locked on his hand for half a beat, and her face tightened in a way that was almost human.

The tremor stopped. Renaud straightened.

He said, very quietly, to Sofia, "Not tonight."

Sofia's head tilted. A question she couldn't ask.

Renaud's voice thinned further, as if the words cost him. "Guide present," he murmured.

Sofia's jaw ticked once. She understood. The inspector wasn't just a judge tonight. He was a constraint. A witness with no allegiance to their hidden rail.

The runner still stood waiting, empty hands, posture trained to receive instruction.

Renaud looked at the runner and spoke with a calm that sounded manufactured. "Take it," he said.

The runner did not move.

The smallest pause. The kind of pause that said the runner did not work for Renaud.

From the corridor mouth, Hale's voice carried for the first time, quiet but clear enough to cut through fan hum.

"Chef," Hale said.

One word. A claim.

Renaud's face remained sealed, but his eyes changed. For a fraction they looked tired. Not physically. Strategically. Like a man seeing the board and realizing a piece had been taken from him without his permission.

Sofia stepped forward half a foot, inserting herself into the space beside the case like a shield that didn't want to admit it was a shield. "We're in service," she said, controlled. Not defiant. Not submissive. A statement of reality.

Hale didn't raise his voice. "So am I."

The suited man behind him watched Sofia's mouth as if recording syllables.

Renaud's nostrils flared once, the only visible sign of breath under pressure. He looked toward the dining room wall again, as if weighing the inspector against the corridor mouth, the stars against the system that claimed to keep them.

He said nothing.

The silence stretched, and for the first time tonight it wasn't the kitchen's chosen silence. It was a contested one.

Sofia's eyes flicked down the line again, fast, landing on Connor.

Connor felt it like a hook. The look was not instruction. It was assessment.

Renaud's voice finally came, low, almost too low. "Sofia," he said.

"Yes, Chef," she answered instantly, as if speed could cover the crack.

Renaud's gaze did not leave the case. "Run the pass."

Sofia's eyes widened by a fraction, then sealed. "Chef," she began.

Renaud cut her off, quiet and absolute. "Now."

It was the first time Connor had heard that tone from him directed at her. Not correction. Relinquishment, forced or chosen, disguised as command.

Sofia stepped into position at center under the lamps. She lifted her chin. Her hands came up, precise, ready.

Renaud took the black case and moved one step away from the light strip, toward the corridor mouth.

Not far. Not leaving. Just shifting his body into a different orbit.

The kitchen kept working, but the air changed. Everyone had felt it.

The center had moved.

And as Sofia began calling plates with a voice that was steady but sharpened by urgency, Connor watched Renaud's back in stainless reflection and understood what he was seeing.

Renaud was not just under pressure.

He was being pulled off the board.

Not erased like a commis.

Repositioned.

Reduced.

A man whose power depended on absolute control was being forced to carry something that wasn't food, while the inspector sat in the dining room measuring perfection that could not include tremor.

Renaud reached the corridor threshold and stopped. Hale's presence swallowed the space around him, ownership pressing in without touch.

For a beat, Renaud did not move.

Then he stepped into the corridor.

The case went with him.

Sofia's voice snapped at the pass. "Walk."

Plates moved.

The brigade obeyed.

Connor kept his hands steady at garde manger, but inside him something locked into place with cold clarity.

If Renaud could be made to step away during the inspector's service, if his hand could tremble under the lamps, then the crisis wasn't about a returned dish or a sabotaged ticket.

It was about the fact that control had started to change hands.

And the kitchen, hungry for a center, would feel it.

Soon.

The corridor swallowed Renaud and the black case without drama.

Sofia's "Walk" snapped the line forward like a switch had been thrown. Plates moved under her voice. Heat lamps burned. The rail advanced. The brigade obeyed because obedience was muscle memory, and because hesitation now would be read as weakness by eyes that counted more than covers.

Connor stayed at garde manger, hands moving in clean, severe geometry, but his attention kept lifting in small, deniable increments toward the pass. Sofia stood centered under the lamps, shoulders squared, chin lifted, voice clipped into pure function.

"Two on four. Fire cold. Walk hot in thirty."

"Heard," voices answered, fast and flat.

She was good. Connor had known that for months. Tonight she was something else: a replacement center thrust into place too quickly, forced to hold a room together while a second service ran underneath the first. Her control was precise, but Connor could see the cost in the tiny tells she couldn't fully erase. The jaw tick. The fraction too-long inhale before a call. The way her eyes flicked, not to plates, but to the corridor mouth between commands, as if her body expected Renaud to reappear and correct the universe.

He didn't.

At the threshold, Hale remained calm as ownership, a shadow with a name. The suited men behind him rotated their attention in slow sweeps. Their stillness wasn't passive. It was supervision.

Connor plated a cold course and sent it with a runner whose hands did not show kitchen fatigue. The runner took it without touching the rim, and Connor felt the familiar chill of recognition. These were not normal carries. These were movements in a system that used porcelain as cover.

Sofia held up one finger.

Hold.

Connor froze mid-placement, tweezers suspended. The hold was too clean, too timed. In stainless reflection, he saw one suited man check his watch. Not for food.

Sofia dropped her finger. “Walk.”

The hold became invisible again, disguised as choreography. But Connor felt the strain in the room, the way a machine began to shake when two hands fought over the same controls.

A minute later, a plate came back.

Not rushed, not clattering, not accompanied by an apologetic server. It arrived the same way returned plates had been arriving since the sabotage began: slid back into the lamp strip with no explanation and no emotion, carried by someone who didn’t belong to either front of house or back.

Untouched.

Connor’s throat tightened. The inspector. The myth made real. A returned dish in this building was never just feedback. It was a signal that the room could not ignore.

Sofia didn’t flinch. She pulled the plate under the lamps and let her eyes travel across it in a way that looked like inspection and was actually triage.

“What table,” she asked.

The carrier answered instantly, too instantly. “Six.”

Sofia’s gaze flicked to the rail. “Ticket.”

The carrier didn't move. He wasn't a runner who obeyed her.

Sofia's eyes sharpened. Her voice stayed calm, but the edge beneath it showed. "Ticket," she repeated, and it was the first time Connor had heard a command in her voice that wasn't meant for the kitchen.

The carrier's mouth tightened. He nodded once and stepped back as if he had received permission from somewhere else. He retreated toward the corridor mouth, not toward the dining room.

Sofia stared at the returned plate again. The dish was correct. Too correct. The kind of perfection that should have been safe.

"Refire," she said, but the word landed slightly off rhythm. Not wrong, just forced.

Hot side called back. "Heard."

Sofia turned her head slightly, eyes scanning down the line, fast and clinical, and Connor felt them land on him like a fingertip pressing a bruise. Not accusation. Calculation. The way Renaud had looked at him when the sabotage tried to hand him over as a body.

She didn't call him up. She didn't have time.

The rail spit another ticket, and another, and the room tightened further. Sofia began to move faster, voice sharper, trying to generate control out of speed.

Connor saw the danger immediately. In this kitchen, speed was not control. Speed was how mistakes became deniable.

Another plate came back, and this time a server's voice followed it, trembling despite training.

"They said it feels… wrong," the server murmured, hovering at the threshold like the air itself could punish him.

Sofia didn't look at the server. She looked at the plate. "Wrong how."

The server swallowed. "They wouldn't say. Just… wrong."

Connor felt his pulse bump once and flatten under discipline. Wrong was the language of people who wanted the kitchen to chase ghosts. Wrong was how you introduced doubt without leaving facts.

Sofia stared at the plate for one beat too long. Connor saw the microfracture in her posture, the slight shift of weight that said her body was about to choose between two rails: the visible service that needed timing and calm, and the hidden service that was trying to make her react.

She lifted her hand.

Not a hold. A gesture toward the rail, toward the printer, toward the only record that could be trusted and had already been proven capable of lying.

And then, for the first time all night, Sofia's voice hesitated.

It was tiny. Almost nothing. A fraction of a second between thought and call.

But the kitchen read fractions.

The suited man behind Hale leaned his head a fraction, interest sharpening. Hale didn't move. He didn't need to. The room itself would do what it had been trained to do when it sensed weakness.

Connor didn't think. Thinking took time. He moved.

He stepped out of garde manger's lane and crossed toward the pass fast without looking fast, posture controlled, hands clean. He didn't ask permission. He didn't announce himself. He simply arrived at Sofia's side in the strip of light where everything could be seen.

Sofia's eyes flicked to him, sharp warning.

Connor kept his face clean and lowered his voice. "Chef. What do you need."

The question was functional. It gave her a handle. It offered her a way to turn his presence into procedure instead of insubordination.

Sofia's jaw ticked once. Her eyes cut to the returned plate. Then, to Connor's hands. Then, briefly, toward the corridor mouth.

"Refire table six," she said, and her voice regained its clipped cadence. "Full course. Now."

Connor nodded once. "Heard."

He turned toward the line and spoke for the first time with a voice meant to carry.

"Garde manger, reset cold components for six. New plates. New towels. No rim marks."

The station answered automatically, relief disguised as obedience. "Oui."

Connor didn't stop. He let his gaze travel, quick, surgical, to hot side. "Hot, refire six. Same timing. Walk together."

Antoine's voice came back, tight. "Heard."

Sofia's eyes narrowed at Connor. Not anger. A warning that he was stepping into a space that could get him erased.

Connor leaned in again, lower. "Your rail is being fed bad returns," he murmured, careful with words. "They want you to chase wrong. Don't."

Sofia's gaze held his for a beat too long, the kind of look that was both instruction and plea. "You don't speak that," she whispered, and then, because she had to be Sofia in front of the room, she added louder, "Less."

Connor nodded once, accepting the correction as cover. "Heard."

He slid into motion at the pass without taking Sofia's place. He didn't stand centered. He stood half a step off, close enough to support, far enough to preserve hierarchy if anyone replayed this later.

Sofia called, "Two on eight," and Connor echoed the timing down the line in the same clipped language, turning her calls into clean execution.

"Fire cold. Hot follows. Walk in twenty."

The brigade snapped into alignment.

Another ticket printed and hung half-caught under the lip. Connor saw Sofia's eyes flick toward it, the smallest tell of irritation. He reached for it first, tore it free, and placed it on the rail with a controlled motion, turning the printer's stutter into something ordinary.

Sofia glanced at him, then back to the lamps. Her jaw ticked once, hard, then steadied.

The refire for six came up from garde manger first. Connor checked the rim without touching it, tilted the plate under the lamps, and felt a familiar cold certainty settle in his chest. In a room where records could be rewritten, the only thing you could control was what left your hands.

"No rim marks," he said quietly, more to himself than anyone else.

Sofia's voice snapped. "Hot."

Antoine's plate arrived a beat later, and Connor aligned the two courses under the lamps so they read as one gesture, one rhythm, one service. He didn't taste. He didn't improvise. He inspected like Renaud: not for beauty, for deviation.

He caught it immediately. A smear near the rim on the hot plate, almost invisible, the kind of mark no diner would name and an inspector might.

Connor didn't pause. He didn't look at Antoine in a way that could be called accusation. He simply slid the hot plate back a fraction and spoke in pure function.

"Again," he said.

Antoine's eyes flashed, but his mouth stayed closed. He took the plate back without argument.

Sofia's head turned sharply toward Connor.

Connor met her gaze for half a beat, then looked away. In this kitchen, you didn't hold eye contact at the pass unless you were ready to be measured by it.

Sofia's jaw ticked. She understood what he'd done. He'd refired without hesitation, preserving a standard the inspector might be hunting for, and he'd done it in a way that didn't require her to show strain.

She turned back to the rail. "Walk cold. Hot in five."

Connor repeated it down the line, voice steady. "Walk cold. Hot in five."

The plates went out together.

For three minutes, nothing came back.

Then five.

Then ten.

The air didn't relax. But it stopped tightening.

Connor stayed at the pass, half a step off center, functioning as an extra spine in the room. He called timing when Sofia's voice needed a breath. He tore tickets cleanly when the printer tried to stutter. He watched the runners who didn't sweat and the carriers who didn't obey, and he treated every return, every hold, every anomaly as a piece of theater designed to make someone flinch.

He did not flinch.

At the corridor mouth, Hale remained still, but Connor felt the shift anyway: the suited man's attention moved from Sofia's face to Connor's hands, reading the way he corrected, the way he refired, the way he kept the line moving without giving anyone a visible crack to pry open.

A returned dish was supposed to remove oxygen from the room.

Connor refused to let it.

Sofia leaned closer, just enough that her words could hide under fan hum. "You're stepping close," she murmured.

Connor kept his eyes on the lamps. "You were about to hesitate," he said quietly. Not accusation. Fact.

Sofia's jaw ticked once, and for a breath her voice went almost human. "Renaud should be here."

Connor's throat tightened. He didn't answer with comfort. Comfort was useless. "He isn't," he said.

Sofia's eyes flicked toward the corridor mouth again. "And if they see you here," she whispered, "they'll decide what you are."

Connor's hands stayed steady. "A point," he said, using Renaud's word, and felt something harden behind his ribs.

Sofia's gaze snapped to him, sharp.

Connor didn't look back. He looked at the next plates coming up, the next timing window, the next chance for the hidden rail to cross the visible one.

He raised his voice slightly, pure function again. "Hands. Tight. Walk together."

The brigade obeyed.

And for the first time that night, Connor felt it: the kitchen's hunger for a center beginning to tilt toward him, not because he was loud, not because he was chosen, but because he was the only thing in the room that was not reacting.

In a system built on control, calm wasn't a personality trait.

It was authority.

A runner approached the pass with a plate that wasn't on the rail, and Connor blocked him without touching him, simply stepping into the lane.

"Ticket," Connor said.

The runner's eyes hardened. He didn't answer.

Connor held his position. No aggression. Just refusal.

Sofia's voice cut, quiet and final. "Ticket."

The runner hesitated one beat too long, then backed away, retreating toward the corridor mouth as if he'd been instructed to test the boundary and report what held.

Connor didn't watch him go. He watched the lamps, the rims, the timing.

He felt Sofia exhale through her nose, controlled. The sound wasn't relief. It was recalibration.

"Walk," she called.

Connor echoed it. "Walk."

Plates left the pass in clean sequence, no stutter, no tremor.

Somewhere in the dining room, the inspector kept eating, unimpressed by anything except deviation. Somewhere in the corridor, Renaud carried a black case deeper into a system that had begun to claim him.

At the pass, under merciless light, Connor did what the kitchen had taught him to do from the first day he stepped into silence.

He executed.

And without asking permission, without announcing it, without ever stepping fully into the center, he began to take command of the only thing left that still mattered.

The service.

Chapter 18

The Pass

The pass lamps made a narrow country out of stainless and heat, and Connor stood at its border like a man learning a new language in the middle of gunfire.

Sofia was still centered, shoulders square, voice clipped into procedure, but Connor could feel the strain in the micro-delays she had to swallow between calls. He watched for them the way he watched rims: not to judge her, to protect the rhythm from showing its fractures.

"Two on eight," Sofia called.

Connor repeated it down the line before the words could lose momentum. "Two on eight. Fire cold now. Hot follows. Walk together."

The replies came back in a single flat breath. "Oui."

The brigade didn't need speeches. They needed continuity. The machine could survive anything except a stutter at the center.

A runner slid in close with a plate for a pickup, hands too clean, posture too controlled. Connor saw the tell now without needing reflection. The kitchen runners moved like they carried heat in their joints. These moved like they carried instructions.

The runner held the plate just a little too high, as if offering it to the lamps rather than to the pass.

Connor didn't reach.

"Ticket," Connor said, quiet and unembellished.

The runner's eyes narrowed. He didn't answer.

Sofia's voice cut without rising. "Ticket."

The runner's jaw worked once. He set the plate down on the stainless just outside the lamp strip, an inch too far to be considered ready, and stepped back toward the corridor mouth.

Connor didn't follow him with his eyes. He followed the plate.

It was perfect. That was the problem. Perfect plates came from the line. These plates were perfect in a way that looked rehearsed, like a photograph of perfection.

Connor leaned in, close enough to inspect without touching. No rim marks. Geometry severe. But there was no ticket clipped. No place in the rail for it to belong. Off-menu without record.

His pulse tried to climb. He pressed it flat.

Sofia's gaze flicked to the orphan plate, then away as if looking at it too long would make it real. Her jaw ticked once.

Connor spoke low, only for her. "We don't walk it."

Sofia didn't look at him. "We're in front of the Guide," she murmured, voice barely moving.

Connor understood. With the inspector present, any disruption would be magnified. But walking an untracked plate was worse. It wasn't just a deviation, it was compliance.

"We refire what's on the rail," Connor said, keeping it functional. "We don't serve ghosts."

Sofia's fingers tightened on the edge of the pass for a fraction. Then she nodded once, almost imperceptible.

"Walk eight," she called, louder.

Connor turned that call into motion, a baton passed cleanly. "Walk eight. Hands. Tight."

Two plates slid under the lamps. Connor's eyes moved across them in a pattern he had absorbed from watching Renaud for months: rim, symmetry, temperature cues, garnish placement, negative space. Not beauty. Control.

He caught a stray dot of sauce near a rim, so small it could be dismissed as steam. In this room nothing was dismissible.

He slid the plate back an inch and said, without looking at the cook, "Again."

Hot side didn't argue. Antoine's hands took it back with a stiffness that was almost resentment and immediately became obedience. The refire began before the plate was fully out of the lamp strip.

Connor felt the line register the word. Again wasn't just a correction. It was proof that someone was willing to burn time to preserve a standard. It was oxygen returning.

Behind him, the printer spat another ticket. The paper fed cleanly this time, but Connor didn't trust clean.

He tore it, clipped it, read fast. Table six again, the one that had returned "wrong" with no language. A cold course, then hot. No allergy notes.

No opportunities for sabotage in print, which meant the sabotage would try another route.

Sofia lifted one finger.

Hold.

Connor froze with his hands close to his sides, posture composed, no visible reaction. Around them, the brigade stopped mid-motion, a still photograph under heat.

Connor listened for the hidden rhythm under the visible one. Watch-check. Footstep. Corridor breath.

He didn't hear it, but he felt the room's attention swing toward the corridor mouth anyway, like a compass needle pulled by a magnet.

Sofia dropped her finger. "Walk."

Connor made it immediate. "Walk. Now."

The line moved again, and the hold disappeared into choreography, but Connor stored it. Holds were signals now, and signals meant someone was timing something that wasn't food.

At the edge of his vision, Dumas drifted close with a replenishment tray, silent as always, towel folded into thirds even while carrying. Dumas didn't look at Connor directly. He never did when it mattered.

He set the tray down and murmured, “They’re testing the center.”

Connor didn’t answer with his mouth. He answered with execution, with the way he checked the rims twice without looking like he checked twice.

Sofia’s voice snapped. “Hot in ten. Cold now.”

“Heard,” Connor said, and repeated it down the line. “Cold now. Hot in ten. Walk together.”

Garde manger sent up the cold course for six. Connor inspected it and felt a grim satisfaction: it was boring. It meant nothing. It could not be interpreted as a message because it contained no personality.

He nodded once to the runner and watched the runner’s hands as the plate was taken. Kitchen runner this time. Fatigue in the wrists. Heat in the joints. Real.

The hot course followed, and when it arrived Connor aligned it with the timing window, held it under the lamps for exactly the right beat, then released it with a single word.

“Walk.”

The plate left.

For a moment, nothing came back.

Sofia's shoulders lowered a millimeter. Not relief. Calculation. She kept calling. The machine kept moving.

Then the orphan plate that had been set outside the lamps began to creep inward, moved by a different set of hands. The too-clean runner returned, and this time he didn't ask. He nudged the plate into the lamp strip as if placing it there made it legitimate.

Connor stepped into the lane again, blocking the runner's path without touching him.

The runner's eyes went cold. "It goes," he said, voice low.

Connor kept his face clean. "Show me the ticket."

The runner's mouth tightened. "It's for a guest."

"Everything is for a guest," Connor said. No emotion. Just logic. "Ticket."

The runner leaned in slightly, not threatening, not quite. A pressure test. Connor didn't move.

From the corridor mouth, Hale's presence seemed to thicken the air. Connor didn't look, but he felt the pull.

Sofia's voice cut in like a blade. "Step back."

The runner hesitated.

Connor understood what the hesitation meant. The runner wasn't deciding whether to obey Sofia. He was deciding whether Sofia had authority to be obeyed.

Connor spoke before the pause could turn into a scene. "We're in Guide service," he said, the same phrase Sofia had used, but weaponized differently. "No record means no plate."

The runner's gaze flicked to the dining room wall, as if the inspector could hear through stone. For the first time, the runner looked uncertain.

Connor pushed gently, no volume. "Take it out of my lamps."

A beat.

The runner's hand closed around the plate. He lifted it and backed away, retreating toward the corridor network.

Connor didn't watch him leave. He watched Sofia.

Her eyes were on the rail, but Connor saw the slight tremor in her exhale, controlled and thin. She hadn't wanted a confrontation. Neither had he. But the pass had to remain a single system. If a second system could place plates under the lamps, then the line wasn't a line. It was a corridor.

Sofia leaned closer, barely moving her mouth. "You're making enemies."

Connor kept his eyes on the plates coming up. "They already tried to make me a body," he murmured. "If I'm going to be something, I'd rather be useful."

Sofia's jaw ticked, hard. For a beat her eyes looked almost tired. Then her voice returned to the room, clean and sharp. "Fire table nine."

Connor echoed it instantly. "Fire nine. Tight. No variation."

The brigade obeyed with a speed that felt like relief. They didn't want politics. They wanted someone to tell them what mattered.

The next ten minutes became a single continuous motion. Connor called timing when Sofia's voice needed breath. He caught a misalignment on a garnish and sent it back before it could walk. He corrected a runner's grip with a glance. He tore tickets as they printed and clipped them cleanly, turning paper into order.

Each time Sofia lifted a hold, Connor watched the corridor mouth in reflection and caught the suited men's watch-checks with a growing certainty. Holds weren't just pauses. They were windows for something to move unseen.

And Renaud still didn't return.

The absence began to press on the room. The brigade didn't say his name. They didn't need to. A kitchen could feel when its center was missing the way a body could feel when a tooth was gone, the tongue returning to the empty space without permission.

A plate returned from the dining room, this time carried by an actual server. The server's face was pale, trained into apology.

He hovered at the threshold. "Chef," he said, voice trembling.

Sofia's head angled toward him. "Speak."

The server swallowed. "Table six again. They… they pushed it away."

Sofia reached for the plate and slid it under the lamps.

Connor leaned in as well, half a step off center, letting Sofia keep the position while he took the pressure. The dish looked correct. The rim was clean. The temperature cues were right. Nothing visible was wrong.

Sofia's lips pressed together. The tiniest hesitation threatened.

Connor didn't allow the room to see it.

He spoke in pure function. “Refire six. New plates. New towels. No one touches rims.”

Sofia’s gaze snapped to him. He met it for a fraction of a second and then looked away, turning the decision into procedure.

Sofia’s voice recovered instantly, sharper now. “Refire six. Now.”

“Oui,” the line answered.

The server lingered, frightened by the lack of explanation. “They said,” he began.

Sofia’s eyes cut to him. “No commentary,” she said, and her tone was gentle only in the way a locked door was gentle. “Go.”

The server retreated.

Connor watched Sofia’s hands. They were steady, but he saw the cost in the tightness of her fingers. She was holding the pass together with discipline, but discipline wasn’t infinite. It wore down. It cracked. And the hidden system was waiting for a crack wide enough to slip a hand through.

Connor lowered his voice again. “Let me call,” he murmured.

Sofia’s jaw ticked. “That’s not how this works.”

"It is tonight," Connor said, and surprised himself with how calm it came out. Not defiance. Reality.

Sofia's eyes flicked, quick, toward the corridor mouth. Then back to the lamps. The inspector was still out there. The stars were still out there. And somewhere in the corridor, Renaud was being handled like a piece.

Sofia exhaled once through her nose, controlled. "Fine," she said quietly, and the word wasn't permission so much as triage. "Don't make it theatrical."

Connor didn't move to center. He didn't take her spot. He simply raised his voice a fraction and began to speak the kitchen's true religion.

"Hands. Listen. We walk what's on the rail. Nothing else."

The brigade's posture tightened, attention narrowing. Even hot side seemed to lean in without moving.

Connor continued, voice clipped, procedural. "No improvisation. No heroics. No curiosity. We execute."

He could feel eyes on him now, not just from the line. From the watchers. From the suited men. From Hale's stillness at the corridor mouth.

But Connor had learned the only safe way to be seen in this building.

Be boring. Be exact. Be impossible to edit.

He lifted the next plate under the lamps, checked the rim, and called without hesitation, as if he had been born at the pass.

"Walk."

"Walk."

The word left Connor's mouth like a latch clicking into place. The runner took the plate and vanished toward the dining room without meeting anyone's eyes. The lamp strip cleared for half a second before the next porcelain arrived, heat and cold trading places in a rhythm the kitchen had always obeyed. Tonight the rhythm felt less like music and more like a code that had to be entered correctly or the door would lock.

Connor stayed half a step off center, exactly where he could be useful without making a claim. Sofia remained the official spine at the pass, but the calls now moved through Connor as well, doubled and reinforced, as if the kitchen needed two signals to believe the world was still one world.

"Two on nine," Sofia said.

Connor echoed instantly. "Two on nine. Cold now. Hot in fifteen. Walk together."

"Oui," came back, flat and immediate.

He watched hands, not faces. Fingers that trembled got steadied by repetition. Knives kept moving. Squeeze bottles stayed upright. Towels were refolded into thirds again and again, a small ritual against the sense that someone could reach in and smear a rim simply to prove they could.

The corridor mouth held its own gravity. Connor did not look directly, but he felt it in the way runners approached the pass like they were crossing a border. Hale's stillness was not a presence so much as an instruction to the room: behave as if I own the air.

A server appeared with a glass of water on a tray, moving too carefully, and paused at the threshold as if unsure whether water belonged in this heat. He wasn't here for water. He leaned in, lips barely moving.

"The Guide," he murmured to Sofia, voice shaking. "They asked to see the kitchen."

Sofia's face didn't change. "No," she said, without volume.

The server's eyes widened. "They said—"

Sofia cut him off with the calm of a sealed door. "No," she repeated. "We're in service."

The server swallowed and backed away, relief and fear mixing into the same expression.

Connor felt his stomach tighten. An inspector asking to see the kitchen wasn't normal, not in a place built on curated illusion. It meant the dining room's silent judge had smelled something behind the plate: a pressure, a control, a fear that didn't belong to food.

Sofia leaned closer to Connor, barely moving her mouth. "They're pushing," she murmured.

Connor kept his eyes on the lamps. "We don't let the pass stutter," he replied, equally low. Not reassurance. Procedure.

Sofia's jaw ticked once in agreement and the tick looked like pain.

A plate came up from hot side, and Connor's eyes went straight to the rim. Clean. He shifted his focus to the sauce line, then to garnish placement, then to negative space. Everything where it should be. He nodded, and Sofia called, "Walk," but Connor saw the runner's hands.

Too clean.

Too careful.

Not kitchen.

The runner reached, and Connor stepped into the lane without touching him, placing his body like a barrier that could be explained as workflow.

"Ticket," Connor said.

The runner's eyes hardened. "It's on," he replied, and his tone carried the faint impatience of someone used to being obeyed.

Connor didn't move. "Show me."

Sofia's voice snapped, controlled. "Ticket."

For a beat, the runner held his position as if testing whose words mattered more: the pass, or the corridor mouth. Connor felt the whole room register the pause. Pauses were where power slipped.

The runner's gaze flicked past Connor, toward the corridor mouth. Permission check.

Connor didn't look, but he could feel it. Hale deciding without moving.

The runner's jaw worked. Then, without producing paper, he backed away with the plate still in his hands and retreated toward the corridor network.

The lamps remained clear. The rail remained real.

Connor exhaled through his nose, controlled. He hadn't won anything. He had simply held a boundary for one more beat.

Sofia's eyes cut to him. "Don't escalate," she murmured.

Connor answered with function. "I didn't," he said. "I asked for a ticket."

Sofia's mouth tightened as if she almost smiled and then remembered smiling was a liability. "Keep it like that," she said. "Clean."

Clean meant a thousand things here. Tonight it meant: nothing that can be replayed.

The printer fed a new ticket. Connor tore it cleanly, clipped it, read fast. Table six again. Of course. The table that didn't use language, only rejection.

Sofia saw it too. Her fingers tightened on the edge of the pass for half a fraction.

Connor spoke before the room could feel her hesitation. "We refire six before they ask," he said, quiet but decisive.

Sofia's eyes sharpened. "We don't refire preemptively," she murmured.

"Tonight we do," Connor replied, and kept it procedural. "Not because they're right. Because we don't give them time."

Sofia's jaw ticked hard. She was weighing standards against theater, the kitchen's religion against the hidden rail's games.

Then she nodded once, small. "Refire six," she called, voice clipped.

Connor turned to the line. "Garde manger, new plates for six. Hot side, match timing. No improvisation. No rim contact."

"Oui," came back immediately, and Connor felt something loosen in the room: not comfort, alignment. They didn't want to guess what to do. They wanted to execute.

As the refire began, a new plate arrived under the lamps from garde manger, and Connor caught a detail that would have been invisible in any other context. The micro greens were correct in placement, correct in quantity, but one leaf lay angled a degree off the pattern. Not wrong. Not to a diner. But wrong to an inspector trained to read control, and wrong to a kitchen being hunted for any sign of drift.

Connor slid the plate back an inch. "Again," he said, without volume.

The commis who'd replaced Jules flinched so quickly he almost made it visible. Connor didn't look at his face. Looking at faces made stories. He looked only at the plate.

The commis took it back with stiff obedience and remade it.

Sofia's head turned sharply. Her eyes said: careful. Her mouth stayed closed. She understood what Connor was doing. He was keeping perfection as a shield. If the only visible service remained flawless, the inspector would have fewer reasons to pry into the kitchen's shadows.

Hot side sent up a dish and Antoine's hands were steady, but Connor saw the faintest tremor in the plating spoon. Not fear of food. Fear of consequence. Last night's sabotage had taught everyone that blame didn't need proof. Tonight's inspector had taught everyone that proof didn't need blame.

Connor leaned in, voice low, meant only for Antoine. "Breathe," he said.

Antoine's eyes flicked up, hard. "Don't talk to me like I'm a commis," he muttered through barely moving lips.

Connor didn't react. Reaction would become conflict, and conflict would become a fracture the watchers could widen. He kept his gaze on the dish. "Then plate like you're not," Connor replied, and it sounded cold because cold was safer than kind.

Antoine's jaw clenched. His hands steadied.

"Walk," Sofia called, and Connor echoed it, sending the course out as if nothing had happened between the two men.

The refire for six built in parallel. Cold came up first. Connor inspected it: rim clean, geometry severe, nothing interpretive. He nodded, and the kitchen runner took it, wrists showing fatigue, the only kind of runner Connor trusted tonight.

Then hot arrived a beat later.

Connor checked the rim first, then the sauce, then the negative space. Clean. He aligned both plates in the lamp strip as a single rhythm and felt the pass settle for a fraction of a second into something almost normal.

"Walk," Sofia said.

Connor repeated it. "Walk."

The plates went.

Time stretched. Three minutes. Five. No return.

Then the dining room wall seemed to tilt, not physically, but in the way front of house energy changed when something expensive had just happened. The slick-haired manager appeared at the threshold, face pale under its practiced polish.

He didn't step in. He hovered, eyes darting to Sofia, then to Connor, then toward the corridor mouth as if checking whether the air allowed him to speak.

Sofia's voice stayed flat. "Speak," she said.

The manager swallowed. "Table six," he began.

Sofia didn't move. "Yes."

"They said it's perfect," he whispered, as if the word itself was dangerous. "They said… it's perfect, and that's what worries them."

For a beat, the pass lamps seemed louder.

Connor felt something cold move through his ribs. Perfect wasn't a compliment here. Perfect could be a threat. Perfect could mean the inspector had stopped tasting and started reading the performance. Perfect could mean: this is too controlled.

Sofia's jaw ticked once, hard enough to look like it might crack. "What do they want," she asked.

The manager's eyes flicked toward the corridor mouth again. "They want to meet Chef Renaud."

Connor didn't look. He didn't need to. Renaud was still gone.

Sofia's eyes narrowed. "He's in service."

The manager's face tightened. "They said they know," he whispered. "They said they saw him leave the pass."

Silence thickened.

Connor understood immediately. The inspector hadn't just been eating. The inspector had been watching the room, the staff, the timing, the holds. If they'd seen Renaud step away during Guide service, then the kitchen's illusion of absolute control was already compromised.

Sofia's gaze cut to Connor, and in it he saw something she couldn't say in front of anyone: we are exposed.

Connor kept his voice low and functional. "Tell them he's overseeing a correction," he murmured. "Tell them he'll return when it's resolved."

The manager stared at him, startled by the fact that a name that wasn't Renaud's was giving instructions.

Sofia made it official without acknowledging it. "Do that," she said to the manager, and her tone turned Connor's words into hers.

The manager nodded too quickly and fled.

Sofia leaned in toward Connor, voice barely moving. "If the Guide asks for him and he doesn't come," she murmured, "that's a fracture."

Connor's eyes stayed on the rail. "Then we keep the visible service flawless," he said. "No returns. No interruptions. No reason for them to dig."

Sofia's mouth tightened. "They don't need a reason," she replied, and her voice held a thin edge now. "They need a pattern."

Connor nodded once. Patterns were how you got erased.

At the corridor mouth, movement finally shifted. Not Renaud. One of the suited men stepped forward, murmured to Hale, and Hale's gaze slid toward the pass like a hand reaching without touching.

Connor didn't look directly. He felt it anyway.

Then Sofia raised one finger.

Hold.

The brigade froze mid-motion.

Connor stayed still, hands at his sides, posture composed, eyes down. He listened. Refrigeration hum. A distant clink from the dining room. The faint whisper of shoes in the corridor network, too soft to be kitchen.

The hold stretched. One beat too long. Two.

Sofia's finger didn't drop.

Connor saw, in stainless reflection, a suited man check his watch.

Synchronization.

A door somewhere beyond the corridor mouth made a sound so small it almost didn't exist. Not a slam. A click. A latch.

Sofia dropped her finger. "Walk."

Connor echoed instantly, voice cutting cleanly through the resumed motion. "Walk. Now."

The line moved again as if nothing had happened.

But Connor felt it with cold certainty: the hold hadn't been for timing plates.

It had been to move something through the building while the kitchen stood still, hands frozen, eyes trained not to look away from their stations.

Precision under fire, Connor thought, wasn't about making food perfect.

It was about keeping the machine's surface flawless while something else moved underneath it.

Another ticket printed. Connor tore it, clipped it, called without hesitation.

"Fire. Tight. No variation."

The brigade obeyed.

And as the lamps burned and the inspector watched from the dining room, Connor understood the real test tonight. Not whether he could run the pass. He could.

The test was whether he could do it while being watched by two different systems, both looking for the same thing: a moment of human error they could turn into proof.

Connor gave them none.

He checked the rim, aligned the plates, and called the only safe word left.

"Walk."

The next plate landed under the lamps with a soft porcelain click that sounded too loud in Connor's head.

He checked the rim. Clean.

He checked the symmetry. Severe, controlled, no personality.

He checked the negative space, the one place where the kitchen's hand always tried to show itself.

Nothing.

“Walk,” he said, and the runner took it, wrists tired, real.

For three minutes, the pass held. Not calm. Holding.

Then the dining room pushed back.

The slick-haired manager reappeared at the threshold, moving like he’d rehearsed every footstep. He didn’t come in. He hovered at the line where heat became jurisdiction. His eyes went to Sofia first, then slid to Connor, then betrayed him again toward the corridor mouth, searching for permission in a shadow.

Sofia didn’t look up from the rail. “Speak,” she said.

The manager swallowed. “They’re not waiting anymore.”

Sofia’s jaw ticked. “Who.”

The manager didn’t say Guide. He didn’t say inspector. As if naming it would make it official. “Table six,” he said, voice low. “They said if Chef Renaud can’t come out, they’ll come back.”

Back meant something different now. Not next week. Not next season. Back with consequences.

Sofia's fingers tightened on the stainless edge of the pass. Her face stayed clean. Her voice stayed flat. "Tell them he is engaged in a correction."

"I did," the manager whispered. "They said they saw him step away. They said they don't accept 'corrections' during service."

Connor felt the phrase land like a knife sliding under the pass lamps. They don't accept. The inspector didn't accept narratives. The inspector accepted only control. And tonight control had been seen leaving the pass with a black case.

Sofia kept her gaze on the rail, but Connor saw the microfracture: a blink that came a fraction too fast, a pause between breaths.

The kitchen felt it too. It wasn't loud. It was a subtle tightening in shoulders up and down the line, like the room was bracing for a blow.

Connor spoke without raising his voice. "Ask them for two minutes," he said to the manager, pure function. "Tell them we are resetting a course."

The manager stared at him, startled again by the fact that a name without a title was giving him an answer that sounded like authority.

Sofia made it official without looking at Connor. "Two minutes," she echoed, turning it into her decision. "Go."

The manager backed away too quickly and vanished.

Sofia leaned closer, just enough that her words could live under fan hum. "We can't stall the Guide," she murmured. The word Guide came out tight, like she hated that it existed in her mouth.

Connor kept his eyes on the lamps. "We're not stalling," he said. "We're buying control."

Sofia's jaw ticked. "And if Renaud doesn't come back."

Connor didn't answer with comfort. Comfort was useless. He answered with the only thing this kitchen respected. "Then the pass doesn't change," he said. "The standard doesn't change. Nothing changes."

Sofia's eyes flicked toward the corridor mouth. The pull was physical, like an unseen hand on her chin. "Except the center."

Connor felt the truth of that sentence hit the room even though she hadn't spoken it aloud to anyone but him. Centers mattered. A kitchen could survive a bad plate. It couldn't survive uncertainty about who had the right to say again.

Another ticket printed. Connor tore it, clipped it, and called, clean. "Fire twelve. Tight."

The line answered automatically. "Oui."

Sofia lifted one finger.

Hold.

The brigade froze mid-motion. Connor stayed still, hands at his sides, gaze down. He didn't have to look to know what the hold meant now. A window. A corridor movement. Something carried while the kitchen pretended it was only waiting on timing.

In stainless reflection, he caught the suited man's watch-check again. That same precise lowering of the wrist. That same patient interest.

Sofia dropped her finger. "Walk."

Connor made it immediate. "Walk. Now."

The line resumed with a controlled snap, grateful for motion. Motion meant the machine still existed.

Then, from the corridor mouth, a shape detached from shadow.

Not Hale.

Dumas.

He didn't cross into the line. He didn't step near the lamps. He just appeared at the edge of the corridor threshold, towel in hand like it had grown there, his face blank with function. But Connor saw something in the way Dumas's shoulders held themselves, a stiffness that wasn't fatigue.

Dumas's eyes flicked to Connor. Not long. Not enough to be called communication. Just a single inventory check.

Then Dumas looked at Sofia and made a small motion with his fingers, a gesture so slight it could be mistaken for wiping something invisible from the air.

Erase.

Sofia's nostrils flared once. She didn't nod. She didn't react. But Connor understood the message anyway.

Whatever was happening in the corridor, it wasn't just Renaud being pulled into a meeting.

It was being cleaned.

Two minutes passed. The manager did not return with relief.

Instead, a server appeared. Not the manager. A server with careful posture and a face trained into neutrality so hard it looked like fear. He hovered at the threshold, eyes down, hands empty.

Sofia angled her head. "Speak."

The server swallowed. "They're coming," he whispered.

Sofia's fingers tightened. "Who."

The server didn't say it. He didn't need to. "Table six," he said, and the words carried the weight of the entire dining room.

The brigade kept moving. Tickets fed. Plates walked. But the air changed, a subtle shift as the kitchen registered that the dining room was about to cross the border.

Connor watched the corridor mouth in reflection without turning his head. Hale stood there, still and calm, as if he'd been waiting for this exact beat. One suited man's gaze moved toward the dining room doors. The other's attention stayed fixed on the pass lamps.

They weren't worried about an inspector.

They were watching for who would flinch.

The door between dining room and kitchen opened.

Not wide. Just enough.

A figure stepped into the threshold. Not wearing a suit. Not wearing whites. Simple clothes. No logo. No status displayed. The kind of anonymity that didn't need to announce itself because it expected the world to recognize it anyway.

The inspector.

Connor couldn't see their eyes clearly from the lamps, but he felt them. A gaze that wasn't hungry. A gaze that measured.

The inspector didn't step into the heat. They stopped at the border and looked at the pass as if it were a plate.

Sofia straightened a fraction, perfect posture, face sealed. "Good evening," she said, voice controlled.

The inspector's gaze moved over her shoulder, scanning the lamps, the rail, the movement. Then it shifted, and Connor felt it land on him.

Not because he was the most important. Because he was doing something.

Because he was speaking.

Because he was making decisions.

"Chef Renaud," the inspector said, voice calm and flat. Not a request. An expectation.

Sofia didn't answer immediately. A fraction too long. The smallest crack.

Connor stepped into it before it could widen.

"He is unavailable at this moment," Connor said, not loudly, not apologetically. Just a fact stated in the same tone the kitchen used for "walk." "I'm handling the pass."

Sofia's head snapped a fraction toward him, warning. You don't speak for the house. Not unless you're ready to be held to it.

Connor didn't look at her. He kept his gaze on the lamps and the rail, presenting his profile to the inspector like something stable.

The inspector's eyes stayed on Connor. "Your name."

It wasn't a demand. It was the kind of question that made your answer part of a record.

Connor knew what naming did in this building. Names got removed from lists.

But there was no safe silence here. Silence would look like fear. Fear would look like guilt. Guilt would become a tool.

"Connor Felwick," he said.

The inspector nodded once, small. No praise. No judgment. Just filing.

Behind the inspector, the manager hovered, sweating in expensive clothing. He looked like he wanted to disappear into the wall.

The inspector looked back at the lamps. "I've had two perfect courses," they said. Thc word perfect landed wrong, the same way it had from the manager earlier. "And one that was returned without explanation."

Sofia's jaw ticked hard.

Connor answered before she could. "Yes," he said. "We refired immediately."

The inspector's gaze slid to him again. "Why was it returned."

Connor didn't say sabotage. He didn't say contamination. He didn't say Hale. He didn't say corridor. Those words would become a story, and stories were where people got erased.

"I don't know," Connor said. "So we treated it as unacceptable and corrected it."

The inspector watched him for a long beat. Connor kept his posture still, his hands clean. He didn't fidget. He didn't overexplain. He didn't plead.

Finally the inspector said, "Who decides unacceptable."

Connor felt the whole kitchen lean toward the question without moving. This was not about food. It never was.

He answered the only way that could survive replay. "The pass," he said. "The standard is the standard."

The inspector's eyes moved back to Sofia. "And Chef Renaud is… elsewhere."

Sofia's face stayed sealed, but Connor saw the cost in her throat as she swallowed. "He is overseeing a correction," she said, using the words they'd chosen as cover.

The inspector's gaze returned to Connor. "You spoke for him."

Connor didn't deny it. Denial would be weakness. "I spoke for the service," he corrected.

A beat.

The inspector nodded again, small, and turned their head slightly, looking past the pass and down the line. Their eyes traveled over stations, hands, motions. They paused on the replacement commis where Jules had been and moved on without registering the absence because the absence had been cleaned into continuity.

Then the inspector looked back at the lamps. "Continue," they said.

Not permission. An order. As if they owned time.

They stepped back. The door eased closed. The dining room reclaimed its border.

The kitchen exhaled without making a sound.

Sofia's shoulders lowered a millimeter. She leaned toward Connor, mouth barely moving. "You just put yourself on paper," she whispered.

Connor kept his eyes on the rail. "I'm already on paper," he murmured back. "That's the problem."

Sofia's jaw ticked. "And Hale heard you."

Connor didn't look toward the corridor mouth, but he felt the shift there. Attention tightening. Interest.

"Let him," Connor said, and surprised himself with how steady it sounded. Not bravery. Calculation.

Sofia stared at him for half a beat as if trying to decide what he was becoming. Then she turned back to the lamps and resumed calling with sharper precision, like she had accepted a new geometry at the center of the room.

"Two on nine," she called.

Connor echoed instantly, voice carrying cleanly down the line. "Two on nine. Fire. Tight. Walk together."

The brigade answered in one flat breath. "Oui."

And Connor felt it, subtle but real, like a weight settling into place.

The line was listening to him now.

Not because he'd demanded it.

Because he had spoken to the inspector without flinching, and the kitchen had not cracked. Because he had held the pass against ghost plates and silent returns and timed holds. Because he had made decisions that burned time and money and pride, and the standard hadn't blinked.

In this place, authority wasn't granted. It was recognized in motion.

A hot plate came up with a rim that looked clean until the light hit it at the wrong angle. Connor saw the faint smear instantly.

"Again," he said, quiet.

The cook took it back without a word.

No resentment. No argument. Just obedience.

Sofia glanced at Connor, and for the first time all night her eyes didn't warn him away.

They measured him.

Then, as if acknowledging what had already happened without ever naming it, Sofia shifted half a step to the side, making space at the pass that she did not announce.

It was small. Deniable. The kind of movement that could be explained as workflow.

But the kitchen felt it.

The center had widened.

Connor stepped into the space without stepping into it, still half a beat off, still careful, still clean. He didn't claim Sofia's position. He simply became unavoidable at the lamps, his voice and hands integrated into the rhythm so seamlessly that removing him would now require disrupting the service.

And disrupting the service in front of the Guide was the one thing even Hale's system couldn't do without consequence.

Connor tore the next ticket. Clipped it. Called it.

"Fire."

The brigade moved.

The pass lamps burned.

Somewhere beyond the wall, the inspector kept eating, unimpressed by beauty, attentive only to control.

At the corridor mouth, Hale remained still, but the stillness no longer felt like ownership of the room.

It felt like observation of a new variable.

Connor checked the rim. Aligned the plates. Released them with a voice that didn't tremble.

"Walk."

And the kitchen obeyed as if it had been waiting for someone like him all along.

Chapter 19

Ascension

The door to the dining room had barely eased shut when the kitchen's rhythm changed again.

Not looser. Not relieved. Sharper, as if the inspector's brief presence had made everyone suddenly aware of their own hands. Plates came up with the same severe geometry, but now every cook moved like they were working under glass.

Sofia stayed close to the lamps, calling with clipped precision, her voice returning to the cadence the brigade trusted. Connor remained in the widened center she'd made without naming it, half a step off, close enough that his words could carry and close enough that any mistake would be his to own.

"Two on nine," Sofia called.

Connor tore the ticket, clipped it, and echoed. "Two on nine. Cold now. Hot in twelve. Walk together."

The answers came back in one flat breath. “Oui.”

The corridor mouth remained heavy. Hale was still there, not intruding, not leaving. A constant that didn’t need to speak to be felt. The suited men behind him had rotated once since the inspector’s appearance, faces changed, posture identical. Their eyes kept sliding to Connor’s hands when he inspected rims, to Sofia’s mouth when she called holds, to the printer when it stuttered and didn’t.

Connor had stopped expecting Renaud to reappear. The absence had become its own presence, a hollow where power used to sit. But even hollows had to be worked around. The service didn’t care who was missing. It only punished stutter.

A plate landed under the lamps. Connor checked the rim first, then the negative space, then the garnish alignment. Clean. He released it.

“Walk.”

A kitchen runner took it and moved fast without looking fast, wrists tired, real. The kind of movement that belonged to work, not instruction.

For the next fifteen minutes nothing returned. No ghost plates tried to slip into the lamps. No silent carrier slid rejection back into the pass. The holds still came, but shorter now, less theatrical, as if someone had decided the visible rail couldn't be pushed too hard with the inspector still close enough to notice patterns.

Sofia lifted one finger.

Hold.

Connor froze, eyes down, posture composed. The brigade turned into a still photograph again: knives hovering, squeeze bottles suspended, hands half-open over porcelain.

In stainless reflection, Connor saw one suited man check his watch. The motion was small and clean.

Synchronization.

Sofia dropped her finger. "Walk."

Connor made it immediate. "Walk. Now."

The line resumed in a controlled snap. The hold disappeared into choreography, but Connor stored it anyway. Holds were never only culinary now. They were windows for corridors.

At the edge of the pass, Dumas appeared with a replenishment tray, face blank, towel folded into thirds as if folding could keep the world in place. He set down clean spoons and disappeared again, but not before Connor caught his eyes for half a fraction.

Dumas didn't communicate with words when words could be replayed.

His look said: it's moving.

The dining room hummed behind the wall, expensive and unaware of the machine's internal recalibration. Or pretending to be unaware. Connor no longer trusted the difference.

A new ticket printed. Connor tore it clean, clipped it, scanned.

Table six.

Again.

Sofia saw it too, the smallest tightening in her jaw. The tick came and went, muscle memory fighting stress. Her eyes flicked toward the dining room wall, as if she could feel the inspector's gaze through stone even when the inspector wasn't in the threshold.

Connor spoke low, only for her. "We do it clean," he said.

Sofia's mouth barely moved. "We do everything clean."

"Yes," Connor replied, and kept it procedural. "No variation. No story."

Sofia nodded once, so small it could be mistaken for breathing. "Fire."

Connor turned to the line. "Fire six. Cold now. Hot in ten. Walk together. New towels."

"Oui."

Garde manger sent up the cold course first. Connor inspected it without touching the rim, tilted it under the lamps, looked for the tiniest deviation in the pattern. Perfect in the way the kitchen meant it: controlled, absent of ego.

He released it. "Walk."

Hot side followed on time. Antoine's hands were steadier now, anger converted into function, fear flattened into obedience. Connor caught a near-invisible streak on the rim that might have been steam and might have been a fingerprint in the wrong light.

He didn't hesitate.

"Again."

Antoine took it back without a word.

Sofia didn't flinch. She called the next table as if refiring a dish was the most normal thing in the world. Because in this kitchen, it was. Money and time were less valuable than control.

The refire came up clean. Connor aligned cold and hot in the lamps so they read as one rhythm, one decision. Sofia watched his hands for a beat and then looked away, as if granting attention itself was too risky.

"Walk," Sofia said.

Connor echoed. "Walk."

The plates left.

Minutes stretched. Ten, then fifteen. No return.

The pressure didn't vanish, but it redistributed, shifting from immediate threat to something that felt like waiting for an outcome. The kind of waiting that happened in a courtroom after the last word was spoken.

Connor kept working. Tickets printed. Plates walked. Holds came and went. Twice more a too-clean runner approached the lamp strip with a plate that had no record, and twice Connor stopped him with the same simple request.

"Ticket."

Each time the runner backed away toward the corridor network, refusing to make a scene in front of the Guide. Connor didn't count it as victory. He counted it as containment.

Near the end of service, Sofia's calls softened by a fraction, not in volume but in urgency. The dining room's hum began to thin as tables paid and departed, laughter moving farther from the kitchen wall, coats being collected, doors opening to night air.

Then the slick-haired manager appeared at the threshold again, face pale under its practiced polish, eyes too wide. He hovered at the line of heat, as if stepping into the kitchen would make his news legally binding.

Sofia didn't look up from the rail. "Speak."

The manager swallowed hard. His gaze flicked toward Connor, then away, then toward the corridor mouth like a reflex. "They're leaving," he whispered.

Sofia's jaw ticked. "Who."

The manager's lips parted, then closed again, as if he was choosing words that wouldn't get him erased for repeating them incorrectly. "Table six," he said. "The Guide."

Connor felt the room tighten anyway, the brigade listening without turning their heads. The inspector leaving wasn't a relief. It was the moment the judgment became inevitable.

Sofia's voice stayed flat. "And."

The manager's throat bobbed. "They asked me to tell you," he said, and his eyes finally lifted to the lamps like the lamps might punish him for lying. "They said the service was… intact."

Intact. Not beautiful. Not inspired. Not transcendent.

Intact meant controlled.

Connor felt a cold satisfaction settle behind his ribs, quickly checked. Satisfaction was a face you couldn't afford to wear.

Sofia nodded once, small, and turned it into function. "Clear the rail," she said, as if clearing paper could clear tension.

The manager didn't move. His voice dropped lower. "And," he added, "they said they will not be changing their assessment."

For a beat, the only sound was refrigeration hum and the distant clink of a glass being set down in the dining room.

Sofia held still, eyes on the tickets like they contained a different answer. "Which means," she said.

The manager's mouth worked. "No loss," he whispered. "No drop."

Stars retained.

No one said it out loud, not yet. Not in those words. Words made records, and records could be used.

But the kitchen understood. The brigade exhaled without making a sound, shoulders dropping a millimeter across the line, hands moving with a slightly different economy. Not less precise. Just less desperate.

Connor saw Antoine's posture ease by a fraction and then lock back into discipline, as if he'd caught himself trying to be human.

Sofia's face stayed sealed. She didn't smile. She didn't thank anyone. In L'Étoile Noire, celebration was a kind of disorder.

"Finish," she said simply.

The manager nodded too quickly and retreated.

Connor turned back to the lamps, to the next plate, because the service wasn't over until it was over. Retained stars meant nothing if the last course came back, untouched, like an insult.

But nothing did.

The final plates walked. The last tickets were torn and clipped and cleared. The pass lamps burned over empty steel.

Sofia lowered her hands to the edge of the pass and held still. The kitchen didn't erupt into noise the way other kitchens might. There was no release valve. The machine simply shifted from service mode to cleanup, the discipline changing costume without changing its face.

"Break down," Sofia said, quiet.

"Oui," the line answered.

Connor began to step back toward garde manger, ready to return to his station and become boring again, when the corridor mouth changed.

Not with sound. With density.

Hale stepped forward half a pace, coat still on, calm unchanged. One suited man remained behind him; the other peeled away down the corridor without looking at the kitchen, as if delivering information to a different rail.

Hale's gaze moved over Sofia at the pass, then over Connor, lingering just long enough to feel like a fingertip pressing a bruise.

Sofia didn't move. Her posture was perfect, a wall made of training.

Hale spoke softly, not to the whole room, not to any single person. "Good," he said.

It wasn't praise. It was confirmation of an outcome he'd expected.

Sofia's jaw ticked. "The Guide is satisfied," she said, making it sound like a report, not a relief.

Hale's eyes stayed on her. "They aren't the only one who matters."

The sentence landed like cold water.

Connor felt the brigade keep working faster, more focused, pretending not to hear. In this kitchen, pretending was survival.

Sofia's voice stayed controlled. "We did not lose anything tonight."

Hale's mouth moved, not quite a smile. "No," he agreed. "You didn't."

He let the pronoun hang there, the implication sharp: you.

Not Renaud. Not the house. You, the machine that had held while a man was moved off the board.

Connor didn't look at Hale directly. He didn't give him the satisfaction of visible reaction. He began wiping the pass edge in single clean strokes, as if cleaning steel could erase the residue of a conversation.

Then, from the corridor, a movement.

Chef Renaud appeared.

Not rushing. Not panicked. Immaculate jacket still on, face centered the way it always was, but Connor saw what the lamps had shown earlier and the corridor had tried to hide. The tiredness behind the eyes. The thinness around the mouth, like he'd been holding his breath in a room with no air.

His right hand was steady now. Too steady. As if steadiness had been applied.

Renaud stepped to the pass and looked at the cleared lamps, the wiped steel, the tickets already clipped away. His gaze landed on Sofia first, then shifted to Connor.

Inventory again.

Not gratitude. Not acknowledgment. Calculation.

Sofia spoke before silence could become a weapon. "Service completed," she said.

Renaud's eyes flicked toward Hale at the corridor mouth. He didn't address him. He addressed the room, because the room was the only thing he could still claim.

"The Guide," Renaud said quietly.

Sofia answered in the same tone. "No change."

Renaud held still for a beat. Stars retained. The house remained untouchable, on paper.

His gaze returned to Connor and held a fraction longer than it should have.

Connor kept his face clean.

Renaud's voice came, quiet and flat. "Good."

Hale's stillness felt like approval without words.

For a brief moment, the kitchen existed in an uneasy balance: the visible victory of retained stars, and the invisible cost still moving through corridors.

Connor wiped the steel again, single pass, as if polishing could make control real.

He understood then that retention wasn't the end of the night's story. It was its cover.

The stars were kept.

Which meant the system that kept them had won another round.

And Connor, who had spoken his name into the inspector's record and held the pass under merciless light, had become something that couldn't be unmade without consequence.

A point, Renaud had called him.

Tonight, that point had held.

And everyone in the building had felt it.

The kitchen did not celebrate the way other kitchens did.

There was no shout, no slammed pans, no champagne sabered against steel. The lamps were wiped, the rail cleared, the burners turned down in clean increments as if the building itself demanded a controlled descent. The brigade moved into breakdown mode without changing expression, the same clipped economy translated from plating to scrubbing.

Connor stayed near the pass, towel folded into thirds, wiping the stainless edge in single strokes that didn't overlap. He had learned, painfully, that repetition was a language here. It told the watchers you were stable. It told the kitchen you belonged. It told yourself you were still inside your own body.

Sofia began calling cleanup the way she called service, calm and precise.

"Hot down. Cold down. Sanitize. Labels out."

"Oui," came back, flat.

A few cooks glanced toward the corridor mouth and then away as if the act of looking might be recorded. Hale remained exactly where he had been, coat on, unhurried, as though time belonged to him more than it belonged to the dining room. The suited man behind him did not relax. His eyes continued to sweep, not to check the work, but to collect it.

Chef Renaud stood at the pass with the cleared lamps in front of him, hands resting lightly on the steel. He did not touch a plate. There were none to touch. He watched the line break down as if watching a machine come apart for maintenance, each piece returned to its place. His face was centered again, but the centering felt imposed, like a mask pressed back onto skin before it had stopped bleeding.

Sofia approached him with a small bundle of paper in her hand: the final service notes, the comp log, the list of tables that had asked questions they weren't supposed to ask. She held it like an offering that could also be evidence.

"Front says the Guide left," she said quietly.

Renaud didn't look at her. "I know."

Sofia's jaw ticked once. "No change," she added, because saying it out loud was how you made it real in this room.

Renaud finally turned his head. His eyes moved to her face, then beyond her to Connor, and then to Hale without lingering there. The motion was small, but Connor saw it anyway: a man checking which hands were on which levers.

“Good,” Renaud said, the word stripped of warmth.

Sofia accepted it as if it were simply a temperature reading. “Yes, Chef.”

The brigade continued working faster, not from relief, but from the need to bury feeling under motion. A pot was drained. A hotel pan was scraped into the bin with controlled efficiency. Someone replaced a sani bucket and aligned it with tape. The metal singing of the dishwasher became the closest thing to applause.

At the far end of the line, Antoine finished wiping his station and paused for half a beat, as if his body had attempted a human reaction before remembering it was not allowed. His eyes flicked toward Connor and then away. The message, if it was one, stayed private. In this kitchen even gratitude could be used as a handle.

Dumas drifted past with a trash bag, silent, his towel still folded into thirds even while carrying weight. He didn’t look at Connor directly, but as he passed he murmured, so low the sound could have been fan noise, “Intact.”

Connor kept wiping. “Heard,” he said, because it was the only safe reply.

Hale's voice cut through the hum with quiet ownership. Not loud enough to startle, but clear enough that it didn't have to compete.

"Chef Renaud."

Renaud turned fully this time. For a moment the pass felt like a border between two jurisdictions. The kitchen's heat on one side. The corridor's cold control on the other.

"Yes," Renaud said.

Hale's mouth barely moved. "A word."

Sofia's posture tightened. It was subtle, a shift in weight that would look like nothing to anyone not trained to read fractions. Connor saw the same instinct that had made her raise holds at the right beats: the urge to control timing even when timing belonged to someone else.

Renaud didn't glance at Sofia. "Continue cleanup," he said to the room, as if their work was a curtain he could keep drawn.

"Oui, Chef," the brigade answered automatically.

Renaud stepped away from the pass and moved toward the corridor mouth. Hale turned without hurry, and the suited man fell into place behind them. They did not disappear fully, not yet. They stopped just inside the threshold, half-visible through the gap, close enough that the kitchen could still feel the pressure of their conversation even without hearing it.

Sofia watched them go for one beat too long, then snapped her attention back to the steel as if she could erase the act of watching by resuming function.

"Faster," she said, not angry, just urgent. "We clear the room."

"Yes, Chef," the line replied.

Connor kept his head down and let his hands work. But the absence of Renaud from the pass, even now that service was over, did something to the air. It created a vacuum that the kitchen tried not to acknowledge. The machine had run without him for hours, and the proof of that sat in every clean, empty lamp and every ticket already clipped away.

A small cluster formed near the beverage station where staff water was poured. No one called it a celebration. They simply stood closer than usual, shoulders not touching, eyes lowered. A junior cook poured water into paper cups with the care usually reserved for wine.

Someone, very quietly, let out a breath that could have been laughter in another life. It died quickly.

The slick-haired manager appeared at the kitchen threshold, face still pale but now wearing a smile that looked borrowed. He didn't enter fully. He never did. He spoke to Sofia with the careful tone of a man addressing a blade.

"They're happy," he said.

Sofia didn't look up. "Who."

The manager hesitated, then corrected himself. "No change," he said, as if using the kitchen's language would keep him safe.

Sofia nodded once. "Good."

The manager's smile twitched. He wanted more. He wanted a visible emotion he could take back to the dining room as proof the house was alive. "We kept it," he said, almost pleading. "We kept the stars."

Sofia's jaw ticked hard enough to be seen. "Yes," she replied. "Now leave the threshold."

The manager blinked, then backed away as if he'd been burned.

A commis near garde manger, the replacement in Jules's old space, lifted his cup slightly toward Antoine. A silent toast. Antoine didn't return it. His eyes stayed on his hands as he folded his towel into thirds again, correcting a corner that wasn't wrong.

Connor understood. Small gestures were dangerous. Small gestures became stories, and stories were what the corridor system used to identify who believed they were safe.

Sofia moved down the line checking stations, not for cleanliness but for order. At Connor's station she stopped and let her gaze travel over the containers and labels that faced outward, the tweezers aligned, the cutting board scrubbed to a sterile blank.

"Boring," she said.

Connor kept wiping. "Yes, Chef."

Her voice lowered. "You did what you did," she murmured, careful. "In front of the Guide."

Connor didn't look at her. "I spoke for the service."

Sofia's jaw ticked. "And you put your name in the air."

"It was already in the air," Connor said, and felt how cold it sounded. He didn't soften it. Softer was a crack.

Sofia's eyes flicked toward the corridor mouth. "They're talking," she said.

Connor's hands didn't stop. "Hale and Renaud."

Sofia didn't answer directly. "This is when people think they can breathe," she said. "This is when they make mistakes."

Connor rinsed his towel, wrung it once, folded it into thirds again. "We don't," he replied.

For half a second Sofia's face almost changed, almost showed something like relief. Then she sealed it away.

"Finish," she said to the line, louder, and moved on.

The kitchen thinned as stations were completed. Some cooks were dismissed with a nod and left without speaking. Others stayed, moving slower now, not from fatigue but from caution. No one wanted to be the last body in the room when decisions were made.

Connor stayed. Not because he wanted to. Because leaving too early could look like avoidance, and avoidance could be interpreted. He kept doing tasks no one had assigned him, making himself useful in ways that were hard to argue with: polishing the pass edge, restocking clean spoons, squaring the stack of plates with a gentle nudge.

In the corridor, voices murmured. He could not hear words, only cadence: Hale's smooth control, Renaud's quieter, clipped replies. At one point a pause fell heavy enough to be felt, and Connor knew without seeing that Hale had said something that landed.

The suited man shifted his weight once. A tiny adjustment that meant the conversation had moved to a new phase.

Then Renaud reappeared.

He stepped back into the kitchen with the same measured pace as always. The difference was in what didn't move: his face remained centered, but his eyes didn't scan the room the way they usually did. They went straight to the pass, and then to Connor, as if checking whether the pass still belonged to him in the only way it could: in the minds of the brigade.

Hale stayed in the threshold, half in shadow, watching.

Renaud walked to the lamps and placed his hand on the steel, right where Connor had been wiping. The gesture was quiet. A claim without drama.

"Sofia," Renaud said.

"Yes, Chef," she answered immediately, appearing beside him.

Renaud's gaze moved to Connor. "Felwick."

Connor's throat tightened, but his face stayed clean. "Chef."

Renaud held him there with a look that wasn't anger and wasn't praise. It was the same look he used on plates: searching for deviation, for weakness, for something he could measure.

"The Guide," Renaud said.

"No change," Connor replied, because it was the only safe language.

Renaud nodded once, a small, controlled motion that could be interpreted as approval if you wanted to survive on interpretations. Then he said, quietly, "Good work."

The phrase was so rare it felt like a threat.

Sofia's jaw ticked at the edge of control. Hale's stillness sharpened, attention tightening like a wire.

Connor didn't thank him. Gratitude would make it personal. Personal could be exploited.

"Thank you, Chef," Sofia said instead, turning it into hierarchy, turning it into routine, absorbing the emotion that might have leaked.

Renaud's gaze flicked to her, then back to Connor. "You stayed in your lane," he said.

Connor heard the lie inside it. He had not stayed in his lane. He had stepped into the widened center and spoken his name to the inspector. But Renaud was offering him a narrative that could be replayed safely.

"Yes, Chef," Connor said, accepting the narrative as cover.

Renaud's hand slid a fraction along the steel, and Connor noticed the way his fingers held tension, too controlled, too precise. The tremor from earlier had been erased, but not forgotten.

Hale spoke from the threshold, voice quiet, smooth. "A disciplined service," he said, as if commenting on a performance he had funded.

Renaud didn't look at him. "The standard held," he replied.

Hale's gaze remained on Connor. "It did," he agreed.

The words landed softly, but Connor felt the shape of them: acknowledgment that the kitchen had discovered a new center tonight, whether anyone wanted that discovery or not.

Around them, the last few cooks finished their stations and slipped out, heads down, leaving the pass more exposed. The kitchen's noise dropped, and in the reduced sound Connor could hear his own breathing again.

A muted celebration, Connor thought, wasn't a lack of joy.

It was discipline used as a lid.

Because the stars had been retained, yes. But the cost of retaining them was now standing in the open, visible in who spoke, who decided, and who was being watched.

Renaud's eyes stayed on Connor a beat longer than necessary. "Go," he said finally.

Connor waited for the hidden condition that always came with permission here.

Renaud added, almost inaudible, "And be here early."

Connor nodded once. "Yes, Chef."

He untied his apron and folded it with controlled hands, not rushing, not lingering. As he turned toward the service door, he felt Hale's gaze follow him like a hand on the back of his neck.

Sofia passed him on her way back to the pass. She didn't speak. She didn't have to. Her eyes met his for half a fraction, sharp and warning.

Be boring, the look said. Even now.

Connor stepped out into the alley where bleach and citrus clung to the stone like an alibi, and the night air felt too wide after the kitchen's controlled heat.

Inside, no one would clink glasses. No one would cheer.

They would simply reset.

And somewhere behind the corridor mouth, decisions would be filed, names weighed, and the machine's next center quietly selected, as if this had been the plan all along.

Connor slept in fragments, the kind that didn't feel like sleeping so much as blacking out between alarms. Every time he closed his eyes, he saw the pass lamps and the inspector's gaze, felt again the moment his name became a record.

When he woke, the city outside his window was gray and indifferent. He washed his hands as if he were already in the kitchen, soap, rinse, dry once. He dressed without looking at himself too long. Looking invited interpretation.

The alley behind L'Étoile Noire was still damp, still carrying bleach and citrus like a rehearsed innocence. The service door yielded under his palm with the same soft resistance as always, as if the building had learned how to accept people without welcoming them.

Inside, the lights were half-on. Stainless accused and forgave in the same breath. The camera above the back hallway blinked its small blue heartbeat.

Dumas was there again, towel folded into thirds, wiping steel in single passes. He glanced at Connor once, then looked away.

"You were told," Dumas murmured, as if confirming Connor wasn't making a mistake by arriving.

"Yes," Connor said.

Dumas's mouth tightened, not approval, not warmth. A warning without words. He drifted away, leaving Connor to prep in silence.

Connor set up garde manger as he always did, labels faced outward, containers squared, tools aligned. He made himself boring on purpose. If anyone watched the footage later, it would show only routine.

By nine, Sofia arrived. Her jacket looked as crisp as ever, but the skin around her eyes had the faint tightness of someone who had not truly stopped working. She did a walk-through that wasn't about cleanliness. It was about drift.

When she reached Connor's station, she didn't correct a thing. That alone was a message.

"You're early," she said.

"You said it keeps you on the list," Connor replied, keeping his tone functional.

Sofia's jaw ticked once. "That was before you put your name in the air."

"It's already there," Connor said.

Sofia looked toward the corridor mouth, then back. "It's there twice now."

Before Connor could answer, the corridor changed density. Not with sound, but with weight.

Hale appeared without hurry, coat on, calm like ownership. One suited man shadowed him, half a step back, eyes sweeping the kitchen as if mapping exits and faces in the same pass.

Sofia's posture went perfect. "Good morning," she said, and it sounded like a report.

Hale's gaze moved over her and settled briefly on Connor, not lingering, not needing to. Connor felt it anyway, like a fingertip testing a bruise.

"Chef Renaud," Hale said.

Sofia didn't move, but her eyes flicked toward the pass.

Renaud stepped into view as if he had been there all along, jacket immaculate, hair precise, face centered. Yet Connor saw what the lamps had shown and the corridor had tried to erase. The tiredness behind the eyes. The mouth set a fraction too tight, as if a new restraint had been installed and locked.

Renaud didn't greet the room. He didn't need to. The kitchen aligned around him out of habit.

"Hale," Renaud said, flat.

Hale inclined his head, a gesture that could be mistaken for respect if you didn't understand how expensive his stillness was. "We need to talk."

Renaud's gaze didn't change. "We talked last night."

Hale's voice stayed smooth. "Last night was a problem solved. Today is a structure."

The suited man's eyes moved, slow and patient, taking inventory of who listened too hard.

Sofia spoke first, carefully. "Chef, we have prep."

Renaud didn't look at her. His eyes stayed on Hale. "Then speak."

Hale stepped forward one pace, just inside the border where heat became jurisdiction. He didn't lower his voice. He didn't need to. The kitchen's silence carried everything.

"The Guide saw you leave the pass," Hale said. "And the Guide saw the pass continue."

A pause, small, controlled. Not dramatic. A statement allowed to land.

Renaud's jaw flexed once. "The stars were retained."

"Yes," Hale said, calm. "Intact."

Connor felt the word again, the way Dumas had said it, the way the manager had whispered it. Intact didn't mean safe. It meant held together under pressure.

Hale's gaze moved toward Connor without turning his head fully. "The pass held because someone else made it hold."

Sofia's breath went shallow for a fraction, then returned to measured.

Renaud's eyes cut, surgical, to Connor. Inventory. Calculation.

"Felwick," Renaud said.

"Yes, Chef," Connor answered.

Renaud didn't ask if Connor had spoken to the inspector. That was already recorded somewhere that mattered. He didn't ask what Connor had said. He didn't need to. He looked at Connor as if Connor were a plate that had returned untouched: not visibly wrong, but unacceptable because it contained an implication.

Hale let the silence stretch, comfortable inside it. "We can't have uncertainty at the center," he said finally. "Not with the Guide close. Not with investors close. Not with the city watching."

Sofia's jaw ticked hard. "The kitchen has a center," she said. "Chef Renaud."

Hale's eyes didn't shift. "Does it."

It was not a question. It was an accusation framed as calm.

Renaud's voice stayed flat. "You're here to keep stars. We kept them."

Hale smiled slightly, not warmth, not humor. A minimal movement meant to show he could. "I'm here to keep more than stars."

Renaud's nostrils flared once. The only tell.

Hale continued, "We need a pass that does not leave. We need a standard that does not tremble under lamps."

Sofia went still at the word tremble. Connor felt her anger like static, contained and dangerous.

Renaud's gaze sharpened. "My hand is steady."

Hale's gaze held him. "Today."

The suited man behind Hale watched Renaud's mouth as if the exact shape of his words could be replayed later.

Renaud's attention moved, not to Hale, but to the pass. To the lamps. To the place where the kitchen's religion lived. He stared at the stainless as if reading something written there that only he could see.

When he spoke again, his voice was quieter. Not softer. Controlled in a new way.

"What do you want," Renaud asked.

Hale's answer came without hesitation. "A clear line. Sofia remains discipline. You remain face. Felwick becomes center."

The kitchen did not react. That was the training. But Connor felt the room's muscles tense anyway, a collective tightening as if the building itself had just been told to change its skeleton.

Sofia's head turned sharply toward Hale. The movement was fast enough to be a mistake in any other context. Here it was a restrained fracture.

"No," she said. One syllable, clipped.

Hale didn't look at her. "You trained him," he said, as if she were a tool reporting to him. "You pulled him into specials. You let him see the underside. Last night you let him speak."

Sofia's mouth tightened. "Last night I kept service alive."

Hale's gaze slid to her at last, mild as poison. "Exactly."

Renaud's eyes stayed on the pass. He did not defend Sofia. He did not defend himself. That absence was its own admission.

Connor kept his face clean and his hands still. He didn't step forward. Stepping forward would look like ambition. Ambition could be punished.

Renaud finally spoke, and the words sounded like they had been shaved down until only function remained.

"Felwick will call under my standard," Renaud said.

Hale nodded once, satisfied. "Good."

Sofia's jaw ticked again, and this time Connor saw the effort it took for her not to speak.

Renaud turned his head toward Connor. His gaze held. Not approval. Not kindness. Something colder: recognition that a change had already occurred and could only be controlled by naming it first.

"You ran my pass," Renaud said quietly.

"I ran the service," Connor replied. The same correction he had given the inspector, because it was the only safe truth.

Renaud's mouth moved, not quite a smile. "Careful," he murmured.

"Yes, Chef."

Renaud took one step closer, close enough that his words could hide under the refrigerator hum and the distant clatter of a pan being set down. "Do you understand what they will do to you if you fail."

Connor didn't answer too fast. Speed looked eager. "Remove me," he said.

Renaud's eyes narrowed by a fraction. "Erase you," he corrected, and his voice made it sound like a technical term, not a threat. "And they will erase anyone who tries to keep your name alive."

Connor swallowed once, controlled. "Yes, Chef."

Renaud held him in place with a look that felt like the pass lamps: merciless, clarifying. Then, very quietly, "Good. Then you will be boring."

Connor heard Sofia's language inside it. Heard the way the building spoke through them.

Renaud straightened and let his voice return to the room. "Sofia," he said.

"Yes, Chef," she answered immediately, but her eyes were hard.

"Station assignments," Renaud said. "Update them."

Sofia didn't move. "Chef—"

Renaud's tone cut, not loud, absolute. "Update them."

A beat. Sofia's jaw ticked once more, then stopped. "Oui, Chef."

Hale turned slightly toward the corridor as if the matter were already closed. The suited man mirrored him, a shadow pivoting on command.

Before Hale left, he looked at Connor fully for the first time, and Connor felt the gaze pin him without touch.

"You did well in front of the Guide," Hale said.

Connor didn't answer with gratitude. He answered with the kitchen's religion. "The standard held."

Hale's mouth moved again in that minimal almost-smile. "See that it continues."

He withdrew into the corridor without hurry, taking the suited man with him, leaving the kitchen with the aftertaste of his control.

Silence remained, but it had changed shape. Not the suffocating silence of service. The silence of a new arrangement settling into place.

Sofia exhaled through her nose, sharp. “This is what he wanted,” she said, low enough that it wasn’t for the room.

Renaud’s eyes stayed forward. “This is what happened,” he replied.

Sofia’s gaze cut to Connor, warning and something else beneath it. Fear, maybe. Not for him. For what he would become.

Renaud looked at Connor one last time, and the look was so controlled it felt like a stamp pressed onto paper.

“Be here at the pass at five,” Renaud said.

“Yes, Chef.”

Renaud’s voice lowered, nearly inaudible. “And do not mistake this for ascension.”

Connor didn’t ask what it was. He already knew.

Renaud stepped away toward the corridor mouth again, but this time he didn’t disappear. He stopped at the threshold, half in shadow, half in heat, occupying the border like a man refusing to leave the only place that had ever belonged to him.

Sofia stood still at the pass, as if bracing the room with posture alone.

Connor returned to his station and began prep with the same severe economy as always, labels outward, containers squared, towel folded into thirds.

Nothing about his hands changed.

But everything about the kitchen's attention did.

He could feel it now, the new line drawn through the room, invisible but absolute. The pass was still the pass. The standard was still the standard. The stars were still above them like a promise and a threat.

Only the center had shifted.

And Connor understood, with cold clarity, that transfer of power in L'Étoile Noire did not come with applause or ceremony.

It came the way everything here came.

Quietly.

Efficiently.

Like erasure, reversed.

Epilogue

The New Standard

At five, the pass lamps came on like a verdict.

Connor arrived at four-thirty because he had learned that time was another surface you had to keep clean. The alley had been rinsed again. Bleach and citrus. Always the same. Always an alibi that never quite covered what lived underneath.

Inside, stainless held the early light without warmth. The camera above the back hallway blinked its blue heartbeat, indifferent and patient. Connor washed his hands. Soap, rinse, dry once. He tied his apron, aligned his tools, and then walked to the pass like it was a station he'd been assigned years ago, not days.

The pass was already arranged. Someone had prepped it for him, and that was its own message.

The heat lamps were spaced in perfect symmetry. The ticket rail had been wiped, the printer loaded, the corner of the stainless polished to a shine that would show fingerprints like confession. A stack of plates sat squared to the edge with a precision that wasn't necessary for function. It was necessary for surveillance.

Sofia stood a step back, clipboard in hand, posture rigid enough to read as calm. Her eyes moved over Connor, not like a friend, not like a rival. Like a sous chef reviewing a knife before service. Sharpness. Balance. The ways it could slip.

"You're here," she said.

Connor didn't smile. "Yes, Chef."

Her jaw ticked once at the title, not because it was wrong, but because it carried consequences. She looked past him toward the corridor mouth. "He's here too."

Connor followed her gaze without turning his head, using stainless reflection the way the kitchen had trained him to. Chef Renaud stood at the threshold, half in the corridor's shadow, half in the kitchen's heat. Jacket immaculate. Hair precise. Face centered.

Still face.

Not center.

He didn't step in. He didn't take the lamps. He held the border like a man refusing to admit a room could survive without him. His right hand rested at his side, too still, the steadiness of something corrected.

Behind him, the corridor held its usual weight even before Hale arrived. Doors that didn't have signs. Footsteps that didn't belong to cooks. A silence with different rules.

Sofia lowered her voice. "Call clean," she said. "No flourishes."

"Boring," Connor replied.

Her jaw ticked again, hard enough to look like pain. "Yes," she said. "Boring."

Dumas drifted by with a tray of folded towels, all of them in thirds. He set them down without looking at Connor directly, but his voice slid under the fan hum as he passed.

"They'll test it," he murmured.

Connor didn't ask who. He didn't need to. "Heard," he said.

By five, the brigade was in position, stations set like territories. Hot side gave off its low, aggressive heat. Cold side held its clinical chill. Knives lay aligned. Labels faced outward. No one spoke unless the words were useful.

Tonight the silence had a different density. Before, it had been fear of Renaud. Now it was a fear of uncertainty. The kitchen had spent months obeying one center and one standard; in one night, it had learned it could obey another, and the knowledge didn't feel like liberation. It felt like exposure.

At five-fifteen, Hale appeared as if the corridor had exhaled him.

Coat on. Calm like ownership. One suited man behind him, half a step back, eyes sweeping the line in a slow inventory that had nothing to do with food. The suited man's gaze passed over wrists and mouths and shoulders, searching for tells.

Hale didn't step fully into the kitchen. He didn't need to. His presence held at the border and made the air behave.

His eyes went to Renaud first, then to Sofia, then to Connor. When they landed, Connor felt the familiar pressure, the fingertip on the bruise.

"Chef," Hale said, and the word aimed itself at the pass, not at Renaud.

Connor didn't correct him. Corrections were a kind of negotiation, and negotiation was theater.

"Good evening," Connor replied.

Hale's mouth moved in that minimal almost-smile. "We're aligned."

Connor kept his face clean. “Yes.”

Hale’s eyes shifted toward the lamps. “No noise,” he said.

“We execute,” Connor answered, the kitchen’s true religion.

Hale lingered half a beat longer, then withdrew into the corridor without hurry. The suited man followed. The border remained heavy even after they disappeared.

Renaud stayed at the threshold. Watching.

Not approving. Not stopping it. Just refusing to vanish.

At five-thirty, Sofia did lineup like she always had, clipped and procedural.

“Allergies as printed,” she said. “No specials unless called. No variation. No rim marks.”

“Yes, Chef,” the line answered.

Sofia’s gaze flicked to Connor. A warning disguised as routine. Don’t make it personal. Don’t make it visible.

Connor nodded once. No theatrics.

At six, service began.

The printer fed its first ticket, and the sound still cut sharper than it should have. Connor tore the paper cleanly, clipped it, scanned fast.

"Two on four," he called.

The brigade answered. "Heard."

His voice didn't rise to fill the room the way a loud chef's voice would. It moved like a blade through the air: clean, quiet, and immediately obeyed.

"Fire cold," Connor said. "Hot follows in twenty. Walk together."

"Oui."

Plates began to land under the lamps. Connor's eyes went where they always went now. Rim first. Always rim. He didn't touch. He tilted under the light, let the lamps reveal what the kitchen's heat could hide.

Geometry. Symmetry. Negative space. Not beauty. Control.

He sent the first plates out with a single word. "Walk."

The runners moved fast without looking fast. Connor watched their hands, always. The real kitchen runners carried fatigue in their wrists and heat in their joints. The others carried something else. Instructions. Timing. An agenda that didn't taste.

The second ticket printed. Connor tore it, clipped it.

"Two on eight," he called.

Sofia echoed down the line as discipline, not as a second center. "Heard."

She stayed half a step back, controlling the machine's edges: timing checks, station resets, towel replacements that were about appearances as much as hygiene. Her jaw ticked sometimes, but her voice didn't.

Renaud stayed at the threshold. He did not intervene. He did not call. He watched Connor's hands with the same intensity he used to reserve for plates, as if searching for deviation in the way Connor held authority.

Ten minutes into service, a runner appeared at the edge of the lamps with a plate held a little too high.

Too clean hands. No fatigue. Posture trained.

The plate was perfect. That was the problem.

The runner didn't speak. He slid it forward as if belonging could be imposed by proximity.

Connor didn't look at the runner's face. Faces made stories. He looked at the empty space where a ticket should be.

"Ticket," Connor said.

The runner's eyes hardened. "It goes," he replied, low.

Connor didn't move. "Ticket."

Sofia's voice cut in immediately, calm and sharp. "Ticket."

The runner hesitated a beat too long, and Connor felt the entire kitchen register the pause without turning their heads. A pause at the pass was a crack in the building's surface.

The runner's gaze flicked toward the corridor mouth, permission check.

Connor did not look. He didn't give the corridor the satisfaction of his attention. He kept his focus on the lamps as if the lamps were the only jurisdiction that mattered.

After a beat, the runner withdrew with the plate, retreating back toward the corridor network.

Connor spoke to the room without announcing he was speaking. "We walk what's on the rail," hc said, voice clipped. "Nothing else."

"Heard," the line answered, relief disguised as obedience.

The machine tightened itself. Towels reset. Containers squared. A lid aligned. The smallest human drifts corrected before they could become something someone might use.

Sofia leaned in, mouth barely moving. "They're checking if you'll flinch," she murmured.

Connor's eyes stayed on the lamps. "I won't," he said.

He didn't say because of pride. He didn't say because he wanted power. He said it the way he would say the oven was hot.

A fact.

The next plates came up. Connor checked rims, aligned, released. "Walk."

Thirty minutes passed without a return.

That should have felt like calm. It didn't. It felt like bait.

Connor could still feel the inspector's gaze even though the inspector wasn't there. Guide present had become more than a slip of paper; it was a permanent condition of the kitchen's nervous system. The myth that any anonymous diner could be the judge. That any plate could be the one that came back untouched and removed oxygen from the room.

Connor didn't allow himself to forget the moment he'd spoken his name into that system. Names didn't wash off stainless easily.

At the hour mark, the printer stuttered for half a breath, then fed cleanly again.

Sofia's eyes flicked to it. Connor tore the ticket before the stutter could become a story.

He read fast.

A familiar table number flashed in his mind like a cold light.

Six.

He felt nothing in his face. Inside, his body recognized the pattern the way a wound recognized pressure.

"Fire six," Connor called, as if it were any other table. "Cold now. Hot in ten. Walk together."

"Heard," the brigade replied.

Sofia's jaw ticked once, then stopped. Discipline returning.

Renaud's gaze sharpened at the threshold. A fraction of movement around the eyes. Not surprise. Recognition.

Connor kept his hands steady as the first plate for six came up under the lamps.

Rim. Clean.

He inspected the negative space. Nothing interpretive. Boring. Severe. Absent of ego.

He released it. "Walk."

The hot course followed on timing. Connor's eyes found a faint smear that might have been steam.

He didn't hesitate.

"Again," he said.

Hot side took it back without a word, resentment swallowed under the standard. A refire began immediately, because the pass had spoken.

For the first time all night, Connor felt the kitchen's attention settle fully onto him, not in curiosity, not in fear, but in acceptance of a simple truth: the center was not the man at the threshold anymore.

It was the voice that could say again and mean it.

Sofia shifted half a step, giving Connor the exact strip of light beneath the lamps without announcing it. Not permission. Confirmation.

Connor aligned the refired hot plate under the lamps. Rim clean. Symmetry exact. No story.

He released it. "Walk."

The runner took it, wrists tired, real.

Connor didn't watch it leave. He watched the lamps, the rail, the space where returns arrived.

He felt the corridor's weight press in, the sense of unseen eyes measuring whether the new center would hold under the old pressure.

Connor kept his posture composed and his voice flat.

"Two on nine," he called.

"Heard."

He tore the next ticket and clipped it as if paper could anchor reality.

The service continued, and Connor stayed at the pass, hands clean, eyes merciless, voice calm. He did not improvise. He did not perform. He did not try to be Renaud.

He executed Renaud's standard with a colder absence than Renaud ever needed, because Connor had learned what this kitchen truly demanded.

Perfection wasn't taste.

Perfection was control, made repeatable.

And as the night tightened around table six like a drawn wire, Connor stood in the strip of light beneath the lamps and felt the building accept him the way it accepted all new rules.

Quietly.

Efficiently.

Without applause.

Like the beginning of something that would be called inevitable later.

The first return came the way returns always came in this building: without shame, without explanation, without the normal theater of apology that other dining rooms used to soften embarrassment.

It arrived on a tray carried level and steady, slid into the strip of light beneath the pass lamps as if it belonged there. No clatter. No urgency. Just the quiet certainty of an object placed to be judged.

Connor's hands did not stop moving, but his attention narrowed instantly, the way the kitchen had trained him to narrow it when the room threatened to change shape. He looked at the plate before he looked at the person holding it, because faces could lie and porcelain could not.

It was the table six course he had walked ten minutes ago. The refire. The second hot plate, the one he had aligned under the lamps with cold discipline and sent out with a clean "Walk," wrists tired on the runner, nothing ghostly about it.

Now it was back.

Untouched.

The sauce line had not been dragged by a fork. The protein had not been cut. The garnish still held its angle like it had been pinned in place. Steam had died, but the dish had not been disturbed.

The carrier stood just outside the lamp strip, hands too clean, posture too controlled. Not a server. Not one of Connor's runners. Another piece from the corridor rail, delivered into the visible service without speaking.

Silence did what it always did. It pressed down. It removed oxygen, not with volume but with attention. Knives paused. A squeeze bottle hovered in place. Someone's foot stopped mid-step.

Connor did not look up. He did not scan the line. He did not allow himself the reflex of searching for reassurance in another person's face. Searching was a kind of dependence, and dependence was weakness that could be used.

He slid the plate fully under the lamps, aligning it with the edge of the stainless so precisely it looked intentional. He kept his fingers under the porcelain, thumbs clear, no rim contact. Then he inspected it the way Renaud had taught him without ever calling it teaching.

Rim first.

Clean. No smear. No print. No accidental confession that someone could later claim was the reason it came back.

Then geometry.

Everything was in its place. Severe symmetry. Negative space intact. The dish was boring in the only way that mattered: it offered nothing for a diner to interpret as personality.

Connor's gaze moved once more across it, not because he expected to find culinary error, but because he was looking for the other kind. The invisible wrong that had nothing to do with salt.

He felt Sofia's presence behind and slightly to his left, half a step back as discipline, clipboard held too still. Her jaw ticked once, sharp as a metronome. The sound was tiny. The kitchen heard it anyway.

At the threshold, Renaud remained in shadow, half in the corridor's cold jurisdiction, half in the kitchen's heat, refusing to be erased even as he was no longer center. Connor did not look at him directly, but he felt the weight of Renaud's attention settle on the plate like another lamp.

Connor looked at the carrier.

"What table," he asked, voice flat.

The carrier's answer came too quickly. "Six."

No ticket appeared. No paper moved. No record entered the rail.

Connor nodded once as if the words meant something, as if the kitchen was allowed to believe what it was told. Then he asked the only question that mattered now.

"Who carried it back."

The carrier's eyes hardened. "They didn't like it."

"That's not the question," Connor said, still without volume.

For a beat, the carrier did not respond. The pause was the same kind of pause Connor had learned to recognize when he asked for a ticket and a runner checked the corridor mouth for permission. A permission check without looking like one.

Connor held still. Not challenging. Not pleading. Just refusing to let the pass become a corridor.

Sofia's voice cut in, calm and sharp. "Answer."

The carrier's jaw worked once. Then, finally, "Server," he said, and the lie sat in the air like a plate that didn't belong on the rail.

Connor didn't call him on it. Calling him on it would turn the exchange into a scene, and scenes were where the hidden system found leverage. Instead Connor did something colder. He treated the lie as irrelevant.

He turned his attention back to the plate and let the room see what he decided. No anger. No theatrics.

He slid the dish a fraction closer to himself, as if claiming jurisdiction over it by proximity alone.

"Refire," he said.

The word landed cleanly, a single syllable with no emotion. Money, time, pride, all subordinate to the standard. The brigade responded automatically because obedience was their only safe instinct.

"Heard," came back from hot side, Antoine's voice tight but controlled.

Connor did not look at Antoine. He did not broadcast blame. In this kitchen, blame was a currency that got traded up corridors. Connor would not spend it unless he meant to buy something permanent.

Sofia leaned in close enough for her voice to hide under the fans. “They’re doing it again,” she murmured.

Connor kept his eyes on the lamps. “I know,” he replied.

“They want you to chase ghosts,” she said, and the words carried the memory of the last Guide night when “wrong” had been used as bait.

Connor’s mouth barely moved. “Then we don’t chase.”

He lifted the returned plate and set it down just outside the lamp strip, not discarded, not thrown away, simply moved into a space where it could not contaminate the rhythm of the pass. It was a small act, almost nothing. In this room, small acts were statements.

The carrier shifted, as if the movement offended him.

“That stays,” the carrier said, voice low.

Connor didn’t look at him. He tore a ticket as it printed, clipped it, and called it out with the same cadence as if nothing had happened.

“Two on nine. Fire cold. Hot follows in fifteen.”

The line answered. “Heard.”

He turned back to the carrier then, calm and absent. “It doesn’t stay under my lamps,” he said. “If they returned it, it’s no longer service.”

The carrier’s eyes narrowed, not quite a threat, more like a test of whether Connor understood the game he was in.

From the threshold, Renaud’s voice came, quiet, from shadow.

“Felwick.”

One word. Not a call. Not a correction. An attempt to pull Connor’s attention sideways, off the plate and onto the politics.

Connor did not turn his head. He kept his focus on the pass. “Chef,” he replied, acknowledging without shifting his center.

Another beat.

Renaud did not continue. Connor felt the restraint in the silence, the way a man trained to command chose not to speak because speaking would reveal which lever he still controlled.

The refire began on hot side. Connor could hear it without looking: pans moved, a burner adjusted, a spoon tapped once, then stopped because noise was a form of disorder. Antoine was fast. Antoine was good. Tonight that didn’t matter. Tonight the room was hunting for a deviation it could use as proof.

Connor reached for a clean towel, folded it into thirds, wiped the lamp strip where the returned plate had sat. Single stroke. No overlap. A ritual that looked like hygiene and was really erasure. He did not allow even the memory of the return to leave residue on the steel.

Sofia watched his hands. Her expression remained sealed, but her eyes sharpened with something that might have been recognition. Connor had become what she had warned him to become: boring, exact, impossible to edit.

The carrier lingered, still standing as if waiting for a different outcome, perhaps for Connor to flinch, to ask why, to demand an explanation, to give the corridor something to hold.

Connor gave him nothing.

"Where is the ticket," Connor asked again, not louder.

The carrier's mouth tightened. "Not needed."

Connor nodded once, as if accepting that the building ran on two systems. Then he did the one thing that made both systems uncomfortable: he applied the visible rules to the invisible action.

"Then it never existed," Connor said.

The carrier stared at him, and for the first time the man's control slipped enough to show confusion. People who lived in the corridor depended on the kitchen pretending corridor actions were normal. Connor's refusal made them visible.

Sofia's voice, still calm, threaded in like a knife. "Step back."

The carrier hesitated, and the hesitation was the whole point. He was deciding whether Sofia had the authority to be obeyed now that Connor was center.

Connor didn't let the pause stretch into a contest. He spoke in pure procedure, as if addressing a commis who had placed a tray in the wrong spot.

"You're blocking the pass," he said. "Move."

No anger. No volume. No negotiation.

The carrier's eyes flicked, a permission check toward the corridor mouth.

Connor held his gaze on the lamps, refusing to look where the carrier wanted him to look. If Connor looked toward the corridor for confirmation, he would admit the corridor had jurisdiction here. He would admit the pass was not the center.

After a beat too long, the carrier backed away, retreating toward the corridor network with the silent resentment of someone who had expected the kitchen to yield. He left the returned plate outside the lamp strip, untouched, as if abandoning it was also a message: this is what happens when we push.

Connor did not watch him go. He watched the line.

A cold course came up for another table. Connor checked the rim, found it clean, released it.

"Walk."

The runner moved, wrists tired, real.

Hot side followed with the refire for six. Antoine stepped up, face composed, eyes too hard. He placed the new dish under the lamps.

Connor inspected it with merciless attention. Rim first.

Clean.

Sauce line. Symmetry. Negative space.

Perfect in the only way that mattered: controlled.

He held it under the lamps for one precise beat, letting heat and light make any hidden smear confess itself.

Nothing.

Connor nodded once.

"Walk," he said.

The plate left the pass with no ceremony.

The kitchen resumed motion as if the return had never happened, but Connor felt the aftershock traveling through bodies anyway: shoulders tightening, breath controlled, the instinct to look toward Renaud, toward Sofia, toward any face that could tell them what the return meant.

Connor did not allow meaning to enter.

Meaning was where fear lived. Fear was where the corridor found purchase.

Sofia leaned in, voice barely moving. "If they return it again," she murmured, and did not finish the sentence.

Connor answered without looking at her. "Then we refire again," he said.

"That's not what I meant," Sofia whispered.

Connor's hands continued their work. Ticket torn. Clipped. Call made.

"Fire table twelve. Tight."

The line answered. "Heard."

Only then, after the pass had reasserted rhythm, did Connor let his voice drop, low enough that only Sofia would hear.

"I know what you meant," he said. "And if they return it again, we still refire. We don't give them a different show."

Sofia's jaw ticked once, hard, the sound of someone swallowing anger and fear at the same time.

In the threshold, Renaud shifted slightly, a movement so small it might have been breath. Connor felt his gaze, heavy and precise, pinned to the returned plate sitting outside the lamp strip like a quiet indictment.

Renaud had built a kingdom where a returned plate meant death.

Connor had just made it mean procedure.

The difference was not mercy. It was power.

The printer fed another ticket. Connor tore it clean.

He kept calling. He kept checking rims. He kept the lamps clean, the rail real, the service intact.

And somewhere behind the wall of the dining room, a table that refused to use language waited to see if the new center would break the way the old center had, if Connor would turn this return into a spectacle they could use.

Connor did not break. He did not raise his voice. He did not ask why.

He executed, again and again, until the returned dish was just another object that had failed to change the rhythm.

Until the kitchen stopped holding its breath.

Not because it was safe.

Because it had learned a new kind of silence.

One that did not belong to fear. One that belonged to a standard enforced so cleanly it did not need explanation.

A dish had returned.

And the room had not died.

It had adapted.

The refire for six did not return.

Ten minutes passed, then fifteen, and nothing slid back into the lamp strip with that quiet certainty. The dining room wall stayed a wall. The corridor mouth stayed heavy. The machine kept moving because Connor kept it moving, and because the kitchen had learned that the only way to survive attention was to look like it had never noticed it.

But the returned dish still sat just outside the lamps where Connor had placed it, cooling into a kind of evidence. No one touched it. No one asked what to do with it. It was not trash. It was not food. It was a message left in the open, waiting to see if anyone would flinch around it.

Connor kept his eyes on the rail, but he tracked the room the way he had learned to track a dining room you couldn't see: by listening to where silence tightened.

A commis at hot side moved a fraction too fast, the kind of speed that looked like eagerness and was really fear. A towel slipped from its folded third and got corrected instantly, corner aligned, stain hidden. Sofia's jaw ticked once, then stopped. She stayed half a step back, not center, but discipline, the edges of the machine held in place so the center could remain clean.

At the threshold, Renaud did not leave. He did not step in. He held the border like a man refusing to accept that borders could be redrawn without his consent. His face remained centered, but the centering was rigid now, not effortless. Connor did not look at him directly. He refused to feed the gravity with his eyes.

Tickets printed. Connor tore them. Clipped them. Called them.

“Two on twelve. Fire cold. Hot follows in ten.”

“Heard.”

“Walk.”

The word landed the same way it always landed now: not as permission, not as performance, but as a door latch closing. The runner took the plates, wrists tired, real. The lamps cleared. New porcelain arrived. The rhythm held.

Then the printer fed a ticket that didn’t sound wrong but felt wrong anyway, because Connor’s body had learned to distrust even clean paper.

Sofia’s eyes flicked toward the rail, and Connor caught her tension in peripheral motion. Not a hold. Something else.

Connor tore the ticket and scanned.

Table six again.

Not a course. Not a refire. A new ticket, cleanly printed, with a timing window that sat too neatly inside the service flow. Like someone had planned it.

Connor kept his face blank. “Fire six,” he called, and made it sound like any other number. “Cold now. Hot in twelve. Walk together.”

“Heard,” the line answered, and their voices held a tightness that wasn’t culinary. Six was a myth now, a pattern the building recognized the way skin recognized pressure.

The cold course came up first. The replacement commis at garde manger stepped forward with the plate, hands careful. Too careful. Connor watched the hands, then the plate.

Rim first.

Clean.

Geometry: severe and absent.

Negative space: correct.

He was about to release it when something caught in the light, not on the plate, but in the way it had been built. A detail so small it wouldn't register as a mistake to anyone who ate with hunger instead of scrutiny. The micro greens were placed with precision, but one leaf had been trimmed differently than the others, a fraction longer, a fraction more visible. It introduced a whisper of personality.

Connor looked at it for one beat and felt the room tighten, not because anyone knew what he had seen, but because the pass had gone still.

He slid the plate back an inch.

"Again," he said, quiet.

The commis's eyes widened, then sealed. He took the plate back without a word, but Connor saw the tremor in his fingers as he turned. Not anger. Fear. Fear of time, fear of waste, fear of being the reason something returned again.

Sofia leaned close, mouth barely moving. "Connor," she murmured, and it was the closest she had come to using his name at the pass in months.

Connor didn't look at her. "No variation," he replied, and kept his voice flat enough to be instruction, not emotion. "Boring."

Sofia's jaw ticked once, sharp. "Yes," she whispered.

Hot side fired the protein for six, the timing window tightening. Antoine's station moved fast without looking fast. Pans didn't clatter. Spoons didn't tap. The kitchen did what it always did when it sensed danger: it got quieter.

The commis rebuilt the cold course. This time the leaf lengths matched. The arrangement was sterile. It meant nothing.

Connor checked the rim again and released it.

"Walk."

The runner took it. Real hands. Real fatigue.

Hot followed on time, arriving under the lamps with clean heat. Connor inspected it with the same merciless attention he had used all night. Rim, sauce, symmetry, negative space. No smears. No fingerprints. No story.

"Walk," he said.

The plate left.

The kitchen held its breath without making sound, the way it always did after a dish for six walked. Waiting to see if the dining room would reject it again without language. Waiting to see if the corridor would try to push a ghost plate into the lamps. Waiting to see if the building's new center would be forced to show something human.

Nothing returned.

Five minutes.

Ten.

The tension loosened by a millimeter, not relief, recalibration. The machine adjusted to the fact that it was still intact.

Then the door from the dining room opened again.

Not wide. Just enough to let in a slice of different air. Less heat. More perfume. The expensive, controlled air of people who did not sweat.

The slick-haired manager hovered at the threshold, face carefully neutral, eyes too alert. Behind him stood a server Connor hadn't seen before, posture stiff, hands empty, expression trained into absence.

The manager didn't step into the heat. He spoke softly, toward Sofia and Connor, and the words landed like a plate.

"Chef," he said.

Sofia's voice answered first, controlled. "Speak."

The manager swallowed. "A plate has been returned," he said.

Not table six.

Connor felt the room tighten again, sharper this time, because a return that wasn't six meant a different kind of problem. It meant the pattern was spreading.

"What table," Connor asked, calm.

The manager glanced down at his hands as if reading something written there. "Two," he said. "A guest asked that it be taken away."

Connor's eyes stayed on the lamps. "No comment."

The manager's mouth tightened. "No comment," he confirmed, and the repetition sounded like apology.

The server stepped forward, and Connor's attention locked instantly on the plate the server carried. Not the food. The rim.

The server held it correctly, thumbs clear, fingers under porcelain. Good training. But training didn't prevent accidents. It didn't prevent sabotage.

The plate slid into the lamp strip, and the kitchen's oxygen thinned again in the way it always did when porcelain came back untouched.

Connor looked down.

It was a cold course from garde manger. Clean geometry. Severe. Boring, in theory.

And yet it was untouched.

Connor did not ask why. Why was the word that invited stories. Stories were how you got manipulated.

He inspected.

Rim first. Clean.

No smear. No print. No accidental confession.

He moved his gaze inward, tracing the arrangement, looking for drift so small it could be denied. Everything sat where it should.

Then he saw it.

A single dot of dressing, nearly invisible, placed a fraction too close to the rim. Not on the rim. Near it. A detail that would mean nothing to a diner but could read as sloppiness to someone trained to look for control.

Or worse: a deliberate near-miss. The kind of error you didn't correct because it wasn't technically wrong, but that a silent judge could use as proof that the machine was no longer absolute.

Connor felt the memory of another lamp strip, another returned plate, another silence that had ended with a question.

Who plated this?

The prologue story had been told so often it had become scripture. A returned dish. No comment. No complaint. Just returned. The kitchen's oxygen removed. A young chef raising his hand like confession. Lucien Renaud saying, "Remove him."

Connor understood now, with cold clarity, why that story had endured. It wasn't about punishment. It was about making the standard a living thing that required blood to stay alive.

Sofia stood half a step back, watching Connor's hands, watching his face for any sign of human conflict. Her jaw ticked once, barely audible.

Renaud remained at the threshold, shadowed, watching like a man watching his own myth get rewritten.

Connor lifted his gaze to the server.

"Who plated this," he asked.

The words fell into the kitchen without volume. They did not need volume. Every person in the room heard them as if they had been spoken into their bone.

Silence became absolute.

No one moved. Not knives. Not towels. Not a footstep. Even the fans seemed louder because nothing else existed.

Connor kept his face clean. He did not look down the line searching for guilt. He did not give anyone the mercy of pretending it wasn't their responsibility. He waited the way Renaud had waited, because waiting was the pressure.

The commis from garde manger, the replacement in Jules's old space, froze at his station. Connor watched him in stainless reflection, not directly. The kid's shoulders rose with a breath he couldn't control.

A beat passed.

Two.

Finally, slowly, the commis raised a hand.

It wasn't dramatic. It wasn't defiant. It was the smallest motion possible that still answered the question. A confession offered because silence was worse than death here.

Sofia's eyes closed for half a fraction, then opened, her face sealing again. She didn't intervene. She couldn't. The question had been asked. The machine required an answer.

Connor nodded once.

Not anger. Not satisfaction. Just recognition of procedure.

"Remove him," Connor said.

The words did not feel like his. That was the point. They were the kitchen speaking through him, the standard using his mouth.

Two senior chefs moved instantly. No violence. No grabbing. Just hands on the commis's elbow, a calm escort that was almost gentle. The commis didn't protest. Protest would only make it personal, and personal didn't exist here.

As they guided him toward the service door, he glanced once over his shoulder, eyes wide with something raw and disbelieving. Not at Sofia. Not at Renaud.

At Connor.

As if trying to find the moment where Connor could have chosen differently.

Connor did not look away. Looking away would be a lie. He held the gaze long enough to make the truth clear: there was no different choice that didn't break the standard, and breaking the standard was a worse death than removal.

The commis disappeared through the door, apron still on, hands still clean, name already beginning to evaporate.

The kitchen didn't move until the door shut.

Then Connor spoke again, and the machine obeyed because it had been trained to obey continuity.

"Refire table two," he said. "New plates. New towels. No rim marks."

"Heard," garde manger answered automatically, a different commis stepping into the empty space without ceremony. The station did not pause to mourn. Mourning was disorder.

Sofia's voice returned, clipped, steady. "Continue."

Hot side fired for the next table. Cold side rebuilt the returned dish with sterile precision. The pass lamps burned over new porcelain as if nothing had happened.

In the dining room, the guest who returned the plate continued eating something else, unimpressed, perhaps unaware of the cost of their silent rejection, or perhaps fully aware and counting on it.

At the threshold, Renaud shifted, a small movement that might have been breath. Connor felt his presence like a pressure change.

For months, Renaud's kingdom had been built on erasure delivered in silence. Tonight Connor had delivered it without raising his voice, without hesitation, without making it theatrical.

History repeating didn't feel like fate.

It felt like design.

Sofia leaned in, her mouth barely moving, and her words came out like a warning and an acknowledgement at once.

"You didn't hesitate," she whispered.

Connor kept his eyes on the lamps. "Neither did the standard," he replied.

Sofia's jaw ticked, and in her eyes Connor saw something he hadn't seen in a long time: a flicker of fear that wasn't about Hale or the corridor, but about what the kitchen had just proven it could do with Connor as center.

Behind them, Renaud remained silent. He did not correct. He did not approve. He watched, and his watching felt different now, like a man observing a successor carry out a sentence that used to belong only to him.

The refire for table two came up. Connor checked the rim. Clean. The dot of dressing sat exactly where it should, far enough from the edge to be unarguable. The plate was sterile, boring, perfect in the only way that mattered.

"Walk," Connor said.

The runner took it.

The lamps cleared.

The machine moved on.

And the space where the commis had stood was already being filled by someone else, hands working, eyes down, name still intact for now.

Connor tore the next ticket, clipped it, called the next fire time as if the kitchen hadn't just erased a person in the span of two sentences.

Because that was the real continuity here.

A returned plate.

A question.

An answer.

A removal.

Service continues.

History repeats, not because anyone wants it to, but because the system is built to make repetition feel like order. And in L'Étoile Noire, order was the only thing that ever earned the right to survive.

www.ingramcontent.com/pod-product-compliance
Lightning Source LLC
LaVergne TN
LVHW050908080826
845145LV00001B/6